WHITE BIRD

BOOK TWO OF THE AURE DUOLOGY

W.K. GREYLING

ISBN: 978-1-9994748-2-9

Edited by Allister Thompson

First edition: November 2018

Get the Audiobook: https://www.audible.com/pd/White-Bird-Audiobook/B07NJD5J4M

wkgreyling.com

CONTENTS

Title Page i

Copyright ii

Map v

PART ONE: CHOSEN 1

    CHAPTER 1 3

    CHAPTER 2 13

    CHAPTER 3 29

    CHAPTER 4 33

    CHAPTER 5 37

    CHAPTER 6 41

    CHAPTER 7 47

    CHAPTER 8 55

    CHAPTER 9 65

PART TWO: CONSPIRACY 73

    CHAPTER 10 75

    CHAPTER 11 87

    CHAPTER 12 93

    CHAPTER 13 105

    CHAPTER 14 109

    CHAPTER 15 121

    CHAPTER 16 129

    CHAPTER 17 139

CHAPTER 18 145

CHAPTER 19 153

CHAPTER 20 165

PART THREE: TOURNIQUET **169**

CHAPTER 21 171

CHAPTER 22 173

CHAPTER 23 183

CHAPTER 24 193

CHAPTER 25 203

CHAPTER 26 213

CHAPTER 27 225

CHAPTER 28 235

CHAPTER 29 245

CHAPTER 30 257

CHAPTER 31 261

CHAPTER 32 271

PART FOUR: THE DREAMING PLACE **287**

CHAPTER 33 289

CHAPTER 34 301

CHAPTER 35 313

CHAPTER 36 319

CHAPTER 37 325

CHAPTER 38 337

About the Author 351

PART ONE

CHOSEN

CHAPTER 1

The sound of an ax biting into wood cracked through the still morning air.

Merisande d'Ivry perched on the felled tree that she and her father, Rives, were slowly reducing to firewood, running her ax blade over a whetstone. Her halfwit brother, Jan, squatted beside a stream, apparently hoping that the sleeping frogs would pop their heads out of the mud to greet him. *You're not spring,* she thought.

Rives set down his ax and groaned, stretching his arms behind his back. He froze that way for a moment and then turned to Mer with a gleam in his eyes. Another riddle, she guessed, and leaned forward in anticipation.

The riddle game had become synonymous with gathering firewood. Mer could not recall who had asked the first riddle or how many years had passed since she and Rives began playing the game. All she knew was that she could not chop wood without riddles.

"The hungry dog howls," he said, "for a crust of bread. His cry goes unheard. It's far overhead."

He picked up his ax and swung.

How could a dog's cry be overhead? She ran her hand over the rough bark, feeling the vibration of the ax in the wood. *Oh.* She drew her tiny bell from her dress pocket and shook it. Rives left the ax in the wood and stepped closer to catch her whispered answer. Since she had lost her voice, that was all she could do.

"The moon," she said.

He snorted, pushing damp strands of dusty blond hair off his forehead.

Rives was a tall, wiry man with heavy-lidded blue eyes and a mouth unaccustomed to smiling. Mer had inherited his height and slender build; she owed the rest to her mother, who had died nearly two decades earlier while giving birth to Jan. Rives, disinherited for marrying the raven-haired farm girl instead of some lord's daughter, had barely settled into his modest life when he found himself without a wife, alone with two babies and only an acre of stony soil from which to eke out a living.

"It was too easy," Rives said. "I can't think when I'm this tired."

"Let me chop for a while," she offered.

"It's not your turn."

She shrugged, flicked a watchful eye at Jan, and slipped the silver bell back into her pocket. It had been a gift from her uncle's wife, Lisette. Mer smiled as she recalled her last visit to Lord Barret d'Ivry's manor. Lisette had been shocked to silence when Mer, wanting to snag Rives's attention during an elaborate meal, tapped her knife against a silver plate. The bell arrived by messenger a week later.

Jan loved the bell, though his thick fingers could not find a way to make it work. One ring meant "Yes," two, "No," and three meant "Come here." Mer could approach Rives and whisper those words to him, but it was easier simply to ring the bell, especially if she was occupied in a task that required constant attention.

Autumn leaves rustled in the branches overhead. Mer picked a leaf out of her braid and leaned her face into the sun.

Life without a voice was not as terrible as she had thought it would be. Harder to bear was the memory of how she had lost it.

Mer still dreamed of Thorsault. Try as she might, she could not banish her memories of the fae city, though it lay on the other side of the island, buried under the lively roots of the Cursed Wood. The knight who had suffered with her in that vile place—her old acquaintance, Sir Avry—had advised her to write her dreams down. *Dreams are more about feelings than happenings*, he had written. *They lose power when described.*

Write them down she did, then on a whim, she had tucked them into one of her short replies to his almost daily letters. A few days later, a stack of his own dreams arrived, and they were not a pleasant read. But they soothed her when she lay awake at night, struggling to cast images from her mind. She knew which were his worst by the way he wrote them: the lines were thick and heavily blotted, and he left grace-marks of ink between the words. Funny, she had once believed Sir Avry to be emotionless, cold, and calculating, but his writing revealed just the opposite—

"Are you watching Jan?"

Mer's gaze flashed to the stream. Groaning, she darted to the edge and coaxed her brother out of the knee-deep water. He did not seem to feel the cold. She pulled off his boots and turned them upside down over a patch of sun-warmed earth. "What were you doing?" she rasped near his ear, not expecting an answer.

Jan drew a wet, folded leaf out of his pocket. "Fa."

"Mmm." 'Fa' usually meant 'father,' but it could also mean 'fall.' She wondered which it was.

Rives lowered his ax, leaned toward her, and riddled, "You must keep it after giving it."

"Your word?" she guessed.

"A red drum sounds without being hit and grows silent when touched. What is it?"

Mer led Jan to a rock where he could sit in the sun. *Grows silent when touched.*

She paced as her father chopped through the felled tree, split the log slab into four chunks, and tossed them onto his hand cart. Officially, those logs were not his. Since the crown owned the forest, it was illegal to harvest trees from it. But Rives had done exactly that for two decades.

"Do you give up?" he asked.

Sighing, she fetched her ax and slipped on her gloves. A wrong answer meant the loser worked.

"A heart," he said.

Mer tossed the whetstone at him. He caught it in a gloved hand and pressed it to his chest in parody. *Heart.* Mer could not help but smile.

Her ax clove the wood, slicing through layers of bark to enter the fibrous flesh. The initial burn in her arms faded to numbness as she found her pace and let herself flow into the repetitive motion of the swinging blade.

Drink, a voice whispered from the past. Mer winced, blinked away sweat, and swung. *Milk of the earth.*

A memory of pain seared across her throat. She swallowed convulsively and slammed her ax into the wood.

Bury deep, pile on stones, she riddled, *my mind will always dig up those old bones.*

"Mer, that's enough." Strong hands gripped her arms and held them steady, preventing her from swinging again. "Let go."

"But it's my turn."

"Let go. Now." Rives's eyes were hard, his jaw firm.

Mer's hand went limp, and her father tossed the ax onto the ground behind him. There was an awkward silence; even Jan was still, watching them with wide eyes.

"Where were you?" Rives demanded.

She shrugged and whispered, "Bury deep, pile on stones, my mind will always dig up those old bones."

"Memory."

She ran a trembling arm across her forehead. "Correct."

Rives shook his head. "We've done enough today," he said, gathering up the axes. He passed her the empty picnic basket. "Come, Jan."

"But it's such a nice day," she protested. "And the cart is far from full."

Her father would not be dissuaded.

***

As evening fell, Mer was grateful that Rives had insisted on heading home early. Her arms ached as though someone had battered them with a mallet. She sought her bed early and slipped into a mire of dreams as elusive as fish in a pond.

She woke to the sound of shutters slamming open against the wall above her bed. Jan, who rarely stirred once asleep, moaned in his bed across the room. Mer got up, wincing at the chill wind, and felt for the iron catch that held the shutters in place.

It was not there. Instead, there were two empty holes where nails had once been. The catch for the deadbolt had been torn right out of the shutter. Mer fingered the holes thoughtfully. *Nails must have been loose.*

"Mehh," Jan moaned.

Mer snatched a blanket off a chair and draped it over him. "It's all right, Jan. There's nothing to be afraid of. Just a gust of wind." Soon he quieted down and resumed snoring. Mer wrapped herself in a blanket and peered out the window to the shadowy line of trees, stroked by the eerie glow of dawn.

Then she froze, heart in her throat.

Something was out there.

A pale form crouched in the wood, only visible because it was lighter than the trees around it. The vestiges of night rendered it shapeless, incorporeal as mist. Mer squinted, afraid to move, afraid even to breathe.

Little by little, the forest brightened; the rising sun glimmered between the trunks, casting diagonal shadows over the field separating the cottage from the wood. Mer's eyes crossed in tiredness. When they focused again, she realized that nothing was there, and nothing ever had been. The tree shadows formed an unbroken line over the ground, revealing no mysterious shape.

She had only imagined it.

With trembling hands, she felt around on the floor until she found the latch, then pushed the attached nails back into their holes and closed the shutters. The bolt slid through with a satisfying click.

Please let there be no more wind, she prayed as she returned to her bed and pushed her face into the pillow.

She lay curled up, shivering, trying to ward off the fear and emptiness that were never more than a breath away.

Those old bones.

Mer had told no one she had killed the fae who destroyed her voice. She held that memory close to her, like a seed swathed in layers of hardened flesh. No one could pry it open.

Her fingers clenched as she remembered his red blood, spilling into the pool of milky poison he had forced her to drink from; the bloodied knife, loose in her hand; the icy water inside the tunnel she had crawled through to escape; the desolation of being lost in a dark forest, without a voice. Without a hope.

She had stumbled on Avry in the Cursed Wood. The knight had held her while she wept soundlessly into his chest. She would never forget the solid warmth of his arms, the moment of utter calm she had felt as she lifted her face off his tear-soaked shoulder.

I should thank him, she thought.

But she knew she never would.

She sighed and rolled onto her back. Perhaps she should seek out the wood woman, barter something for valerian root. Her stash had long been exhausted.

Unable to sleep, she dressed quickly in the chill air, tiptoed down the hallway to the common room, and set about starting a fire in the hearth. Amid the snapping of twigs came the creak of floorboards as Rives walked about his bedroom, dressing. Moments later, he came out and squatted beside her, his knees cracking as they bent.

"It's a cold morning," he said.

"Windy."

He pursed his lips. "No, it's just cold. Cold for early October."

She set a log on the fire and fanned it with the bellows. "The wind blew the bedroom shutters open this morning. Tore the catch right out of the wood."

Rives stiffened. "Both nails gave way?"

She nodded. "I pushed them back into their holes, but they won't stay like that—"

"The devil's hairs," he muttered and marched down the hall to her bedroom. He returned moments later and pulled on his boots.

Mer fetched her own and followed him out the door.

The land between the cottage and the wood was bare and brown. Clumps of squash plants and the leafy tops of root vegetables appeared here and there like a sprinkle of tossed coins. The other crops had been withered by frost. A stone well stood to one side of the yard, encircled by vine and weeds that no one had thought to pull.

"It hasn't rained in a week," Rives complained as Mer knelt beside him. "If it had, we might have found some footprints."

"Footprints..." She eyed him with a frown. "Do you really think someone was out here?"

He ran a hand over her shutters. "There is no mark on the wood. Did you hear anything? Footsteps, voices?"

She shook her head. "All I heard was wind." She refused to tell him that she had imagined a pale shape in the trees.

His brows rose. "You heard wind?"

"Heard it. Felt it. It woke Jan, and I had to throw an extra blanket over him."

He slumped against the cottage wall. "That catch was well fastened. It hasn't budged since I pounded it in two decades ago."

"The nails might have been loose," Mer pointed out, shivering. She should have grabbed a coat.

They both turned at the sound of approaching hoofbeats. "That must be the messenger with your daily letter," Rives said.

They came around to the front yard and surprised the messenger, whose gloved hand was raised to knock on the door. Jacques was a short, thick-set man whose nose and chin constantly sought to touch one another.

"Lord Rives, Lady Merisande," he greeted them, tilting his head in a show of respect for the meaningless titles they still held. He handed Mer the letter. "I'll be at my usual place until noon.

No other messages to deliver today, thanks be to God." With that he turned, threw himself on his dappled mare, and trotted off to Lord Gille d'Avrance's estate, where his brother worked as a stable master.

Mer never made Jacques wait long. If she replied—and she usually did—the fee was paid by Sir Avry. Waiting incurred additional charges, which Jacques had hinted at once or twice when the weather was bad.

Rives held the door open and she went in, sighing with relief at the warmth that greeted her.

***

Later, they sat around the table eating smoked rabbit and mushrooms. Jan swayed with tiredness. He probably would have slept on his plate if it did not contain his breakfast. Mer held Avry's letter under the table, surreptitiously leafing through the pages. There were always at least three, brimming with Avry's small but elegant script. His thoughts were as effortlessly expressed as wind through an open window. They revealed a world foreign to her: life inside the keep and its weapons yard, the intricacies of sword play. Even the king was not exempt from Avry's unembellished narrative.

And here and there, like a startling color that appeared in the warp of a weave, were hints that he never stopped thinking about her. She caught one as she read.

The armory received a gift from Faolin today. I am sure you have heard of that place, wedged between Ann and Lys. Their short swords are coveted, and they have gifted us ten. The box they arrived in is extraordinary, carved with animals and flowers, the wood so rich and dark that it reminded me of your hair.

She bit her lip, feeling a twinge of remorse. Try as she might, she could not manage to view Avry as more than a friend. That they had grown this close was surreal, a possibility she would have scoffed at half a year ago. She took a bite of rabbit and chewed over the problem.

After a time, she looked up to find her father watching her, and in his eyes lurked a conversation she desperately wanted to avoid.

CHAPTER 2

The isle of Aure was encircled by steep cliffs. Every morning, merchant ships lined up outside a slender opening at its southernmost tip. Once through the gap, they made their way up the widening estuary to the docks, where goods were unloaded and deals brokered. From the docks, shop owners hauled their cache of expensive fabrics, spices, and wines up the port road to the city markets.

The city was a maze of cobbled streets and carriageways. Its oldest, wealthiest quarter clung to the sides of a hill like barnacles hanging on a ship's hull. The castle rested on top. Its shape was recognizable to the smallest child: four towers piercing the sky, each connected by curtain walls topped by battlements. The tower keep, situated in the center of the castle yard, was a six-story pillar of polished white stone. Its inner wooden beams had been intentionally blackened with bitumen, a style that called to mind the ruins of an ancient city that had once thrived in Aure and still littered it, here and there, with charred stone and pottery.

By decree of the king, any man could train at the castle's yard if he owned a bow or blade and had the patience to become proficient with it. Despite this boon, no more than a dozen men trained there at any one time (full-time soldiers trained at the barracks). Many came in hopes that their efforts would garner them a knighthood. There were two ways to attain it: by birth, or by skill. King Ghislain offered the title to any man of noble birth who could swing a sword. He did not knight commoners unless they displayed extraordinary ability. For that reason, King's Knights—those who lived and worked at the castle—were usually commoners.

Sir Avry of the house Eleuthère was a rare exception.

***

Even on a still day, the castle yard was riotous with wind. Banners snapped, wooden shields knocked together, archery targets creaked on their poles. In autumn, the trainees who climbed the winding road to the castle arrived in sturdy woolen coats and caps. If the day warmed, these extra garments would be tossed aside and forgotten for a time.

Despite the chill morning, a pile of discarded garments had already gathered along the wall. Avry nudged a cap under a coat so it would not blow away. He was a tall man in his early twenties, with dark, thickly waving hair and eyes so pale a brown that in sunlight they appeared yellow. His lean jaw, combined with his eyes, had earned him the nickname "Pup," though only a handful of men called him that to his face.

Avry trained those who had worked their way through the beginner and intermediate stages of swordsmanship. If they bested Avry, they could move on to Sir Neville, Master of All Things Sharp.

Crossing his arms, he cast a tired gaze over the yard. An aging man had dragged his bones up the hill to whack away at a practice dummy, and three boys no older than sixteen were launching into their first week of training. Avry watched them idly, his head tilted to the side as he noted their strengths and weaknesses. Then he went still, remembering himself at that age.

"You'll be here a month," his trainer promised him. "Men of the houses only train to a ceremonial degree. They don't need to fight. Commoners do the fighting for them."

"Is that a rule or an observation?" Avry had wondered out loud.

"It's the way it is," the trainer replied.

Pain was Avry's closest friend those first few weeks. It rocked him to sleep every night and breathed fire on him during the day.

The king sometimes strode into the yard, as if his feet had led him there by happenstance. On the day Avry completed novice training, King Ghislain took the sword from the trainer and let Avry see how much further he could go. His ice-blue eyes had posed a question, and Avry could not help but answer it. *Yes. And yes. And yes again.*

Avry got to know the sound of Ghislain's tread on the paving stones. Every morning for half a year he listened for it, unthinkingly, and in time, longingly. He watched for the smile that breezed across the king's lips when Avry pleased him, and he pushed himself harder, wanting to glimpse that smile again.

Avry was the last student Ghislain trained and the only man of noble birth employed as a King's Knight. Strangely enough, these distinctions had earned him nothing but suspicion and disfavor from those of the upper houses. Some accused him of scheming to gain Ghislain's attention for his own ends, while others disdained him for choosing a profession belonging to commoners. Strangest of all was the rumor that he had renounced his family name and would only be called "Sir Avry."

The one person whose opinion would have truly mattered to Avry had remained indifferent, unimpressed by his skill with a blade. For years she had scorned him at dances and avoided his eyes when they ate together at his father's table.

Mer had warmed to him after their shared experience in Thorsault, but it had taken effort to keep the coals of that fire burning. Distance made visiting her a challenge, and Avry, not knowing how she truly felt, feared that if he stopped writing her, she would not ask why.

A feeble friendship is better than no friendship, Ghislain had once said. The words struck Avry as profoundly true, though not in the context Ghislain had intended them.

A sharp pull at the back of his head made him start.

"What a convenient cap," came the rumbling voice of the senior trainer. "It hides the shaggy dog you keep on your head."

Sir Neville was a rangy giant of a man whose broken nose and missing teeth should have deterred women. Instead, he was the most sought-after man in the yard.

"Morning yourself," Avry replied, dropping a hand on the trainer's arm, then that hand shot up and seized the clump of copper hair Neville had combed back over his bald spot.

Cursing, Neville tried to catch Avry in a chokehold, but the youth slid through the man's meaty arms, got behind him, and knocked him down in a leg lock.

"All right, that's enough," Neville said with a strained chuckle, struggling to fix his hair before anyone noticed.

As Avry straightened, brushing dirt off his hose, color snagged his eye.

A slender figure cloaked in a brilliant red surcoat had sauntered into the yard. The visitor's gray eyes flicked over Avry like a snake's tongue, then he turned to one of the beginning trainers and said something. The trainer—Marcus was his name—bobbed his head, uttered some sort of brief reply, and headed straight for Avry and Neville.

"Patric d'Audamar," Neville murmured.

"Why won't he just talk to us?" Avry said, smothering a twinge of anger.

Neville shrugged. "Who knows? Men of the houses are as fickle as women." Avry flashed him a look, and the senior trainer grinned. "It's true."

Marcus arrived, slightly out of breath and still sweating from a training session. He was a thick-set man with a wide mouth that seemed to eat words as he spoke them. His awkward speech made people think him unskilled. They were always proved wrong. "Sir, Lord—"

"Patric is not a lord," Avry corrected him, trying to control his irritation. "Lords must own land."

"Patric d'Audamar," he stumbled on, "wishes to train with you, sir."

Avry had suspected as much. The young noble would not wish to lower himself by training with a commoner. He shot another glance at Patric, who had unsheathed his blade and was swinging it like a farmer's scythe. His uncertain grip on the handle had convinced others to give him a wide berth. "What did you tell him?" Avry asked.

"That I would bring his request to your attention, sir."

"You didn't ascertain his skill level first?"

"That would have been pointless, sir. He only wants you."

"He wants," Avry repeated slowly with a raised brow. "Since when does someone's wants supersede the rules?"

Marcus's cheeks flushed pink. He said, flinging a stiff finger at the waiting noble, "When that someone is Patric d'Audamar, sir."

A hush had fallen over the yard. Patric did not look their way, but his supercilious smile suggested he had been listening.

The pale-haired, lace-cuffed Patric was not special. His name was.

Audamar was first of the houses. The connected house, the *ruling* house. And if that were not enough to give one pause, there was a good chance that Ghislain, bereft of sons, would elect him as successor.

No one wished to make an enemy of Patric.

Avry touched Marcus's shoulder, drawing him away from onlookers. "Remember our maxim here," he said.

"*Peritia supra nomine*," Marcus muttered.

"Which means..."

"Skill above status."

Avry gave a slow nod. The real meaning was "skill above name," but no one translated it that way. "If we allow Patric to bend the rules, we'd be turning that principle on its head. Worse, we'd be placing him above the king, who founded this system of training. Do you see how that would be dangerous?"

The trainer's lips compressed. "Yes, sir," he said stiffly.

But Avry sensed other words in the air between them. Vile, poisonous words. *The king is sick. The king may die. What good will his rules be then?*

Nearly two weeks had passed since Ghislain had fallen ill. He had shown no signs of grippe or stomach upset since he had crawled onto his mattress and remained there. His only symptom was fatigue.

Despite a lack of evidence, his physician stubbornly maintained that he was being poisoned. *I've seen this before*, he had commented in Avry's hearing. *It doesn't end well.*

Ghislain had countered that argument by pointing out that his own servant tasted his food and drink before every meal. However, the physician would not be dissuaded.

Avry, forced to watch the once vigorous man weaken day by day, woke in dread every morning, expecting the toll of bells.

"Pup." Neville's familiar, sturdy presence made Avry loose a breath he did not know he had been holding. "Patric is gone. He just walked off, still swinging that pretty sword of his."

Avry's gaze swung to the spot where Patric had been standing. The space was refilling with students. Patric was indeed gone. Had he given up, Avry wondered, or would he return the next day? "Marcus," he said absently.

"Yes, sir."

"You may go. We'll talk again later."

As the trainer mumbled a reply, the keep's back door swung open, and Avry's name cracked against the bustling yard.

"King wants you earlier than usual," Neville remarked as Avry unhooked his training belt and tossed it by the wall next to his jacket. "Do you think…?"

"I don't think anything," Avry said briskly, hoping the lie would not show on his face. "He was well enough when we met yesterday. Someone on death's door wouldn't bother discussing a lack of cesspits in the immigrant quarter."

Neville snorted.

Twice a week for the past month, Avry had been summoned to see the king. They discussed unsolvable problems such as poverty and illegal trade. And there was the endless list of items the king wished to attend to. Avry had no idea why Ghislain sought his advice. Mer thought it was the king's way of keeping Avry under his thumb. But Ghislain had kept Avry under his thumb for years. At first, Ghislain had permitted him to visit his family only on weekends. Then only on Sundays. And now...while Avry was still free to make the three-hour journey to his father's estate—as long as it did not interfere with his duties—he could not spend the night there. Avry might have protested the restriction, but the king's new illness made him fear to leave, even for a single day.

"I may be gone a while," Avry warned Neville. "Let me know if Patric...well, just let me know."

The keep was cold and quiet in the early morning. Rows of narrow windows cast bright bands across the floor, lending an illusion of depth to the marble flagstones. Avry strode through the welcoming light, passing the banquet hall, with its intricately carved pillars and sweeping arches, to the foot of the grand staircase. The second floor contained the Hall of Kings—a memorial to the former rulers of Aure—the knights' chamber and the royal library. The third and fourth floors housed the castle's guests and permanent residents. The fifth was the king's, the sixth, the servants.'

Avry forced his fingers to unclench as he stepped off the landing onto the fifth floor and headed down a slender corridor. It was a cheerful, if silent space. Light filtered through stained glass windows, flecking the floor and walls with brightly colored gems. Of the six rooms, only one was occupied. The queen rarely slept in her chamber; she spent most of her time in the southeast tower, looking out to sea where she had last seen her daughter.

Guards bowed to Avry as he approached the chamber's double doors, then it seemed as if two wings opened, ushering him into darkness.

Avry entered a vast, shadowy space. Lamps flickered, illuminating tapestries and delicately wrought mouldings. The chamber's sizeable windows were closed but not fastened; soft sounds filtered through: sea birds crying, the chatter of men and steel from the training yard, a ship's low bellow. As Avry approached the four-poster bed, the slender figure of the king's servant rose, offered Avry a brief bow, and scurried out of the room.

Avry waited until the doors had closed then dropped into the chair by the bed and bowed until his forehead grazed the sheets.

Ghislain's hand came to rest lightly on his shoulder. "You smell of sunlight and fresh air," he sighed.

"Those old friends miss you, My Lord."

The king chuckled, releasing him. "It's cold outside. Cold in here."

It was not cold at all. A merry fire crackled in the hearth, brushing the walls with orange fingers of light.

Avry allowed his gaze to settle on the pale figure on the bed.

The king was encased in a cocoon of silk and wool. Shadows lurked like bruises under his eyes; hard lines of pain were etched around his mouth and between his brows. His breath was stiff and shallow, fluttering a few strands of gray hair that lay across his cheekbone. Avry cleared his throat, afraid of the sound that would come out when he spoke. "Have you eaten something?"

"It's early yet. I've had a little wine and some bread." The king shifted onto his side and frowned his white, bushy brows at Avry. "And that, my boy, will be the last of your mothering. Bring me the papers."

Avry opened the top drawer of Ghislain's bedside desk and drew out several sheets of stained, rumpled vellum. "The top page is blank," he remarked. It always contained two or three sentences, written in the king's stiff, jerky hand, each sentence expressing, in the simplest terms possible, a need or a want. Sometimes a dream.

"You will write for me." His finger gestured to the desk. Normally bare, it now held a serviceable lamp and a variety of writing tools. Avry's heart sank, recognizing that Ghislain could no longer carry out even this simple task.

The king was waiting.

Avry set the paper squarely in the center of the desk. His fingers slowed as he pinched the corners, lining up the pages. Writing always made him think of Merisande. Without conscious thought, his mind was already sifting through the morning's events, deciding which to reveal to her. The ritual woke in him a deep sadness and restless longing. He needed to see her, at the very least to know if anything had changed between them.

Despite all the small compliments he had paid her in his letters, she had not responded with a hint of romantic interest.

But did that truly mean anything? They had not spoken face to face for a month, not since that warm evening at the edge of his father's land. Since then, she had replied to every one of his letters. Every one. Did it matter if they were brief? She must feel something, or she would not continue writing him.

He chose a fine bone pen from an assortment of quills, affixed a nib, and uncapped the ink jar. "What shall I write, My Lord?" After a silence, Avry glanced at the bed and realized with a twinge of alarm that the king had been watching his face.

"Write this: Sir Avry will no longer call me 'Lord' while we speak together in confidence."

He almost dropped the pen. "Then what should I call you?"

"You know my name. Use it."

"Very well," he agreed, knowing very well that he would not. He dipped the pen. His lips compressed as he stared at the blank page, an urge to fill it with his own needs and wants, his own dreams nearly overcoming him.

When Ghislain did not speak, he asked idly, "Is there news from the second mission to Thorsault?"

"The team searched two more of the castle's upper floors, found a couple more dead slaves, but no fae." He paused to clear his throat, as if the word "fae" had fluttered down his windpipe. "They couldn't have flown over the Cursed Wood, could they...?"

Avry resisted the urge to sigh. How many times had the king raised this question? Either he was losing his memory, or he refused to accept the answer. "Certainly not," he said firmly, biting back the added, "My Lord." "The fae are like flightless birds. Even the strongest of them couldn't have flown for more than a mile."

"Perhaps they attempted to fly over it and were trampled to death by the trees."

Avry pursed his lips. "Perhaps..."

"Or," the king added ominously, "the fae are spirits."

Avry shook his head. "I've seen their bones. They are as mortal as we are."

"Their bare bones?"

"Yes, My—"

"Where—where did you see them? And why wasn't this in your report?"

Avry knew it had been in his report but chose not to contradict him. He drew a tight breath, recalling the stench of stale air. The silence of the dead. "After escaping my cell, I was in the deeps of the tor, searching for a way out. I opened a door and stepped into a mausoleum."

The king gave a violent shudder and drew the covers more closely around him. "Let us speak of something else. Something living."

"Immigrants?" Avry suggested, recalling their last conversation.

"Gandel."

Avry ran a slow finger over the vellum pages. "I always assumed he died in the trees."

"Not according to the lady's narrative."

Early in the summer, Merisande had been asked to provide a report of her experience in Thorsault. The king referred to it now and then, but Avry longed to read it himself, wanting all the details she had either forgotten or intentionally kept from him.

"Merisande wrote," the king added as Avry leaned forward in interest, "that Prince Gandel left the city two days before its destruction."

"Disappeared," Avry amended quietly. "She told me that his father tore apart his chamber looking for him."

"Either way, he might still be alive, lurking in the north wood, or perhaps even in Aure City."

Avry frowned. Though he had never met the fae prince, he had learned enough about him to be sorry if he had died. *The prince and the king are enemies,* a slave in Thorsault had once told Avry. *If Gandel lives to become king, he would free us.*

"Prince Gandel was Merisande's only friend in that place," Avry pointed out. "He tried to free her and would have freed all the slaves, had he the chance. If he lives, then he is no threat to anyone."

"A threat!" The king groaned and ran a hand over his eyes. "Gandel is a valuable source of information. He could answer all our questions about Thorsault, and some we haven't thought to ask." He pointed a shaky finger at the vellum. "Write this: Find Prince Gandel."

Avry dipped the pen and scratched obediently. "Anything more?" he asked without looking up.

"Yes. Write: Decide whether or not to allow fishing on the eastern banks of the arm."

The pen slowed only briefly before plunging on. "Only fish?" he wondered out loud as he drew more ink from the jar.

"Surely not live there. The Cursed Wood has receded from the shoreline, but it could return at any time."

Avry finished writing and leaned back against the hard wooden chair. According to Gandel, the Cursed Wood had sprung up around the fae city and its surrounding farmland decades after they had settled there. In the ensuing years, the fae had learned, whether by trial and error or by accident, that the trees' powerful roots relaxed when told stories. But no one could stop an entire forest on the move.

"I wasn't suggesting you encourage people to live there," Avry said. "But the fisherfolk will want docks, huts to shelter in during storms. And after a few years, some may want to settle there."

Ghislain was nodding. "Well done, my boy. You're learning to delve deeper into these thorny problems. You're beginning to see that passing a law isn't as easy as stamping a seal on a document. Important questions must be raised and answered. For example: Do the benefits outweigh the risks? Do I have a way to ensure that the law is not abused? And if there is no way to avoid abuse, do I have a way to reduce it, perhaps by way of fines?"

One of the shutters creaked open a crack. Avry, listening to a gull's cry, wished with sudden fervor that he could fly away with it. *Don't be selfish,* he scolded himself. The king was sick; perhaps he needed Avry to work through these thorny problems. "I suppose you could station a few guards along the eastern shore," he mused.

"It's a pity we can't just burn the wood down."

Avry shuddered at the thought of destroying the wood. The trees had a collective intelligence, a sentience that no one fully grasped. Fortunately, a moisture they excreted protected them from the lick of flames.

Ghislain's eyes drooped then darted open again, and Avry was appalled to see him clench his fists and use the pain of his nails biting into his palms to keep himself awake.

"Would you like me to fetch you water?"

"God, no. I don't have the patience to fill another chamber pot."

"Then is there something else I can do to ease your discomfort?"

"Yes. There's a small chunk of marble in the drawer. Clenching it helps keep me stay awake."

Shifting through the various odds and ends, Avry found the cool, gray stone and placed it in the king's upraised palm. Stiff fingers curled around it, dragging it down under the covers.

"That's better." Ghislain drew a long breath. "Where were we?"

"The Cursed Wood."

At the words, a memory of trees filled Avry's mind, the quiet sigh of wind through branches. The Cursed Wood had seemed serene when he and Mer walked through it after escaping Thorsault. But at the first sign of dawn, the ground opened and roots bit down on Avry's leg. The pain had been so severe that he could barely speak, never mind call back the dozen or so tales he had stored up in his memory. Merisande might have helped, but her voice had been ruined. In desperation, she had whispered for him to recount how the fae mistreated their slaves.

As the story spilled out of him, the roots eased open, allowing him to go free. For a time, all was quiet and still. Then the earth trembled violently, and they were forced to climb the nearest tree. The wind wailed. Branches pinned him to the trunk. The world shuddered, and he lost consciousness.

Mer had jabbed him awake. He could still picture her face when he had turned and looked at her, the profound relief in her deep green eyes.

It was a moment he would never forget.

"You've wandered off again, boy," Ghislain grumbled. "Where are your thoughts?"

Where indeed. Sighing, Avry told him. Ghislain nodded along to the familiar tale, his hand moving like a small animal under the sheets, toying with his worry stone. "I do hope you've taken my advice and concealed the true version of events," he said when Avry had finished.

"I haven't said a thing," Avry sighed. "People remain under the misapprehension that it was my idea to tell the story that destroyed Thorsault, not Merisande's." The deception would have bothered him more were she not so content with it.

"It works out for the best," Ghislain promised.

"How can twisting the truth work out for the best?"

The king chuckled. "You're still an idealist. I was too at your age. It doesn't last.

"At any rate," he went on when Avry said nothing, "it doesn't hurt to be thought of as a hero. Whether or not the story was yours, you told it well enough to stir the heart of the wood. You vanquished your enemy with words."

"Not everyone feels that way," Avry pointed out, watching firelight stroke the wooden snout of a beast curled around a bed pole. "The lion of Audamar still hates me."

"Audamar will always hate you," Ghislain said flatly, then snorted. "A lion indeed. The house has grown fat and lazy. A lion drunk on its own piss doesn't harm anyone."

Avry's mouth twitched up in amusement and then straightened. He stared down at the dark flagstones.

"What's wrong now?" Ghislain demanded.

"Nothing. I just...don't want to lose you."

The fire in the hearth cracked and settled, like someone readying to sleep. "I believe that is the first time you've admitted any sort of fondness for me." The king paused and then hissed out a laugh at Avry's discomfort. "Ah, well. We must move on. Write: Return Patric d'Audamar's hereditary land."

Two years ago, Patric had lost a hefty sum while gambling. To cover the cost, he sold the land he had only just acquired from his father to Lord Pere of Bereux, who owned the neighboring lot. By law, land had to remain within the house it belonged to. When Ghislain learned about the illegal transfer, he confiscated the land, forcing Patric to return the money. Lord Pere was fined, and Patric's father reluctantly paid his son's gambling debt.

"Well?"

Avry set down the pen. "I'm sure you have your own reasons for returning the land."

Ghislain's mouth hardened as he stared up at the gauzy canopy above the bed. "Patric will never be king. His younger brother would have made a better choice, but..." He raised his hand in a shrug. "Neither will do. But that doesn't stop people from speculating. Many—including Patric—believe I will name him my successor."

"But you won't, so this is a means to soften the blow," Avry guessed, breathless at the revelation that Patric would not be king.

"Just so. And it will remind people why Patric shouldn't be king."

"Who *will* be king?" Avry asked, caught on the edge of fear and anticipation.

Ghislain threw him a sharp glance. "What makes you think I should tell you that?"

"Nothing. Arrogance, perhaps."

The answer bought him a fond smile.

For a while, neither of them spoke. Ghislain stared at the ceiling again, awake, though his hand was motionless under the blankets. "Write one more thing," he said abruptly, a strange note in his voice.

Avry dipped the pen. The nib hovered over the page. "Yes?"
"Convince my heir to accept the kingship."
Pen touched paper. "Why would he need convincing?"
"Because my heir is you."

CHAPTER 3

"This isn't something to jest about, My—"

"I'm not jesting." Ghislain raised himself up on shaking arms, clinging to the edge of the desk for balance. Some of the covers fell away, revealing a gaunt form draped in blue silk. As the fabric settled, his hand shifted from the desk to Avry's shoulder. Strength of purpose suffused his face, giving it a brightness that rendered everything else dim.

The hair on Avry's arms rose as he looked back at that face, and the pen slipped from his chill fingers and wobbled to the edge of the desk, where it rested precariously.

"You are my heir," Ghislain said, stressing each of the words as if they were their own continents. "I've formally named you, stamped my seal on a document before witnesses, declaring you my successor. I was only waiting for the right moment."

Avry swallowed hard. Alarm surged through him, making him dizzy. His heart thundered, his ears rang. He was worried he would throw up on the king's bed sheets. "The right moment…?" he managed.

"To tell you what you are. What you will be."

He struggled to order his thoughts. "But I'm not of Audamar."

"That doesn't matter. Anyone can be chosen from any one of the twelve houses." He shook his head at Avry's stunned expression. "I'm amazed that you haven't guessed this."

"How could I?"

Ghislain drew breath as if to speak then fell still. His expression grew vague and dreamy. "I'll never forget the day you strode into the knights' chamber, a gangly boy of sixteen who'd spent his adolescent years in a book. As you held your first sword, I watched you mouth the tiny words engraved on the underside of the hilt: *Under Light*. No one else had noticed the inscription, but you saw the small things and understood their meaning.

"*My boy*. That's what I called you. If you only knew what that term meant to me." His lips curled in a fond smile. "I'm well aware of your faults. You haven't always made the wisest decisions. But neither have I. Neither has anyone. No one is perfect; they are merely suitable." Dropping his hand from Avry's shoulder, he loosed a long sigh. "Well, have you nothing to say in answer?"

Avry mouthed a word or two, but no sound came out. Ghislain's brow furrowed as he studied Avry's face, then he reached over and touched his hand.

"My god, you're in shock."

"I'm fine," he croaked and then flinched as the king shook a hand bell.

The chamber door whispered open, and the servant stepped in.

"Fetch me the physician," Ghislain ordered.

***

Some time later, Avry passed an empty mug, still reeking of bitter tea, to the figure kneeling beside him. The king's physician was a pale, lanky man with a full head of thick white hair that stood out from his head like porcupine quills. His voice was always gentle, even when his words were grim. "You should get some rest," he advised Avry.

"I'll rest later. Thank you."

Inclining his head, the physician rose to his feet with surprising grace and slipped through the door. When the room was quiet again, Avry stole a glance at the bedridden king, who looked as though he had bitten down on an unexpected bone. "Forgive me," Avry muttered.

Ghislain shook his head. "The physician is right. You ought to get some rest." He dropped the stone into Avry's palm. "Come back this evening when you've given this some thought."

Avry clenched the chunk of marble, feeling its lingering warmth in his chill hands.

He could not accept the kingship.

Not only was he profoundly unqualified, but he was not of the ruling house. No matter what Ghislain did to legitimatize him, Avry would still be an imposter, and Audamar would have every right to take back what was theirs, not by force, perhaps—the Lion had no army, no means to overthrow a rightful sovereign—but there were other ways to strike: paid assassins, false accusations that could poison men's hearts. And Audamar could use its alliances with important traders to strangle Avry's house and any houses supporting him.

Ghislain must have reflected on these possibilities, yet he had chosen Avry regardless.

My boy.

Avry had known that the king favored him over other knights, but it had never occurred to him that Ghislain would—or even could—come to view him as a son.

The revelation ought to have stirred his heart, but when he searched inside himself, he found nothing but the creeping sludge of his own dread.

He set the stone on the desk. Light from the hearth breathed color into it, giving it a soft glow. "I don't know what I'm supposed to think about. Evidently, you've been planning this for some time. You've even signed the papers."

Ghislain pinched the space between his brows. "You still have to agree to it, boy. I can't *make you* be king, no more than I could keep you from wandering into the Cursed Wood after Merisande."

You punished me for that, Avry recalled darkly.

"Give me your objections," the king offered. "I'll try to keep an open mind."

Avry snorted. He had already given an objection, and Ghislain had flicked it aside like an unwanted bug. "I'd prefer to ask questions."

"Go on then."

He fingered the pen, catching a drip of ink before it soiled the desk. "By making me your successor, you would be removing the kingship from a house that has held it for centuries. That act will be viewed as an indictment against your own family. It will shift the order of houses, demoting Audamar to second place. Are you truly willing to suffer the consequences of that decision?"

"I would give up more to keep Aure alive," Ghislain said. "Remember that. Aure is more important than a name."

Aure supra nomine.

Avry leaned into his hands with a sigh. "Why me?" he muttered through his fingers. "Why *my* name? I don't know a thing about ruling a country."

"Nor did I. Nor does anyone. A man doesn't learn to be king from study and observation—he learns by doing. You must trust me, Avry. Trust that I know better than you do who would make a good king."

They regarded each other in silence, then Avry rose to his feet. Though he had other questions, it would have been pointless to ask them. The king, who had spent months, perhaps even years reflecting on this scheme, would have an answer to them all. "I do need time to think," he admitted.

Ghislain caught his arm. "I want you to do something for me."

"Yes, My..." he cleared his throat. "Yes?"

The king relaxed back into the pillow. "When you are in the quiet of your room, I want you to imagine me dead."

Avry recoiled from the thought. "But—"

"You must. I am dead, and Aure has no king. Now, I want you to think of a man you trust. Someone who hasn't sequestered himself in his country house, whiling away his time and money. Someone you would willingly serve. When you think of such a man—and be sure that he is of Audamar, since you consider that so important—come give me his name."

"And if I can't?"

The king's eyes closed. "Then you will agree to be king."

CHAPTER 4

Across the sea, the country of Ann had begun to feel the effects of the changing season. The last of its grapes had been harvested, and the wheat fields were bare and gray, soil upturned to accept the new winter seeds.

It was the season for campfires. One, wedged between a stone fence and the shadowy edge of a forest, had begun to burn brightly. Autumn leaves whirled in the sky above it. A few tangled with the smoke and flames, coming to rest on the fire's edge like scorched butterflies.

Night was approaching.

Fingers shaking, Prince Gandel slowly unwrapped a bandage clinging to his now wingless shoulders and upper back. The cloth darkened as he peeled off the last few inches. Cool air slid across his wounds. The very act of unwrapping tightened the skin across his back, making him wince. But he had grown used to the pain. *Imagine that*, he thought wryly.

As always, the last bit of cloth stuck, and he had to lie on his stomach and pick the stiff fabric away from the scabbing sores. The task done, he wiped his bloodied fingers on the clean end of the bandage and tossed it into the fire. He watched it burn, ignoring the blood trickling down his back. *Replace it every couple of days,* the physician had advised him. *Don't reuse it. And don't bury it. An animal will drag it up the next day. Just take it off and burn it.*

Gandel had left Thorsault with no more than a sack of coins and the clothes on his back (these were a plain brown tunic and hose, buried under a jacket he had filched from a field slave). Having crossed the gorge, he made his way down to Aure City, where he spent the summer drifting from inn to inn, lingering at public houses and wandering the dockyards. Most people avoided him, casting uneasy glances at his humped back, slender hands, and dandelion-fluff hair. *I'm looking for a discreet surgeon,* he murmured over and over again to anyone who would listen. At last, an olive-skinned sailor dropped a name. For a coin, he scratched a map into the wet sand, naming towns, holdings, long roads winding through forests and vineyards. *Board a merchant ship,* the man advised him. *This time of year, it's the only way you'll get to Ann.*

Gandel smiled sourly, recalling the surgeon's face when he glimpsed what the prince concealed under his heavy jacket. "I wish to rid myself of this deformity," Gandel had said with a loathing that was not entirely feigned. He had come to hate his wings and all they represented.

The physician, having warned him that he might die from the surgery, accepted the coin and went on with it.

He almost did die. The bleeding would not let up, no matter what the physician did to try to halt it. Gandel had fainted twice from the pain. And after being burned by hot irons and squeezed by heavy cloths, after lying face down on the same table for two days, smelling blood, tasting it, feeling it wrap him in chill fingers, he was barely conscious and beyond caring when the physician announced that the bleeding had stopped.

Another week passed before he could walk again. Weakness was only a part of it. Without wings, Gandel had trouble finding his balance and swayed with every step.

The physician had not let him leave until the fae could negotiate the path from the front door to the road without stumbling.

He was on his own now, as free as he had ever been. Lonelier than he had ever been.

But it was a different sort of loneliness. Gandel had hope now, a chance to live the way he wished. Free from the burden of his inheritance. No one in his line had made the choice simply to walk away. Not in four centuries. Since he had done so, he had felt as if a weight was lifted from him. Even his nervous twitches had disappeared.

Tossing his head back, he drew a long breath of cool air. He scented damp leaves, wood smoke, cooking meat. The rabbit had been an easy kill. The forest was teeming with small animals, and the sturdy bow he had fashioned from a willow branch was as good as the one he had left behind in Thorsault. Soon he would need to think about shelter. He had been skirting the edge of a forest for nearly a week, gradually making his way to a town where he hoped to find some light work.

He unraveled another length of cloth and began wrapping the wounds. His fingers trembled again as they brushed that bare place between his shoulder blades. He could still sense his wings, like twin ghosts perched on his back. The eerie sensation robbed him of the liberation he had wanted to experience. "The feeling will fade," he promised the fire. One day he would be completely healed, and then…

He could pretend. Without wings, there would be nothing to give him away. True, his bones were longer and lighter than those of humans, but not grotesquely so. At best he would be considered thin, at worst, deformed.

Human, either way. A human in a sea of humans. Like a blade of grass in a meadow.

He smiled as he tore the cloth and secured it with a pin.

CHAPTER 5

At two hours before midnight, Avry dragged his feet up the stairs to the royal floor. Lamps flared as he passed them. The flickering shadows only served to deepen the feeling of unreality. He strode through the chamber's double doors, blinking at the sudden brightness. The king's chamber was lighter at night than during the day. All the lamps in the room were lit, and decorative wax pillars graced the corners, their braided wicks topped with lively flames.

The king's long, gaunt form lay stretched out on the mattress, enveloped now by a single sheet. Only the faint rise and fall of his chest and the cracks of his open eyes revealed that he was not dead. Avry pushed back the chair and knelt on the floor by his side.

They regarded each other for some moments before Ghislain cleared his throat. "Well, have you a name?"

There had been dozens. Avry had spent hours filling pages with them, a bottle of apple brandy in one hand and a pen in the other. Aure was a small kingdom, settled three centuries before by adventurous young nobles from Ann. Their lineages had been scrupulously maintained over the years, even the births of acknowledged bastards, though they could not hold titles. At present, the majority of people living on the isle were commoners: farmers, crafters, miners, smelters, fishermen; the nobility huddled in their midst like a dysfunctional family.

The king regarded him expectantly.

"I was forced to disqualify most of them for 'sequestering themselves in their country houses, whiling away their time and money.'"

"What did that leave—about twenty?"

Avry gave a tired nod. "I spent the afternoon poring over the remaining ones."

Poring did not begin to describe what he had done. If names were onions, he had peeled them open, eyes streaming and hands reddened, until nothing remained inside but the delicate slivers of green. Only a handful of names had survived being scored out. A handful of men he trusted.

But for various reasons, they could not be king. Charles and Giles d'Audamar suffered from chronic health problems; Lord Dimetre had fathered twin girls with dwarfism—a defect considered unlucky in Aure—and Lord Robert had given up the church. Avry had contemplated making a list of potential queens, but since the king had married off his only daughter to the prince of Ann, crowning another young woman—especially one from another house—would have been unforgivably cruel.

He had crushed the lists and chucked them into the fire. Turning once around his chamber, he had snatched up a second bottle of brandy and strode out of the keep into the cold darkness. Torches flared along the outer walls of the keep, casting a sickly yellow glare over the pale stone blocks. Nodding to the guards, he crossed the front yard to the western wall, which offered some measure of privacy. Though his legs were stiff from long hours of sitting, he was barely aware of the discomfort, and the chill air that seeped through his tunic cleared his thoughts.

Ghislain's illness had hung about the castle for days, breathing death down everyone's backs. Avry had thrust aside the worry so often that doing so had become reflex. Still, the prospect of Ghislain's death stole over him from time to time, and worse than knowing he might lose a friend was the fact that no one was suited to rule in his place.

No one had included himself.

You must trust me, Avry.

He almost could. The desire to rise to the challenge, as he had once done on the training yard, hovered close to the surface. It sneered at death and gathered confidence around it like clothing.

But he could not embrace it and certainly could not maintain it.

He gazed up at the clear night sky. Mer had pointed to the stars one evening as they lay on their backs on the edge of the gorge, exhausted after crossing the Cursed Wood and the vast plain beyond it. Her face had been cool and serene. *The stars seem changeless,* she had written him later. *They exist in a permanent state of tranquility.* Avry smiled at the memory, and at that moment he sensed the true reason he did not want to be king: because it would destroy any future he might have with Merisande. Mer would recoil from the prospect of being queen, a position that would subject her to constant scrutiny. There would be no forest for her to retreat into, no place where she could truly be alone, free to be herself. He took a long pull of brandy.

It was not enough. He could not tell Ghislain that Merisande was the reason he would not be king. Ghislain would not accept that answer. *The concerns of a kingdom outweigh those of a single man,* he had once said, and those were no empty words. Ghislain sacrificed much by selecting Avry as king-in-waiting. Had he settled on Patric, he would have retained his good standing with his house and avoided conflict. But his subjects would have paid for it dearly. A bad king threatened the most vulnerable: those without titles and holdings, immigrants and tenant farmers. When the crown was rotten, the people suffered. How could Avry live with himself if he allowed that to happen? Could he even serve such a monarch? He drained the brandy and flung the empty bottle at the moon.

***

"There are no names left," he told the waiting figure on the bed.

"Then…"

"I will be king."

CHAPTER 6

"Where is Jan?" Mer's breathy whisper caught Rives mid-swing.

He set down his raised ax, wiped his forehead with the back of his sleeve, and lifted a wry brow at his daughter. Were there three words more annoying than "Where is Jan?" He doubted it. "You shouldn't come so close to me while I'm swinging. Use your bell next time."

"I did, but you didn't seem to hear it. Jan?"

"I don't know. I suppose he wandered off while you were speaking to the messenger." He glanced at the unopened letter stuffed down the front of her dress and wondered what Avry would think if he knew where his letter had ventured. "I don't know," he repeated as she strode away, heading for the door.

Rives stretched his stiff back. The chill air made his muscles ache, but the pain worsened if he stood still, allowing the cold to seep in. He swung again, taking pleasure in the clean crack of the ax driving through wood.

Mer did not reemerge. Rives tossed the chunks of wood onto the pile and set down his ax. Jan liked to be outside while Rives chopped. What mischief had he got up to inside?

Brushing off his dusty tunic, he strolled into the house.

Pitiful moaning came to his ears. He followed it to the pantry, a small room tucked away at the northwest corner of the cottage. The scent of honey filled his nostrils as he swung open the door.

For several moments he could not speak, could not even draw breath.

Jan lay sprawled on the pantry's stone floor, his face, hands, legs—every part of him but his bare chest—smeared with honey and berries. Mer knelt at his side with a bucket of well water, trying to remove the sticky mess with a cloth. His soiled shirt lay in a heap by his head, and next to it were the broken shards of a ruined honey jar, which must have been pulled off a shelf.

Jan met his eyes, licked his wet lips, and burped.

Rives lost control. Laughter exploded out of him, shuddering his whole frame and making him bend double. Jan's moan joined to the sound like a discordant note.

Mer leaned back and smiled. "I don't remember the last time you laughed," she said when there was a pause for her to whisper into.

"Neither do I."

She shook her head at the empty space on the shelf. "What a waste."

Rives understood her pain. Jan had destroyed half their berry preserves. It had cost them a day's work to gather the honey and berries and prepare it all for bottling. The remaining jar would not last the winter.

Rives knelt down and gathered up the sticky pieces of pottery, thinking that he and Mer would have to give the floor a good washing later. After depositing them outside, he returned to the pantry, hauled Jan to his feet, and dragged him out the door to the well. He stripped his son naked and scrubbed him until his teeth chattered. Mer came out with a blanket, and together she and Rives steered Jan inside.

Rives watched Mer from the corner of his eye as she tugged a fresh tunic down over her brother's head and helped him into some clean hose. Rives's son was a boy no longer. Had he been born a normal child, he would have been in his senior year of schooling. At nineteen, he could have been married with children, but instead he would himself remain a child. Forever.

Rives frowned as Mer led Jan to the hearth and coaxed him to lie down. She should not sacrifice her happiness for her brother. But it was happening. Day after day, Rives let it happen, and now she was in her twenty-second year, unwed and stubbornly clinging to a life she should have long left behind.

My god, Rives thought, *if the only naked male she ever sees is Jan, perhaps there is a reason she remains unwed.*

He shook the thought away. With Mer, nothing was that simple.

Jan was on the floor by the fire now, snoring heartily. Rives kicked off his boots and plunked himself down into one of two chairs encircling the hearth. He flicked a glance at Mer, who was seated in the second chair, head bent over Avry's letter.

Suddenly her fingers tightened convulsively, and she straightened, cursing under her breath.

Astonished, Rives asked her what was wrong.

"Nothing. It's not worth mentioning."

Rives did not have to strain to hear her. The chairs, which used to be a foot apart, had been pulled together so they almost touched.

"If it's enough to make you curse, then it's worth mentioning."

She shrugged and then acquiesced. "Avry can't attend the quarterly dance. He must stay by the king, who is apparently ill."

An amused smile crept up the sides of Rives's face.

"Don't say it," she said.

"Say what?" he asked innocently.

"You were about to point out that this news would have cheered me a few months ago."

"The thought had crossed my mind, but why voice it? You know quite well that your opinion of Avry has changed since the last quarterly." But did she recognize just how much it had changed?

There was a silence. Rives ran a finger over the chair's wooden arm. "My brother said something about the king's health when we spoke last week."

"Oh? What did he say?"

"I don't recall," he admitted, embarrassed by his poor memory. "Something about a debilitating weakness." A twinge of anxiety knotted his stomach as he contemplated Avry's news. Could the king be near death?

But of course not. If that were true, he would have announced his heir. "Has Avry written about the illness before?"

Mer shook her head. "He said only that the king has been tired lately."

Rives sighed. "Well, it's untimely, to be sure."

"I'll miss his dancing more than anything." She curled the paper under her palm and stared wistfully into the fire. "He coaxed me into dancing with him at the last quarterly. I was annoyed at first, and then astonished. He dances as if he were born to it. As if he's music's incarnation."

Rives nodded, unsurprised. He wondered if she were aware of the ripples of gossip their dancing had sent through the twelve houses. No, Lisette would not have told her, and Mer would not have learned it from anyone else.

"Well, there's always another quarterly," he said.

"I'm still going." She waved to the neatly folded dress on the sewing stool by her chair. "It would be ungracious not to wear Lisette's beautiful fabrics."

"But who will you dance with?"

"Whoever gives me their card."

Rives shook his head, stunned by her lack of social understanding. Mer was so intelligent in other ways. How could she fail to grasp something so simple? "But what of your courtship? Do you expect others to sacrifice their cards on you while you're being courted by Sir—?"

"I'm not being courted by Sir Avry."

Rives suppressed a groan. "You write each other nearly every day."

"Friends write. If we hadn't agreed to be friends, I wouldn't have asked him to write me."

"*You* asked?"

Mer set the letter on the chair arm and went to stoke the fire. Jan stirred at the sound of wood shifting and cracking but did not waken. "I was concerned about his welfare," she explained when seated again. "After all, I'm the reason he was imprisoned last summer. If he hadn't gone into the Cursed Wood to rescue me..." Her voice trailed off. Rives sighed at the word "rescue." While it was true that Avry set out to find her, he did not rescue her. Mer escaped Thorsault on her own and happened upon him by chance later that night. *Rescue* was a word belonging to the alternate version of events King Ghislain had spun and spread; the King's Truth, as Avry called it.

"He's not imprisoned now," he reminded her.

Mer twisted her brown braid around her neck. "He is, in a way. After his release, the king reassigned him to combat training, which has kept him leashed on the castle grounds, unable to get away long enough even to visit his family. Avry has lost his independence and may lose more if he tries to break free…" She paused, drew a hesitant breath, and said lamely, "I asked him to keep me informed about how things progressed."

Rives pulled at the stubble on his chin. Did Mer truly believe that Avry's situation was this dire, or had she used the idea as a pretext to continue their correspondence?

"I know how it sounds," she went on, watching his face. "But I feel as if I'm involved in this mess. Not to blame for it, but drawn in nonetheless."

"I wouldn't worry about Sir Avry, Mer. The king has kept him on a tight leash since he knighted the boy six years ago. Lord Piercy d'Eleuthère was always proud of that fact. He used to say that his son had two fathers, as if Avry would be king one day." He chuckled, remembering how the old lord used to invite nobles from Audamar to his table, only to regale them with stories of Avry's chumminess with the king.

Mer had fallen still, staring at the flames as though they contained a hidden message. "Are you suggesting I stop writing him?"

"No." He leaned forward and laid a hand on her wrist. "I'm merely suggesting you reexamine *why* you are writing him. The man loves you. Whether or not he agreed merely to be friends is irrelevant. It doesn't change how he feels. And it won't change how others view your correspondence. I—" His voice broke as Mer sprang up and tossed the letter into the fire. The room brightened as it burst into flames.

"There," she said curtly, falling back into the chair. "It's finished. I won't write him anymore."

A sudden snore from the floor punctuated her sentence. Rives, torn between amusement and frustration, stared at the burning sheets until they broke apart with a soft rustle and settled into the grate. "What will you tell him?"

"Nothing, until I see him in person."

"And you will," he assured her.

Mer nodded morosely.

Rives, watching light fan over the tight lines in her face, felt a pang of guilt. What if she unknowingly loved Avry? Had Rives just disrupted something fragile and unacknowledged?

"I'm going out to check on some traps," he announced and crossed the room before Mer could reply. He needed to think.

As he pulled on his boots, a spot of honey on the toe reminded him of Jan's sticky skin. "I don't want you seeing your brother naked anymore," he decided. "Nor," he added, inspired, "should you sleep in the same room with him."

Mer turned in her seat and stared as if he had suggested that they rebuild the cottage.

Rives smiled, his conscience already soothed by the sacrifice he was about to make. "Jan can sleep in my room."

CHAPTER 7

Mer stepped out of the dainty carriage her aunt had loaned her for the night, allowing the driver to take her hand.

Light from the falling sun cast a warm glow over Rose Hall's stately facade. The twelve pillars holding up the great porch cast spindly shadows. Each represented a house, and because they all looked exactly alike, young men had taken it upon themselves to scratch names into them. The line of houses marched from left to right: Audamar, Eleuthère, Arcy, Bereux, Briomme, Ivry, Corbet, Artois, Aubry, Reviers, Valois, and Avrance.

Mer felt luminous as she mounted the great stair and swept through the open doors. Her gown was of deep burgundy, accented by lace cuffs and rabbit fur trim at the neck and hem. She fingered the silver pendant at her throat, remembering the evening late last summer when Avry had given it to her. Since then, it had inhabited a dark corner of her desk drawer. Not wanting to feel her father's questioning eyes, Mer had waited until she was in the carriage before securing it around her neck.

It isn't stamped with his name, she thought, *so why not wear it?*

She sighed and let her hand drop. Her decision to stop writing Avry still felt raw. The reasons behind it made sense one moment, and the next they felt insufficient and empty.

Like her father said, she needed to spend time thinking about why she had kept up such a regular correspondence.

The hall's opulence overwhelmed her even more than it usually did. The paneled walls, richly carved and painted with shades of red and gold, ascended to a gilded hammer-beamed roof. Tapestries hung here and there, illuminated by lamps set in gold sconces. Mer's eyes rested on one of the hall's open windows, recalling something Avry had said when they last danced together. Glimpsing the night sky, he had asked her which of the luminaries she liked best. *I like the moon,* he had confessed when she could not find an answer. *It sees through darkness.*

The musicians were setting up on a raised platform at the back wall. Mer had arrived neither early nor late in hopes she would earn less notice, but as people trickled in she began to feel the weight of their eyes on her.

An ostentation of peacocks huddled by the food stands, flicking fingers at her like feathers. Mer recognized the leader of the group and shook her head. Pale-haired Patric d'Audamar had decked himself out in royal garb: a blue sleeveless robe over a doublet and breeches of embroidered gold. Scarlet hose and soft leather shoes completed the ensemble. Mer turned away from his sneering eyes only to find herself face to face with Charles d'Aubry.

"My Lady," the tall youth said, offering her a courtly bow as he passed her on the way to the food stands. Mer returned the bow, flustered by the respect in his eyes.

Her cousin Thierry walked in just as the musicians made their first few bleats and blasts.

Mer turned to him with relief. She could handle being stared at, but this sort of attention felt different, like she had walked in naked or tackled the doorman with a candlestick. Thierry pulled up short when he saw her.

He was four years her junior, a stocky youth with thick, curling red hair and a wide, freckled face that resembled his mother's, her aunt Lisette. Mer wondered how his first year of schooling had gone.

"I'm surprised to see you here," he said.

Mer opened her mouth to answer and then snapped it shut with a frown.

"It's too noisy," he agreed, casting a surreptitious glance around them. Mer had never seen him so uncomfortable. His arms were stiff as logs, and his fixed smile might have been plastered on. Had they not grown up together, she would have assumed he disliked her.

He had even forgotten his usual bow.

She was startled when he tugged her toward the door. "There's a bench behind the hall. We can talk there."

They slipped through the door and stole around to the back of the building.

The evening was unusually warm. The glow of the setting sun hung over the field behind the hall. Thankfully, the bench was deserted, though she doubted it would be for long.

"I didn't see Avry," Thierry remarked as he settled down beside her.

"He isn't here," she whispered.

"I heard you write each other. Frequently." He shot her a wry glance. "There aren't many secrets on this silly little island."

A silence fell as Mer fought the sudden onslaught of frustration and sadness. Her father had been right about the gossip after all. Somehow, people knew about her correspondence with Avry. Her choice to stop writing him had been for the best, then. "I'm not writing him anymore," she admitted, the words feeling jagged in her mouth.

"I see." Thierry gave a thoughtful nod. "Do you still resent him for that time he helped his brother beat up Jan?"

Mer had forgotten she told him about that. "Not anymore. His brother was a bully then, and Avry was only twelve. I know him well enough now to admit that I judged him too harshly." Indeed, she had held it against him for years. Regret joined the other emotions, and they swirled in an ugly squall.

"Has he apologized for it?"

"No. And I haven't brought it up."

Thierry leaned back and began to crack his knuckles one by one. The childhood habit resurfaced whenever he was nervous. Was she making him that way? "I'm sorry you lost your voice," he said flatly.

Mer shrugged and forced a smile. "I'm used to it now. And I have this when I need to get someone's attention." She pulled the bell out of a pocket she had sewn into her skirt and handed it to him.

"My mother gave you that," he guessed.

"She did indeed. Got tired of me tapping plates with my dinner knife."

His face broke in two as he guffawed. Mer winced. The laughter had come too fast and was laced with tension. "Well," he said, catching his breath, "you've developed a deafening whisper. You might even blow your potatoes away, if you aren't careful."

She grinned but said nothing.

Thierry pushed at his knuckles and gave up. "I don't think you'll find many cards in your box tonight."

"Probably not. I'm beginning to see that my father was right."

His voice lowered. "About...?"

"About staying home."

The unease had returned to his face. "What's wrong?" Mer asked then added, "What are people saying about me? You must have heard something."

"I've heard plenty. The school is a quagmire of gossip these days, and the pubs..." His voice trailed off, and he drew a long, slow breath. "Would you like to hear the good first, or the bad?"

"It doesn't matter. Just tell me."

"Those who love and respect Sir Avry—the King's Knights, those of the lower houses, and the common folk—consider him a true hero, someone who can do no wrong. And his devotion to you makes them admire you."

"Most of them have never met me," she pointed out.

"Doesn't matter. What they don't know, they imagine. That's just the way these things work."

"And the bad?"

He tried his knuckles again and managed a snap. "Audamar and those connected to it claim you were ensorcelled by the fae, cursed forever."

Mer's mouth went dry. "And...?" She cupped the bell over her chin. "There's more, isn't there?"

He gave a slow nod. "They claim you were molested by the fae and are no longer a virgin. Some even assert that you shouldn't be allowed to live."

Mer recoiled in horror. "They can't mean it." How could people who did not know her be so cruel?

"Some don't. But some probably do." He touched her arm. "Mer..."

"I wonder if Avry knows."

"He might. Or he might not. It's not something someone would be eager to tell him." He studied her face. "I'm sorry."

Mer did not answer. A dull pressure was building behind her eyes. How many inside the hall were aware of this rumor? And of those who knew, how many believed it?

Thierry's arm curled around her shoulders. "It's just a rumor, Mer."

"What do *you* believe?"

"I don't think you would have allowed a fae to summon you against your will, as the story goes."

"And the rest...?"

"Is nothing more than Lion sop. Words. Empty words."

Lion sop referred to rumors started by those of the ruling house, usually for political reasons. If Audamar resented Avry for his new popularity, they may well have created the rumor to injure him. Implying that his rescued lady was soiled—worse, was ensorcelled by the fae—would cast mud on his reputation. That was if everyone believed it. *And they don't,* she thought, recalling Charles d'Aubry's respectful bow, her cousin's earnest face. Relief touched her. But it was a cold sort of relief, one that would not last.

"I'd love to know the true story," Thierry murmured.

Mer eyed him in the growing darkness. She had a sudden desire to tell the tale, even if it were only to her cousin. "I can give you some of it, but you must be circumspect."

"I'll be whatever spect you want."

She leaned back against the wall with a sigh. "You probably heard about how Jan loosed Gille d'Avrance's bull. The animal ran two dozen of Percy d'Eleuthère's sheep over the gorge."

"That was back in June," he mused. "I didn't think much about it, because it had all been worked out, the debt cancelled. Two dozen sheep seems like a lot, but Avry's father has hundreds, and he must have known he couldn't have squeezed a penny out of Rives if he bled him dry."

Mer was nodding. "All of that is true. However, there are other forms of payment than money. That very morning we received a letter from Lord Piercy, offering to cancel the debt if I'd marry Avry."

Her cousin stared at her with an open mouth. "Was Avry behind this?"

"I thought he was. It had never occurred to me that Piercy would make an offer like that without his son's approval. But that's exactly what he did."

"How odd," Thierry said. "To start with, why would Lord Percy want his son bound to the daughter of a disinherited lord?"

"Apparently it was at Avry's mother's urging. She was aware of Avry's feelings for me and saw this as an opportunity to give him what he wanted."

Thierry rubbed his chin thoughtfully. "What did Rives think about all this?"

"He was furious but couldn't see a way out of it. He told me I would have to marry Avry. So I ran. I felt trapped, terrified to marry a man who would purchase me like livestock in exchange for twenty sheep. And I thought—I had hoped to return. After a little while. When the whole thing had blown over."

"How did you cross the gorge on your own and get through the Cursed Wood?"

"I didn't." She paused, then, studying him. This was the part he would not like. "A fae took me."

His brow furrowed. "But—"

"Let me tell you a story. Nine years ago, a fae prince named Gandel wandered into the Cursed Wood after his runaway horse. He spent the night telling every tale he knew, and when morning came, he emerged, but on the wrong side of the wood. With no stories left to tell, he couldn't go back through the wood. So he crossed the gorge, and I found him in a cave shortly thereafter, crouched like a frightened animal. I brought him food and a bundle of my grandmother's stories. In return for these gifts, he gave me one of two stones he wore around his neck. If I were ever in danger, he said, I could speak his name into the stone and he would come to me.

"So that's what I did. I wrote my father a letter, crawled out my window, and met Gandel at the gorge. He was reluctant to take me to Thorsault, but in the end he honored his promise, flew me over the water, and we traveled together to the fae city."

Thierry had not moved while she told him the story. Mer did not have to observe his face to know he was upset. She had kept something from him for years, and he could not understand why. She rolled the bell between her palms.

When she looked up, her cousin had vanished; Avry sat there instead, looking just as he had when they had last spoken together. The impression only lasted for a heartbeat, then it was gone. Mer sucked in a breath, torn between wanting to see Avry and dread of that very same meeting.

"I remember that stone," Thierry said quietly. "It was shaped like a wheel, wasn't it? You wore it on a silver chain around your neck."

She felt the hollow in her throat. "I don't have it anymore."

"Why didn't you tell anyone—about the fae, about how to get through the Cursed Wood?"

"I don't know," she said honestly. "Part of me worried that if I did say something, no one would believe me." Until Thorsault was discovered, the east side of the island had been thought to be uninhabited, carpeted by a vast forest that buried trespassers and never returned them. The fae had existed only in tales.

She touched his stiff shoulder. "Don't be angry, Thierry."

"I'm not angry. Just taken aback." His mouth crooked. "You never were very good at sharing secrets."

Mer said nothing, knowing it was true.

Thierry stood and stretched his arms. "I like your story better— or at least the little I've heard of it."

He had not heard much.

Mer looked north over the field. Crickets buzzed. A song ended inside the hall, and there came a smattering of distant laughter. Loneliness touched her like a cold hand. She had once taken pride in her ability to switch from the girl who gathered mushrooms and dug for potatoes to the well-mannered lady who glided over the dance floor and picked through food like a hummingbird sipping nectar. Lisette had trained her well. But now she wondered if that facet of her life had come to an end. If this would be her last quarterly.

She glanced at her cousin and sighed. "I'm keeping you from dancing."

"Nonsense. I wouldn't have missed your story for anything." He added, with a wistful smile, "One dance?"

Her heart sank. "I don't think I should. But you go on in." She peeked around the corner to the misty line of waiting carriages. "I think I'll head home."

CHAPTER 8

Avry stood at his chamber's open window and stared down at the blue finger of the estuary. The rising sun sprayed a shimmer of diamonds over the water. Fishing boats drifted through it like seabirds, their rigging tangled in the effervescent light. He leaned forward into the chill air and breathed in, scenting saltwater, a waft of smoke from extinguished lamps, the elusive scent of autumn.

A clang of swords made him realize how late it was. The training yard would be filling with men who had risen early and trickled up the sides of the hill with their heavy weapons and armor to practice in the yard. Avry would not be with them. Ghislain had surrounded him with chattering servants who took his measurements and schooled him on what to say and do during the ceremony. One was the castle's steward, who also happened to be the king's adviser.

Senet had appeared in the king's chamber while Avry signed his life away.

He was slender to a fault; people joked that the aged man ate air instead of food and walked with invisible strings hanging from his arms and legs. He had lingered by Ghislain's bed as the last of five witnesses—all knights—applied their seals to the fateful document.

"Was it a taxing night, sir?" Senet had asked Avry.

Avry met the steward's placid eyes and relaxed. Senet was like calm water next to a rushing current. "You could say that."

"Ah, Senet." The king tensed in the covers. "Help me up."

Senet slid an arm under the king's back and lifted him to a sitting position. Avry, looking on, stifled a twinge of jealousy. Ghislain had never asked Avry's help to sit up. In fact, the king had applied his seal while propped up on pillows.

"There you are, My Lord," Senet murmured.

Ghislain patted his steward's shoulder then reached past him and caught Avry's arm. "Is it done?"

Avry glanced back at the document and said heavily, "It's done, My Lord."

"Good, good. The ceremony will be held in a week. Until then, your appointment must be kept secret. Senet will advise you about how you shall dress and act. Trust his advice."

The familiar thud of a spear slamming into a practice dummy brought Avry's mind back to the present. Heaving a sigh, he latched the window and pulled on his boots. *Forget the seamstress,* he thought. All he wanted now was a good meal and a stroll in the fresh air. He would sneak down to the refectory and see what he could scrounge from the kitchens.

He secured his chamber door, took two steps down the hallway, and almost collided with Patric d'Audamar.

They were of a height, but Patric, having led a sheltered, sedentary life, was as smooth and slender as a spring fawn. His hooded eyes drooped as he offered Avry a mocking bow, then he turned and disappeared down the stairs. Avry trailed along behind. He had assumed Patric was on his way to the refectory, but the young noble chose the third floor instead of the first.

Avry lingered on a step, wondering if he should follow and find out who Patric visited at this hour in the morning, but his rumbling belly drove him on.

The refectory was a spacious, unadorned room wedged between the kitchens and the great hall. Row upon row of long wooden tables occupied the space. Maids scurried between them, collecting dirty dishes. One noticed Avry standing in the doorway and shot him a swift smile.

"I'll tell the cook you're here," she said.

"And me," came a familiar voice behind him.

Avry felt a rush of affection and relief as he turned to meet his squire. Édouard was a stocky youth in his fifteenth year. His coppery hair fell to his dimpled chin in a neat bowl shape, framing his deeply set blue eyes and wide mouth. "You look better," Avry commented.

Édouard wiped his reddened nose with a cloth and cleared his throat. "I am, sir," he said hoarsely.

Édouard was the youngest son of a tenant farmer. He and Avry had met in the city markets three years earlier. The knight, drawn by the boy's open, honest face and capable manner, had watched him in secret for a time, noting the respect he received from vendors, impressed by the ease with which he carried enormous sacks of grain over his shoulders. Avry paced him for half a mile, weaving through stalls and carriageways, squeezing past the warm, malodorous bodies of pigs and goats, before Édouard finally turned and asked what the good sir wanted.

"Your name," Avry said simply, for that was how every friendship started.

Avry was one of the last knights to enlist the services of a personal squire. The practice had gone out of fashion. Tasks traditionally done by squires now went to servants appointed by the king on the knights' behalf.

Avry had not wanted merely a servant, but rather an ally. A companion. Someone he could train to watch his back. Édouard served as a page for eighteen months before becoming a squire. Now he was nearing the end of his novice training, and if he stuck with it, he might garner a knighthood.

Avry's food arrived, and they fell into some chairs at a long, empty table.

Avry stared down at the eggs, sausage, and mushrooms, all of which had been laid neatly onto a bread trencher. "Have you seen Patric d'Audamar around the keep?"

"I saw him just yesterday, sir. He passed me in the guest's hall, all decked out for the quarterly in blues and purples."

Avry tore off some bread and snagged some yolk in it. "Don't remind me of the quarterly. It's painful enough that I couldn't attend, but knowing that Lady Merisande might have gone anyway, might have danced with—" He shot his squire a dry look. "With the likes of Patric, just makes me want to rip my skin off and use it to strangle him."

Édouard's face crumpled with laughter at the idea. Avry grinned at him, glad he was able to distract the boy from the discomfort of his illness.

"Do you really think she would dance with him, sir?" he asked, dabbing his nose again.

"No. I don't."

"Maybe she didn't even go."

"There's a good chance she didn't," he agreed, taking a bite of sausage. "I'm not sure what Patric wants here. He was in the yard a week ago, demanding I train him. When I refused, he just stalked off."

"Could he hold a sword, sir?"

"Barely. A passing insect might have knocked it from his grasp."

Édouard stared at Avry's trencher, perhaps wondering where his own meal had got to. Then his face froze in a rictus of horror, and he slapped a mushroom out of Avry's hand.

"How many of those have you eaten, sir?" he demanded.

Avry frowned at the little brown mushrooms resting beside the remains of his sausage. "None, yet."

"Thank God," he muttered, almost under his breath.

"Édouard..." Avry's voice trailed off as the boy dragged the trencher to the far side of the table, causing a mushroom to bounce onto the floor.

"That is false morel, sir. Morel is always boiled, because if it's not, it tastes bad. But those mushrooms are raw. False morel is deadly when it's raw."

"Perhaps they forgot to cook them?" Avry offered. Or perhaps Édouard's illness had muddled his brain. "I haven't tasted them to know if they're sharp."

"They're not the right color, either, sir." He stood abruptly, almost knocking the chair over, and snatched up the trencher. "If you allow me, sir, I'd like to make some enquiries on your behalf."

Avry had never seen the boy so impassioned. His mouth was a firm line, and his blue eyes shone with the grim determination of a soldier about to do battle. Anxiety stuck a claw into Avry's belly as he contemplated the chance that his squire was right. He rose, placing a hand on the boy's shoulder. "Very well. Perhaps I should accompany you…?"

Édouard shook his head. "I'd rather go alone, sir. The staff won't say as much if you're there, if they made mistakes, or didn't report something they should've."

"And if you're right, and the perpetrator is right in front of you, armed with a kitchen knife?"

A hidden blade peeked out of Édouard's sleeve. "If he lunges at me, sir, I will kill him."

Avry looked from Édouard to the knife and shrugged. He did not doubt that Édouard would do it, efficiently. "I trust you will be discreet."

"I will, sir."

The egg yolk was dripping off the side of the trencher onto Édouard's fingers. Sighing, Avry turned toward the door. "I'll be upstairs."

***

Avry strode down the hallway on the second floor, passing the knights' chamber and the royal library. He slowed at the doorway to the Hall of Kings. His eyes snagged on a silver figure standing to one side of the entrance.

The suit of armor lay neatly over the wooden limbs of the mannequin that propped it up. The pieces were slightly mismatched, with one greave slightly larger than the other, one gauntlet shorter and missing fingers. He walked around behind it and studied the opening in the back where wings would have protruded.

After the Cursed Wood had picked up its roots and moved east, artifacts that had not seen light for centuries had become exposed, baring their faces to the sun. No one knew how the fae soldiers had come to be there, whether they had perished in a slave uprising or if the wood had killed them, dragging their bodies down under its roots. Fae armor was remarkably resilient, immune to the elements, difficult to dent, puncture, or warp. It was superior to any armor in the known world. Ghislain had sent pieces off to all the smiths in the kingdom, but none could duplicate the metal.

The suit, composed of the most intact pieces available, had been a gift from the royal smithy. No one knew why Ghislain had placed it at the entrance to the Hall of Kings. But since it had appeared there, fewer people visited the hall, and some avoided the floor entirely.

Even Avry, who had seen living fae in the armor, felt a shiver move through him as he stared into the empty eye sockets. "Where are your bones?" he whispered, but only silence answered him.

He strode past the armor into the room and stepped into a fat beam of sunlight. The Hall of Kings was possibly the brightest room in the keep. Rows of windows stretched like pillars from ceiling to floor, allowing unobstructed light to reach out and touch the stone busts that marched along the opposite wall.

Avry walked slowly down the line of kings, reading the names engraved on their golden plaques. King Alum d'Audamar, King Reyner d'Audamar, King Donatien d'Audamar, King Everard d'Audamar...

Their alabaster eyes followed him, perhaps asking who this usurper was and how he could possibly imagine he belonged alongside them.

Three centuries of kings, all of them of Audamar.

As he came to the last, he fell to his knees on the cold marble floor. His breathing had turned fast and sharp; his heart raced. He saw his hand, scarred and callused in a ray of brilliant light, and swallowed back a choking sound in his throat. What had made him think he could be king? He had as much right to the title as the fae whose armor graced the entrance.

Sinking forward in a kneeling bow, he prayed feverishly, his lips trembling inches from the floor.

After a time, a bird came to one of the windows and sang into the open space. Avry turned and looked at it, amazed that such a tiny creature could produce so much sound. It made the hall seem empty, its kings insubstantial.

The bird is alive, he thought, *and I am kneeling among the dead.*

He rose stiffly and exited the chamber.

***

"Sir!"

Avry pulled up short, nearly colliding with his squire. He had been walking aimlessly around the third floor, hoping to spot Patric. A flush burned his cheeks. He had completely forgotten the mushrooms. The slip made him realize how little he believed it was attempted poisoning.

Édouard retrieved a handkerchief and blew his nose.

"Go on, Édouard," Avry prodded.

"I tracked down the head cook and showed him the mushrooms, sir."

"Did he agree they were poisonous?"

"He did, sir. In fact, he grabbed a handful of them and marched right into the kitchen to question his staff. The maid who served us the food broke down in tears. She said she didn't know the mushrooms were poisonous, or she wouldn't have served you the trencher. The cook said she had run out of mushrooms yesterday and couldn't have conjured more from thin air. The spit boy hadn't moved from his post the whole morning, and the mincer was away. The only person who hasn't been questioned is the dishwasher. And he's disappeared."

Avry stroked his chin, hiding a worried frown. "So what did you do then?"

"I told the steward, sir, and he ordered a search of the castle grounds."

Avry's hand strayed to a concealed knife at his side. "I'm guessing that the guards never saw the dishwasher leave the castle."

"No, sir. They did not."

"And they won't. Mark my words, Édouard, the dishwasher won't be seen again."

Édouard contemplated that, his red nose twitching. Watching him, Avry felt a sudden rush of gratitude and pulled him into a rough embrace. "You saved my life, Édouard."

"That's my duty, sir."

"Well, I won't forget it." Avry stepped back from him just in time to avoid an explosive sneeze.

"Why would someone want to kill you, sir?" Édouard said when he had recovered.

Avry shook his head. Ghislain had asked him to keep his appointment secret until it could be announced at the naming ceremony. But someone—the seamstress, perhaps—must have talked. The secret would have been worth something, if offered to the right ears.

What would Ghislain do when he learned what happened? Avry looked about him uneasily. He knew what the king would do: place further restrictions on Avry's movements. He could already feel the iron fist closing around him, keeping him from leaving the castle.

"I have to see Merisande," he said, more to himself than to his squire.

The lady had not written him for a week, and while there could be a dozen reasons for her silence, he imagined the worst: that she had taken ill, or had an accident, or had finally succumbed to her ghosts and slipped into a deep depression.

But concern for her well-being was only half the reason he wanted to see her.

Avry still had no idea what she felt for him. Their relationship hung like a question mark, unresolved, and very soon, unresolvable.

Mer had never been at ease among the gentry. Long ago, Avry had guessed that she was really only herself when she was at home with her father or foraging in the wood. She would not marry a king-in-waiting. The approaching ceremony might well end their communication forever.

But if he found so much as a glimmer of affection in her eyes, he could carry that back with him, that simple validation. No matter what else happened, at least he would have that.

He moved with a firm step toward the stairs.

"Sir!" Édouard scrambled to catch up with the knight's long stride. "If you wish to leave now, I'll fetch the horses."

Avry paused then said gently, "Thank you, but no. You're not well enough to travel, or to be doing anything else, frankly. You should return to your bed and rest."

Édouard's head sank in reluctant assent. "Very well, sir. What should I tell the king if he asks where you went...?"

"That I've gone riding and will return by sundown."

CHAPTER 9

Avry cantered up the old North Road, leaving the bustling city behind him. Rolling hills painted with oranges and greens filled his line of sight. Clouds moved like heavy ships over them. Farms and cottages appeared and disappeared, tucked away in soft folds in the land. Avry dragged in a draft of cool autumn air and sighed. The city had not seemed tiresome until he knew he would have to spend the greater part of his life in it.

If he survived to live his life.

The sun was past its zenith when he turned up the slender, weedy path snaking up to Rives's cottage. Without asking permission, he led his weary horse to the well and dragged up a bucket of water. He fingered his saddlebag, tracing the outline of a book he had brought for Mer. He knew she had access to her uncle's collection, but this work was rare. Avry had copied it himself from a dozen scrolls in the royal library.

"Sir Avry." Rives's bemused voice touched him on the shoulder like a familiar branch. "Have you come straight from the city?"

"I have." He offered Rives his hand. "How are you? How is Mer, I mean Merisande?" he corrected, scolding himself for not using her full name.

Rives did not seem to notice. "Mer is foraging in the wood," he said, then added, his voice tinged with concern, "Is all well with you?"

Avry hid his disappointment behind a courteous smile. "I'm fine, thank you. Will she be gone long?"

"Very likely. You may come in and wait for her, if you wish."

Avry was always uneasy entering the small cottage, not because he was unfamiliar with modest dwellings—Édouard's family lived in a four-room hut equipped with two hearths and sturdy box beds to keep out the smoke—but Rives's cottage was a disaster. The roof had been patched so many times that its weight had begun to warp the overspanned beams that held it aloft. The chimney was filthy, the cedar logs badly peeled. A scent of rodent droppings hung in the air, which was perpetually chill and drafty. In short, it was a cottage built and maintained by a disinherited lord, a man who had probably never lifted an ax before he had felled his first tree and had survived day to day from sheer strength of spirit.

Avry respected him. But that did not make seeing the cottage any easier.

Rives rekindled a dead fire in his hearth and offered Avry a chair. "It's warmest here."

"Thank you."

"Would you like some mead?"

"Only if you're having some too."

Rives flitted into the pantry while Avry stared into the feeble flames. "I remember the last time I sat here," he said as Rives returned and placed a cup in his hands. "Mer had just disappeared."

"And you thought she was lost forever," Rives recalled. "I did too. But you didn't give up."

Avry sipped the mead to hide a frown. "This is nice."

Rives accepted the compliment with a cautious smile. "I'm sure it pales in comparison with what you're used to."

"Mead isn't a popular drink at the keep, but my father was always fond of it. It reminds me of home."

"Ah."

Avry shifted in the chair so he was speaking to Rives instead of the fire. "You should know that the king-in-waiting ceremony is being held this Saturday. A crier will undoubtedly come through these parts to announce the event."

Rives seemed unsurprised by the news. "How *is* the king? I've heard he's not well."

"In truth, he may be closer to death than people suppose," Avry admitted, gritting his teeth at a pang in his stomach, which seemed to recur every time he thought about Ghislain dying.

Rives turned his glass. "Do you know who'll be named?"

"I do. But I'm not at liberty to say."

"You don't seem too happy about it."

Avry nearly hissed out a feverish laugh. Instead, he drained his cup, picked up the poker, and stirred the fire. "When the storm clouds arrive, you can't wish them away."

"Ghislain has been a good king," Rives remarked calmly. "I can't imagine he would choose someone unsuitable. Would you like more mead?"

"No. Thank you." Avry threw a glance behind him. "How is Merisande? She hasn't written in a while."

Expression flickered into Rives's face, but it was gone before Avry could decipher it. "Much better than she was two months ago. But you know how Mer is. She keeps her thoughts to herself."

Avry perched on the edge of the chair. "I missed the chance to see her at the quarterly."

"I imagine she missed you too. Your dancing, especially."

So she *had* gone without him. Avry clenched the chair arms, wanting to spring up and track her in the wood. He considered the sky through the window. It was well past noon; he had promised the king he would visit him that evening. "Does Merisande go to a specific place to forage?"

"Not usually. If she always went to the same place, there would be nothing to pick."

"Of course." *Idiot.*

A silence fell. They watched a log burn until it crumbled into blackened fragments. At last, Avry rose with a sigh. "I can't stay. Thank you for your hospitality."

At that moment, the door burst open and Jan tumbled in, his face and hands purple with berry juice.

Mer was close behind him, dressed warmly in a green woolen coat trimmed with rabbit fur. "We found some wild grapes," she said in a remarkably loud whisper. Then she spotted Avry, and the basket almost slipped from her fingers.

There was no mistaking the look of anxiety that washed over her face. Her eyes were wide, her mouth gaped; she even drew back as if readying to flee. It was abundantly clear she did not wish to see him. Perhaps ever again.

Throat closing, he offered her a swift bow and squeezed past her through the door. His hands shook as he prodded Dancer out from between piles of wood along the side of the cottage.

The sound of a tinkling bell made him pause before riding off. Mer, freed of her basket, had darted in front of his horse and wrapped the reins twice around her hand, effectively trapping his mount. The move was so unexpected, so bold, that he was rendered speechless.

"I'm sorry," she said, "but you took me by surprise. Did you want to talk?"

It had been a mistake to look at her, because now he could not take his eyes away. His fingers longed to draw her hair back from her cheek. Strands, caught in her lashes, shifted as she blinked. Lingering on her soft, berry-stained lips, he imagined pulling her onto his horse and riding away from everything. If she asked him to, he was not sure he could say no.

He found his voice. "I wish I could. Stay and talk. I've missed you." He remembered the book and fished it out of his saddlebag. "A gift," he said, placing it in her free hand.

She opened the book over the horse's neck and glanced over the headings.

"It's a record of every war that has been waged in the known world," he said and almost smiled. It was not the sort of gift a man would give a woman but exactly the sort Mer would covet.

"You transcribed it yourself," she said, her whisper tinged with amazement. "It must have taken some time." After a silence, she closed the book and tucked it under her arm. "Thank you. I'll treasure it."

Neither moved for a while. Finally, Avry, unable to speak, reached forward and grasped the hand imprisoning his reins. Fingers loosened under his palm then slid away until all he held was leather.

"Until Saturday," he said in a harsh breath, which was all that would come. "Farewell, My Lady."

***

Mer trudged back inside and shut the door firmly behind her. "What is Saturday?" she asked, leaning on Rives's chair.

"The king-in-waiting ceremony."

"He came to tell us that?" As she spoke, a cold shadow of foreboding stole over her.

"Avry knows who'll be named," Rives went on, "and he doesn't seem happy about it. In fact, I haven't seen him so uneasy since the time you disappeared into the Cursed Wood."

"I wonder who's been chosen." Mer, seeing Patric's leering face in her mind, set the book on her sewing stool and slumped on the floor beside the hearth. Avry must have heard the rumors: that she had been molested and cursed and should not be allowed to live. Lion sop was harmless until the lion became king. What then? Would she be condemned to die, as some witches were in Ann? Could anyone prevent it? Could Avry?

No wonder he had been anxious.

"Merisande."

Her cold fingers tightened around her arms. "Yes?"

"King Ghislain is a wise man. He wouldn't have chosen poorly."

"Apparently Avry thinks he has."

"Avry hasn't spent thirty years on the throne. Between the two of them, I'd trust Ghislain's judgment in this matter."

"But what if he chose before knowing all the facts?"

The chair creaked, and Rives squatted on the floor beside her. "What facts? I'm tired of you keeping things from me."

"It was just a question."

"No, it wasn't. There's something you're not saying."

Mer met his eyes stubbornly, while inside herself she banished the specter into the roiling darkness where her other terrors lived. No one but she deserved to see them. "There's nothing," she lied.

"Mer—"

Leaving him on the floor, she fled out the door into the afternoon sunlight.

***

Avry, not wanting to tax his mount, trotted back to the city. He was hungry, tired, and emotionally drained. His encounter with Mer had left him without answers. All it had achieved was to remind him of the power she had over him, and would continue to have.

He ran his hand down the reins, stroking the purple stain she had left, like a parting gift to remember her by. A thickness gathered in his throat, and he blinked away tears.

This had to end. If Mer had feelings for him, she would never willingly own up to them. And that was probably for the best. If she did feel something, some ephemeral glimmer of love, would it be right to make her acknowledge it, knowing what lurked in his future? No. He ought to leave her alone. Better to let the wound heal than to keep picking at it, causing them both pain.

He forced his shoulders to straighten. It was time to move on, not to put her behind him—he could never do that—but to find a way to live with the idea that she would never be his.

He turned his horse off the old North Road and began his downward ride toward Aure City.

The sun cast a reflection of fire over the estuary. Avry shaded his eyes, trying to pick the boats out of flame.

His hand froze.

What he had taken to be sunlight ate through a mast and sent it plunging into the water. A boat was on fire, and as he squinted, he found that two others were shattered, split in pieces as if torn by a giant hand.

Avry had barely registered what his eyes beheld when something new tugged at his peripheral vision. It looked like a cloud at first, a graceful drift of white, moving as if propelled by vigorous winds toward the castle on the hill. Then wings the size of freighter sails opened, and a giant bird touched down on the southwest tower. But it did not mean to land. With a great burst of energy, the bird beat its wings, while its talons scraped and pulled at the aged stone. Avry, as far away as he was, heard the sound of the tower roof breaking. Its conical spire crumbled. Half of it tumbled to the ground outside the castle walls and the rest imploded as it fell forward, likely dropping tons of heavy rock into the tower's upper floors.

And still the creature pulled and scraped. Then, for no reason Avry could discern, it loosed a bone-chilling scream and shot backward. The giant bird reeled in the air, flew in a jagged circle over the city, then climbed into the sky until it disappeared from view.

It was some time before Avry could move again. His hand was still frozen to his forehead; his legs were so stiff, they felt locked in place. He did not remember halting his horse, yet she grazed at the side of the road as if nothing unusual had happened. The pealing of bells drifted through the air like a scattering of raindrops.

His fingers shook as he wiped sweat from his brow. How many had died in the attack?

Perhaps it was too soon to ask. The creature might not be finished yet. It could return at any moment.

Spurring his mount, he galloped down the road into the city.

PART TWO

CONSPIRACY

CHAPTER 10

Dusk had settled over the north wood. The ferns surrounding Esperance's cottage rustled in a gentle breeze. She emerged from the trees with a pheasant dangling from each hand and a slingshot stuffed under her belt. Her wet toes wriggled in discomfort. While she had done her best to bleed the birds, some drops had leaked onto her legs and feet as she walked home.

Next time she would have to wear shoes.

She pushed through the ferns until she reached the old well behind her cottage, then she drew up a bucket of water, squatted on the hard ground, and washed herself, using the end of her long auburn braid to wipe away dirt and blood. She shook her head as she worked, rebuking herself for bathing before plucking. A summer of living in deer form had made her unaccustomed to the rituals of human existence, like washing, plucking, walking. It seemed that every autumn she had to relearn what it meant to be human.

Having rinsed her braid, she tossed the water at the ferns and drew up another bucket.

"Astrid," she called out in a friendly voice. "Why don't you come out here, girl, help your poor mother pluck some birds?"

A troubled moan drifted from the open window. Esperance had expected nothing less.

Her daughter was not well.

In the week since Esperance had helped her across the gorge and half-carried her home, she had lain like an injured animal beside the fire, eating only when forced to and preferring to urinate on the floor rather than use a chamber pot. Her fits came and went throughout the day and night, and they varied in intensity. At times she merely stiffened and held herself in a tight ball, while at others she thrashed and moaned, often biting her tongue in the process. Esperance suspected what was wrong, but until the young woman talked to her, she could not confirm it.

The wind rose, lifting the plucked feathers into the air. "Flicky sticky flickers," Esperance muttered, wiping uselessly at her face and hair. They were always flickers when she plucked them. "Feather" was too nice a word for the flimsy fluff that stuck under her nails and toes.

She finished the second bird then dumped the bucket of water over her head and wiped and shook and stamped until she felt flicker free. Her lips pursed as she considered what remained on the ground. Once, she would have gathered the feathers up and stored them. When mixed with mud, they made an excellent daub for the ridging on her roof. But she had neither the energy nor the patience to bother with them now.

Snatching up the birds, she went around to the front of the cottage and kicked open the door.

Her home was a large room heated by a fire pit at the center. Smoke leaked through an aperture in the roof. Esperance slept in the loft, a protrusion of old boards that had been thrown over the capstones, accessible only by ladder.

"You let the fire go out," she complained to the huddled figure on the floor. As she bent to stoke the fire, the scent of blood assailed her nostrils, and her heart gave a little jolt.

With tentative fingers, she drew her daughter's blonde hair back from her face and neck. Both were covered in blood, as if someone had smeared her with the stuff. Her hands were clenched at her chin. Esperance pried them open and almost jumped when she glimpsed the gouges in her palms. *My fault,* she thought, clucking her tongue. *I should've remembered to cut her nails.*

Esperance tore strips of cloth from her own hem and bound up Astrid's palms, tying them so firmly that her small fingers bulged. The young woman was awake now, watching without interest. Esperance bathed her face with soapy water, trimmed her nails, and sanded them down with a pumice stone. "Your dress should come off too," she decided. It was as filthy as the flickers. Astrid made a weak sound of assent and rose to a sitting position so her mother could unfasten her frock.

Esperance's nose crinkled as she scented the fabric under the crotch. "Lift your bottom." Astrid obliged, kicking the dress free from her legs. Her mother resisted the urge to toss it into the flames. It was one of the few dresses that fit.

Afterward, she stood regarding the thin, naked form of her daughter crouched on the floor. For years she had longed to see her again. Day after day, she had hiked to the gorge to watch for her. She had even given the knight, Sir Avry, her daughter's story in hopes that it would reach Astrid's ears and she would recall her humanity. Apparently the story had aided him during his first trek through the Cursed Wood, prompting his friend, or possibly his lover, to find Esperance and thank her.

Astrid was back now. But was it a true homecoming? Had her runaway daughter made a conscious decision to return, or had she been driven to it by desperation? Would she go away again as soon as she recovered? Esperance's mouth turned down, and she swayed with helpless fatigue.

"All these years," she muttered, "and you come back to me like this. Why did you wait so long? What were you doing?"

Astrid's untidy head shook over her knobby knees.

"You don't know," her mother said flatly. "And I don't know. No one knows." Wind nudged the shutters, making them creak. It was a lonely sound.

***

Avry went to the docks first, wanting to know what had befallen the men on the boats.

The brisk current had carried away the wreckage. Only one burning boat remained, smoldering under a cloud of smoke. His eyes ran over the two dozen or so men crouched on the boardwalk.

Blankets were draped over them, concealing any injuries they might have sustained. Women too old to worry about their lives had emerged from their homes with hot drinks and woolens for the sailors. Most of the men were still in shock, their pale faces frozen in fear. Some rocked back and forth as if to calm themselves, while others prayed into their hands. The women spoke to them soothingly while pressing drinks into their hands. Avry was so absorbed in the scene that he did not notice the skiffs laden with soldiers and rescued men until they pulled into the dock alongside him. Avry seized the ropes thrown to him and secured them to a post.

The twenty wet soldiers remained hunched in the boats for a time. They were exhausted, and for good reason. They had just spent their supper hour dragging men out of the sea.

Avry helped unload their five insensible passengers and haul them to the boardwalk.

"That's the last of them, sir," the leader of the twenty told Avry.

The knight flashed him a smile that came straight from his heart. "You did well. Better than well."

"Thank you, sir."

Avry leaned in and asked quietly, "Can you tell how many died?"

"No, sir. The current carried away the bodies."

"How many boats were attacked?" He had only glimpsed three, but there could have been more. He caught himself holding his breath for the answer.

"Three, sir."

"Fishing boats?"

"Yes, sir."

Fishing boats rarely held more than a dozen men, yet nearly thirty were huddled on the boardwalk. Could it be that most had survived? Hope rose in him, but he tempered it with the thought that some in the castle might have died.

Avry left them then, promising to send a physician, and rode up the winding road to the castle.

The city was jarringly quiet, its windows shuttered and some hastily boarded up. Even the chimneys were dead, though the day was growing chill. It was as if Aure held its breath, caught like prey in the eye of a hawk.

The castle was exactly the opposite.

Men swarmed on the battlements, bows ready in their gloved hands. On the ground, most of the commotion centered around the southeast tower. Soldiers had built a ramp to the tower door by piling rubble along the sides of the wall. The air was thick with dust and rank with sweat. As he watched the scene, two men emerged from the tower carrying a bier. On it lay a slight figure wrapped head to toe in purple silk. Avry closed his eyes in sudden pain as he realized who it must be.

The queen was dead.

He had forgotten that she had taken residence there. What a terrible blow for the king. For Aure. If a kingdom could not protect its queen, who could it protect? The king's men had failed. Avry saw it in their hanging heads, in their heavy steps as they marched with the bier toward the chapel. He wished he could comfort them, but what could he say? He felt like an outsider now. A soldier who arrived after the battle was little better than a ghost.

"Sir Avry!"

The king's physician had stepped out from the procession and was eying him keenly.

"I'm fine," Avry said as the physician approached him. "Are many injured?"

"Surprisingly few. Three soldiers and a maidservant were crushed to death under falling stones. One man survived with a broken leg."

Avry lowered his voice. "And the queen."

His lips tightened. "And the queen. But thanks be to God, she did not suffer."

Avry rested a hand on the physician's back, leading him away from the soldiers. "I assume the king has been told." What he really wanted to know was whether the king was lucid.

"I told him myself. He's wide awake now, as if his eyes have been pried open by fish hooks. He wants you."

"I'll go at once. If you're not needed here, there are thirty men squatting at the docks, half-frozen and perhaps injured—"

"Say no more," the physician said breathlessly and ran off toward the stables.

"Bring a torch!"

Having found a servant to take his horse, Avry swept through the doors of the keep and took the stairs two at a time.

The royal floor was crowded with servants and soldiers, most of them milling about aimlessly. Avry laid a hand on a soldier's arm to get his attention. "Hold still," he breathed then drew the soldier's blade halfway out of its scabbard and slammed it back in.

The sound had an effect like lightning. The restless bodies went still, and in the ensuing silence, the king's voice could be heard drifting through his closed door. Avry could not make out the words, but the ominous tone sent a shudder through his heart.

He eyed the men around him. "Have any of you been called to see the king?"

It was all he needed to say. The men shuffled toward the stairs, and soon the hallway was empty again.

***

The king's chamber was cool and damp. All the shutters had been flung open, allowing the twilight wind to blow mercilessly into the space. Lamps flickered wildly, and the canopy of Ghislain's bed undulated like a slack sail.

Knights huddled around the bed. The king's steward lingered behind them with folded hands. He flicked a glance at Avry as the knight entered, but Ghislain was speaking, so he remained as silent and unobtrusive as a shadow.

Avry swallowed as he looked on the king's face. Ghislain was shaking, his mouth quivering as if in anger. Sweat glistened on his brow as he struggled to hold his head erect, his back straight on the pillows that propped him in a sitting position.

"A shot to the thigh, though it stalled the attack, is worse than no shot at all." This was directed at Sir Neville, who stood at the king's right side. "It will have angered the creature so much that when it does return, a forest of arrows will not deter it."

"I agree, My Lord. But to speak plainly, what's done is done. We can't go back and change it. All we can do is prepare for the next attack so we won't be taken unawares."

Avry's breath caught, astonished at Neville's brusqueness. What had Ghislain said to his first knight to provoke such a reaction?

Then he knew.

"You shot the arrow," Avry said and then instantly regretted it.

Neville seemed to sense his remorse. He flung him a wry smile.

"Avry," the king exclaimed. "Thanks be to God. Did you just arrive in the city?"

Avry offered him a belated bow. "Not exactly, My Lord. I turned off the North Road at about the supper hour."

"Then you witnessed the attack."

"For the most part, yes." Avry folded his arms against his chest. He was acutely aware of the curious gazes and listening ears of the other knights. He hoped the king would not ask him where he had spent the afternoon.

"Where did you go after that?"

"To the docks, My Lord." He paused, looking for censure in the king's face. There was none. "I was worried about the fishermen. But when I arrived, there they were, hunched under blankets on the boardwalk. Most of them survived, thanks to the efforts of your men." He fingered his chin as he recalled how few casualties there had been in both attacks.

"What are you thinking?" Neville asked him.

Avry waved his hand, not wanting to draw attention. "Nothing that hasn't likely already been discussed in my absence."

"Speak your mind," Ghislain muttered.

"Very well, My Lord. The bird had the look of a raptor about it, with its powerful claws and long wingspan. Raptors attack to feed or to protect their eggs from predators. But it seems this assault had neither aim. Only five died in the castle, and not one of them was personally assaulted." He faltered, glimpsing a shadow of the dead queen in Ghislain's eyes. "At least," he amended, "no one was carried off by the bird as its prey. It makes me wonder what the bird was really after…"

Neville snorted. "Maybe it wanted something shiny for its nest."

The king's mouth opened then snapped shut again as his advisor squeezed past some broad shoulders to be nearer the bed. "My Lord, if I may speak—"

"Go ahead, Senet."

He tented his slender fingers. "Commander Neville just introduced an important word, perhaps without even realizing it: nest. We all know the rule for invading animals: If you see one, there are others. Might I suggest, My Lord, that you consider this possibility when preparing a defense?"

The room had gone deathly silent. Avry shuddered as fear skittered up his back. Could he be right?

The king expelled a harsh breath. "Thank you, Senet. That was a most cheering thought."

"My Lord." Senet dipped his head in a bow and retreated back behind the men.

The king pinched the space between his brows. "All this is merely conjecture, useless without more information. All we can do, as was pointed out earlier, is prepare for the eventuality of another attack." He fixed his eyes on Neville. "Drag out every crossbow and ballista in the armory. I want every tower armed, including the sentinels farther south. Station warships along the length of the estuary. I want every man, both on land and sea, armed with a crossbow and trained to use it."

Neville's breathing had accelerated during this speech, and his foot was already pointing toward the door.

"It will be done, My Lord."

"Good. Then you may go. You may all go." Ghislain's eyes closed, and he relaxed back against the pillows.

Avry stood without moving as the men filed out. Ghislain's hand, in a movement scarcely discernible, had trapped his wrist and held it on the edge of the mattress.

The door closed, and footsteps in the hall pattered softly away until all he could hear was the king's breathing and the creak of shutters in the wind. He licked his dry lips. "I'm sorry, My Lord. Sorry I wasn't here to help you. Sorry your wife died."

Ghislain's eyes creaked open, but he looked at the ceiling instead of at Avry. The trembling was gone from his face. Sadness replaced it, a deep emptiness that darkened his eyes and softened his wrinkled lips. "I want you to send a letter to Ann. On my behalf. You've spoken to Modeste before. My daughter should know that her mother is dead and that I may not last much longer."

Avry blinked, wondering if he had heard him right. "You'd prefer me to write it myself, rather than—"

"Yes. That's what I'd prefer."

"All right, then." The idea made him uncomfortable, but he would have done it even if Ghislain were not king. He gave a respectful bow. "I'll return to my chamber and—"

"Stay. Please," Ghislain said, gesturing to the chair at his bedside desk.

Avry complied, and for a while neither of them spoke. Stealing a glance at the king, Avry wondered if there was a lonelier creature in the world. Ghislain had no immediate family left in the kingdom, no one with whom he could be completely open and vulnerable. Being king did not make him less human.

"I'm glad you're here," Ghislain said, driving Avry's nail of pain in deeper.

Avry's head sank into his chest. Other words lurked beneath those, words that had already been spoken but remained unacknowledged:

My boy. That's what I called you. If you only knew what that term meant to me.

Avry knew. And as he reflected on all the ways Ghislain had shaped him over the years—nudging, prodding, honing him like an unfinished blade—something inside him eased open. Looking on the king's bleak face, he felt a sudden welling of love and grief.

"As am I, Father," he said firmly.

The king turned burning eyes on him. "You only say that out of pity."

"I say it because I feel it. You've been more a father to me than my own ever has."

Ghislain exhaled harshly out of parted lips, then he struggled to a sitting position and grabbed hold of Avry as if he were a piece of wreckage in a wide-open sea. Avry returned his hold and was not surprised when Ghislain began to weep, those deep sobs that a man reserves for a private place or for someone trusted. Avry's own feelings were more akin to happiness than sorrow. He gripped his father in both arms and felt the closeness he had always yearned for but had never received from Lord Piercy d'Eleuthère.

"I'll fetch you a handkerchief," Avry mumbled when the king broke the hold.

"Third drawer."

"Would you like your marble, too?"

"Please."

Avry found the items and piled them into the king's hands.

"I'm not sorry you had to see this," Ghislain said after he blew his nose. "Life can be rubbish sometimes. If you learn that now, you won't be taken by surprise later."

Avry dashed a tear away and grinned. "You're too late to teach me that lesson. I've already learned it."

"Have you?" Ghislain's mouth crooked. "Well, perhaps you've dipped your toes in the water." He eased back into the pillows, clutching his worry stone. After a long silence he asked, "When you were in Thorsault, did you see or hear anything about a white bird?"

Avry shook his head, taken aback by the idea. "Nothing comes to mind."

"Perhaps I should reread the lady's account. By the way, I sent runners to check on those outside the city to make sure they are safe."

Avry gave a wordless nod and hoped the king did not notice the flush in his cheeks. Ghislain had said nothing about his intrepid ride north. For that he was grateful. "Will you delay the king-in-waiting ceremony?"

"No. And that reminds me of what happened this morning."

"The mushrooms," Avry sighed.

"I've had a dog sent to your chamber. Make sure she tastes every meal before you eat it. And drink no wine. You should also choose a guard to shadow you—"

"I have Édouard," Avry interjected, annoyed that Ghislain thought so little of his ability to protect himself. But the irritation vanished when he recalled how close he had come to being poisoned. If Édouard had not been there...

"Has the boy's health improved?"

"It has. A great deal."

Ghislain's eyes closed and his breathing deepened. "Good. Good. You may tell him about your new appointment. He ought to know." The hand holding the marble relaxed then, and he began to snore.

Avry studied his face in the flickering light, memorizing lines, storing them for a time when Ghislain might be just another statue in the Hall of Kings.

Live, he urged him silently, as if the word were a spell.

CHAPTER 11

"There may be frost tonight," Rives warned as he shut the front door with his booted foot and rearranged the stack of firewood balanced precariously on his arms.

Mer waited until he had deposited it by the hearth before leaning in and whispering, "Jan's asleep in your room. Now you two can compete to see who snores the loudest."

"We'll compete in our dreams."

"I can't fathom this sudden urge you have to hold us apart. Did your brother suggest it?"

Her father snatched a ratty sweater off his chair and pulled it on. "No. It was my idea."

As she waited for him to elaborate, pounding on the door made them both jump. Mer reached it in three strides and pulled the latch. A soldier, looking chilled to the bone in his fine green uniform, stood holding a torch against the clear night sky.

"Come in," Rives said before the words reached Mer's lips.

The soldier shook his head. "I can't, but thanks for the offer. Are you Lord Rives d'Ivry?"

"I am."

He offered a hasty bow. "Then may I ask if everyone in your household is accounted for, My Lord?"

Rives rubbed his chin, his brows furrowing in a puzzled frown. "They are."

"And have you seen or heard anything unusual this evening?"

"No. Why do you ask?"

"Because there has been an attack on the city. A flying creature destroyed three boats and pulled down the roof of a tower. The queen is dead, along with at least a dozen others."

The words had piled out without emotion. Rives and Mer stared at him speechlessly, uncomprehendingly, until the soldier added, "If you have no further questions, My Lord, I'd like to move on."

Mer lurched forward, her heart beating out a sharp staccato against her ribs. "Is Sir Avry safe?"

"He wasn't one of the casualties, My Lady."

"What do you mean by a flying creature?" Rives demanded.

The soldier shrugged. "No one can say for sure. It looked like a bird. A giant white bird." He tapped his booted foot on the ground. "Will that be all, My Lord?"

The question was met by stony silence.

"Very well. If you see or hear anything unusual, inform the king immediately. Farewell, My Lord, My Lady." Offering them another a hasty bow, he mounted his horse and rode off.

Rives slammed the door behind him and collapsed into his chair. For some time he simply stared into the fire, his face a mask. Mer ran a cold hand over her neck. She was remembering the morning her shutters had blown open and how in the frail dawn light she thought she had glimpsed a pale form in the trees...

"I wish I wasn't alone in my room tonight," she said.

Rives looked at her grimly. "I'd wager a lot of people are feeling the same way."

***

Two days had passed since the attack.

The castle buzzed with new life. The armory had been emptied, its weapons counted and carted out on wagons. When it was discovered that there were not enough ballistae, men went to work making them, enlisting the help of carpenters, smelters, and smithies from every corner of Aure. The activity had raised everyone's spirits, except perhaps those of the knights, who remained grim and snappish. Sir Neville in particular was uncharacteristically cross.

Avry was sorry for him. Not only had he been tasked with arming Ghislain's men, but he also had to train them. Only a handful of soldiers could handle the unwieldy ballistas, and of those only two were spry enough to devote entire days to training others.

The deficiencies in Aure's defenses stood out like dirty linen on a line. Airing it out had shown everyone just how reliant they had come to be on Ann.

For years, Aure's true defense had fallen to the powerful king across the water, whose vast fleet of ships patrolled the channel separating the island from the continent. If Aure were ever in danger, no one doubted that Ann would come to their aid.

But so far, no ships had been sighted on the arm, and Avry questioned whether Ghislain would want them if they did appear. "The thin edge of the wedge," he had once called them, and, "An unwanted foot in the door."

But these were dangerous times. Very likely, his view had changed.

Avry went in search of Édouard. The boy had been resting when Avry visited him last, and though he had made a valiant effort to appear well, he could not hide his reddened nose and swollen eyes. If Avry did not see an improvement today, he would be forced to find a temporary replacement.

As he reached the staircase, a pattering of footfalls made him turn to look behind him.

Senet flashed Avry a crinkled smile. "Good morning, sir. I was hoping to stumble on you this way."

Avry tossed an arm over the rail and molded his face into a semblance of friendliness. What would the king's steward want from him today? "Good morning yourself. Are the preparations for the ceremony going well?"

"Quite well, sir, for the most part. However," he leaned forward and lowered his voice, "it appears that the seamstress won't be allowed to finish your garment."

"I'm not surprised." Not surprised was putting it mildly. Avry had considered it a foregone conclusion. "Has she confessed? It would be good to know who she sold the—" he glanced around them furtively, "—the secret to."

"She hasn't, sir. Not yet, at least."

"And what is to be done about her servants?"

"They are all being held, sir, as a precaution." He cast a sidelong glance at Avry. "I happen to know a seamstress who works wonders on short notice…"

"That won't be necessary," Avry said cheerfully. "I have my own idea about what to wear."

Senet pursed his lips. "The king will want to know, sir."

"He will have to know."

They parted ways on the third landing, Avry heading for his squire's chamber.

Édouard was up and dressed in a freshly laundered tunic and hose. His wispy red peach fuzz had been shaven off, his hair clipped and tidied. But what made Avry's eyes close in relief was his clear complexion and strong voice. "You're feeling better."

"I am, sir. Truly this time." He stepped aside, and Avry took a turn around the chamber Édouard shared with two other young men, both of whom were absent. He frowned at his squire's battered clothes chest, warped bedframe and moth-eaten blankets. Édouard had stubbornly clung to these relics of his past, refusing to consider the idea that he might have outgrown them.

One thing at a time, Avry thought.

Leaning against the window frame, he called his squire over and gave him the astonishing news of his appointment. Édouard reacted as Avry had expected: his mouth dropped open, his eyes bulged, and he stood as stiff as a statue for several moments. Avry waited for his happy smile, his joyous exclamation; instead, his head sank down and he slumped like a lifeless marionette against the shutter.

"Congratulations, sir."

Avry drummed his fingers on the window frame. "That's the least sincere word you've ever said to me."

Édouard raised his head and met the knight's eyes. "I'm proud of you, sir. No one would make a better king. Aure would be lucky to have you."

He meant it, and yet the words had come out in a monotone, as if he had read them from a page. Despite this, Avry smiled impulsively. "Thank you, Édouard. I'll take that, despite my own feelings to the contrary." He cleared his throat. "So why the long face?"

The boy swallowed. His expression was remarkably similar to the one he had worn when Avry had revealed he would be going off on his own to find Merisande.

"Perhaps you worry that I'll put you aside, forget you?" Avry ventured. "Well, that won't happen. I mean to keep you near me as my servant and friend. As long as you wish to be those things."

Édouard made a valiant effort to smile. His lips compressed, and the corners struggled to turn up. It was an amusing sight, and at any other time Avry would have been hard pressed not to laugh, but all he felt was growing concern.

Exasperated, he grasped the boy's shoulders and shook him. "Speak your mind. What is it about my appointment that bothers you?"

Meeting Avry's eyes again, he said, quite seriously, "Your sure death. Sir."

CHAPTER 12

Rives and Mer, dressed in their finest clothes, clung to the arms of their carriage seats as the contraption bumped along on the old North Road. Rives's brother, Barret, and his wife, Lisette, traveled in the carriage behind them, and ahead were a long string of carriages slogging their way to Aure city. Jan had been left in the care of one of Barret's servants. Rives wished his brother would offer more often to take Jan off his hands, but until now, a dinner invitation was the only circumstance which had prompted one. *Jan does not belong at a finely laid table,* Barret had said, and while the words hurt Rives, he could not deny their truthfulness.

Mer whispered something, but it was lost in the clamor of rattling wheels and creaking wood. Rives leaned in and asked her to repeat it.

"You look troubled. Are you thinking about the attack?"

Rives sighed. "I wasn't. Are you?" He looked at her more closely. They had both been on edge since the soldier's visit, but Mer's tense reserve dated back to the moment she had learned about the king-in-waiting ceremony. Rives wished he had kept Avry's anxiety over who would be chosen to himself. She had taken it up like a torch and would undoubtedly carry it until the moment Ghislain's heir was revealed.

"No," Mer replied. "But perhaps I should be."

As they neared the turn off, the sides of the road became cluttered with vendors, most of them selling small wooden crowns painted bright yellow. Some of the carriages had pulled to the side so the passengers could make purchases. Their children gathered around the vendors like eager, chirping birds.

Juxtaposed against the festive scene was the startling view of the castle, with its southeast tower pointing a torn fingernail at the sky. Rives heard Mer's sudden intake of breath as she spotted it, and he bent forward to catch her whispered words.

"It's frightening to think of how large the beast must have been to wreak such damage. The people must have been terrified."

"And yet…" Rives gestured to the busy vendors. "Here they are, braving the open sky to sell capes and crowns to children." But even as he spoke, a shiver went through him. With so many gathered in one place, another attack would be devastating.

Sensing his daughter's eyes on him, he forced his tight face to relax, his hands to unclench from between his thighs.

The carriage train turned onto the city road, wobbled down a steep incline, then turned again, moving inside the shadow of a stony ridge, which ringed the city in a half circle. The king-in-waiting ceremony was to be held at the southernmost tip of the ridge, where the stone curved in, forming a natural amphitheater. A century ago, masons employed by the king had worked the rising stone into twelve terraces, one for each of the twelve houses (the order going from greatest at the bottom to least at the top). Stairs cut through the terraces like spokes on a wheel, allowing people to reach their designated platform. Those who arrived late or were too old to climb simply continued along the north road until the pavement ended. Then it was only a short walk to the grassy top of the amphitheater, where commoners were permitted to gather to hear the ceremony.

Rives had only been a boy when he had attended Ghislain's coronation, yet he remembered the day with a strange clarity: the enormous, enthusiastic crowd, the brightly colored pennants, the stone platform extending like a plank at the amphitheater's base.

He did not recall a ballista perched on top of the ridge, nor such an amount of armed guards.

After a halting drive up an uneven road, he and Mer alighted from the carriage and followed Lisette and Barret to the entrance pavilion, a wide, open-air gallery with a marble roof held aloft by pillars. Guards stood at the pillars, making sure that people entering did not carry weapons. Once past the guards, visitors had to give their names to the secretaries. If someone was not of the houses, it was usually discovered at that point.

Ivry's terrace was more or less in the middle of the twelve. Lisette, ever concerned about comfort, offered Mer an embroidered cushion to sit on so her niece would not have to endure the cold stone. She was a plump, dark-haired woman of middle years, with a kind face and expressive hands. Barret was her opposite in every way: slender, blond, and as stiff as chalk.

Mer draped her arms over the stone railing and flashed Rives a tense smile. "At least it's a nice day." She had to hiss the words into his ear to be heard above the din. "Do you think most people will be here?"

"No. I doubt even half will come. A lot of people don't care who takes the throne."

"Oh, I think they do," interjected Barret, who was perched on a cushion behind him. "But they may not want to spend their afternoon sitting on—"

"Surely not that long, dear," Lisette cut in cheerfully. "It's much shorter than a coronation ceremony. The knights come out, and then—"

"No, the flag-bearer comes out first," Barret said.

Lisette brushed him away with a gloved hand. "Then the knights. Followed by the king-in-waiting. Then the king sets the ceremonial cape on his shoulders, and a priest flicks him with water—"

"Holy water, Lise. Water blessed by His Holiness."

"Water is water, dear. If a blessing makes it holy, then the priest could use milk or wine..."

They rattled on as the terrace filled up with uncles, aunts, and cousins that Rives had not seen in decades. Rives, casting an ear to the chatter around him, heard more talk about the ballista on the ridge and the chance of another attack than about who might be appointed king-in-waiting.

A distant hand waved to them. Mer straightened and waved back. "It's Thierry," she hissed. Lisette and Barret dropped their argument then and spent some useless moments trying to convince their son to leave his place and join them.

A horn call brought them all to silence.

The king's crier had emerged from one of the elegant tents arrayed across the front of the amphitheater. Dressed in bright, heavy garb, he mounted the steps to the platform with a cautious, deliberate gait, all the while holding his horn like a baton. When he had reached the end of the platform, he bellowed out the rules everyone had to follow or be forcibly removed from the theatre. Most of the rules had to do with creating disturbances, such as throwing objects and allowing children to play on the stairs. After he had taken his leave, a soldier appeared carrying the standard of Aure. Knights, dressed in full ceremonial armor, followed him up and formed two lines on either sides of the platform.

There was a long pause. No one in the audience moved, or, it seemed, even breathed as they waited for the chosen to come forward.

A cool breeze swept down from the ridge, making the standard snap like a sail. Amid that sound, another drifted in: the creaking and rattling of metal. The knights had rattled as they walked, but this was different. It was not a well oiled, even sound, but an unwieldy clamor of screeching, clanking, and thudding that reverberated across the space like strange music. Rives found himself unable to move as he watched the maker of the sound take the stairs one creaking step at a time and begin his ungainly walk down the platform.

It was a knight dressed from head to toe in the strangest armor Rives had ever seen. The fact that it did not fit him and showed signs of being hastily adjusted by a blacksmith did not detract from the overall impression it made, which was one of deep menace. Rives tried to understand what made it look so threatening. It might have been the angry shape of the visor or the exquisitely smooth plates, which mimicked the curve of muscle to an eerie degree. Or it might have been the ethereal gleam of the metal, a silver that would have dragged down the sun if a cloud had not passed overhead. Prickles danced down Rives's back, but they were more from awe than dread. What sort of man would don such armor?

The knight had reached the end of the platform. For a moment he stood without moving, and there was blessed silence. Then he unlatched the helm and tugged it off his head.

A familiar set of amber eyes gazed fearlessly up at the crowd. Rives gaped, and for a time he did not hear the murmurings around him or feel the chill of the stone rail he clenched in his hands. *Sir Avry d'Eleuthère, King-in-Waiting. King Avry, of the house Eleuthère.* The words wheeled in his head like birds. He could not make sense of them, no matter how he tried. Yet there stood Avry, in armor that did not fit him, and with enough steel in his eyes to proclaim that he did not care.

Movement at Rives's side intruded on his reverie.

Mer had slumped against the rail as if she had fallen asleep. Rives reached for her but was prevented by one of Lisette's heavily swathed arms.

Cooing like a mother hen, she pulled Mer against her skirts and rocked her gently. "Too much excitement, poor thing. You go ahead and watch the ceremony. I'll take care of Mer."

Worried, Rives touched his daughter's slack hand. Had she passed out in shock, or had the revelation of Avry's appointment upset her?

His questions died away as he became aware of what was going on around him. The audience roiled with barely contained emotion. Avry's name had reached the ears of those on the ridge, who would have been too far away to see him clearly. Their excited murmuring contrasted sharply with the low muttering and restless shifting of those on the first terrace. Rives could almost feel the ruling house's deep discontent. It was like that of a caged, pacing animal.

His spine stiffened with unease. *We should get out of here*, an inner voice told him. But how could they, in this crush of bodies?

Avry turned then, revealing a curious gap in the armor below his shoulders. Something gold peeked through it, cloth perhaps, or gilded chain mail. He crouched low in an awkward bow. The knights, too, fell forward as a sedan chair lumbered up the platform.

The audience grew silent in the presence of their king. But was it a silence of respect, Rives wondered? Or of shock, for Ghislain was as frail as a wraith. Most of him was hidden under his flowing scarlet robes, but what peeked out was sunken and sallow. His eyes were deeply shadowed, his gray hair like a film of cobweb clinging to his scalp. The crown was in danger of sliding off his head; only the back of the chair kept it steady.

When the litter reached Avry, the soldiers carrying it lowered it to the ground. A bony old man Rives had not noticed before walked out from behind it with a gold cape on his outstretched arms. He draped it over Avry's back, and then the king, who would have placed it there himself, reached out with trembling hands and pinched it at the shoulders.

As his arms fell, he straightened his slouched back, and like a man half-dead on the battle field gathering strength for one last stand, he cried hoarsely, "Rise, Sir Avry d'Eleuthère, King-in-Waiting!"

Avry creaked to his feet, and for half a breath nothing spoke but the quiet wind. Then a cheer like nothing Rives had heard before thundered down from the ridge.

***

Crystal goblets tinkled as a servant moved around the dinner table, topping off wine. Mer drained her glass with a steadied hand and allowed the servant to refill it.

The dining hall at Lord Barret's estate was spacious and dark. The walls were of polished wood carved into a variety of exquisite designs. Paintings of exotic animals graced them: hyenas, crocodiles, great, toothy cats. Mer stared at them fixedly, wishing she could lose herself in their feral eyes.

She took another long swallow.

Lisette had insisted Mer ride back with her. Reluctant at first, Mer quickly realized that her aunt's endless chatter would keep her from having to think. When Barret had invited them to diner, Mer agreed before Rives could open his mouth.

The four ate quietly at one end of a table that seated twenty-four. Mer wished that someone would speak. Even a comment about the weather would have been welcome. She might have initiated a conversation herself, but she did not want the attention. Rives had been fishing for her eyes ever since she regained consciousness. She had avoided looking at him for so long that she had forgotten what he was wearing.

Drawing a steadying breath, she forced herself to lift her knife. She had to at least appear to be eating.

Her fear of who would become king was gone. It seemed trivial now, ephemeral, like a childhood terror of the dark. The beast that had taken its place had torn the floor out from under her, sent her flailing into the murky deeps of her own powerful, incomprehensible emotions.

How long had Avry known he would be king? And why would he have donned the battle armor of the fae when it represented something so evil?

As difficult as those questions were to ask, they were not what drove her anguish. She could toss them aside and still feel the dark shape of the thing hovering at her edges, making her throat burn and her stomach sicken.

Her knife landed a little too hard on the table.

"My, it's quiet in here," Lisette said, as if the sound had nudged her awake.

"When the food is good," Rives said, "the guests are quiet."

She smiled at the compliment. "Thank you, dear. But there is so much to talk about. Sir Avry's armor, for instance. I'm sure it was pure silver."

Mer, unable to stop herself, rang her hand bell and whispered, "It was fae. Fae armor."

Knives rattled against plates as her aunt and uncle stopped eating and stared at her in surprise.

Rives hid his face behind a napkin. "I had wondered," he said quietly.

Barret leaned back, tugging on his bearded chin. "It was a smart move then to wear that armor. Even if it didn't fit well."

"Why do you say that?" Lisette asked.

"Because it makes so much sense. In times past, soldiers considered it a right and a privilege to wear the arms and armor of their vanquished enemy. The man who bested a king's champion always stripped him of his armor and wore it himself for a few hours, even if it didn't fit right. By wearing fae armor, Avry reminded everyone of his part in bringing down the fae. And," he said, raising a finger as if Lisette had been about to interrupt him, "that he wore it so calmly says something about him to others: he fears nothing. And a fearless king is exactly what people want right now. It will comfort them in this time of uncertainty."

Mer turned her wine glass with pursed lips. It did make sense, and if the king had asked him to do it, what else could Avry do but obey?

"Few would have recognized it as fae armor," Rives pointed out dryly. "That fact will take time to spread."

"But spread it will," Barret said with a confident smile.

"Did it comfort *you*?"

Barret waved his hand. "I'm not worried. The attack was a one-off. The creature won't be back." As if to emphasize that point, he raised his goblet and said, "To the king we needed."

After the toast, Barret tilted his cup toward Mer. "Well, my dear, you should've snatched him up when you had the chance."

"I don't think she ever had an interest in that boy," Lisette said, winking at Mer as though she had done her a favor.

Barret's brow crinkled, but thankfully he did not mention Mer and Avry's correspondence. "No matter," he said, setting down his cup. "Very likely he'll marry one of King Alaric's daughters to forge a stronger tie with Ann."

Lisette wagged a carrot at him. "Or he'll marry into Audamar."

"He may choose to marry into neither," Rives murmured, glancing at Mer's carefully neutral expression.

Barret shook his head. "That would be unwise. Audamar is fuming right now for being snubbed. If Avry marries into another house, he would lose any remaining good feelings, and may incite a rebellion. No, if he does not wish to marry into Audamar, he'll have no choice but to marry into the royal line of Ann. That, Audamar would understand. Of course, he may not have to make a choice at all. The king may arrange his marriage at any time."

Mer set down her knife slowly and stood, leaning her hands on the tabletop. "I have a headache. The dust and noise has made me ill." Her whisper sounded dusty, harsh in her ears. Rives rose and took her arm.

Lisette laid a hand on Mer's shoulder. "Of course. Let me see you out, dear."

***

The loaned carriage rattled over the stony path that led up to Rives's cottage. Mer sat with clenched hands and endured her brother's pinching and patting, his troubled moans. She had begged her father not to speak, and so far he had obliged her. But she did not expect his silence to continue past the front door.

She pushed a hand over her burning eyes then leaned into both hands and hissed out what would have been a groan of pain.

This was the end. A gulf had opened between her and Avry, and there was no bridge to span it, nothing but the parched sigh of her own dead voice to fill the empty space.

She was startled when the carriage came to a jolting stop. Crickets poured into the silence like rushing water. Shaking off Jan's clinging fingers, she flung open the carriage door and dashed down the overgrown path to the front steps. She felt her way down the hallway to her room, closed the door behind her, and jammed a chair against the latch.

She paced in the darkness. Wind from the unshuttered window blew hair across her eyes. Her fingers came back wet after brushing away strands.

"Open the door, Mer." The latch rattled. "You shouldn't face this alone."

This. She choked out a sour laugh. If only she had known sooner what *this* was. Now it was impossible for her to deny her feelings. It would be like denying she needed air or water. She needed Avry. Loved Avry. Nothing could rid her of the powerful emotion that had taken root when she was not looking. She cupped her throat, wishing she could cough out the wretched pain in her heart, as she had once coughed out her voice. She had learned to live without her voice. She could live without her heart too.

"My brother was wrong," Rives said through the door. "He's forgotten one important thing: that Avry loves you. Has loved you for years. And he won't budge once he's made up his mind. He won't allow himself to be sold off like a prized stallion to the highest bidder."

Mer collapsed against the wall. *If only that were true.*

"Merisande—"

Loosing a rough sigh, she kicked the chair away and let her father open the door. Lamplight flooded in, making her blink. Rives set the lamp on her desk. His eyes widened as they landed on her face, and she guessed that he had not heard her quiet sniffling through the door.

"He is not Sir Avry any more," she told him. "He is king-in-waiting. His every action will be scrutinized, and he knows it. He is every bit as calculating as King Ghislain."

He gripped her shoulders. "He is still Avry. Remember, he rebelled against the king's order when he set out into the Cursed Wood to find you."

"And after finding me?" she demanded. "Remember, I escaped on my own."

"That was different. An army was gathering to strike Aure. He had to warn the king."

"Indeed. He put Aure first, as he should have done."

"But—"

"I'm so tired." She dropped onto the mattress and closed her eyes. "So tired of everything. Sometimes I think the world would be better off without me in it. Goodnight, Father."

CHAPTER 13

"Be as you wish to seem."
—Socrates

Gandel smiled as he regarded the slender man in the mirror.

After days spent creeping along the edge of the wood, he had finally reached the village. In exchange for a few small coins, he had received a meal, a hot bath, and a warm bed.

His freshly laundered clothes had dried overnight. He breathed in as he pulled the tunic over his head, scenting soap and clean air. The room was not large, at least not by his standards, but it was warm and dry and smelled of polished wood. A mirror half the length of his body hung on one wall. Gandel fingered the new beard that clung to his face in soft, wispy curls. He ran the back of his hand down his shoulder blades, feeling the slight outline of his neatly wrapped bandage. A smile jumped into his face. No lumps hinted at hidden wings. Nothing suggested he was anything other than human.

He turned away with a whoop and did a little dance. He had never been so happy, so free. Here he was, in a country where no one knew him and his entire life ahead. The chain binding him to Thorsault held him no more. He would not let it hold him. The fact that he had removed his wings proved he could fling off anything.

He peered out his window to the busy street and saw two men pushing wheelbarrows and a boy carrying a chicken. Work. He needed to find work.

The inn's pub seemed a good place to start looking.

It was a large space, taking up the entire first floor of the building. On one side was a merrily burning fire, on the other a shiny wooden counter ringed by stools. Gandel rested his bow and sack against a stool and grinned at the three men seated at the counter who had all turned to look at him. Only the youngest returned his smile.

The innkeeper, a well-muscled man with a tidy beard, emerged from a swinging door at the back of the bar and refilled the men's goblets.

"I'll have what they're having," Gandel said.

The man's meaty hands moved with amazing dexterity as he tipped the beaker, filling the cup without spilling a drip. Gandel's nose wrinkled as he brought the unfamiliar reddish liquid to his lips. Mead had been the drink of choice in his father's court, but honey was hard to come by. It must be rare here, too, or they would have been drinking it. *You must learn to be poor*, he told himself, and poured poverty down his throat.

If he could have cursed while swallowing, he would have. The stuff was horrid, sour, and biting, with the rancid tang of old fruit. He coughed, swallowed, then coughed again. "What is this?" he asked the innkeeper, who had been watching him with amusement.

The young man at his side snorted. "It's Vin de Perce. From the Oule region. But they say old Perce ages it in shipping crates sealed by tar."

The innkeeper shook his head over the counter. "That's a load of pig slop, and you know it."

"It's what they say."

"Perce is midrange," one of the older men muttered and waved a finger at Gandel. "Look at him. Skin's as soft as a baby's bottom. Probably hasn't drank worse than Vellotet."

Gandel trailed a hand surreptitiously over his sun-browned arm. It did not seem soft.

As the men resumed their conversation, the innkeeper leaned toward him on the counter. "Where are you from?" he asked with quiet interest.

"Cabart," Gandel replied. It was the name of Thorsault's slave village, spelled backward.

"Never heard of it."

"I'm not surprised." He forced himself to take another sip.

"What brings you to these parts?"

"Work."

"Ah." The man tugged on his beard a few times then said, "You might find it at Malborne."

"Where is that?"

He pointed his finger toward the wall behind Gandel. "East. You can't miss it. Just look for the castle on the hill."

Gandel smiled into his cup. "Thank you. I'm grateful for your help."

The innkeeper winked. "You know where I am," he said mysteriously, and tossing his bar towel over his shoulder, he swept through the swinging doors.

The fae tilted his cup, watching the red liquid gleam purple as it caught light from the unshuttered windows.

"...the towers are bigger than Malborne's," one of the three men was saying. "My uncle was there in a merchant ship. He saw what he saw."

"No bird is big enough to take a roof off a tower, let alone snap a mainmast in half."

"It's what he saw. Anyway, all this is old news. I just came in from Alsward, and half the town is talking about it..."

Gandel's cup had frozen at a tilt. He sat without moving, his heart crashing painfully in his chest.

"...some folks worry the creature will cross the ocean and make off with their cattle."

"Where did this happen?" Gandel interjected hoarsely.

There was a pause as the men shifted on their stools to look at him.

"In Aure," the youngest said cautiously. "Five days ago."

The fae stood so fast that his stool toppled over. For several heartbeats, he strove to control his breathing. The men stared at him with slack mouths. "Forgive me," he spluttered. "I just realized I need to write an important letter. Would one of you be kind enough to tell me where I can purchase supplies?"

No one moved but the innkeeper, who had entered at the sound of the stool overturning. "A messenger always comes by here round noon for a drink," he said gruffly, righting the stool. "He'll have your supplies."

Gandel clasped his hands together. "Thank you."

CHAPTER 14

Avry sat at his desk, doing surgery on his food. The spaniel he had named Tips waited patiently at his side, swallowing excess saliva as she watched Avry trim corners off his bacon, sausage, and mushrooms.

"Don't make me feel guilty for this," he said, feeling a twinge of guilt nonetheless. He had grown fond of the little brown and white dog that woke him every morning with wet kisses and followed at his heels wherever he went.

He scooped the food into her bowl and waited while she ate. Inevitably, his mind turned to Merisande, and he wondered, possibly for the tenth time since the ceremony, what she thought of his new appointment. Did the words *King Avry* make her wince? How would he feel if they did?

"Stop it," he muttered. If she had something to say to him, she would have written. It did him no good to think about her all the time.

Chair legs scraped the floor as he rose and went to the window. The cool, salt-touched air was thick with of the sounds of clanging swords and thudding arrows. Avry had grown weary of the clamor. It would have been a novelty to hear birds in the early morning hours, or a quiet rain shower. He forced his drooping eyes to widen.

Last night's feast in his honor was the largest he had ever attended. Avry might have enjoyed it if his father had not been there. Lord Piercy d'Eleuthère, his face flushed, his eyes gleaming, had gloated over his son all evening. Avry had finally silenced him by asking the royal bard to play "Summer's Passing." The sweet, melancholy tune was a favorite of Lady Belle d'Eleuthère, whose debilitating illness had kept her home for thirteen years.

I should visit her, he thought. He had not spoken to his mother for six weeks. Too long.

Tips's tail lashed against his leg. Avry was about to scoop her up to show her the view out the window when a distant horn call sounded. He counted the blasts: four short ones, followed by a pause, then two more short ones and a long one. After another pause, the message repeated.

Tips whined.

"There's no danger," Avry assured her as he regarded the glittering arm of the estuary. The message from the sentinels was clear: war ships from Ann were creeping up the arm. Avry wondered if King Alaric meant to force Ghislain to accept them or if this was but an offer of good will. Alaric had sent no letter ahead of him, or if he had, Ghislain had kept it to himself.

He crossed the room a few times, pushing a hand through his untidy brown hair. Ghislain had passed out after the ceremony two nights and a day ago. No one had been able to rouse him, not even the physician. If he did not regain consciousness this morning, Avry would have no choice but to meet whomever King Alaric had sent as his representative.

He swallowed down his breakfast while standing and only barely remembered to hold the door open long enough to let Tips out.

Knights and soldiers milled about in the keep's entryway. It did not take long for Avry to notice who was missing. Without Neville's sturdy presence and commanding tone, the men were lost.

"No one has seen him this morning," said Sir Fennick, a swarthy knight with heavy-lidded eyes. "Not at breakfast or at the training yard. Perhaps he's sick."

"That wouldn't have stopped him," Avry said under his breath. "Even sick, he would have dragged his bones down here at the sound of that horn. I wonder if he left the castle for some reason."

"I could question the guards at the gate," Fennick offered.

"Please do."

"Sir?" Turning, Avry found his squire behind him. "There's a crowd of knights at Sir Neville's door, but no one will go in. If you wish, I…"

Édouard's voice trailed off as Avry shook his head. "Not yet. Or at least not until other possibilities have been explored. Neville is a private person. He won't even allow servants to enter his chamber, unless," he added with a grin, "they mean to share his bed. I'm going up to see the king. Come with me."

Avry entered the king's chamber with Édouard and Tips trailing behind.

Senet rose from the bed, flicking water off his fingers. "I can't wake him, sir. I've sprayed him with cold water, blown whistles into his ears, dabbed gin on his tongue…"

Avry held his hand over Ghislain's mouth and felt breath, as frail as moth's wings. His eyes closed in pain. "He's not dead," he said, more to himself than to anyone in the room. "He may still recover. Where is the physician?"

Senet drew a folded sheet from his belt pouch and handed it to Avry. "He slid this under my door, sir."

Avry unfolded the paper and began reading. *My apologies, Steward, but I have received a note, ostensibly from my brother, begging me to visit my sister, who has fallen ill with a deadly fever. If I decide to stay longer than an hour or two, I will send another physician of good repute to the castle. In the meantime, keep doing everything in your power to wake the king. He will not live long if he remains unconscious. Please share this note with King-in-Waiting Sir Avry.*

Avry sighed as he returned the paper to Senet. "I hope he sends someone, and soon."

"Would it make a difference, sir?"

Avry chose not to answer. He went to the window and flung open the shutters. "Did you hear the horn call?"

"I heard it, sir. Very soon we'll have guests to entertain. I've already warned the kitchen staff."

Avry's mouth relaxed in a grateful smile. "Thank you, Senet. You do your job well." At that moment, horns sounded again, this time from the castle towers. Tips scurried to Avry's side and barked.

"I believe they're already here," the steward said.

***

By the time the castle gate opened to admit the travelers from Ann, Avry had arranged the knights and soldiers into two lines, creating a welcoming walkway from the castle gate to the keep. Édouard had remained behind with Tips.

Sir Neville was still missing. The guards had not seen him leave the castle. If he were not in his room, Avry would have to order a search of the keep.

At the moment, though, finding Neville was not on his list of priorities.

As he watched the enormous, gilded carriage driven by four white horses glide through the gate, he wondered if King Alaric himself had deigned to pay them a visit. But the man who stepped down on soft-slippered feet was far too young. Avry made a sound of surprise as Princess Modeste came out after him.

So this was the man Ghislain's daughter had married. Prince Archard, Alaric's heir.

Avry lowered his head in a respectful bow. Archard merely tilted his chin; Modeste followed suit, only a moment late.

She had scarcely changed since Avry last saw her, nearly seven years ago. Despite having borne children, she had retained her girlish figure, which was draped in a simple gown of rich red wool. Her pale, lank hair had been gathered into a clasp at the top of her head. But much of it had spilled out and was so stiff with brine that Avry guessed she had spent more time above decks than below.

"Sir Avry. I hear you have been made king-in-waiting." A hint of sarcasm belied the warmth in her voice.

"It was your father's wish."

She smiled, but it did not reach her eyes. "Of course it was."

The prince stifled a yawn. He was a plain-faced man of medium height and build, with unremarkable brown hair, undisturbed by the slightest wind. His blue tunic rippled as he shifted from one foot to the other.

A drift of perfume wafted in the air. Was it Modeste's or Archard's?

"I'll go up and see him now," the princess said in a tone that broached no argument. "You may accompany me, Sir Avry."

To Avry's surprise, the prince chose not to go with her; he and his entourage of knights followed the steward into the feasting hall.

The royal chamber was cool and bright. Avry winced as Modeste exclaimed over the chill.

"Who left these windows open?" she demanded, slamming them closed.

Avry, knowing full well who had opened the windows, fled to the hearth and piled wood on the fire.

"I wonder where his servant has gone?" she said.

Avry had wondered that himself. "Would you like me to fetch him?"

"Perhaps later."

The chair creaked as she sat down by her father's bed. Avry remained crouched by the hearth and let her have her privacy. She must, he imagined, be shocked to see her father so changed. Avry had witnessed his decline over several weeks, and he still could not look on the king without feeling unsettled.

At last, she rose with a sigh and called Avry's name. In the faint light of the fire, he could see that she had been crying. Her face was red and swollen, her hair in disarray. But she was not ashamed of it. Her large blue eyes pierced his with all the mastery of her father's.

"For how long has he been unconscious?"

"Two nights and a day, Lady."

"Your letter implied he was dying, but I didn't believe...I..." her words broke off in a choke. "He looks terrible, so much worse than I had imagined."

Avry drew a sooty hand over his face, afraid of what his own would reveal. "I'm sorry."

After a long pause, she moved listlessly to one of the windows and opened the shutter a crack. "He won't be able to sign the document," she said.

"Which...?"

"The one that must be signed if King Alaric's ships are to remain here and protect this kingdom."

"I see." He worried his lip. If only he had taken an interest in law. Ghislain had taught him much by word of mouth, but there was so much more, and he had no time to learn it. "Well, he may yet waken. Tomorrow perhaps, or the next..."

"You don't have that long." As she turned, Avry glimpsed some private anguish in her pinched mouth and rigid jaw line. "My husband only meant to stay an hour, two at most. Just long enough to see that the document was signed."

He blinked, astonished by her words. "But he knew your father was sick. Surely he didn't expect Ghislain to meet with him and sign that document before noon." He shook his head. "No. He'll simply have to wait."

"He won't wait. He has already agreed to attend an event tomorrow in Ann. So he can't stay. You must sign the document on the king's behalf."

His head was shaking again. "I can't. I'm not regent."

"You are king-in-waiting. Where is my father's physician? He could declare him incapable."

The coldness of her tone shocked him. A moment ago, she had wept over Ghislain's sickbed, but now it seemed that he was just an arm with a pen. "The physician left the castle to visit a sick relative. He said," Avry went on as she opened her mouth to protest, "that he'd send a replacement if he thought he'd be gone more than an hour or two." He paused, pulling on his chin. "I could send someone to look for another."

"There isn't time." She latched the shutter, crossed the space between them, and fixed him with an indomitable stare. "Aure needs those ships. She needs the additional ballistas and crossbows and all the men who know how to use them. If you don't sign that document now, and the creature returns tomorrow, you, king-in-waiting, will be held responsible for the loss of life. Are you prepared to accept that?"

Avry swallowed and curbed an impulse to rush to the bed and shake Ghislain until he woke.

If only it were that easy.

"I'll speak to the king's adviser."

"Will you speak to him now?"

"Now," he agreed tightly.

"Good." She passed a trembling hand over her eyes. "I missed my mother's funeral. Was it well attended?"

He struggled to recall it. "Well enough, Lady. Considering the times."

"I assume her tomb is in the chapel?"

He assured her it was, and they parted ways.

Avry found Senet on the stairs, walking up to meet him. Avry was more than a little relieved to see his calm face. He felt as if he had been caught up in an angry storm, with no sturdy branch to cling to.

Some of that chaos stemmed from his frustration over how Archard was treating Aure. If Ann was a guest, then she had traipsed in with muddy boots, demanding food and drink, only to stomp out after a few bites. Prince Archard should have allowed Ghislain a few days to sign the document. He should have left the warships in the channel until a decision could be made, instead of showing them off to all of Aure so that everyone would know what they were losing if Ghislain—or possibly Avry—turned them away. The whole incident hinted at an acute lack of diplomacy.

Senet leaned against the handrail. "Sir Avry, I was just coming up to see you. Prince Archard demands written consent before he'll allow the ships to stay. When I told him about the king's condition, he demanded that you provide that consent, and now. He's waiting in the green room."

"Modeste just told me the same thing," Avry said, sinking onto a stair.

"What will you do, sir?"

Avry's mouth crooked as Senet lowered his old bones down beside him. "I was just coming to ask you that very thing. I've never studied the intricacies of the law, but nothing about this sounds right. How can I act as regent before the king has been declared incapable? I don't even have a regent's seal. I would have to use the king's."

The steward nodded calmly. "You'd have to sign on His Lordship's behalf."

"And you think that would be acceptable?" When the man did not reply, Avry asked bluntly, "What do you advise, King's Adviser?"

Senet met his gaze squarely. "I advise you to do what is best for the kingdom, sir, even if you find that distasteful."

Trust his judgment, Ghislain had said. Avry smiled, feeling as though a great weight had been lifted from him. "Thank you, Senet. I will do just that. Could you fetch me the king's seal?"

"Certainly, sir."

***

Avry peered around curiously as he took a seat in a soft leather chair across from Archard.

The Green Room was only opened when the king met with foreign dignitaries. The walls were decorated with faded green tapestries depicting the early days of Aure, when Avry's people cleared away miles of forest and the ancient, burned remains of the previous settlement to start something new. From such humble beginnings, a thriving kingdom had sprung.

Snatching the parchment off the table, he began reading. His teeth clenched as Archard drummed his fingers on the chair arms.

"It's quite straightforward," the prince complained.

"Perhaps a little too straightforward," Avry said, leaving out "My Lord." If Archard refused to use Avry's title, Avry would not use his. "No where does it state how long the soldiers are to remain in Aure."

He waved his hand. "Until you or the king sends them back, of course."

"That clause appears nowhere in the document."

"It doesn't have to. It's obvious."

Avry crossed his arms. "Perhaps. But until you add it in, I can't in good conscience sign this—"

"Petre," Archard called without moving, "fetch my stationery."

In a few moments, Archard had scratched a sentence into the margin and passed the document back to Avry.

The ships will remain, it said, *until King Ghislain or his regent sends them back.* "That will do," Avry decided. Drawing a steadying breath, he reached for the heated wax and seal.

The mark had barely dried before the prince plucked up the page and passed it to his secretary. A hint of perfume lingered in the air as he rose and went to the door. "We'll be off, then," he said, flashing Avry a quick smile. "It was a pleasure."

"The same," Avry managed.

As the door opened, the princess strode in, surprising them both. "I wish to remain here a few days with my father," she declared.

Anger flared in Archard's face, and without a word of reply he shoved her forcefully toward the door. Rather than fight him, her shoulders sank and she stumbled forward under the weight of his palms until they had both disappeared down the hall.

Avry's hand dropped from his mouth. The prince's treatment of his wife reminded him so powerfully of his brother's bullying that the hairs on his arms stood on end.

He went to the door and listened to the sounds of their retreating footsteps, Archard's shouts to his men. *I should have said something,* he thought. *Stood up for her.* But would it have made a difference? He doubted it. It probably would have caused more harm than good. Archard, humiliated by Avry's protests, would have seethed all the way to his ship, and Modeste would have suffered for it later. Avry knew these behaviors only too well, having been a victim of them for years.

He meandered down the empty hall to the foot of the stairs, listening to the rumble of carriage wheels and a drift of Senet's amiable voice as he bade farewell to his guests. Then the door to the keep boomed closed, and blessed silence enveloped him.

Avry's mind felt numb as he tried to recall the other matters that pressed him that day. He still had to request a regent's seal from the secretary, send a servant to fetch a physician...

Sir Neville.

He found his squire in the training yard, batting a dummy with a wooden sword. Tips barked at Édouard's feet, wanting to join in the game. Avry sent them both into the keep to look for Neville. "If he's not in his room, take a piece of clothing with you and have Tips sniff it. You might just find him in the servant's quarters, passed out drunk on some maid's bed."

"Where will you be, sir?"

It was a good question. Édouard was supposed to be guarding Avry's back. He could hardly fulfill that task while running errands.

Avry dragged the tips of his fingers over his eyelids. "I don't know. Maybe to see the king. His servant is missing."

"If I see him, sir, I'll send him up."

"Thank you, Édouard."

***

The princess had left no sign of herself in Ghislain's shadowy chamber, not a hint of fragrance, not even a hair. Avry stood over the king's bed, observing the slight rise and fall of his chest. "I did something you probably won't like," he murmured. "Or maybe you will. I don't know. Such a bizarre set of circumstances..." His voice faltered, and he felt a prickling at the nape of his neck. He looked past the bed to the streaks of light spearing in through the shutters, seeing the princess standing there, offering her feeble explanation for why Archard could not stay. "And there's Neville's disappearance," he added, "and the physician's family emergency."

A pressure was gathering behind his eyes. *Something isn't right.* It was all a little *too* bizarre.

His thoughts scattered at the sound of footsteps in the hallway. Then all of a sudden the door burst open and four guards stamped into the chamber. One, a man he had spoken to on occasion, winced as he announced, "King-in-waiting, I'm sorry to tell you that you are under arrest for treason."

Avry crossed the room to the door. "What do you mean?"

"Did you not make yourself regent and use the king's own seal to sign a contract?"

While his mouth worked to form words, he glimpsed movement in the hallway. "Senet," Avry snapped. The steward stepped into the doorway, face calm as a winter lake. Avry snared his eyes. "You," he said, voice cracking as he recognized the trap that had been laid, "advised me to do it."

Senet managed to look authentically startled, even affronted, as he declared, "I did no such thing."

CHAPTER 15

Mer spent the day after the ceremony in a cloud of her own activity. She foraged and bottled what she gathered. She sliced some meat Lisette had given her and hung the strips on pegs inside the hearth to dry. She even dusted the flies out of the window sills— something she was ashamed to say she had never done. Her father watched her with half an eye, but he knew better than to say anything. He had already said enough.

She swallowed a few bites at dinner to please him, then tidied up the table and went to bed.

Alone in her room, she stared sightlessly up at the ceiling, wishing she could weep again. It would be another thing to do. A distraction. But the tears would not come. At last, she fell into a fitful sleep.

Dreams assailed her. In one, she wandered down a dark hallway. A door opened, but before she could step through, someone shoved her from behind and she plunged into a pool of milky water. A voice bubbled up from its depths: *Drink.* Her jaws tore open, and the bitter water flowed in. With a terrible scream, she burst asunder. The seed of her pain sprouted and became a blood-red sea that ate everything: light, life, even death. It left her nowhere to hide.

She gasped as she woke.

Wrapping herself in blankets, she piled out of bed and paced the room with a restless energy. The sea raged inside her, an angry storm of memories that never went away. Killing the fae who destroyed her voice was not the worst, though it returned to her most often. Worst was the moment when she had looked out across the treetops in the Cursed Wood and spied the ruin of Thorsault. One fae's death was but a drop in a bucket next to the city's destruction. The Cursed Wood had trampled both the fae and their human slaves alike. And what had prompted that ruin? Her story.

Mer ground her fists into her eyes. She thought she had squashed her guilt over the city's ruin. Why did it return to her *now*? Hopelessness welled in her. Hands trembling, she lit a lamp and rummaged through her desk until her fingers closed around Avry's bundle of dreams. But as soon as she found them, she let them go.

What was she doing? How could reading his dreams make her feel better now? They would only remind her of what she had lost. She shoved them back in the drawer, curled into herself on the mattress, and closed her eyes. *Sleep,* she commanded herself firmly. And after a while, sleep found her.

***

She slumped at the table the next morning and regarded her breakfast as if it might cause her some injury.

"Aren't you going to eat?"

She glanced up from her plate. A familiar dread haunted her father's eyes. He had seen her like this before.

Heaving a sigh, she shoved pickled cabbage into her mouth and forced herself to chew.

"You should get some rest today," Rives said. "I'll take care of Jan."

The cabbage went down in a rough gulp. "What am I supposed to do here?"

"Finish smoking the meat. Read the book Avry gave you. I'm sure you'll find something to do." He snatched Jan's fingers just as they closed around a handful of Mer's cabbage.

"Let him have it." She got up from the table and pushed in the chair with more force than was necessary. "I'll stay inside," she agreed, forcing calm into her voice. "But only for a day."

The cottage was horribly quiet after Rives and Jan were gone. Mer paced again, unable to settle on any one task. Despite herself, she yearned to pull on her boots and head south, and she was reminded of a fragment of poem she once found, shoved between the pages of a book in her uncle's library:

I will rise now and go about the city,
in the streets and in the squares;
I will seek him whom my soul loves.
I sought him, but found him not.

She was on the brink of grabbing pen and paper and jotting down the poem when a firm knock landed on the door.

"Good day, Lady," Jacques greeted her as she threw it open. "I have a letter for you, from Ann of all places." He pulled a rumpled scroll out of his side bag and handed it to her reverently.

Mer stared at him in surprise then leaned in and whispered, "I don't know anyone in Ann."

"But the name on the scroll is yours all the same. There's only one Lady Merisande in Aure."

"I see."

He tapped the paper with a fingernail. "There isn't a return address, so unless they've included one inside, you won't be able to reply."

Mer fingered her chin as she eyed the formless glop of wax holding the pages together. Only one person living as far away as Ann might have written her. If that person had indeed sent this letter, she would have to inform Avry. Her mouth quirked at the thought. "Will you be with your brother until noon?" she asked.

"I can be. But, Lady, I should warn you that a letter to Ann is costly, more than it was two weeks ago."

"It won't be going to Ann."

Mer bid the messenger farewell and shot across the room to her chair by the hearth. She popped the wax seal, shook the last page free of the others, and stared at the signature.

Gandel.

"Hah!" A flare of happiness brightened her gloomy mood. Prince Gandel was alive after all. And somehow he had traveled as far as Ann. What had he done with his wings? Surely he could not have kept them concealed for long.

Eagerly, she began reading.

Lady Merisande,

I know you must be surprised to read these words. We didn't part on the best of terms. And then I took off, leaving you at the mercy of my father, who was readying to attack your people and carry them off as slaves. I don't think he would have succeeded, but that's beside the point.

You probably think I'm a coward. And you may be right. But I hope that by the time you finish reading this, you'll at least understand why I chose to leave Thorsault.

Turn your mind back to the day we picnicked under the pine tree. Remember how surprised you were when I told you about the continent my ancestors came from, a land to the west, far across the sea? Naturally, you asked me why they ever left and came to Aure. I answered: they were exiled. Again, you asked me why. Why were my ancestors exiled? I didn't answer you then. It didn't seem important for you to know.

Now it is. Vitally important.

Mer was clutching the letter so hard that a fingernail had pierced the paper. Forcing her hands to relax, she read on.

Five centuries ago, in that land across the sea, a young fae named Genningas started a family near a mountain range. These particular mountains were, and perhaps still are, inhabited by long-lived animals held sacred by the fae. In the ancient language of my people they are called "skin shifters."

Have you ever spied a leaf insect? They are difficult to spot because they blend so well with the leaves. Skin shifters are the same way, but with an important difference: they don't simply mimic a thing—they become it, be it a tree, a fish, or a horse.

Mer paused, reminded of the wood woman, Esperance, and her daughter, Astrid. Both could shape-change into deer, and both were long-lived and reclusive. Could they be related to this creature Gandel spoke of?

If they were, then skin-shifters were anything but dumb animals.

My young ancestor was warned to stay away from skin shifters, for they are known to draw fae into relationships with them, and if these relationships grow strong enough, bindings can occur.

All shifters are born bound to their parents by means of invisible communication strands. At adulthood these strands snap, and the shifter may toss them to others, so two or more can communicate from a distance. Between mountains, for example.

Some shifters choose to devote their lives to the objects of their affection. To do this, they toss their loved one a "dedication strand." Normally, such a strand can be snapped with ease. Not so if the strand connects a shifter to a fae. When a shifter devotes his or her life to a fae, the tossed strand puts down roots, as it were, and becomes a permanent vehicle for the fae's will to be conveyed.

Allowing a relationship to progress to the point of binding was illegal in my ancestor's land. In fact, if it became known that a binding had occurred, the fae involved would be put to death and his children banished.

Genningas lived to a ripe old age before his crime was discovered. In fact, his heart gave out on him before his executioner could finish him off. But his offspring paid the price for his folly. More than thirty of his descendants, together with their spouses, were set adrift on the open sea. Banishment meant sure death, for there was no place to go. Few could negotiate the dangerous waters along the coastline, and they would've had to travel far to find a vacant stretch of land. But my ancestors had a secret that gave them hope: the shifter's binding still held. In her passion, she had extended it to every firstborn heir. Forever.

So as soon as the ship left land, the shifter, in the form of a giant bird, grasped the ship's head and towed it out into the open sea. For weeks, she pressed on until Aure bared its green head.

A giant bird.

Mer's hand flew to her mouth as she recalled the broken tower, the drowned men. A huge white bird had done it, the soldier had said.

Gripping the pages, she read on.

I'd like to say that everything went well from then on, that my people were free and learned to be content with that freedom. But that is not what happened. Within half a century, they raided the people living on the island, burning their homes and making them slaves. When the slaves revolted, the new king of Thorsault compelled his shifter—who had become known as "The White"—to attack them.

That act drove a wedge between The White and her binder.

Angry and likely feeling betrayed, The White left the fae and made her home on the west side of the island, somewhere in the range your people call "The North Mountains." Her binder, rather than force her back home, retaliated by dashing the white bird emblem from his standard and replacing it with a griffin. He also set guards on her, but these lost their minds. In fact, all guards who have ever been sent to watch her have gone insane. "Crazy as a mountain guard" is a common saying among my people.

For four centuries, the binding continued to pass from father to son, generation after generation, and The White lingered in the mountains, wounded and lonely, broadcasting her relentless cry of pain to her binder, down to this day.

Now comes the part you won't like, Merisande.

While I was still in Aure, I heard about Thorsault's ruin. However, I can say with absolute certainty that some of my people survived. You see, the binding did not pass to me. So at the very least, my father lived. Most likely he and a few others escaped through the tunnels under the tor, which stretch all the way to the mountains. To avoid the Cursed Wood, they would have traveled to the west side of the island, settling in the trees on the fringe of the north mountains, where they could hide and live off the land.

Mer dropped the letter with a sudden gasp.

If Gandel was right, the fae king and others had settled only a few miles north of where she sat now. Her skin crawled as she reflected on the days she and her father had spent on the very edge of the north wood, chopping down trees. How much farther were the mountains? A dozen miles? Less?

"It doesn't matter."

Her whispered words gusted into the charged silence. If the fae king wielded The White, no one in Aure was safe, regardless of where they lived.

Her hands shook as she lifted the last page.

I wanted nothing to do with my father's war, so I left Aure and crossed the ocean to Ann, hoping to put enough distance between myself and The White that when my father did pass, I wouldn't feel the binding. I even had my wings removed and can walk among others with gratifying anonymity.

Imagine my astonishment when I heard about the shifter's attack on Aure. It felt as though the old bones of the past had been torn out of their resting places and strewn on the street. I was angered, perplexed, and ashamed. I can only conclude that my father has lost his mind. But what can I do, short of killing him? I could never dissuade him from anything.

This letter is the best I can do. Pass it to someone you trust. Someone with power.

To that person, I offer the following advice:

You have but two choices: either deal my father so swift a blow that The White doesn't have time to respond to his distress and save him, or hunt down and kill her outright. Either option is fraught with peril, but doing nothing is just as dangerous.

The White will attack again.

I wish you all the luck in the world,

Gandel

CHAPTER 16

Avry dreamed of darkness.

He wandered with outstretched arms while the air shivered around him and the earth rumbled under his feet. No matter how long he searched, his fingers found nothing but empty space. Blackness. Then the ground opened, and he plunged headlong into a void.

He jerked awake, then groaned, touching his bruised head. It was sticky with blood. *My fault*, he thought. Though he rarely gave in to anger, he had flown into a rage against Senet, and all four guards had struggled to hold him back. Avry had incapacitated two of them before the chamber guards joined in. Someone must have knocked him unconscious at that point. He did not recall being carried down to the castle dungeon.

He was lying on the stone floor of a tiny cell. A barred window set high in the wall across from the door glared at him like a bright eye. His wrists were shackled together, the iron cuffs separated by a short chain. Wincing at a pain in his side, he curled his knees into his chest and patted his ankle. No pen knife. The guards had done a thorough search.

A clang of metal broke the silence, and he rose shakily to his feet. Footsteps echoed off the damp stone walls. Avry stiffened, wondering if someone had been sent to kill him.

But it was Édouard who stepped into the dusty light.

The boy's face was so stiff and white that it might have been chiseled from stone. "Sir," he croaked, "are you in pain?"

Avry moistened his dry lips and tasted blood. "I'm fine."

"Are you hungry, thirsty?"

"I suppose I should force myself to eat something."

"I'll fetch you something, sir."

"Thank you, Édouard."

Avry closed his eyes and leaned his head against the bars. His mind drifted back to the morning Patric stole off down the third floor. Senet's chamber was on that floor. The two men had probably colluded.

He slid a chill hand across his face. He would not be here long. Someone would slip into his cell and kill him. It was inevitable.

Édouard returned with a flagon of watered mead and a loaf of bread torn into pieces.

"Sorry about the bread, sir. The guard thought I might have hidden a knife in it. You can use the cloth it's wrapped in to clean your face."

Avry squatted down, shook the bread into his lap, and folded the cloth into a manageable square. He eyed Édouard furtively as he dabbed his forehead. The boy's hands were clenched so tightly that an old scab had cracked open and was oozing blood.

"Sir," he spluttered, smearing blood on a knuckle. "I have some terrible news."

Avry stiffened. Could this get any worse? Yes. It could. "Go on," he said cautiously.

"Senet ordered a search of your chamber. The guards found a sack of something…a green powder the steward calls devil's thumb. Senet says it's a slow-acting poison and that you've been using it to murder the king."

Avry dropped the cloth. He sat without moving, one hand gripping a bar as if it were the only thing keeping him from tumbling into the void. "I don't suppose," he managed in a tight voice, "that anyone thought to ask the king's steward how he could identify such a herb and its uses?"

"I don't know, sir. I wasn't there. I got the news from Sir Fennick."

"The bastard probably had a ready excuse."

"You think Senet poisoned the king, sir?"

"Yes, I do." Avry regarded him closely, looking for doubt in the wide brown eyes. There was none. He lifted the flagon awkwardly and took a long pull, barely tasting the watered mead. His hands trembled with anger at the thought that Ghislain might die from this, that such a great man—master swordsman, wise king—could succumb to Senet's sly fingers. What a fool Avry had been to trust him. He cleared his throat and said evenly, "This is all part of an elaborate plot to set Patric on the throne."

"Patric." Édouard's mouth gaped. "Why would Senet do this for Patric?"

"I don't know."

"And Ann? Do you think King Alaric is part of this scheme?"

"Not Alaric, but certainly his son, Archard. Patric must have promised the prince something, perhaps gold or white stone, if he helped get me out of the way."

"But Archard couldn't have known you would accept those ships in the king's name."

"No. But he made it difficult for me not to. He gave me an ultimatum: sign the document before noon or lose the ships. Senet encouraged me to sign. *Do what's best for Aure,* he said. Aure needed those ships."

"Did anyone overhear him say that?"

"No one." The chain separating his wrist irons tinkled as he took another swallow of mead. "Senet played his part well, first by poisoning the king so he wouldn't wake, then by drawing the physician away so that Ghislain couldn't be declared incapable."

"The physician is still away," Édouard informed him, and Avry's jaw tightened. The man was very likely dead.

A sudden thought made him set the flagon a little too soundly on the floor. "And what of Sir Neville? Did you find him?"

Édouard's back straightened. "I did, sir. He was lying on his bed, moaning, with a chamber pot full of vomit by his head. He said he was poisoned."

Avry rose up on his knees, not caring that the bread scattered onto the floor. "When was he poisoned?"

"Last night, sir. But he says he's survived it, that the worst is over."

Avry flung his hands sideways through the bars, caught his squire's shoulders, and held them in a steel grip. "This was their one mistake. Neville wasn't supposed to live. But he does. He does. I have to see him, Édouard. Go back and tell him all I've told you. Then bring him here, before the supper hour if possible."

As commander, Neville had authority over all the king's men. He was also hard to kill, which was why Senet had gone to such trouble to end his life.

"Yes, sir. Right away."

Avry relaxed back against the wall with a sigh. "Thank you, Édouard."

"Oh," Édouard exclaimed as he scrambled to his feet, "I almost forgot the letter." He wiped his hands on his hose then drew a scroll out of his tunic and passed it to Avry. "I had to bribe the guard to get it to you. It's from Lady Merisande."

Avry stared numbly at the clean white thing in his hand, not knowing if he should embrace it or wish it away. Soon enough, she would find out what had happened that morning. What would she think of him then? *I should write her back and explain things,* he thought. But it might just come across as one long excuse for his behavior.

"Édouard…"

"Yes, sir?"

His mouth opened; he tried to form the awful words he needed to say. "I hope I didn't give you the impression that I'm entirely free from blame."

His squire shrugged a shoulder. "You were framed, sir."

"Perhaps. But in the end, the decision to sign that document was mine and mine alone. Do you understand? I willingly made myself regent and used the king's own seal illegally. It was a foolish thing to do, and it may cost us a great deal."

He waited impatiently for Édouard's response. But the boy's eyes withheld expression. Avry sighed, giving up on an answer. "Be careful, Édouard. You are a target now too."

"I will, sir." With a slight bow, he turned and disappeared down the hallway. Metal clanged as the prison door slammed shut.

Avry's head sagged between his knees, and he moaned. It felt as though his heart had migrated from his chest to his head. Every beat was a rush of pain. Tentatively, he fingered the wound at his temple. The entire right side of his head was sticky, but at least it was not still bleeding.

He finished what was left of the mead and wiped his hands on the cloth. Then he popped the wax seal and loosened the paper. Mer's note only inhabited the first page. The last four, which were wrinkled and stained by road dust, were part of a letter addressed to her. Gandel's name shot from the final page like an arrow, making Avry gasp in surprise. So the fae prince had survived after all. What had moved him to come out of hiding?

Sir Avry, Merisande wrote, *I apologize for this letter's brevity, but my trembling hands won't let me write more than a few lines. First, allow me to congratulate you on your new appointment. I hope you are faring well. If you have not looked over the letter tucked behind this one, then I'll tell you that it's from Prince Gandel and includes some information of deadly importance. In fact, I have committed its main points to memory in case it gets misplaced or damaged. I trust you will share its contents with the king. I wish I had better news. I suppose it's better to be in light than in darkness. But how such brightness blinds! Your friend, Merisande*

Avry, hardly breathing now, picked up the prince's letter and read it through slowly. Once. Twice. A third time.

Finally, it dropped from his hands and he leaned back against the wall. The world swayed behind his closed eyes. Everything was spinning away, leaving him flailing in the blackness of the void. His hands clenched in the wrist irons. How dangerous was this creature? Could it adopt an even deadlier form?

What did the fae king have planned for Aure?

His jaw firmed, and he drew a steadying breath. His eyes were clear when they opened, his back straight. Senet's scheme did not intimidate him any longer. He could not allow it to. If he did not thrust it aside, like someone clearing a tabletop, Aure may be swept away in the coming storm.

***

Having dispatched the letter to Avry, Mer tackled all the tasks her father had recommended. The smoked meat was stored away in the cellar under the kitchen floor, the fireplace swept, Avry's book removed from its place in her desk drawer. She ran a hand pensively over the cover.

Her father had been gone all morning. She kept listening for his footsteps but heard only the shutters creaking gently in the wind. What if Jan had wandered off while Rives was busy setting traps? Though he seemed clumsy, her brother could travel far and fast. In a few hours, he might find himself in the shadow of the north mountains.

"That's ridiculous," she muttered. But she could not shake the thought from her mind. She set the book aside, snatched her coat off a hook, pulled on her sturdy boots, and strode out into the afternoon sunlight.

The grass, dry and brown from weeks without rain, crunched underfoot as she crossed the stony field to the wood. Green was a color the world had forgotten for a while. Reds, oranges, and browns had taken its place.

She dragged her hands through the branches, trapping leaves in her fingers. She let them fly into the wind, catch light and sparkle. *Jan would have loved this*, she thought. She was bound to find some sign of him on the path. Torn or crushed leaves, a discarded scarf.

A soft thud made her pause midstep. She opened her mouth and nearly shouted her brother's name before remembering that she could only whisper.

As she scanned the trees, a voice caught her like a claw.

"I'm right behind you, girl."

Mer turned so fast that she almost crashed into a tree.

Esperance rested a steadying hand on her shoulder. Mer did not feel comforted as she looked back at her, feeling the full weight of those dark green eyes, still tinged with wildness, as if she had only just become human.

Probably she had.

Mer shuddered. What if Esperance *was* The White? *Skin shifters don't simply mimic a thing,* Gandel had written, *they become it, be it a tree, a fish or a horse.*

Esperance dropped her callused hand with a snort. "Calm yourself, girl. I'm not about to throw you into my pot."

Mer hissed out a nervous laugh. What was she thinking? Esperance could not be The White. The woman lived in a rickety cabin, not a mountain range, and the only form Mer had glimpsed her in—aside from human—had been that of a red deer. "I'm sorry, you startled me is all," she said in her loudest whisper.

"Never mind. I need your help. My daughter is sick."

"Your daughter..." Mer's eyes widened. "Has Astrid returned to you? Has she crossed the gorge?"

"You ask too many questions," the wood woman snapped. "Will you help me help her or not?"

"I'm not a physician."

"Doesn't matter."

Mer burned with curiosity. Her brother could wait, she decided. He and Rives were probably back home anyway. She wished she had left a note. But no matter. Her father knew she was out of valerian root. He would assume she had gone to fetch more. "I'll come," she said.

As soon as the words left her mouth, Esperance seized her hand and wrenched her off the path into the trees. Mer lurched along behind, too startled by the woman's strength to protest. If a sword had wrapped itself around her knuckles and pulled, she would have been less surprised.

The ground raced by. Esperance charged through the undergrowth as if it were a fine mist. Mer gave up worrying where she stepped, what she might be treading on, and let her feet land where they would. Just when she thought she would collapse with exhaustion, Esperance dropped her hand.

"Take some time to catch your breath," she offered as Mer collapsed on the spongy ground, panting and clutching her sore wrist.

They rested thrice more during their journey through the north wood, and when at last they entered the clearing and waded through a field of swaying ferns, it was all Mer could do to keep upright.

Esperance's cottage lay like a sleeping beast in the sunlight, its thatched roof softened by feathers and fur and other material Mer had no desire to identify.

Esperance paused in the doorway, her tight mouth straining to shape a smile. "Tea?"

A rancid scent assailed Mer's nostrils as she stepped inside. It did not take her long to identify its source. A young woman lay curled by the fire like a stray kitten. Her dress was no more than a rag, soot-stained and soiled by bodily fluids. Her face and hair were clean but shockingly pale against her grimy clothing.

Mer wriggled a worn blanket out from under the girl's legs and draped it over her. She laid a tentative hand on Astrid's forehead.

"She's as cool as a toad," Esperance muttered as she placed a steaming cup on the floor.

"How long has she been like this?"

"A few weeks. I came to the cliff one morning and saw her lying there, naked as the day she came into the world. So I found some lengths of rope, tied them together, and brought her across. She hasn't spoken a word."

Mer, looking from the bandages on the girl's hands to Esperance's pinched mouth and hooded eyes, muttered, "You know what's wrong with her, don't you?"

"Was that a question?" the woman asked testily and then gave up with a shrug. "I suspect something, but I can't confirm it until she talks to me. But she won't." She twisted away, hiding her face behind a fall of auburn hair. "Maybe she'll talk to you."

Mer wanted to ask her why. Why would Astrid confide in Mer instead of her mother? And why had Esperance chosen Mer for this task? The last time they spoke, the woman had all but thrown Mer from her cottage for implying that there might be a connection between Astrid and the Cursed Wood. She sipped the tea. "I'll try."

"Thank you," Esperance said and withdrew into the shadows.

Mer took the girl's face in both her hands and tilted it toward her. "Do you remember me, Astrid? We saw each other more than once in the forest near Thorsault. Remember how Prince Gandel nearly shot you with an arrow?"

Astrid's large eyes fluttered open. Mer was instantly entranced. They were a pale, liquid blue, like sunlight on still water. And they were the white doe's, bright with that innocence only an animal knew. Mer's throat burned, but she found the words to go on speaking. "Remember the night we last saw each other? I was alone in the dark trees, not knowing where to go or what to do. You found me and led me to the Cursed Wood."

Astrid nodded faintly. Her rigid mouth had relaxed, and the tight lines around her eyes had smoothened. Mer grasped her bandaged hand. "My name is Mer, and I'd like to help you, like you helped me. Can you tell me what's wrong?"

Her lips parted, but no sound came out. Mer leaned her ear over the girl's mouth. "Go on," she breathed.

Warm air tickled Mer's hair, then a desperate whisper, "She calls."

"Who calls?"

"Her."

Her? Mer was baffled. Was she speaking about Esperance?

All of a sudden Astrid's body went rigid, and her teeth snapped together like rocks cracking. She shuddered twice, violently. Horrified, Mer gripped her shoulders and fought to steady her. "Astrid, what's wrong?"

The girl's face seemed to blur as she looked at Mer, and when she spoke, the sound might have come from anywhere. "Stay with me."

"I'm here. I will." *I owe you.*

"Stay."

Mer felt a hand on her shoulder and turned.

Something large crashed into her then, slamming her against the wall. Her next breath was filled with smoke. As she choked out a painful cough, there came a sound like wood splitting. Wind tore through the space, beating her hair back in smoky waves.

Mer, twisting her neck to look up, glimpsed a huge form shooting through the ruined ceiling into the sky.

CHAPTER 17

"Out!" Esperance shouted behind her. "Now!"

Mer shielded her head with her arms. Panic fluttered in her belly. The roof was sinking in, dropping blackened wood and thatch onto the sizzling remains of the fire. The pot had overturned and lay several feet from the pit. Astrid was gone. The creature must have torn the roof open to get at her. Or at least, that was what seemed to have happened. She dove for the door just as a rafter above her began to fall. Esperance seized her wrist and pulled her outside.

"Let me go," Mer said as she stumbled out of the ruined cottage.

"Why? So you can stagger about like a drunken mouse? You need to get away from here."

Mer lost her footing and tumbled to the ground, coughing into her freed arm.

Esperance crouched over her with hands on hips. Her jaw was set with determination. "Get up, girl."

"Did you see what happened?"

She tossed an arm at the wood. "Do you see those trees? That's where you need to be."

"We need to find Astrid." Mer peered at the swaying ferns and the empty sky above them. "She was there and then she was gone, and I did nothing to help her."

A tear glittered in the corner of Esperance's eye. "There's nothing either of us can do."

"Did you see which way—?" Her whisper broke off as a piercing cry shook the clearing, silencing the birds and crickets. Mer scrambled to her feet in a panic. "What was that?"

Esperance's head shook, and Mer guessed she had not heard her. "Poor Astrid," the woman sighed. "Poor little girl. If she were only a little stronger. But she's been away too long..." She jabbered on, her wet eyes looking past Mer to something in the distance.

A shadow was moving over the field.

Mer looked up and felt all the blood leave her face. She stepped back, her heart hammering in her throat, her braid snapping behind her in a sudden breeze. Then huge white feathers brushed her, and something firm clamped around her middle.

With a sickening lurch, the ground fell away.

Mer choked then vomited into the empty air. Blackness enveloped her for an instant, but she pushed it back, terrified of what would happen if she lost consciousness.

The forest was an orangey-red blur far below. If the bird dropped her, she would die. And it could at any moment. Waves of terror flooded through her. A terrible pressure drilled in her ears. The gray wall of the mountains loomed ahead, growing nearer with every breath. Shivering, she pulled up her dangling arms and dug her fingers under her belly, between the bird's talons and her wool coat.

The air grew colder still as the bird swooped higher, skimming past jagged rock formations toward some lofty peaks in the distance. Mer glimpsed her death as she looked out over them, for she would surely freeze.

Then all of a sudden the bird's wings pulled in, its body tipped down, and it plummeted.

***

Mer woke to find stone under her back instead of air.

When she got up the courage to look around her, her heart gave a little lurch. She was lying on the inner rim of what appeared to be a volcanic crater. The seemingly bottomless hole at her side was perhaps twenty yards across, sighing out warm, stinking air like a mouth. The crater's jagged rim varied in width from several yards to barely a foot. The walls ascending from the rim were slate gray. Orangey-red sacs clung to them like pustules, seeping a dark, mysterious liquid. The substance had pooled on the inner edges of the rim, trapping feathers and fragments of bone before leaching in slender rivulets toward the hole. Mer squinted up at the sky, wondering if she could scale the crater walls. But they were too high and sheer, and the pit would not spit her back up if she fell into it.

She was trapped in The White's den in the cold heart of the North Mountains. "I may as well be on the moon," she breathed, despair welling up in her. There was no water. How long could she last here? She pushed her face into her hands, swallowing back the sour residue of her vomit.

A soft moan made her stiffen. She peered around and then behind her. Astrid was crouched in an indentation in the wall. Her eyes were tightly shut, and she rocked back and forth on her heels, hugging her legs with her arms.

Mer smiled grimly. She had found Astrid, and while the situation was dire, at least they were together. Mindful of the hole, Mer crawled over to her and wriggled into the gap by her side.

Astrid stopped rocking and grasped her hand. "I'm glad you're here with me," she said in a voice rough from disuse.

Mer snorted. "I can't say I am. But it's nice that we're together. She brought you here fast."

"She?"

"The White."

Astrid shook her head. "I brought myself here."

Mer stared uncomprehendingly back at her. The truth dawned on her then, and she sucked in a startled breath. "That was you. You brought me here." She tried to take her hand back, but Astrid held it stubbornly. A thought made Mer blanch. "Were you the one who attacked the city?"

"I've never been to a city. Never and never." Her gaze settled bleakly on the hole, and she began to rock again.

Mer, eying her slender legs, her drawn face, struggled to reconcile this young woman with the beast that had shattered Esperance's roof, plucked Mer off the ground as easily as a hawk snatching a mouse, and flown her over the mountains. "Well," she sighed, giving up. "At least I won't die. If you brought me here, you can bring me back."

"You said you would stay."

Mer grimaced. She tried to call back the sympathy she had felt for the girl earlier, but the pain Astrid's talons had wrought on her middle made it difficult. *Stay* seemed more a threat now than a plea. *I should have stayed home,* she thought sourly. Rives would have returned by now. Finding her missing, he would search the wood for her, unaware of the danger Gandel had revealed in his letter. "But why must we be *here*?" she protested. "This place seems to frighten you. It certainly frightens me."

"I *am* frightened. I didn't want to face her alone. That's why I brought you with me."

Mer's throat went dry. *Her* must be The White. "What can I possibly do against the sort of being that frightens *you*?"

"Nothing." She rocked harder, and her grip on Mer's hand tightened. "Nothing and nothing."

"Couldn't your mother have helped you?"

"No. She has always stayed out of this."

"This...?"

"The White's misery. Her troubles with the fae. Mother used to say that one shouldn't fight pain by pushing it on others."

"You're hurting my hand."

Abruptly, the rocking ceased and Astrid went as still as death. Mer yanked her hand free and massaged her numb fingers. Then she too went still.

A sound like the scratching and scraping of an insect whispered up from deep in the earth. The noise grew swiftly until it seemed that the entire crater crawled with invisible legs. But it was all an illusion, for moments later a giant bird burst out of the hole and landed with a thud on the top edge of the crater rim. Its pale wings opened to the sinking sun, and it let out a long, low cry. Mer found her eyes drawn to an angry wound on its leg. Had it been struck by a spear?

A silence fell. The crater darkened, and mist rose up from the hole. Just as the moon peeked over the crater, the bird's wings lowered and it dropped with a whoosh onto the inner ledge. Mer met its intelligent gaze in the dusky light. Wonder washed over her, along with a strange desire to be closer, to touch, to understand.

The bird bowed its great head, the tips of its wings rippled, and a strange smell wafted out.

"No!" Astrid's voice slammed across the space with enough strength to knock all the stars from the sky. But it could not clear the fog that had climbed into Mer's head. She sagged against the girl's shoulder, closed her eyes, and let blackness take her.

CHAPTER 18

Avry, weary from his injury, had kept himself awake by standing at the barred window and watching the lengthening shadows. It was about the supper hour when the dungeon door clanged again and heavy footsteps sounded in the hall. The visitor stopped and started several times as he neared Avry's cell, all the time breathing heavily. At last, the bulky form of Sir Neville slumped against the bars of Avry's cell door with a relieved sigh. He regarded Avry from under red bushy brows, his eyes taking in the head injury, the bloodied cloth on the floor.

Shooting Avry one of his famous dry smiles, he said, "Just look at us, Pup. Look at the state we're in. Anyone would think we'd spent a night and day in the pubs."

Avry grinned, more in relief than in amusement. His relationship with the first knight remained intact.

Neville scanned the hall, as if there might be a chair to fall into.

"I would invite you in, but…" Avry gestured with cuffed hands to his tiny cell.

"The floor will do," Neville grunted and plopped himself down like a sack of potatoes.

"I assume Édouard reported to you."

He gave a weary nod. "I'm here, aren't I? God, but I feel awful."

"What happened to you?"

"Didn't Édouard tell you? I was poisoned."

Avry sat with legs crossed, knees grazing the cell door. "Yes, but how?"

"Last night I found a bottle of Velotet outside my door, with a note saying it was from a secret admirer. As you can imagine, I was thrilled. How often does a whole bottle of Velotet come your way? So I dug out a fancy crystal goblet and poured myself a glass. The goblet saved my life. I'd only taken a sip before I noticed the wine was murky. I grabbed my chamber pot and tried to vomit, but nothing came up until it was too late. After I'd filled half the pot, a numbness spread through me, and I thought I would die. I called out, but all I could manage was a whimper. I didn't come to until after midday."

"I'd like to see that note," Avry muttered. "I'd bet you anything it was written in the same hand that penned the letter to the physician, calling him away."

"I still have it. Stashed it somewhere safe."

Avry pinched the space between his brows. "They would probably pin it all on me anyway, say that I wrote the letters *and* poisoned you. After all, I poisoned the king."

Neville slipped a meaty hand between the bars and patted Avry's forearm. "Don't despair, Pup. The knights I've spoken to suspect Senet, not you. I reminded them of the mushrooms." He scratched his bearded chin. "If there's even a chance Senet poisoned the king, he should be confined and his chamber searched."

"Indeed. But not just yet."

Neville's brow crinkled. "Do you have a plan?"

"I have the seed of one. Whether or not it bears fruit depends on many things." Avry drew Gandel's letter out of his shirt. "But first: this."

"What is it?"

Avry's chest tightened. His first impulse had been to conceal the contents of the letter until he hopefully got free, but Neville was Military Commander as well as First Knight. He was owed that information. Keeping it from him, even for a short time, would damage their rapport. "Something that will make all this seem like nothing at all. It's a letter from Prince Gandel, forwarded to me by Lady Merisande."

Neville's face went slack. "The *fae* prince?"

"There's no other." He pushed the letter into his hand. "Read it."

"I—can't. Well," he cleared his throat, "I can, but not well."

"Oh." He retrieved the pages sheepishly. "Sorry. I should have remembered."

"I should learn. What does the letter say?"

Avry leaned into the bars and read it in a tone just above a whisper. When he was done, Neville had gone utterly still, his breathing shallow. Suddenly he pressed his hand over his face. "God have mercy," he said through his fingers. "What do we do?"

"One thing at a time. We must deal with the present problem before we can tackle the next."

Neville lurched to his feet, swaying before managing to steady himself. "Tell me what to do, and we'll get it done."

Avry pursed his lips. In Neville's present state, it would be a miracle if he made it through the evening without collapsing. He stood so they were at eye level. "I assume that Patric is away from the castle."

"Édouard said he hasn't seen him. The boy searched every inch of the castle today, looking for myself and the king's servant. He didn't see Patric anywhere." His mouth closed, opened again. "You do realize that the king's missing servant is Senet's younger half brother?"

Avry groaned. "No. I didn't know that. No wonder he's missing. He was probably the one administering the poison. Senet probably stashed him somewhere so he couldn't be questioned."

Neville shook his head. "I don't understand this at all. Why would Senet conspire to place Patric on the throne? Senet's position as steward is secure—or was, at any rate, and you've given him no cause to fear you."

"I don't know, but I expect you'll get some answers tonight." Leaning into the bars, Avry whispered, "Close the castle doors and order a pair of knights to watch them. Then find out which of the guards are on duty tonight, bring them in quietly, and interrogate them. If I'm right, at least one will be in collusion with Patric and Senet."

Neville's eyes widened. "Do you expect an ambush?"

"I expect that Patric will return to officially declare Ghislain incapable and take the throne."

"Over my dead body, he will."

Avry gave a solemn nod. "And mine too, if we're not careful. He won't come alone."

"Would you like me to report back what the door guards say?"

Avry drew a long breath and loosed it slowly. "No. I think you'll know what to do with the information they give you." Trust, Avry thought, was like taking a step into empty air.

"Very well," the commander said huskily. "Wish me luck, then."

"Neville," Avry said as he lurched down the hall. "If we succeed, I'm still guilty of using the king's seal."

Neville paused with a grunt. "So you are. What would you like me to do about that? Give you a few lashes? A public scolding? I'm not your da, but for a few coppers I'd be willing to..."

"Get out of here."

"Certainly, My Lord Regent, King-in-Waiting Sir Avry of the house Eleuthère."

***

Rives, exhausted from a day of walking, sat on a clifftop overlooking the gorge and watched the purple twilight darken to deep indigo. When he had returned home that afternoon, he was surprised to find the cottage empty, without so much as a note explaining why. Jan had burst anxiously into Mer's room a dozen times before Rives had dragged him to the hearth and thrown a blanket over him.

"She'll be back soon," Rives had assured him. But as the afternoon wore on, he began to doubt the soundness of his own words. Fear danced up his spine. He went around the back to see if he could find a trail, but the ground would not talk.

Not knowing what else to do, he left his son in the cottage and strode back into the wood alone. His mouth twisted as he hiked up the trail toward the gorge. Another father would have gone to the neighbors first, asked around. But he knew his daughter too well. In her depressed state, the trees would have been her only refuge.

And something else drove Rives into the wood: a fear, however irrational, that Mer had crossed the gorge again.

He had arrived at the cliff at sunset, panting with exertion, his eyes blurring to the beat of his heart. But there was no Mer and no evidence that she had ever been there. *No rope*, he thought mordantly.

The slender hook of the moon peeked out of the trees across the gorge. Rives drew flint out of his sack and went about lighting his lamp.

He was afraid for his daughter. Even if he found her, either back at home or wandering on the trail, she would still be lost, like someone wandering around and around inside themselves. In the weeks following her return from Thorsault, Rives had feared she would die. She had eaten almost nothing, rarely slept, and worked until she was little more than skin and bones. He had given her every opportunity to talk about what disturbed her, but she remained as silent as the grave. Perhaps she had buried her hurt so deep that she could not put it into words.

By September she had recovered from the worst of it. Her flesh softened, and she slept through most nights. But the Mer he knew— the confident, teasing, carefree girl that had both infuriated and amused him—was no more.

Rives stretched his stiff legs and rose to his feet. The light wobbled as he threaded his way around a stony rise and found the trail again.

Mer was sliding back, spurning rest and food, disappearing for hours on end. He could not stand to watch it happen again. If she were lovesick, then he would urge her to write Sir Avry and tell him how she felt. The knight would be thrilled to receive such a letter.

Just let her be home, he prayed.

***

The wind had risen, but Astrid could not feel it anymore. Something cold and hard pressed her into the crater wall, and a voice—either spoken aloud or into her mind—said her name.

A whimper gathered in her throat like tears. She had fought this for so long. Struggling in the dark of her own mind, she had clung with tattered nails to freedom. Even when her will began slipping, she did not let go.

After a week of torture, she had allowed her mother to take her back in, not because she believed that Esperance would free her from The White's incessant call, but because she did not want to suffer alone.

Two more weeks passed—too long, and when her mother brought Merisande to her, something inside Astrid had snapped. The woman had looked on her with pity. Pity instead of wonder. How far had Astrid allowed herself to fall?

I'm a coward, she thought. *Only a coward would have dragged an innocent woman along just because it felt good.*

Now Mer hung like a wrapped fly in a crevice in the wall. Astrid could not see her anymore, but she had watched what had been done to her. The White had let her watch.

All was quiet now, though her name flowed through her still, like the deep thrumming of a chord. Swallowing hard, she twisted her hand and touched the darkness that held her.

Her fingers brushed solid stone.

Astrid. Granddaughter.

A growl sprang from her throat. "Don't call me that."

Why? That is what you are.

"A true grandmother wouldn't torture her kin."

I called, but you would not come. Perhaps that made you uncomfortable for a time...

Astrid was inarticulate with anger. Her heart pounded, and she wanted to pull herself into a hundred different shapes, but The White held her with the inflexibility of stone. She spoke through clenched teeth. "Why didn't you just come to *me?* I wasn't far."

If I had, would you fear me as you do now?

"What do you want*?"*

What I want does not matter. I stopped wanting long ago. I have only needs now. I need *the binder's heir. The prince named Gandel.*

"Gandel…" In her mind, a pale-haired fae lifted an arrow to her heart. She had been in deer form, then, and he had been hunting. Mer had called him "Gandel."

Where is he?

"I don't know. He isn't with the other fae?" She had glimpsed them months ago, creeping like injured dogs along the edge of the gorge.

No, he is not. I need you to find him for me.

"But he could be anywhere. He might even be dead."

Find him and bring him here, like you brought the woman. If you do not, you will have no sleep, no peace, and no hope.

As those last terrible words rumbled through Astrid, The White loosed her abruptly, and she fell forward onto the rim. At once, she changed shape and shot like a spear out of the crater. She fled to the moon, higher and higher, until her eyes ached from the chill air. Still she ascended, letting the wind drive everything away.

Almost everything. A terrible thought clung to her like spider's silk: What would become of Mer if Gandel remained missing?

Loosing a cry, she tilted sideways and soared away from the mountains.

CHAPTER 19

Avry opened his eyes and struggled to lift himself off the floor. His injured head throbbed. He did not recall falling asleep.

"Idiot," he muttered. Someone could have easily shot him through the bars of his cell door while he slept. Or through the window.

He stumbled over to the shadowy square and pressed his face against the bars. Night had fallen. Wind swept over the castle yard, snapping banners and whipping torch flames sideways. He licked his lips, tasting brine. A storm was approaching, and if he could already taste the ocean, it would be fierce. He wondered how Neville had fared. Patric would arrive at the castle door soon. He could not afford to wait another day.

If it *was* Patric. It had occurred to Avry, in the moments before he drifted off, that another in Patric's line might have conspired to steal the throne. But who might that person be? Gossip had placed Patric as the likeliest choice for king-in-waiting. He had even taken residence in the castle, like a crow hovering near a sick animal, waiting for it to die.

But Neville was right. It made no sense for the king's steward to risk his life on behalf of the young, spoiled noble. What could he hope to gain? Greed was a common motive in such cases, but unlikely in Senet's. The steward had never shown a fondness for luxuries, and as far as Avry knew, he had no children on which to bestow an inheritance. Perhaps he wanted power. A man as weak as Patric could be swayed to do almost anything.

Thunder rolled across the sky. The wind lifted, spraying dust into Avry's eyes. He wiped the grit away then froze as a new sound stole into the yard: the creaking of the castle door. After the space of a few heartbeats, another creak sounded, followed by a sturdy thud. Thunder rumbled again.

As he wriggled to get a better view of the castle wall, lightning brightened the sky, and in that moment he glimpsed a shocking sight: archers swarming on the battlements, shooting arrows over the wall. Then darkness fell like a curtain, and for several moments he saw nothing but a searing memory of light. He leaned on his other senses. Shouts mingled in the raging wind, but they were too muffled to have come from inside the castle. *Must be the men outside*, he thought. *The ones being shot at.* He clenched the bars, begging the sky for another flash, but the rain came instead, and within seconds his face and hair were drenched. Still, he could not pull away. Why had Neville ordered the door to be opened? Who had he let in? Possibilities tumbled through Avry's sleep-fogged mind.

Had Neville been murdered, and Patric's men taken over the castle? Were the ones being shot at reserves from the barracks, making one last stand? He dashed rain out of his eyes. A torch along the wall went out, and a man relit it. Avry shouted to him, but the driving wind and rain tore the sound away.

He was being irrational. No, he was thinking clearly. He should stand by his cell door and prepare for an attack.

No, he should wait patiently until Neville sent him a message.

The clang of the dungeon door made him turn so fast, he almost whacked his head on the window casing. The steps of several men thudded down the hallway. Had they come to finish him off?

Heart hammering, he cast about for a weapon. His hands darted over the walls, tugging at loose stones. One came free, but his heart sank as he weighed it in his hand. Too small. Still, he had nothing better, and he was out of time. He moved to the side of his cell door so they could not skewer him with an arrow, formed a warrior's stance, and listened with dread to the approaching footsteps.

A lamp dimmed as someone passed in front of it. Elongated shadows streaked across the floor then vanished. After a few more steps, a door down the hallway creaked open. A key rattled in a lock. Someone shuffled through. Another clang, another click, and the footsteps started up again.

Avry flattened himself against the wall, muscles tense, hands clenched around the stone. Someone had been imprisoned. Might be Patric or Senet. Or it might be Sir Neville. He could not afford to be optimistic.

The men halted outside Avry's door. Keys rattled, and the lock clicked open.

"Regent Avry?"

Fennick. Avry slumped forward. His relief was so strong, he could barely stand. What a fool he had been to worry. He should have had more faith in Neville. In all of Ghislain's loyal men. "God, but I'm glad it's you, Fenn."

The knight swept through the door and laid a gloved hand on Avry's shoulder. His face was paler than Avry had ever seen it. "Let's go," he said quietly.

***

The storm had reached its full strength as Avry stepped outside. Torches on the castle walls had guttered out. Men clasped lamps to their breasts like mothers with bundled babies. Avry, glimpsing a line of bodies on the ground and more being dragged through the castle door, almost came to a complete stop.

"Keep walking, Pup." Sir Neville's ragged, weary voice caught him from behind.

"Who were they? What happened?"

"They're soldiers from Ann."

Avry wheeled. "Ann," he repeated hoarsely.

Neville wiped water from his eyes. His red hair clung to his face like ocean weed. "They came in off the warships, two hundred, perhaps more. Patric's alliance with the prince must run deeper than we thought."

"Where *is* Patric?"

"We just locked him up. You didn't see him come in?"

Avry shook his head. He disliked twisting the truth, but admitting that he had hidden behind his cell wall would have been many times worse. He could confess to being a coward, but he would never confess to a lack of faith in the commander and his men. "I didn't see his face."

Neville shrugged into his jacket as wind gusted across the yard. "We have the physician, too."

"The physician lives?"

"He's with the king."

"Is the king awake?"

"No." They were shouting now, trying to be heard over the wind and rain. Swallowing his questions with an effort, Avry followed Neville into the keep.

Knights milling about in the entryway quieted as Avry passed them on his way to the stairs. Neville seemed too tired to acknowledge them. His boots sloshed as he dragged himself up the stairs, leaning heavily on the railing. Avry ascended uneasily behind him. It was unlike the commander to show weakness in front of his men.

"Is Édouard with the physician?" Avry asked as Neville paused on the third landing to catch his breath.

"I hope not. I sent him to his room hours ago. He's a good lad but useless when he gets worked up about something."

Avry made a noncommittal sound, torn between a desire to defend Édouard and an urge to know what had upset him. In the end, he added it to the long list of questions he doubted would be answered that night.

New guards had been stationed at the king's chamber. Avry's hands were tight at his sides as he walked through the door. Ghislain had been unconscious now for three days; how much longer did he have? And in what condition would Avry find him?

"Good morning, sirs." The new servant, an aged man with curly white hair, bowed awkwardly while holding a shutter closed.

"Where did the physician go?" Neville asked.

"Back to his room, sir. But he said he'd be back with another latch for the shutter, if he could find one."

With a grunt, Neville plopped himself down on one of two chairs beside the bed.

Morning, Avry thought. It might as well have been the darkest hour of night. Wind crept in from around the shutters, making the lamps flicker and the gauzy canopy around the bed undulate like a sail. The valiant efforts of the fire had done little to keep the room warm and dry. Avry joined Neville, and they both stared at the king's marble face.

"He breathes," Neville whispered. "There's still hope."

Eying him, Avry swallowed a harsh breath. He had begun to resemble the busts in the Hall of Kings: cold, silent, chill as stone. Avry's eyes closed. "Report to me, Commander."

"I hardly know where to start."

"What did you do after you left my cell?"

Neville scooped up a bottle of wine left by the chair and took a long pull. Avry wondered how he could stand the taste of it after being poisoned. "I found out which guards were on duty tonight and arrested them. I told each of them that the others had squealed, and we knew everything. If they didn't cooperate, they'd be killed on the spot and their families would suffer." He looked sideways at Avry. "It was nasty but effective."

At least, Avry thought, he had not chopped off their fingers. "How many did you question?"

"The four sentinels, the door guards, and the dungeon guard. Everyone outside the keep."

"And they were all implicated?"

"One and all." He passed Avry the bottle. "I'm itching to question Patric. Among other things, I'd like to know how these men got scheduled together."

"The captain of the guard?"

Neville shook his head. "Wasn't implicated. He thinks the men swapped their scheduled watches with others in order to be together at the same time. Says it would be easy, since no one wants the night shift."

Avry brought the bottle to his mouth then lowered it abruptly as a new thought came to him. "Where is Senet?"

"Dead. When I found out the guards were taking orders from him, I barged into his room and had it searched. We uncovered a hoard of poisons in a secret compartment in his desk, along with some vile-looking weapons. But the guard watching over him didn't pay enough attention, and while his hands were cuffed, Senet slipped a tiny knife out of somewhere and drove it into his own throat."

Avry drew back in horror.

"So we can't learn anything more from Senet," Sir Neville said.

"What about the king's missing servant?"

"None of the men I questioned knew he was involved. Or where he went, for that matter."

"Patric might know." *Or he might not.* Avry shook his head as he brought the wine to his lips again. "What a mess. We'll have to haul in every man and woman working in the castle and question them."

"Do we have time for that?" Neville asked in a low voice.

Avry's hand moved to the bulge under the front of his tunic, where Gandel's letter lay hidden. "I haven't forgotten about that. Like I said: one thing at a time."

"Until we run out of time." Neville took the bottle from Avry and drained it. "Every time I think about that letter, my skin crawls."

A strong gust raked the shutters, and the canopy swelled in, sagging over the mattress.

Avry cleared his throat. "So what was the plan tonight? What did the guards tell you?"

Neville's chair creaked as he leaned back in it. "The prison guard shoots you dead with a concealed shortbow and drags you out into the yard, then the keep guard summons Sir Fennick, saying you want him. As soon as Fennick steps outside, the sentinels shoot *him* dead, and the keep guard drags him over to…er…your body. The prison guard bashes a rock against his own head to make it look like Fennick attacked him. Finally, the castle door guard opens the gate, and Patric and his men rush in."

Avry, who had been nodding along at first, grew tense and still as he realized how close he had come to death. "What was your response?"

"I imprisoned the dungeon and keep guards."

"Where?"

A line formed between his brows. "In the dungeon, of course. You must have been asleep when they came in."

Avry fingered his head wound worriedly. "Must have been," he muttered. "What did you do with the others?"

"I ordered the sentinels to their places, with a reminder of what would happen if they disobeyed, then I assembled all the archers I could rally and had them hide in the battlements. I told the door guard to let Patric in and then close the door quickly and bar it. If he had trouble closing it, my men would help him."

"How many men?"

"A dozen hid behind the door, most of them knights. But we didn't need them in the end. The guard had no problem closing the door."

Avry smiled. Neville had taken Patric's men by surprise. "So what happened next?"

"Patric's men began shoving at the castle door, so I had the archers shoot a round onto their heads. That sent them scurrying." Neville snatched up the empty wine bottle, shook it, then set it down and wiped his hands nervously on his legs. He said in a hushed voice, "I didn't know they were from Ann, Pup. Not until the physician told me."

"Did the physician come in with Patric?"

"No, Patric came in alone. The physician showed up when we opened the doors to bring in the bodies." His hands tensed on his knees. "I'm not happy about what happened tonight."

"I don't see why. You thwarted an attempt to steal the crown, and you did it admirably." Avry slapped him on the shoulder. "Imagine what would have happened if you hadn't acted. Come dawn, those in the castle would have wakened to a mess: Fennick and I dead on the paving stones and the yard filled with soldiers from Ann. Senet would have told everyone there had been a conspiracy to free me and set me on the throne. So he sent Patric—the only man he could be sure wasn't implicated—with a letter to the commander of the warships, asking for aid. And it was a good thing they came, for look what was prevented!

"Some may have doubted him, but most would have agreed with what their eyes had seen, and with the evidence that had already been collected: poison found in my room, you dead and the king halfway there. The physician would have been forced to declare the king incapable, and in no time Patric would have been king. But none of that happened. Because you took action."

Neville's mouth quirked in a half-smile, but his hands still gripped his knees. "I know, Pup. But the way I see it, all I've done is exchanged one problem for another. Soldiers from Ann lie dead in the yard. What do you think will happen when Alaric finds out? Ann is our protector and ally. But in the flip of a coin, she could become our greatest enemy. I'd have taken Patric over that."

The shutters had ceased rattling, and the room was so still that Avry was worried the servant could overhear them, though they had been speaking in hushed tones. "Alaric had nothing to do with this. If he wanted Patric to be king, he wouldn't have chosen such a sneaky, underhanded way to arrange it. There are easier, more honorable ways for a man with power to get what he wants."

"Then you think his son schemed behind his back?"

"I'm almost sure he did. Alaric wouldn't have done something like this. He may have given Archard men and ships, but if he knew what his son had planned for them, he would have been angry indeed."

Neville's gaze lingered on the canopy, and Avry could almost hear his mind working. At last, the commander offered an assenting nod. "You're right," he said, his voice tinged with amazement. "For once, you're right. Treasure it." His hands loosened, and he slapped them on his thighs as if to drive home a joke. "What's Alaric going to do when he finds out?"

A twinge of anxiety clawed into Avry at the thought. "I'm certainly not going to tell him. The prince will be king one day. If his father punishes him for this, Archard will remember it and hold it against me." Avry recalled how cruelly Archard had treated his wife and shuddered. He would make a frightening king. "How many of his soldiers died?"

"Perhaps forty. Fifty at most."

"Then it would be best to send the bodies back to the ships and let the prince dispose of them. I'm sure he'll think up a passable explanation for his father. Maybe they got drunk and were swept away in the storm. It happens."

Neville's eyes had a wandering look. All of a sudden, he stood and walked around the bed to the windows. "Don't worry about the shutter, Jean," he told the servant. "The storm is on its way out. Could you check on the physician, see if he's all right?"

"Very well, sir. Which room is his?"

"Third floor, second door on the right."

"Thank you, sir."

The door closed, and Avry joined Neville at the windows. "What's the physician's story?" he asked.

"He says he was attacked on his way to his sister's house. His captors warned that if he didn't do what he was told, his sister would be killed. So he went with them to the warships, and when night fell, he was placed in custody of a company of soldiers that were to gather at the top of the hill. He stayed with them until the arrows rained down, then he escaped and crept along the front of the castle. My men spotted him while they were dragging in the bodies. I promised him I would send men to his sister's house as soon as the storm broke. I suppose that would be now."

The door opened then, and the physician trudged in with the servant in tow. Avry nearly gasped at the sight of him. His cheek was swollen, his lip cracked and bleeding, and dark bruises painted his arms. His eyes touched Avry's, and a rueful smile strained his split lip.

"This is for you," he mumbled, holding out a sealed scroll. "It's what I was brought here to do, so I thought I'd do it."

Avry did not want to take it, but his hand closed over it anyway. "You've declared the king incapable," he said tightly. Frost crept into his veins. "Is it true then, that he will not wake?"

In response, the physician drew a small leather sack from his bag and tugged open the strings. "Sir Neville let me borrow this, along with other poisons found in Senet's chamber." Avry, shifting to allow light into the sack, glimpsed a fine green powder. "Its common name is devil's thumb. Some have used it in small doses to help them sleep, but taken over a long period of time it can cause permanent weakness and fatigue. Increase the dosage, and a person may never waken." He tightened the strings and shoved it back into his bag. "It's nearly tasteless. Mixed into the king's food, it would have been untraceable."

Avry leaned back and gripped the sill. Anger flowed through him again, and a part of him wished Senet were still alive so he could inflict on him the humiliation and weakness Ghislain had suffered. "You didn't answer my question."

The physician's shoulders sagged. "I don't know the answer. We can't even be sure that the king ingested devil's thumb. Just because Senet planted it in your room doesn't mean he used it. Senet had six different poisons. He might have used devil's thumb initially before switching to something more fatal. Or he may not have used it at all." He walked slowly to the bed. "All I know is that the longer the king remains asleep, the less likely it is that he will waken." He fell into a chair and drooped like a wilted plant.

Neville placed a hand on his shoulder and shook him a little. "You should go back to your room, get some rest."

"I can't," the physician mumbled. "Truly I can't. Not until I've made reparation for what I've done."

"What you've done..."

"What do you mean?" Avry asked at the same instant, his voice blending with Neville's.

"Tell the servant to leave. What I'm about to tell you is confidential."

CHAPTER 20

With the servant whisked away and a third chair dragged from the hearth to the bed, the physician began to speak.

"Men in my profession are so used to keeping secrets that we do so even when we shouldn't. Two years ago, Senet, myself, and three others witnessed the king seal a document declaring Avry his successor. Until recently, people believed Patric would be named king-in-waiting. I can still picture the dismayed look on Senet's face when the king revealed it would be Avry. King Ghislain either didn't notice or didn't care. But I noticed, and even though I knew what sort of person Senet was, I kept quiet." His voice caught, and he pushed a hand across his eyes.

Neville's chair creaked. "Why did Senet so badly want Patric on the throne?"

"Because Patric is his son."

There was a shocked silence. Even the king, as still as he was, seemed somehow attentive.

"How do you know that?" Neville asked in a strangled voice.

The physician leaned back in his chair. "My late wife was a helper to the midwife on the night of Patric's birth. While she was cleaning up behind the bed curtain, Patric's maternal aunt entered the room, and they whispered together about whether or not Henri Audamar should know that Senet was Patric's true father. The revelation shocked my wife so badly that she let it slip to me while we were at dinner that night. She made me swear not to breathe a word of it to anyone, and I kept that promise."

"How was Patric's mother acquainted with Senet?" Avry asked.

"Back then, he was caretaker for Henri Audamar's estates. After Patric's birth, Senet applied to work at the castle and gradually worked his way to the position of steward."

"God's tits." Neville threw his arm across the back of the chair in amazement.

Avry was silent. This information might have saved the king's life, and yet Avry could not scold the physician without feeling like a hypocrite. They had both endangered the kingdom by their mistakes. Was one worse than the other?

***

Dawn had finally broken through the dirty gray clouds when the last of the bodies were piled into covered wagons bound for Ann's ships. Avry passed a scroll secured with a newly minted regent's seal into the head driver's hand. "See that the officer in charge gets this," he ordered. It had not been easy to dismiss the ships, but after the night's attack, Avry could see no other option.

The wagons rumbled through the gate and down the hill. Shortly thereafter, the men Neville had sent to the physician's sister's house returned to say she was safe and unaware of any unusual happenings. The news prompted Neville to march straight down to the dungeon and interrogate Patric. Avry went with him to watch.

Patric sat on the floor with arms tight to his chest, pale eyes flicking about nervously as Neville's men arrayed around him. He answered Neville's questions in a flat, dull voice, only becoming animated when something physically discomfited him: the stink of Neville's breath, his gnawing hunger, the soreness in his back and buttocks from having to sit so long on a cold stone floor.

Neville promised to alleviate each of these sufferings once his questions were answered. Patric warmed up a little then, and Neville wrung out of him what he could, which turned out to be very little. Like the guards and sentinels, Patric had merely followed Senet's orders. The only real piece of information the commander got from him came at the end, when Neville calmly revealed that Senet was dead. Patric's response had been dramatic. After a stunned silence, his face had crumpled and he wept like a child.

Neville and Avry had looked at each other with the same thought: Patric knew who his father was.

At the tenth hour, a trumpet blast summoned everyone to the yard. The seamstress and her helpers, freed from confinement, stood at the front of the crowd. In the absence of the steward, a knight with a strong voice had been chosen to announce Avry's position as regent and to give an account of all that had passed during the previous day and night. Avry had decided not to conceal Ann's involvement in Senet's plan. However, he kept Archard's part in it secret. Instead, he suggested that one—if not more—of Ann's high-ranking officers was to blame. Having succumbed to bribery, they had led their own men on an attack of Aure castle.

As for Patric, Avry saw no reason to reveal that Steward Senet was his father.

After the account was read, the physician stepped forward, and there was a hush of anticipation as the crowd waited to hear what the battered man had to say. Avry wanted to hide his face. Try as he might, he had not been able to dissuade the physician from giving this speech.

"My dear friends," he began fawningly and launched into a retelling of all he had suffered at the hands of Senet's men. "But as battered and bruised as I am," he declared, "my abduction has injured Sir Avry more, for it prevented him—at least in the eyes of some—from legally acting as regent. Being absent, I could not declare the king incapable. However, that does not change the fact that the king *was* incapable at the time Avry signed on His Lordship's behalf. So it can be said that Avry legally acted as regent." He smiled and raised his palms, hoping perhaps for cheers, but all that came was a rustle of smothered laughter and a few embarrassed groans.

Neville flashed Avry a mocking smile. "For a few coppers..." he murmured before Avry turned him roughly away.

"The White," Avry reminded him in a menacing whisper. "Gather the knights. There will be a meeting tonight in the knights' chamber."

PART THREE

TOURNIQUET

CHAPTER 21

A little girl's hand dipped into cool river water and shattered ripples of sunlight into tiny flecks. Fingerlings darted through the flecks, their silvery backs gleaming. As she grabbed at them, a leaf fluttered down and landed on the back of her arm. Some kind of warty growth had marred the leaf's underside. The girl slipped her hand out of the water, plucked it up, and ran her thumb over the warts.

Mer rode within the girl's body like a ghost. Seeing, hearing, smelling, feeling. She was also privy to every drift of thought and emotion emanating from the girl's mind. And on rare occasion something Mer experienced through the girl tickled her intuition, and she could almost predict what the girl would do next.

But not this time.

Disgust flowed through the girl, and she picked the warts off one by one until a jagged tear formed. She tossed the leaf back in the water and stared up at a squirrel in the branches overhead. "What are you doing to the leaves? Peeing on them?"

The squirrel chittered, and another warty leaf fell.

Suddenly it was as if the air itself shimmered. Branches blurred, and dizziness struck Mer like a fist. She could do nothing to prevent the sickening jolt that followed, wrenching her away from the girl, the tree, the cool river water, thrusting her into a void where all senses vanished. Into a place she called The Current.

This was the blackness between dreams. And it was where she dwelled on all that might have happened to her since entering The Dreaming Place. She suspected she was still in the crater, but what had become of her body? Days might have passed since she had gone unconscious. Trapped as she was, she could not know if she were in physical danger, and there seemed no way to break free.

At least she had gained a measure of self-awareness in the dreams. When they had first started, she *was* the girl, without a thought of her own. Only in The Current had she recalled who she was and what had befallen her. Then her terror had been so strong that it became a protective garment, wrapping her as she slid into the next dream. She had become the ghost then, watching the mysterious girl age from dream to dream without ever seeing a face.

The blackness started lifting. Mer made a final, desperate attempt to break free. Her mind writhed against the terrible force thrusting her forward, but it was useless. She felt as weak as an ant caught in a windstorm.

Finally, The Current loosed her.

A hearth fire swam into view. Unease trickled through Mer. Until now, all her dreams had been outside, in fields and forests, by lonely rivers. Where was she now?

The flames danced a long while before the girl shifted her gaze. Footsteps landed beside her. The scent of mead floated warmly in the air.

A familiar voice slipped into the shadows.

"Jan is asleep. It's time for bed, Mer."

CHAPTER 22

Avry frowned at a blank page.

His pen lowered, kissed the paper, then jerked away. Sighing, he dropped it into the ink jar and unstoppered a bottle of brandy. It was still early in the day, but he needed fortification if he was going to squeeze out a single word.

It should have been easy—thank Mer for her letter and assure her that the information would be put to good use. A sentence would have done the trick. But his heart urged him to write more, to tell her everything, without reservation. He longed for confidence with her as much as he longed to touch her again.

He sipped the brandy with half closed eyes, and almost without meaning to, he called back memories he had intentionally repressed: the night they danced at the quarterly, the long, slow morning they had spent together on the edge of the gorge, their reunion at the border tree. And the most searing memory of all: the feel of her body pressed against his as he held her in the Cursed Wood.

"Stop torturing yourself," he muttered into his cup. That was all it was: self-inflicted torture. Though it brought him pleasure, it did him no good. It was like tearing off a scab to relieve an itch. It felt good until the blood ran and another scab formed. Then the itch returned and the cycle continued. Perpetually.

He groaned and dragged a hand roughly through his hair.

He was being selfish, sitting there thinking about Mer while so many other things needed doing.

Seizing the pen, he scratched down a single sentence, signed the note, and sealed it. "Done," he muttered, and after dispatching it via a servant, he headed down to the refectory.

It was the lunch hour. Men sat elbow-to-elbow at the tables, their voices raised to be heard over the din of rattling dishes and the shouts of kitchen staff. Avry scanned the tables for Édouard. His squire had taken off after the assembly in the yard that morning. Avry wanted to know what Édouard had done to irritate Neville, but he had little time to wheedle the answer out of him. The king's military strategist was due to arrive at the castle, and Avry did not want to keep him waiting.

A perceptive maid offered him a trencher wrapped in cloth. Thanking her, he took it up to his squire's room and kicked at the door.

"Come in!"

Awkwardly, he elbowed the latch and ventured inside.

Édouard stood by his bed, tossing soggy bits of bread to Tips. His perfunctory bow was deeper than usual. But everyone's was. Aure had not had a regent in more than a century, and never one who did not own land. "Lord" was not a title Avry had merited, but some were already calling him that, as if he were a foreign vegetable everyone called potato because it looked like one.

Tips yipped excitedly as Avry crossed the room and perched on the boy's worn mattress. "I didn't get a chance to thank you for the part you played in yesterday's affair," Avry said, peeling open the cloth. "Without your help, I doubt Sir Neville would have dragged his bones out of bed in time to do what he did."

Édouard swallowed a bite and sat down next to him. "Sir."

And that was that. They ate in silence while Tips looked on, snout pointing from Avry to Édouard as if not sure which of them would throw her food. Avry suppressed his irritation at the boy's sour mood, telling himself he would address it later, along with whatever Édouard had done to irritate Neville.

He wiped his hands on the cloth and stood.

As he turned to go, Édouard finally found his voice. "He shouldn't have kept you locked up as long as he did, sir. After he found the poison in Senet's room, he should have let you out."

Avry's stomach sank at those words. Cautiously, he asked, "Did you really argue with Sir Neville, Édouard?"

The boy's mouth slammed shut.

Not a nod, Avry thought. Not even a "Yes, sir." He drew a sharp breath. "Then you should be grateful," he snapped. "Another man of his rank would have thrown you out of the castle for such insolence. Don't forget yourself, Édouard. Or you will be forgotten."

Hypocrite, a voice whispered as he left his squire sitting open-mouthed on the bed. But what else could he do? Édouard had learned an unfortunate lesson when Avry made himself regent and signed in the king's name. If he did not correct his squire's behavior now, it would only get worse.

Knowing it was the right thing to do, however, did not make him feel better about doing it.

"My Lord?"

His face emptied of expression as he met the eyes of the portly woman on the stairs. Formerly the head maid, Agne cared for Senet's duties now, and a new girl Agne had recommended held her former position. It was a temporary arrangement, but so many things would be while the king hovered between life and death.

"Yes, Agne?"

"The military strategist is here. He seemed tired, so I offered him a drink. He's in the feasting hall."

"Thank you, Agne. You may send him up to the king's chamber."

She bobbed her head then wavered in hesitation.

"Is there something more?" Avry asked.

"My Lord, folk keep lining up outside the castle wanting the king to settle their disputes. Some have been waiting weeks to be heard."

"Of course they have." He pressed a hand to his brow. This was just another of the many tasks that had fallen into his lap since becoming regent. "Have the secretary take down their complaints, and I'll review them later."

"Thank you, My Lord."

Avry's steps were heavy as he climbed the stairs. With an effort, he cleared his mind of the concerns draping it like cobweb and focused on the one most pressing: ridding Aure of the threat posed by The White.

He strode into Ghislain's airy chamber. Dismissing the servant, he opened one of the shutters a crack and inhaled the salt-touched air. Would the strategist scoff at his ideas? Was he no better than a child playing with a wooden sword? Or worse yet, a real one? *We could use another skull around here,* Neville had said when Avry had begged him for advice, *one with a few gray hairs poking out of it.*

The man who limped through the door and bowed like a stiff hinge had little hair left at all. He was astonishingly old, a stooped, quivering figure leaning heavily on a cane. The skin under his chin drooped in leathery folds, and his wrinkled face was immobile, as if it wore a leather coat.

Pale, watery eyes blinked as they fixed on Avry's face. "Regent," he said in a wavering voice. "My, we haven't had one of those in... at least a century. And I haven't stepped into this room since that man's father wore the crown." He jerked a knobby finger at Ghislain.

"That was well before my time," Avry admitted and gestured sheepishly to a chair by the bed. He had known the strategist was an older man, but if he had known just how old, Avry would not have summoned him to the second highest floor in the keep.

The strategist, Marc, creaked his way to the chair and slid onto it like stew into a trencher.

A silence fell. Avry's face warmed as he looked from Marc to the still form on the mattress. Why *had* he chosen the king's sickbed as a meeting place? Did he feel Ghislain's presence would lend credibility to his words?

He flung the strategist a furtive glance.

A bastard from the house of Valois, Marc had spent most of his life in scholarly pursuits, poring over ancient texts in his quest for knowledge. It was said that he knew every battle, on land or sea, that had ever been recorded. Avry did not envy him. Aure was a veritable desert for someone interested in military strategy. The continent would have served him better.

After exchanging the usual pleasantries, he slid Gandel's letter from his tunic and spread it out over his thigh. He did not insult Marc by reiterating who Gandel was and what had happened to Thorsault. If Marc had forgotten something, the letter would bring it to mind. "Yesterday morning," Avry began in measured tones, "Lady Merisande received a surprise letter from the fae prince, who is apparently living in Ann. How are your eyes in this light?"

Marc seemed to have stopped breathing. "Not good," he said finally. He did not stir as Avry read him the letter. Only his clenched hands and tightly set mouth revealed the state of his emotions.

Avry lowered the letter and cleared his throat. "Gandel gives us two options: either kill the fae king or kill the creature."

"There is a third," Marc said, and when Avry raised his head in interest he added, "Do nothing."

"Nothing. I can't do nothing. The White will return. Gandel assures us of that."

"Gandel assures..." He let the words hang in the air. "Forgive me, My Lord, but it would be foolish to take that letter at face value. Gandel urges you either to kill his father or his father's greatest weapon. Why? What makes you think he's sincere? This may very well be a trap."

Avry folded the letter. "Gandel has no love for his father or his people. It wasn't a coincidence that he abandoned Thorsault just as the fae were readying to attack Aure. He wanted nothing to do with his father's plans and still doesn't." He flicked his thumb at the folded page. "He wishes us 'all the luck in the world.' I think he hopes we'll kill his father."

"Then he's a fool as well as a coward. Even if his father dies, the problem of the bird remains."

"Gandel thinks he has put enough distance between himself and The White that when the binding does pass to him, he won't feel it. But regardless of what happens, without his father wielding the bird as a weapon, it ceases to be a threat." Avry flicked a finger at the pages. "That's what he's trying to tell us."

Marc ran a bony finger over the jagged line of his mouth. "So you plan to assassinate the fae king and leave the bird in the mountains?"

Avry nodded. "Kill the swordsman, and the sword ceases to be dangerous."

"A sword is not alive," Marc muttered.

Avry's mouth opened then snapped shut. He was about to point out that The White only acted violently when compelled to, but the source of that information was Gandel's letter, and Marc did not trust it. "Once the fae king is dead," he said resolutely, "the bird must be left alone. I won't send soldiers into the mountains after a creature that can change shape."

Marc wheezed out a cough, tugged a yellowed handkerchief out of his sleeve, and dabbed his cavernous nostrils. "Have you sent someone to spy out the village yet?"

"I will. Tonight."

"Much will depend on what he finds. We'll need to know how many fae there are and if they're in a position of strength or weakness. We'll need a map of their settlement and the placement of their guards. Once you kill the king, what then?"

"Fall on them, and if possible capture them and take them prisoner."

"You would be better off poisoning their water supply."

"No." The word fell heavily. "There may be slaves and children."

"Casualties of war." Marc's watery eyes fixed on Avry's. "Consider this well, Regent: if the assassination attempt goes wrong, then the fae king will retaliate, and The White will attack us once more."

Avry swallowed dryly. "I know. But I still can't. I won't do to the slaves what the fae did to them. I couldn't live with myself afterward."

"Even if the spy learns that there are no slaves, no children?"

"Even then."

Marc's shoulders sank, and he crossed his arms over the small bulge of his belly. "The fire seems to have gone out," he muttered. "This poor fellow needs to stay warm."

Avry called the servant back in then sat down again next to Marc. He listened to the shuffling of wood and the hiss of flames.

"I have one last suggestion," Marc said, "if you care to hear it."

"I'm listening."

"Employ the king's assassin as your spy. They say he can sneak up on a bloodhound undetected."

Avry's mouth fell open. "King Ghislain employed an assassin?"

"Every king has an assassin, whether he uses him or not."

"What's the assassin's name?"

Marc wheezed out a laugh. "If I knew that, then he wouldn't be a good assassin." He jerked a thumb at Ghislain. "He would know."

"He's not about to tell us," Avry said from between clenched teeth.

"No. I suppose not." Marc dabbed his nose again. "Back when I still lived in the keep, there was talk that the assassin used a page as a go-between—a boy named Oscan."

How long ago was that? Avry thought. Too long. "Surely that same assassin wouldn't still be working."

"Perhaps not, but Oscan may serve whomever the assassin trained as his successor."

The clang of a poker brought Avry's attention to the elderly servant. He turned in his chair. "Jean."

The servant's back straightened. "My Lord?"

"Do you know of a page named Oscan?"

Jean leaned back with a thoughtful sigh. "I did know of an Oscan, My Lord, but he passed away last year."

"Ah."

"But he left a son, a lad named Garrant."

"Garrant."

"Yes, My Lord. The lad works as a page here in the castle."

Avry clasped his hands together and grinned. "Thank you, Jean. That was most helpful."

Eager to find the page, Avry dismissed Marc with a promise to summon him as soon as he learned more. The strategist refused help going down the stairs, so Avry left him and strode through the servants' corridors. His questioning led him to the training yard, which was being tidied by a small army of servants and pages. The storm had cracked archer targets, tossed arrows out of their buckets, and scattered them over the paving stones. The wooden practice dummy leaned crookedly on its post. Neville had postponed training to allow time for repairs.

"Garrant!" Avry tossed the name out like a fishhook. It caught.

A boy no older than fourteen froze while scooping an arrow off the ground. His deep-set eyes focused on Avry's. "Sir?"

"Your name is Garrant?"

"Yes, sir, um, My Lord."

Avry waved him over. "I'm looking for the king's assassin," he said in a low voice.

Garrant blanched. "How did you know?"

Avry hid his relief with practiced ease. "That's my business. Will you take him a message for me?"

"I will, My Lord. But must we talk here?" His words were barely audible.

"We have nothing to talk about. I need to see him. That's all. Just tell him to find me."

"I will, My Lord. Right away."

Avry thanked him and wandered around to the side of the keep.

He paced by the wall, his legs growing heavier with every step.

What if he was doing something wrong? There was no one to check his decisions now. No one to say, "You can't." Because he could. He could do anything he wanted.

It was like the time he had gone off alone into the Cursed Wood after Merisande. There had been no one to check his movements then, no one to tell him which way to go, what he should do.

Was it much different now? No matter what others advised him, he knew he would do what *he* judged was best. But this time he had more than just himself to worry about. The kingdom trailed behind him like a ball and chain. If he went the wrong way, people would suffer. And he would suffer, knowing his decision had hurt them.

It was not how he had wanted to live his life, but there was no other way. No other path. Unless the king revived, Avry's way was all there was.

CHAPTER 23

The hall fires had been lit and the windows shuttered for the night as Avry reached the knights' chamber and strode through the door.

The chamber's high ceiling made it seem larger than it was. On one side was a painted map of the known world, on the other a blackened stone hearth. Steep windows lined the walls on either side of the hearth. They were shuttered now, but in the morning they shed dazzling spears of light across the flagstones. The murmur of men's voices quieted as Avry, passing the king's chair, took his usual place at the long table.

For a time, only the fire spoke. Avry regarded it blindly while a thickness gathered in his throat. If he turned his head, he should see the king, he should hear his booming voice fill the room like wine in a flask, warm, reassuring.

It was too much. He rubbed his hand over his forehead and swallowed harshly. Why did this onslaught of grief have to happen now, instead of when he was alone in his room or at the king's bedside? He strained his eyes open to keep them dry. *Don't look to your left*, he told himself. If he looked at the king's empty chair, it would all be over.

Taking measured breaths, he raised his head and peered at the other fourteen knights, who were hunched in their chairs, staring down at their hands. Only Sir Neville sat up straight, his eyes moist and full of sympathy as he regarded Avry. The rolled map on the table in front of him brought their task sharply back to focus.

Avry cleared his throat. Meetings in the knights' chamber always commenced with a short prayer in Latin, but Avry could not lead them in it. It would feel too much like the king was already dead.

"Before we discuss anything," he began, "I must apologize for my inexcusable behavior yesterday. I should not have signed on the king's behalf using his seal; I should not have made myself regent before he was declared incapable. I remain unpunished for these crimes simply because there is no one above me. If Ghislain wakes, he will judge me. In the meantime, my position as regent is by no means set in stone. If the king revives—and I pray he does—then power will be restored to him. What this means is that any decisions I make now could be reversed." He paused, letting that information sink in. "However, I—*we*, must forge ahead as if nothing will be reversed." *As if the king will never wake.*

He drew an unsteady breath. The men had not moved, and if they were surprised by anything he said, it did not show on their faces. "Sir Neville, could you report what has happened since…the events this morning?"

"Certainly, Sir Avry." Neville sat erect in his chair, his eyes clear, his mouth free of mockery. He wore his commander's face now like a tailored suit of armor. "The warships from Ann have left the harbor. The sentinel at the mouth sighted them heading back across the channel this afternoon. I've assigned two interrogators to question everyone in the keep regarding possible ties to Senet. Every chamber will be searched, including our own. The guards who were part of Senet's scheme will stay locked up until the king revives or—or until Sir Avry succeeds him." He coughed behind his hand then added, "Patric d'Audamar was escorted by guards to his father's estate late this morning. He has not been charged."

Avry hid a smile at the muffled gasps and exclamations that followed these final words. Sir Fennick raised the hilt of his sword, signifying a request to speak. Avry gave him permission.

"My Lord, you don't plan to punish him?"

"Patric's reputation is ruined, Sir Fennick. Punishing him further would accomplish nothing and may well create resentment in members of his house."

"But is this justice, My Lord? Why should Patric go unpunished while others languish in the dungeon? He may not pose a threat, but he's still guilty of treason."

Avry smiled faintly at the word "threat." To ensure Patric's future compliance, Avry had threatened to expose the true identity of Patric's father. The young noble had cringed into the silk of his neck scarf. Suffice to say, they would hear nothing more from Patric.

"It isn't like you," Fennick went on, "to give special treatment to the gentry."

"You're right," Avry admitted. "It isn't. But I can't make choices based solely on what's fair. Ghislain taught me the power of strategy. He viewed people like chess pieces. Everyone has a price, he told me. Including himself." He pressed his lips together, soured by his own words. In truth, he could never play king's chess the way Ghislain did. He did not have the stomach for it. But he could not reveal that weakness to his men. The knights had to believe Avry would always emulate their king, even in distasteful ways. "I must use a measure of strategy when I make judgments," he finished. "It's the only way to succeed at this."

Fennick's mouth had twisted like he had bitten down on something rotten. Avry smothered a twinge of self-disgust and rapped his knuckles on the table. "If there are no other questions, I'd like to move on. We have more pressing matters to deal with." He resisted letting out a tight breath. Being the only noble in the room, Avry had felt compelled to justify his decision concerning Patric. But had it come off sounding foolish?

He *felt* foolish, as if he were only playing at being regent. Somehow, he had to find a better balance between kindness and sternness, even if it meant stepping on some toes.

When no one spoke, he tugged Gandel's letter out of his belt pouch, and after a brief preface, he read it out loud for the third time.

The knights were stiff and pale as he reached the end, some covering their eyes, others staring at the hearth as if a creature made of flame might leap out of it. Avry suspected that if he peeked under the table, he would see hands on sword hilts. Even Neville was edgy, pulling on the neck of his tunic as if the room had grown hot.

Now Avry summarized his strategy. He expected a question or two, but the knights remained mute with shock. It would take some time, he realized, for them to digest the information. Avry asked Neville to unroll the map.

"It's a bit stiff," the commander warned. "I had to fetch the archivist to find it for me. And even he didn't dare to open it."

Avry's eyes narrowed at the map's ragged, yellowed edge. "Then how did he know it was a map of the north wood and mountains?"

Neville held up something resembling a curled, discolored leaf. "This page was folded against it. The archivist called it a 'ticket,' but there's more written on it than the map's title."

Avry's curiosity burned. "Pass it to me, please."

"Just the ticket, or—"

"Everything."

Neville slid the map and ticket across the table, leaving a trail of brown fragments like shattered, dry leaves.

The paper smelled musty. Avry slid his forefingers gently into the gap between the top of the map and the rolled section under it. Bracing it against his chest, he attempted to pry it open.

The paper gave way with a dry crack, and a jagged strip—the top three inches of the map—rustled onto the table. Wincing, he repeated the action again and again until the map lay in four sections. "How old is this?"

A smile as dry as the map quivered on the commander's lips. "Three centuries, Sir Avry."

Avry ran a hand across his face, smelled the map on his fingers, and dropped it. "And this is the only map we have of the north? Can it be that no one has been to the mountains in three centuries?"

"It's the only map," Neville confirmed then added, "As far as we know. The Ivry and Eleuthère lands lay closest. You could ask Lord Barret d'Ivry if his ancestors ever explored the north. He may have an old map in his library."

Another old map. Avry nudged a strip. The paper was littered by age spots and other discolorations, but he could still make out the finer details. His finger hovered over a range of jagged peaks. Mountain passes, caves, and canyons were clearly marked in ink faded to a dusty brown. The trees just below the mountains had been rendered larger than those near the Ivry border. A ragged line labeled "thornes" ran though the length of the wood from east to west. Avry drew a wondering breath. The thorn wall. Incredible that it had existed even then.

Gradually, he became aware of the inquisitive eyes on him. He waved the knights over.

"What does the ticket say?" Fennick asked quietly.

"Good question." Avry nudged it onto his palm and held it in the lamplight. The script was small and barely darker than the paper, but with an effort he was able to decipher it. "It says—and I paraphrase—that the mapmaker was one of twenty men who went on an expedition to the mountains. The king wanted to know what sort of metals were in the rock. The miners found veins of ore, which are marked by X's, but these are 'not plentiful or accessible...'" He fingered a crumbled edge. "There's more, but I can only read it in snatches. 'The cave is...leach from the rock...memories...place... signed Carles, mapmaker to King Audamar.'"

"The first king of Aure," Neville said with wonder.

The men's eyes had drifted back to the map. Fennick asked about the varied sizes of the trees, and Neville conjectured that the larger ones belonged to a section of forest that had never been cut down. They talked about spies and strategy, wings and weapons, while the moon shed soft yellow light through gaps in the shutters. Only when the knights started yawning did Avry remember how little sleep they had gotten the night before. He dismissed them with a reminder to keep everything they had learned secret.

Neville lingered behind. "How's your head, Pup?" he asked, reverting to his usual persona as easily as shedding a robe.

Avry resisted touching the injury. "Healing, I suppose. How about you? Are you still feeling the effects of the poison?"

"I'll live." Neville drew a flask out of his tunic and unscrewed the cap. His hand trembled slightly as he took a swig. "Your squire tracked me down today and apologized. I thought you should know."

Avry took an impulsive step forward. "When?"

"This afternoon." He chuckled. "Look at you, with that foolish grin. Anyone would think I was speaking about your son instead of your squire." He offered Avry the flask. "You've done right by that boy, Pup."

Avry swallowed a mouthful of brandy, silently vowing to commend Édouard as soon as possible. "Thank you," he said, handing back the flask.

Neville gave him a rare, private nod of respect, then lumbered to the door and closed it behind him.

Avry drooped over the back of a chair. He spent a few moments poring over the map, hoping to spot something he had missed before. Wood shifted in the grate, setting off sparks. He thought nothing of it until there came the unmistakable thud of a log being fed to the fire. Loosing an imprecation, he stumbled back and drew his ceremonial sword.

A diminutive form stood by the hearth, completely surrounded by light. For an instant Avry could not breathe for fear, then his superstitious dread changed to anger, and he shouted, "Who are you, and how did you get in here?"

"Who asks?" The voice was so thin and shrill that it made his skin crawl.

"Your regent asks."

"Ah." The figure folded in a smooth bow. "Then I am pleased to make your acquaintance, sir. And to answer your questions, my name is Havent, and I came through a door."

A door. Avry gritted his teeth. How long had the man been in the room with him, and how had he entered without Avry knowing it? A quick glance told him that the door was still closed. Surely he would have heard the sound of the latch falling. Unless there was another, secret door. But how had the stranger divined where it was?

Then his eyes closed with understanding. This was no stranger. It was the king's assassin.

"There's no need to be afraid." Havent's voice hovered on the edge of laughter. "I promise to protect you from me."

Avry slammed his sword into its sheath. "I don't appreciate the intrusion."

"I beg forgiveness, My Lord," Havent said solemnly, hiding his face behind another deep bow. "Old habits are the hardest to vanquish."

With an effort, Avry thrust aside his irritation and approached the intruder.

He was scarcely taller than a dwarf, his hair white as fresh snow, his skin smooth and pink except where time had marred it, the lines so sharp and deep, they might have been carved by a blade. He had to be at least fifty-five, and yet he looked as lithe as a young cat.

Avry hauled a couple of chairs over to the fire. Havent hopped into one. His feet dangled like a child's over the edge. His watchful eyes gleamed as they fastened on Avry.

Unsettled, Avry snatched up the poker and stirred the fire. "I assume you are the assassin I summoned this afternoon?" At a nod from Havent, he said gruffly, "Then I thank you for coming, though I hope it wasn't for nothing. The work I have for you may not be... suitable to someone of your profession."

"Let me be the judge of that, My Lord."

"Very well." For a fourth time, Avry opened the letter and read aloud the prince's words. But unlike on the previous three occasions, his listener did not react. Havent showed no signs of anxiety. His expression remained fixed. His fingers tapped on the chair arms as if drumming to a distant song.

"Do you understand the situation?" Avry probed when he had finished reading.

The fingers slowed. "I may be half-sized, but I'm not half-witted. Have you sent a spy?"

"I was hoping *you'd* accept that challenge."

"I can…on the condition that I work alone."

"Agreed," Avry said, relief mingling with worry. He hated giving such an important assignment to a man he knew nothing about. But Marc *had* recommended him.

"And after the spying, My Lord, what then? Will you have me kill the king?" The eyes gleamed again.

"We can talk about that when you return. As for the spying, I need to know the size of the settlement and its situation, where the king lives, his habits, how the place is protected. If there are sentries, I'll need their schedule. If there are hidden snares, I'll need their locations. If there's a daily hunting party, I'll need that information too…"

Havent flapped a hand back and forth. "Yes, yes, yes. And so much more. How long will you give me?"

"No more than five days."

His lip twitched, but thankfully he did not argue. "Then I'll aim for five. Where is this place? Your letter seemed vague and uncertain."

Avry led him to the map. He said, running his finger over the trees below a ridge of mountains, "We think it's somewhere along here. We haven't pinpointed a likely place for habitation yet, but—"

"No. *I* haven't," the assassin interjected, and it was a moment before Avry caught the joke. He resisted rolling his eyes. "We haven't talked about payment, My Lord," Havent added.

"What would you ask for something like this?"

The assassin stared long and hard at the map. At last, he lifted his gaze to Avry's. "For the spying and assassination, I'll require ten years of service from your firstborn child."

Avry's mouth dropped open in shock, but before he could speak, Havent loosed an ear-splitting squeal of laughter. "It was a jest, a jest!" he said, clapping his tiny hands.

Avry pinched the space between his brows. He would go mad if he did not get away from this creature soon.

Havent chuckled at Avry's discomfort. "As for payment, the kings of Aure have covered my living costs and supplies for the past thirty-five years. I assume that arrangement will continue."

"Of course."

"Good." He flicked his finger at the map. "A detailed copy of *that* must be in my hands before dawn, My Lord. I'll gather my things while you prepare it." Bowing deeply, he added, "Good evening, fair regent."

CHAPTER 24

Gandel lay on his back under an apple tree, his eyes closed, his ears attuned for birdsong. His staff lay at his side, ready to use if he heard a single chirp. Eight other workers, men and women who for one reason or another had chosen not to attend church that Sunday morning, loitered under the trees. A breeze smelling of apples, sunlight, and rain-drenched earth stirred the blades of grass next to his ears.

Gandel had arrived at Malborne shortly after posting his letter to Merisande.

The castle stood like a jewel on the hill, its battlements as smooth as glass, its eight slender towers as elegant as columns in a great hall. The guard at the gate demanded Gandel's name and purpose. Yes, they were hiring. He would have to see the castle steward to learn more. Gandel agreed and was promptly escorted through countless doors until he found himself seated on a couch in an exquisitely appointed chamber, with a ceiling so high it almost made him miss his wings. He was offered a drink called cider and spent the remainder of the afternoon slipping in and out of slumber. Each time he woke, he found his fingers clenched, his jaw stiff, as if he had captured something between his teeth. His facial twitches had not returned, but he feared that they were only a breath away.

Fortunately, he was awake when the door swung open and a servant admitted a slender, middle-aged woman wearing a creamy gown and matching puffy hat. Gandel shot to his feet and offered her a courtly bow.

The woman halted when she caught sight of him and for a few breaths did not move or speak. Gandel stared fixedly at the floor. He nearly flinched when the door closed.

"I am Steward Hestence," she informed him in a voice as soft as silk. "And you are...?"

"Gandel."

"Gandel. What an unusual name. You came here looking for work?"

Was there sarcasm in her voice, or had he imagined it? "Yes, Lady."

"No, say, 'Yes, Madame Hestence.'"

"Yes, Madame Hestence."

"Turn for me, Gandel."

His brow puckered. "You mean...?"

She danced her finger in a circle. "Turn so I can look at you."

Gandel obeyed her promptly, and her gaze whisked over him like a soft-bristled brush, lingering on his face, his hands, his crotch. Probably his backside, too. The intense scrutiny gave his absent wings a ghostly twitch.

She smiled as he finished the turn and tucked gray hair behind her ears. "Very good. Please sit down."

Puzzled, he returned to the chair and draped his hands over his knees. Hestence claimed the chair across from him. A plain leather folder had appeared as if by magic in her hands. She opened it out on the low desk between them, revealing an orderly array of nibs, quills, paper, and ink.

"Where are you from?" she asked as her tapered fingers attached a nib to a quill, uncapped an ink jar.

He cleared his throat, "Cabart."

"Ah. And where is that?"

"Just over the Lednag Mountains."

Her pen hovered over the page. "Lednag. Isn't that your name, spelled backward?"

His face froze for an instant before he remembered to smile. "You're right. I never noticed that."

Frowning, she scratched down a few words, then redipped the pen. "Why did you leave?"

"Family trouble."

"Who are your family? What house do they belong to?"

Her questions fell like a rain of arrows. Gandel replied to them calmly, but none of his carefully crafted answers pleased her. She exhaled noisily as she wrote, until at last she set down her pen and regarded him frankly. "Shall we start over?"

He shrugged. "If you wish."

"Where are you really from?"

"Cabart—"

He flinched as her pen slammed onto the page. She glowered at him, her mouth an angry line. "Lance!"

The door opened and the servant stepped in. "Yes, Madame?"

"Escort this man out of the castle." She rose from her chair and crossed the room without offering Gandel a parting glance.

Gandel barely had time to react before the man seized his arm and hauled him to his feet. "I can walk..." he protested, horrified by the thought of being dragged down a dozen hallways in full view of the castle staff.

"Wait," Hestence sighed. Her gaze swept over the visitor again. Gandel almost hoped she would let him go.

"Madame?"

"I've changed my mind. Send him to the master of the orchards instead. If he wants work, he'll have it. But it won't be soft." Squeezing Gandel's arm, she murmured, "When the sun blisters your pretty face, you'll reconsider your answers."

Lance allowed him to return to the inn to fetch his things. On the way back to Malborne, he stopped in a field to bury his silver along with whatever jewelry he owned, concealing the loose dirt with a heavy stone. It was a wise decision. On his first night in the compound, workers pinned him down and searched his pallet. He lay there like a limp puppet, heart pounding while their rough hands ran over him, narrowly missing the fragile space between his shoulder blades. At last they wandered off, leaving him with a few drunken kicks to remember them by.

The work was hard, but he got used to it. He refused to be "soft," as humans were fond of calling him. So he clenched his teeth and endured the long days, the incessant muscle aches, the scorching sun.

It would not last forever. The work was seasonal. In a few short weeks he would be let go, and if he did not come up with a believable story by then, he would have to dig up his silver and move on to another town.

A flutter of wings brought him jerkily to his feet. He jabbed his staff into the leaves, harrying the bird onto a high branch where there were no apples, only clear blue sky and hot sun. He stood, still as a stone, and watched it. Memories of Thorsault drifted through his mind: the tor road whipped by wind, the scent of farm fields budding in spring, the breathy whispers of an old slave who used to visit his chamber. His mother had been dead for ten years, and yet he could still call back her scent, a mix of rosewater and lorisen blossoms.

The bird opened its wings.

Gandel shut his eyes, capturing the splayed image behind his closed lids. What if that was all a memory was made of? A fading image of light, trapped behind one's eyes for a while before time banished it to oblivion? The idea was vaguely soothing.

***

Three men—a tracker, a builder, and a master of hounds—fidgeted uneasily by Avry's chamber window. Their rough woolen tunics reeked of sweat and moss, and their hose was torn and muddied. "Sir," the tracker begged him, "at least let us remove our soiled boots."

Avry wiped grit out of his eyes with a cold, damp hand. "If it makes you feel better." He poured himself a brandy and shot it down his throat. Rives's letter lay open on his desk. It had arrived on the same morning that Havent left the castle. Upon reading it, Avry had broken into a cold sweat. The ground beneath his feet tilted like a ship climbing a swell, and he grasped the wall to steady himself.

Sir Avry, Rives had written, *I regret to inform you that Merisande is missing. I last saw her the morning before the storm. She was feeling tired, so I took Jan with me trapping. When we returned home she was gone. I searched for her at all her favorite haunts, but found nothing. After the storm, I went to my brother's place, but Barret and Lisette were away, and their servants had not seen her. On the way home, I recalled a conversation Mer and I had last summer.*

Two months ago, Mer returned from a long hike carrying a bundle of dried valerian root (used to make a calming tea). When I asked her where she got it from, she said that a woman living in the north wood had given it to her. To be honest, I thought she was lying. If a woman lived in the wood, I ought to have seen her tracks. My skepticism seemed to free Mer's tongue, for she told me not only where her cottage was but what it looked like.

Mer's stash of valerian has since run out, and she hasn't been sleeping well. Given these facts, it seemed possible she sought out the woman for more. So I set off into the wood again, moving north this time.

It took me several hours to find the place. But once again, all my efforts came to naught. The cottage was empty and ruined, its roof destroyed, probably by heavy storm winds. Clothes and household items were strewn everywhere. There was no trace of Mer. She might have been there when the storm occurred, or she mightn't have gone into the wood at all.

I know how you must feel now, reading these words. We've both felt it before: the fear and helplessness, the ache of not knowing. If it's within your power, send men to help me search for her. She may yet be alive. Rives.

It had taken all of Avry's resolve not to jump on a horse, round up ten men, and gallop after her. But the measured tones of Rives's letter reminded him of the value of careful thought. Instead, he fled alone to the knights' chamber and paced through the slender bars of light cast by the windows.

Mer had written him on the day before the storm. Had she received the prince's letter that morning, while her father was away trapping? Had something she read made her want to seek out Esperance? Mer believed the woman could change shape. Perhaps she had reasoned that Esperance would know something about The White.

But Mer would not have spent the night at the wood woman's cottage without telling Rives. And even if she had, the storm could not have destroyed Esperance's roof. Avry had taken a good look at it when she invited him in. He had admired the smooth, well placed rafters, the expertly laid thatch. The cottage was as solid as a hoary old oak and far enough away from the surrounding forest that it was not in danger of being struck by a falling tree.

He had lurched against the hearth then, his face drained of blood. One possibility remained, and the longer he dwelled on it, the more certain he was of its truth.

Three pairs of boots now lay in a pile by his chamber door.

"What did you find?" he asked, addressing both the tracker and the master of hounds at once. He had managed to keep their errand a secret by sending them off at night, and not from the castle. He hoped it would remain a secret.

The master of hounds answered first. He was a thick-set man with limp yellow hair and a wide, mobile mouth. "Nothing, I'm afraid. Lord Rives lent me a piece of the lady's clothing so my hounds could pick up her scent. But no trails led either to or away from the wood woman's cottage. That's hardly surprising, though, considering the rain we just had."

"Had she been there—at the cottage?"

"She had, sir. The hounds picked her scent off a filthy blanket that had been tossed into a corner. They got a good whiff of the woman, too, but again…" He shrugged. "I'm at a loss, sir. The storm was brief, and my hounds combed through miles of forest, from the thorn wall to the edge of the Ivry lands, and from the gorge to the

Briomme Hills. The women might have cut their way through the thorns, but not without leaving something of themselves behind. A piece of clothing or hair."

Avry nodded soberly. It was exactly what he had expected the man to say. "Thank you. You've done well."

"Sir," he said, bowing.

"Tracker?"

The tall, fidgety man sank into his shoulders. "The same, sir. The men you gave me cast a wide net over the wood. After a hard rain, you'd expect to find some hint of a trail, but the only tracks belonged to Lord Rives."

"Did you find anything unusual at the woman's cottage? Evidence of a struggle?"

His lips pursed. "No, sir. But the storm made quite a mess of things. The whole area was littered with thatch and debris."

Once more, Avry expressed his gratitude, then he dismissed the first two, asking them to put on their mucky boots in the room rather than carry them out the door. It was more tempting to eavesdrop while in stockinged feet.

"Take a seat," he said kindly to his remaining guest as the footsteps faded in the hallway.

The raven-haired builder still bore the scowl he had worn when Avry tore him away from his work on the damaged tower. But there was something new in his eyes now: a tinge of fear. He sank heavily into the chair.

Avry stood by the desk, his fingers splayed over the polished wood. Sweat dribbled through his hair, tickling his scalp. Had he been calmer, he might have grabbed a cloth and wiped it away, but anything he held now would end up in pieces. "Tell me about the stone cottage."

"It's at least a century old, My Lord, and so small that its roof has lived happily all those years without a center beam. There's no rot, no water damage to speak of. It was extremely well maintained." He dragged his hands over his thighs.

"So what made it come down?"

He gave a nervous snort. "I can't say for sure, My Lord, but I can say what it wasn't: not a branch and not the wind. Some of the rafters and collar ties had been snapped clean in half, as if they'd been struck by an enormous hammer and chisel." *Or a bird's beak,* Avry thought grimly. "And," the builder added, "these breaks didn't occur where you'd expect them to if the roof had caved in naturally."

"Were there any scratches in the blackened wood?"

"No, My Lord, nothing like what was done to the tower."

"When would you say all this happened?"

"When…?"

"If the damage wasn't caused by the storm," Avry explained patiently, "then it might have happened earlier." It might even have happened on the day The White attacked the castle.

The builder shook his head. "No, My Lord, it had to have happened the night of the storm, or a few hours earlier. Rives said there were still some smoldering coals deep in the pit."

"I see."

There was a lengthy silence. Avry looked past the man to the sunlight rising over the estuary. A helpless fury was building in him, like too much water in a skin. He wanted to tear apart the desk under his hands and dash the pieces into the ocean or ride until the briny wind made him sightless and stunned.

"My Lord…" The builder's voice was uneasy.

Avry cleared his throat. "You heard what the others said. What do you think happened?"

"I…" He turned aside from Avry's burning eyes. "I think this was an attack, My Lord. I think the bird harried the women out of the cottage, then carried them off."

After a moment, Avry found his voice. "Thank you. Thank you for your honesty. You may go now."

The builder started to bow but then stopped. "And what about the…the other thing, My Lord?"

"The other…oh." Avry squeezed the space between his eyes. He was not thinking clearly. "Lord Rives's roof. How is it?"

"A disaster, though it's not in danger of falling in, at least not yet. I offered him a few suggestions while we went…ah, trapping."

"Excellent. Then you know what to say if someone asks you where you went."

"Yes, My Lord. Though…" He frowned, chewing his lip. "To be honest, it won't make you look good."

"That is exactly the point. It's so awkward that no one would question it."

Avry waited as the builder pulled on his boots and shuffled out the door, then he threw himself into the chair and mashed his face into his hands. How fast had the bird taken Mer into the air? Did she pass out? Vomit? Was she struck by a falling beam? Had she suffered internal damage from the pressure of its talons? How did it set her back down? And where?

He shot out of the chair and paced the chamber. There were two places it might have gone: to the fae village or to the mountains. The village seemed the likeliest option. The fae king, having run out of slaves, might have willed The White to fetch him more. Mer and Esperance would have been easy targets in that isolated, unprotected cottage.

Another possibility occurred to him, though it was so unlikely that he was tempted to dismiss it out of hand: that the fae king, having learned by spying that Avry had precipitated the destruction of Thorsault, had taken Mer out of revenge…

He pushed damp fingers through his hair. If the women were in the village, Havent would spot them. The assassin could hardly fail to notice Esperance, with her wild eyes and fire-colored hair.

His fingers froze. Could Esperance herself be The White?

After a moment, he shook his head. Neither he nor Mer had actually witnessed her shift into a deer. And even if she could, that did not necessarily make her The White. Esperance had lived a long time in the wood, not in the mountains. And not accompanied by fae guards. Add her runaway daughter to the mix, and it was simply too far-fetched.

Rapping at the door wrenched him from his reverie. Avry flung it open and blinked as the shadows arranged themselves around the form of the king's servant, Jean. If he had not been smiling, Avry would have assumed the worst.

Jean gave a hurried bow. "My Lord, the king is awake. The physician…"

"I'm coming," Avry said breathlessly, only narrowly remembering to secure his door before following the servant up the stairs.

CHAPTER 25

"When did he waken?" Avry asked Jean.

"Only moments ago, My Lord. The physician and I were changing his clothes when he opened his eyes and looked around. It was eerie."

And perhaps fleeting, Avry thought, steeling himself for disappointment as he entered the royal chamber.

A cool breeze spun around the heated space. The drawn bed curtains revealed a gaunt figure propped up on pillows, his head lolling over the physician's arm as he gulped whatever mixture was being held to his mouth. Avry made a sound in his throat. He did not remember crossing the room and kneeling at Ghislain's side, but he was suddenly there, prodding the withered hand out from under the covers. "He needs his worry stone," he murmured and rattled through the desk for it.

"Are you looking for this?" The physician motioned to a dark object beside the pillow. "I found it in the sheets."

Avry snatched it up and placed it in Ghislain's limp hand, holding it closed with both of his.

For how long had he been unconscious? Five days. And it was only just morning. By nightfall, he might be able to speak. Avry would tell him everything. He had no fear of chastisement. On the contrary, he desperately wanted guidance.

"Frog shwabble," came a gurgling voice from the pillows. "Ishe...I shhhit on. Oh..." His eyes rolled as the physician rested his head on the pillow. His neck and chin glistened with fluid.

"Bring me water," the physician barked at the servant.

Avry leaned forward warily. "What's wrong with him?"

"He's delirious. And to be honest, he may remain that way indefinitely. If you don't mind, I think I'll move my cot next to his bed."

Avry loosed the king's hand. The stone fell from Ghislain's twitching fingers.

***

Astrid crouched in human form under a ragged hedge and watched sunlight seep like molten gold over the city.

The task of finding Gandel had not seemed so hard at first. If the prince lived, she had reasoned, then he was somewhere on the island, and unlike her, he could not change form.

In eagle's shape, she had flown south along the gorge until the oppressive shadow of the mountain vanished behind her. Gradually, the wood gave way to lush pastures dotted with sheep. The steep banks lowered, and a chill breeze smelling of brine and beached kelp told her she had passed the point in the estuary where freshwater met salty ocean tides. Ships of all sizes speckled the turquoise water, most staying close to the western bank.

She circled the castle three times before gliding down the hill and moving inland. As night fell, she took an owl's shape and flew low over fields, peering into cottages and manor houses. She became a sparrow at sunrise and watched men trickle into the fields to harvest wheat. She passed over hills and valleys littered with white stone and skimmed over a stream, catching winged insects in her gaping beak. She sheltered in an old barn during a storm and then followed grain carts down a winding road that took her back to the city.

Hunted creatures did not wander in open spaces, she decided; they crouched in the mire, under stones, or in the hollows of rotting logs. They slunk into dark, smelly places squirming with other hidden things.

The city was that place. Astrid padded into it in cat's form, her paws damp with sweat, her heart thudding anxiously at being around so many people. For two nights, she stole through the docklands, slinking into warehouses and boat sheds, resurfacing to watch people mill about on the piers. The sweet scent of fish drew her to the gutting lines. But other cats had got there first. One attacked her viciously while a group of beggar boys looked on. Ears scratched and bleeding, she retreated to the maze of residential streets. She flitted in moth's form from window to window, glimpsing people loving each other, beating each other, mothers giving birth, aged people dying.

Days passed, and she lost herself. She did not know how it happened or when. It was as if she had fallen asleep. Her thoughts frayed, like clouds burning under a noonday sun, and then she just...went away.

Something must have clawed her back, a drop of water or a forceful word. It did not matter. Her mind resurfaced, faint as a flame glimmering in dark space, then her own panicked scream filled her, and the light became a flash. Dropping back into human form, she huddled under a bush and wept.

Gandel was probably dead. But she would never convince The White to accept that. Astrid would have to dig up his bones first and bring them to her in a sack. *By then,* she thought, *that's all Mer will be. A sack of bones hanging inside a crater.*

***

Havent arrived back at the keep in the early hours of morning, six days after he departed.

Avry, who had finally slipped into a deep, dreamless sleep, was jerked awake by the scraping and skittering of fingernails on his chamber door. In an instant, he knew it was Havent. Who else could dream up such an exquisitely disturbing sound?

The assassin shook his head when Avry asked him about slaves. "There were none," he said flatly. "Not a human in sight. And I was close enough to have smelled them."

Avry's mouth slackened. He took a step back, caught the edge of the desk, and held it. Havent's face wobbled in the hazy light.

"Are you well, sir?" the assassin asked uneasily.

He steadied himself with an effort. "I'm just...tired. I haven't slept a full night in days."

"How unfortunate. I've slept like a babe. Would you like me to come back in a few hours?"

"Yes. Please do."

Once he was gone, Avry dressed methodically, nudged his face into an acceptable expression, and ghosted down to the stables.

The stable master, bleary-eyed and half-dressed, looked at Avry blankly a moment before tilting his head in respect. "Sir."

"I'd like Dancer's reins changed."

"Certainly, sir."

"Now, if you please."

Wiping grit from his eyes, he did as Avry requested while the knight looked on.

Avry took the mare's old reins back to his room and held them up to the morning light. The smear of berry juice now looked like old blood. With loving care, he sharpened his pocket knife, lay the reins flat on his desk, and cut them into pieces. He fashioned the section containing the stain into a wristband by punching holes through both ends and threading them through with tough leather string. Finished, he deposited the tools and leather fragments in his desk drawer and slammed it shut.

The band hung on his wrist now. He sat in utter stillness, one hand clenched over the band with so much pressure that its edges dug into his skin. This was his shackle, and the oath he bound to it was deadly. He spoke it aloud under his breath, his lips quivering, his forehead slick with sweat: "I will find Merisande d'Ivry, dead or alive, if I have to weave through every cave, tunnel, and gorge in the mountains. If I do not find and free her, this band will become my tourniquet."

The thought of taking his own hand off made him shudder, but it would be nothing compared to the torture of never knowing if she were dead or alive, if his failure cost her her life, or even worse—the slow destruction of her mind. *Mad as a mountain guard.*

To recover her, he had to locate The White. Neither Mer nor Esperance were in the fae village, so that left The White's lair as their likely prison. Finding it would be difficult, but not impossible. Prince Gandel would not have suggested killing The White if she were too hard to find.

Avry would help Neville round up the fae then quietly break off from the others and enter the mountains using the miner's route.

A hiss of laughter burst from him as he considered the audacity of such a plan. To walk alone into the mountains after a skin shifter, leaving the rule of Aure in the hands of Sir Neville.

His mouth straightened, and he pushed his face into his hands. He thought about enlisting the help of others and decided against it. If he approached with armed men, The White might simply disappear, bearing her prisoners off with her. One man, however, posed no threat. Avry would enter her home and speak to her, find out what she wanted, and promise her that in exchange for Mer and Esperance.

If he were lucky, the fact that he had freed her from the fae king would be payment enough.

He drew a steadying breath. For the first time in days, he felt a brush of true relief. *I abandoned Mer once before,* he thought. *I won't do it again.*

***

Hours later, Avry sat at a meeting in the knights' chamber, his back stiff and straight, his face void of expression as he listened to the high-pitched, sing-song voice of the king's assassin. The chamber had a gray, wintry feel. The shutters hung open a crack, just enough to let in the patter of the rain. Havent sat cross-legged on the tabletop, fingers stabbing a map as he described the fae village. The other knights regarded him with varying degrees of tolerance. Some leaned forward in rapt attention, others leaned back as if Havent might, at any given moment, scramble across the table and bite them.

Avry had kept Havent's identity as king's assassin secret to all but Sir Neville. The others thought he was a mercenary hired on the advice of military strategist, Marc. That he still went by the name "Havent" suggested it was fake. But Avry had suspected that from the beginning.

Avry's eyes drifted closed. He slid his hand over the band around his wrist and caressed the purplish stain, drawing his fingers gently over it. The action soothed the rawness in his heart.

At last, Havent's shrill voice died, and he threw a clear-eyed glance at Avry. "I may have missed something, My Lord, though I very much doubt it. Will that do?"

Avry jerked his shirtsleeve over the wristband and rested both hands on the tabletop. The rain had slowed, and cheerful slivers of light were peeking through the shutters. Avry thought over everything Havent had said.

The fae village was wedged between a sheer stone wall and the gorge, with a dense crescent of trees closing in its southwesterly side. Fae sentinels armed with bows had claimed three of the trees. These changed shifts twice daily and once at midnight. Only forty fae lived in the village, and of those, twenty-five were soldiers. The rest were members of the royal household and their staff.

The villagers lived in beehive huts built from stone scavenged from the mountains. Red clay from a nearby stream had served as mortar. The dwellings were arranged in a tightening spiral, with the royal quarters at its center. The king never left his hut. Havent, who had glimpsed him through a crack in the mortar, believed he was too fat to walk. Soldiers armed with short swords took turns guarding his doorway.

Hunting parties went out every day at dusk. They traveled west, creeping along the edge of the mountains. Havent had found no snares, either for animals or humans.

Avry dragged a tired hand over his eyes. All this information would be next to useless if Havent failed to kill the king.

The fae king wielded the greatest weapon of all—The White. And he could summon her from the mountains in a breath. For that reason, Neville's troops would have to lie in wait outside the village until the fae king was dead. Only then could they move in and secure it.

"Thank you, Havent. Before I open this to discussion, do you have any suggestions?"

Havent replied almost before Avry had finished speaking. "Yes, My Lord. I certainly do."

"Go on."

"I assume you wish to attack the village and take the fae prisoner."

"That is our plan."

Havent drew a long, noisy breath through his nostrils. "Then there are two key tasks that must be done perfectly. The first is either to kill or incapacitate the three sentinels. The second is to assassinate the king. I wish to perform both these tasks myself, My Lord. In fact, I will do both, or none at all."

Avry sat back in his chair. The silence in the room was profound. "How will you kill the sentinels on your own? If one falls from a tree, the others will be alerted."

"Not so, My Lord. The sentinels perch so securely in the branches that they often fall asleep. There is little chance that they will fall."

"Not even from the punch of an arrow?"

A slow, sinister smile bloomed on Havent's face. "I don't use arrows, My Lord. My own weapons are far more effective."

Avry stiffened. "What weapons?"

He almost regretted asking. Havent, in a motion so smooth it was barely discernable, plucked from his tunic what appeared at first glance to be a couple of snakes. The knights jolted back. Three were on their feet, blades drawn, before they got a good look at what threatened them.

Two slender pipes lay harmlessly on the assassin's open palm. Havent's mouth twitched, and his eyes danced merrily as he met the sheepish gazes of the men around him.

Avry made an effort not to smirk. "I believe those are blow pipes, one for short range and one for long. Do you mean to kill the sentinels with poison darts?"

"Kill, or incapacitate, My Lord. Whichever suits your fancy. The poison works fast, so you won't have to wait long."

Avry tented his fingers. Havent had already shown a talent for sneaking up on people unaware. Perhaps he was better suited to approach the sentinels than the stealthy archers Avry had planned to send.

Neville raised the butt of his sword.

Avry nodded to him. "Commander?"

"Do the sentinels carry horns?"

"No," Havent answered. "They communicate by making bird calls."

"So if a sentinel found the dart before the poison spread, he could alert the others."

A sliver of wood sprouted from between Havent's thumb and forefinger. "This is the dart. It's so tiny that it's usually brushed away like an insect."

Neville grunted. It looked, Avry thought, like something a tree might have shed. "I suppose that wouldn't raise their hackles," the commander said gruffly. "Of course, you're assuming that the poison will work on fae as well as humans."

"I know it will. I've tested it."

Avry jerked forward in his seat. "You did what?"

Havent raised a placating hand. "I had to, My Lord. Only a fool would attempt an assassination without being sure of their weapon. I took down an old guard while he was hunting. His comrades thought he'd had a heart attack."

Neville shot Avry a meaningful glance. Avry ignored it and rubbed his temples, which had begun to ache as if some small, relentless creature was burrowing into them. "Havent, if you feel you must do something we haven't talked about, please inform me first."

"Certainly, My Lord. If I can." He smiled faintly as he added those last words. Avry chose to ignore it and moved on.

"Any more objections?"

They talked until the morning chorus of birds quieted to a few chirps, and Havent, squirming on the hard table, finally declared that his small buttocks were numb, and if the meeting did not end soon he would have to elect a volunteer to massage the blood back into them.

No one offered.

Avry dismissed everyone but Neville, who looked as haggard as Avry felt.

The commander opened a shutter wide and then shut it firmly with a curse. "It's sickeningly cheerful out there."

"Close them all, if you wish. It makes no difference to me."

Neville dropped his hands and paced the length of the chamber, sword hilt flashing in the stripes of light burning through the shutters. Avry retrieved a satchel that he had placed under his chair and unwound the string holding it closed.

"I don't trust him," Neville said in a low voice.

"I understand."

Neville's boots scuffed on the floor as he halted. "Do *you*?"

"King Ghislain trusted him, and his father did before him. That's good enough for me." He slid two sealed scrolls out of the satchel and arranged them in a tidy line on the table. "I appreciated your restraint this morning."

Neville had not moved, and Avry could feel the weight of his eyes burning into his head. "Is something eating you, Pup? You have a look about you…"

"It's nothing." His finger twitched toward the band then went still. He could not tell Neville what had happened to Mer. If the commander learned the truth, he would tie Avry up like a sack of grain and stuff him into some dark corner of the keep to rot until the mission was over. "Nothing more than what everyone else is feeling. Sit with me a moment. There's something we need to talk about."

"Oh?" The commander's voice was laced with worry as he fell into a chair beside him. "And what is that?"

"A fallback. If, for whatever reason, I don't return from this mission alive."

"Pup…"

"Let me speak." He rested his palm lightly over the scrolls and then rolled them toward Neville. "The first is a letter I've written the king. The second is a document I've signed in front of witnesses, declaring Lord Charles d'Artois regent if I die. The secretary has both, but in case something happens to him… Choose a man you trust, perhaps one of the four knights who are staying behind. Give him the letter and document to keep safe until I return. If I die and King Ghislain does not revive, the knight must send for Charles and present him with the document. If the king revives while I'm away and the physician declares him capable, the knight should give him both letter and document." He paused. Would the document mean anything to powerful nobles of Audamar? If Avry perished in the mountains, would some power-hungry noble seize the throne?

His lips compressed in a hard line. It was the best he could do. "Have I missed anything?"

Neville drew a flask out of his tunic and took a long swig. "You wouldn't die if you stayed at the keep." He offered Avry the flask. "Stay here with the king. Let me handle the mission. You shouldn't risk your life needlessly."

Avry corked the flask without drinking and handed it back. "I'm going, Neville. The decision has been made, and you'll have to accept it."

Neville rose to his feet with a defeated growl, but his meaty hands were gentle as he scooped up the scrolls and tucked them safely under his arm. "You're not to fight," he said sternly.

"Whatever you say, Commander."

"I'm serious. I will restrain you if you attempt it. Myself, if I have to." He waved the scrolls in the air. "I don't care what this document says. You're all we have. All."

"Then you don't have much," Avry muttered as Neville walked out the door.

CHAPTER 26

"It's too rocky here."

A boy's voice, Mer thought, and vaguely familiar. She wished the girl would look up from the ground and let Mer catch a glimpse of the speaker.

She drank in the information the girl's other senses gave her. The air smelled of fresh manure. Sunlight warmed the crocuses, which peeked through the soil here and there like short green tongues. Her feet were tiny under her skirt. She remembered those stout shoes. Her aunt had sent them to her on her tenth birthday.

She had reluctantly come to grips with the fact that these were not true dreams, but rather memories. And the girl was not a character— she was Mer herself. Reliving a past she scarcely remembered was frightening at times. Feelings she had suppressed, events she had forgotten, all came rushing back. And she could not evade them. Unless she broke free, she would be trapped reliving her memories. Until she died.

"There's softer ground at Gille's farm," the girl said.

"But you'd have to pull the grass up first."

"That grass is strong."

"Yeah, it hurts to touch it, like it's made of knives."

I could pull it up, the girl reflected, *but then he'd make fun of me for my rough hands.*

At last, she looked up.

A boy no older than seven walked ahead of her in a wide-open field. A dead mole dangled from his left hand; in his right was a gardening trowel. He paused and glanced about him.

A young Thierry. How could Mer mistake that freckled face, that thickly curling red hair?

"It'll have to be here, then," he decided.

"I'll dig."

"No, you'll get your dress dirty."

Like she'd care about that, Mer thought.

"Like I care about that," her younger counterpart said only a heartbeat later. Mer cringed at the echo.

Thierry offered her the mole. "I'll dig, and you hold Moley."

Sighing, she took the tail from him and stood by while he jabbed at the ground. Her feet shifted from one to the other. *He's not going to let me do it. I just know he won't.*

When a sizeable hole had formed, he tossed the trowel aside. "Done. Give me Moley."

The girl's jaw clenched. "I want to do it."

"But I found him. I get to put him in."

Her lower lip jutted out, and she stamped her foot. *Why does he get to do everything?* "It's not fair!"

Thierry pried the mole from her clenched fingers and placed it into the hole. The girl, gazing at its tiny hands and upturned face, forgot her anger. A feeling of wrongness pushed into her. Mer went still inside as she relived the sensation. Up until this point, the memory had been unfamiliar to her, but it resurfaced now, and she knew what would happen next.

The girl thrust her small hand into the hole and turned Moley face down.

"Why'd you do that?" Thierry exclaimed.

"I don't want to throw dirt on its face." That was not the true reason, but the girl could not articulate the true reason, so she had come up with a believable excuse.

Thierry's red brows pinched together. "But why? He's dead. He's not going to come back to life and get free."

The girl stared down at Moley. *He's right,* she thought. *But he's still wrong.* It did not occur to her to wonder how he could be both at the same time. She flinched as Thierry flung a handful of dirt into the hole. While he was busy gathering up more, she snatched Moley out of the hole and tossed it at his feet.

"Hey!"

"What?"

"You *know* what. You just threw him at me!"

"No, I didn't." She patted the bottom of the hole. "Oh, he must have got free."

"Liar." But there was doubt in his voice. Mer heard it, though her younger counterpart seemed oblivious. Thierry returned Moley to its grave and covered it over with dirt. They both stood then, waiting to see if the loose earth would tremble and a snout peek through.

A cloud passed over the sun. The ground blurred as it darkened, and Mer, anticipating a shift from one memory to the next, made a sudden, urgent attempt to escape. If the memories continued, sooner or later she would find herself in Thorsault. A fae guard would hold a knife to her throat, make her drink poison from a silver chalice...

The blackness lifted. As she entered the next dream, her anxiety eased. But she retained more of it than she usually did, as if her sense of self was strengthening.

The thought gave her hope.

***

When the last glimmer of light died on the horizon, ten men dressed in sturdy brown woolens hefted packs over their shoulders and marched out the castle door. A half hour later they would be followed by another ten, and then another, until one hundred men would have exited the castle. Each team was to take a different way down, ghosting through quiet streets and carriageways until they would come to the main road and follow it out of the city. By dawn, the last of the men, reaching the end of the north road, would cut through the stony field near Rives's cottage and vanish into the trees.

Avry had insisted on this stealthy arrangement, not merely to avoid causing a panic but also as a precaution in case the fae king employed spies. Neville had heartily agreed with him. "One hundred men marching north in broad daylight would make the dead wake up and notice," he had said.

Avry's team was the second out. Édouard marched alongside him, his young frame buzzing with excited energy as they descended the hill, passing quiet, stately mansions, their windows shuttered against the chill night air. The sky was as cold and clear as a spring stream; leaving the city behind, the men seemed to walk into it, treading on stars instead of paving stones.

Avry lifted his face to the glittering darkness. The lofty peaks of the north mountains gathered around him, ringing him with their cold, indifferent silence. He swallowed, tasting dust, ash, a shard of ice as brittle as bone...

"Sir..." The buzz of crickets rushed back in, and he found Édouard jogging beside him, his face pale in the moonlight. "You're leaving the others behind."

Grimacing, Avry forced himself to slow.

"Could we talk, sir?" his squire prodded. "That might help."

Avry threw him a sideways glance. Though he had spent an hour with the boy that afternoon, reviewing Gandel's letter and a summary of their plans, Édouard still itched with questions.

"Sir...?"

"Not now," he said quietly, and his squire sighed.

Avry's feet ached by the time he reached the end of the road and ventured into the murky blackness of Rives's field. He flicked a wary glance at the cottage, which was little more than a smudge against the sky. Avry had sent Lord Rives a letter asking him to keep Mer's disappearance a secret for as long as he could. In the meantime, Avry would do everything he could to find her.

It was not much, but Rives never asked for much. That was one thing Avry respected about him.

For a third time on the journey, they paused to eat and drink. Then Avry lit a lamp, and they plunged into the trees. The air was heavy with mist, redolent of wet autumn leaves and moss. They walked in a northerly direction until they reached Mer's foraging trail—a slender track, picked clean of stones and weeds, that ran almost to the gorge. After following it for about a hundred yards, the frail light of a soldier on watch duty became visible. The rest of his team lay in a bundled line on the ground. Avry's men settled in behind them.

With a weary sigh, the knight dug a blanket out of his pack and wrapped himself, coat and all, in the rough wool. Then he switched off his lamp and tried to sleep.

Avry had been sure Édouard would keep him awake with whispered questions, but the boy was asleep almost instantly, his slow, deep breathing joining the arrhythmic chorus of the other sleeping men.

Rustling leaves brought Avry's eyes up to the web of branches above him. A small horned owl perched on a tree, its stout form silhouetted by moon-brightened clouds. Avry stiffened. Gandel had written that The White could take many forms. A giant bird seemed her shape of choice, but what was to stop her from taking the shape of an owl or another such animal?

Could she be watching him now?

He suppressed a shudder. Too many uncertainties. Avry had steeled himself not to fixate on them, but he could not assume others would do the same. Fortunately, Neville had not stoked the men's fears by ruminating on vague possibilities. *We can't be prepared for every contingency*, the commander had said to Avry that evening while they waited in the castle yard.

Avry patted his belt pouch. A copy of the old miner's map was stowed safely inside, the path into the mountains marked by red ink. This was the contingency Neville could not have anticipated—that Avry would break away from his team and head off on his own perilous quest. How and when Avry made that exit would be vitally important. He must not give himself away.

***

"Sir Avry."

Avry grunted and rolled over, blinking as a shaft of light speared him in the eye. Sir Neville stood over him, chuckling at his discomfort. "Up and about," he bellowed in the direction of the other slumbering men.

Avry extricated himself from the blanket and stuffed it into his pack. Édouard was already up, devouring a stick of jerky as if he thought it would be his last meal. The path was littered with blankets and open packs. Soldiers were scattered throughout the wood, relieving themselves. Avry followed their example, not caring who saw him. On this mission, he was just another knight under the command of Sir Neville. Of course, he could veto any decision the commander made, but he hoped it would not come to that.

He returned to find Édouard sharpening his short sword. Avry dug a lump of sharp cheese and a half-full bottle of cider out of his pack.

His squire set aside the whetstone and shook some oil onto a cloth. "Sir, can we talk now?"

Avry cast a furtive eye at the soldiers. "Quietly."

Édouard swiped the cloth down the blade. "What if The White decides to investigate how her binder died?"

"She might."

The cloth went still. "But what if she sees us hiding in the wood?"

"She might," Avry repeated with a half smile. "Half the leaves are down now, and birds have excellent eyesight."

Édouard's eyes bulged. "Sir, are we prepared to fight thirty fae soldiers and…" He lowered his voice. "And the bird?"

"Twenty-six. Four will be dead. Édouard, why would The White attack us?"

"To protect the fae, sir."

"And you think she'd choose to do that on her own?"

"It's possible," Édouard said, popping cheese into his mouth.

"Possible, but not likely. Gandel's letter implies that she only attacks when forced to." He slipped the letter out of his belt pouch and found the relevant passage. "'*When the slaves revolted, the new*" *king of Thorsault compelled the The White to attack them. That act drove a wedge between The White and her binder. Angry and likely feeling betrayed, she left the fae and made her home on the west side of the island, somewhere in the range your people call "The North Mountains."'* The letter goes on to say that she has been wounded and lonely ever since."

He replaced the letter in his pouch. If The White hated violence, then why had she taken Mer and Esperance? The question had nagged at him for days, but he was no closer to solving it than he had been the moment he learned of their abduction.

"Isn't *likely*," Édouard echoed.

Avry shrugged a shoulder and looked away. He did not want to tell the boy that Havent had given Avry's team poison for their arrowheads. The fact made a bird attack seem inevitable. "If she does appear after the king dies, she'd be more likely to attack the fae than us, considering how they've treated her."

"Unless the canary fails…"

"The canary?"

The oiled short sword whispered into its scabbard. "That's what Sir Neville calls Havent, sir."

"Don't imitate Sir Neville, Édouard."

"I wasn't, sir. It just came out that way."

Avry's mouth quivered with amusement then abruptly straightened. The boy would be fine, he told himself firmly. With or without Avry.

They were on their way again at noon, moving as quietly as one hundred men treading on dry leaves could. Squirrels chittered at them, their claws scraping on tree bark. Magpies cawed out a warning. A stiff autumn breeze stirred the branches, shaking sunlight over the ground.

If Avry had been alone, he might have drowned in memories. The last time he had hiked through a dense forest was when he fled from the ruined fae city.

His hands clenched as memories of Thorsault returned, unbidden. He could almost smell the decaying odor of dead and dying slaves, the stale air of the servants' corridors. His fingers moved, shaping the hand signs he still remembered from the time he worked with other slaves doing the king's laundry.

What did the fae king have planned for Aure? Was he really as deranged as his son believed him to be, or were there things Gandel did not know?

Anything was possible. But the village at least held no mystery. Havent had sifted through it with a thoroughness even Neville had begrudgingly admired.

At last, they reached the thorn wall. Earlier that morning, Havent had guided two scouts through a hole he had carved through the canes. The assassin had led the scouts in a reconnoiter of the fae village. Their report had put a spring into Neville's step.

The commander now stood by the wall, booted feet firmly planted in the ground while he watched four men widen Havent's hole. The other soldiers, still formed in their teams of ten, waited like leashed hounds, glittering eyes fixed on the opening space in the thorns.

The wall was three yards thick, and Avry suspected it was even wider in spots. Its existence was as mysterious as the Cursed Wood. It stretched nearly the entire length of the forest from the gorge to the Briomme Hills, and as far as Avry knew no one had crossed it since that early expedition to the mountains three centuries before.

He drifted closer as the men hewed down the final branches and began clearing away the brush. The wood beyond was shadowy, flecked here and there by lonely patches of light. "Do you see Havent?" he breathed to his squire, who stood quietly at his elbow. When Édouard shook his head, Avry pointed through the gap at a gnarled oak. "He's there, in the hollow of that tree."

Spotting the assassin had been a pastime that afternoon. Havent always seemed to be missing, yet he would inevitably appear just when Neville wanted him, as if he had been hiding in plain sight.

Édouard squinted at the tree. "You're right, sir. He's right there, watching us in the shadows."

The teams slipped through the hole like syrup through a cracked jar. Every team was headed by a knight. Avry's was comprised entirely of archers. Each team had at least one servant, a page or squire; these bore the team leader's packs, serviced his weapons and armor, and even rubbed his feet. Avry had caught other squires eyeing Édouard with a mix of resentment and envy, for he would become a king's man one day.

Or perhaps not.

Fortunately, Édouard had never been petty. Petty men rarely overcame misfortunes well.

Once through the gap, they strode in single file along the edge of the thorn wall. Two of the four men with falchions charged ahead, thrashing a path through the underbrush. The other two busily sharpened their blades. Soon enough, they would step in to relieve the first two, who would then go on to sharpen *their* blades. The process would be repeated over and over until the teams reached the gorge.

The wood grew denser, darker. The trees seemed to nudge closer, as if investigating the intruders. Caught between the hoary trees and the thorns, the men were forced to leave the wall and weave a ragged path through the undergrowth.

They approached the gorge at dusk. The trees thinned, giving way to flat, sunken boulders the color of bone. The sky was patchy with clouds. Avry ran a sleeve across his soggy nose. The air had turned so damp, he could have swallowed it.

They made camp in the stunted trees along the edge of the gorge.

While the men refilled their bottles at a nearby stream, Neville took Avry aside to review their plans.

Once Havent did away with the sentinels, Avry's archers were to position themselves in the trees surrounding the village. "It would be prudent," the commander said between sips of brandy, "if they kept half an eye on the mountains. That way, if the bird comes out, we'll have a better idea of where it nests."

Avry tugged on his chin, grateful for the shadows concealing his face. He had already ordered his men to do that very thing. But any information they gleaned was to be Avry's, not Neville's. Avry did not want Neville to know where the bird hid.

"I agree," he replied with a calmness he did not feel, "though I doubt The White will make an appearance." And if she did, he would order his men to lie to Neville about what they saw. He snatched the brandy and took a long pull.

Nothing would be left of his reputation when this was over.

The layers of wool did little to keep out the dampness that night. Avry contemplated shifting closer to Édouard for warmth. It would mean losing a stretch of ground that held no stones or jabbing roots, but the alternative was just as uncomfortable.

He drifted asleep before he could choose. Vivid dreams rattled through his mind. He woke trembling, his jaw as stiff as an ax blade. His clenched fingers opened as he sought for his sword hilt, then abruptly closed. What was he doing? The night was calm and still. Autumn leaves whispered in the branches, and all around him men snored.

He turned onto his side and gazed sleepily at the bare rocks edging the gorge. The moon, shot through by racing fingers of cloud, cast a bleary eye on them. The steep drop beyond was so dark, it seemed to eat light.

His eyes closed then immediately popped open. Prickles danced down his neck and back. Resisting the urge to wake Édouard, he propped himself up on an elbow and peered around. The man assigned to the last watch leaned sleepily against a tree. His candlestick cast a dim light on the camp. Avry's gaze traveled past the bundled men to the gorge.

For a long while he did not move. He barely even breathed.

Something pale and shapeless rested on the cliff stones. Avry felt the presence more than he saw it. He had never sensed another's eyes on him so intensely; they were like hands coldly searching his body. He wanted to flinch away, find a hole to wriggle into like a rabbit fleeing a fox, but he found he could not move. Clouds ranged against the sky. A wind, dry rather than wet, blew up from the south, carrying with it a hint of brine.

When the moon peeked out at last, the pale shape had resolved into an upright boulder. Avry regarded it incredulously for a moment then threw himself down on the ground with a muffled curse.

The mission was starting to affect his mind. If he did not force himself to be calm, he would see phantasms in every rock and tree.

CHAPTER 27

Havent wakened the men a couple of hours before dawn.

Avry ground a fist into his eyes and struggled to free himself from the blanket.

"I can't even see what I'm eating," Édouard complained as they fished what they could out of their packs. "How will I see to walk?"

But they did. The small army stole through the stunted trees rimming the gorge, Havent at the front, his lamp dancing like a cheerful firefly from his upraised hand, followed by Sir Neville and Avry with his team. The rest shuffled along behind in single file.

Time dragged on, but Avry would not allow his mind to drift. His attention was divided between being as quiet as possible while creeping through the wood and listening for potential assailants. Havent's night's scouting had revealed a village deep in slumber. No one was about. But that could change in a short time.

During yesterday's reconnoiter, the assassin had flung drops of some whitish, chalky liquid on hanging branches every ten yards to mark the distance traveled. The splatter resembled bird feces so well that Avry winced when Havent grazed one with a finger, smudging it down the bark.

Avry's stomach churned as they neared the village. Every rustle of a leaf falling through the canopy made his heart leap into his throat.

At last, Havent halted and looked behind him, his eyes moving from Avry to Neville. "The village is a hundred yards hence." He offered the commander the lamp. "Proceed quietly. I'll return as soon as I can."

Neville gave a sharp nod, and the assassin disappeared into the trees.

The army shuffled west, away from the gorge. After three more markers, Neville's steps faltered. He waited, lamp raised, until the last of his men had ranged themselves behind him, then he snuffed out the light.

Several eternities passed. The intermittent creak of leather and shifting of weapons were the only sounds that could be heard. Even the air was still, as if the world hung suspended between one breath and the next.

Finally, Havent's whispering voice slid into the shadows. "The sentinels are dead. I go to kill the king." He was so breathless, he could barely speak. Avry wondered if it was due to excitement or exertion.

"Sick little bastard," Neville breathed, apparently deciding on the former. He jerked his head forward. "Go on, Pup. He'll be fast."

Dawn was breaking. A glimmer of light as tender as new leaves hung over the wood, brightening the fog that was gathering everywhere. Waving his men forward, Avry trailed after the eager assassin.

***

Havent's heart thrummed contentedly as he flitted through the village, pausing behind huts to look about him as he cut a line toward the center. He did not remember the last time an assignment had excited him so, and that was odd, for it did not challenge him in the slightest. Months of calm isolation had given the fae a false sense of security. A laziness. Why, two of the three sentinels had been asleep when he shot them!

His confidence ebbed as he spotted some new repointing on the huts. Was this sort of maintenance done regularly? Sir Avry had not allotted him sufficient time to find out. Havent could easily have spent weeks sniffing around, gathering valuable information. Five days—two of them spent traveling—were worse than worthless.

He halted at a hut adjacent the king's and surveyed his quarry.

Sure enough, the royal residence had been repointed too, the gaps in the mortar plugged with fast-drying clay. He could not use the hole he had marked days earlier as a place to fit his weapon. He could not even glimpse who was inside.

Sweat trickled down his back. There was nothing he hated more than a sloppy job. If he could, he would have retreated back into the wood, retrieved the darts from the sentinels, and spent another week reconstructing his plan, but the army waited, and he sensed that Sir Avry would not accommodate his wishes.

He had to kill the fae door guard and hope that the king was alone with his servant. His hands trembled slightly as he slipped his pipe and dart box out of his coat. The box cover popped open on well-oiled hinges, revealing a row of tiny darts, their tips sitting in a gelatinous glob of yellowish poison. The act of loading his weapon calmed him, and his breathing slowed and deepened.

Now.

Glancing about, he darted to the king's hut and sidled around to the front. Unlike the sentinels, the door guard had no branch to lean on. The fae stood with his winged back against the curved stone wall of the hut, head bobbing into his neck as he fought to stay awake. Havent calculated that the guard would slide to his knees before falling face down on the packed earth. He inserted the pipe into his mouth, aimed for the back of the guard's neck, and blew.

The guard came awake with an indrawn breath, blinked a few times, then nodded off again. Almost a minute passed before his legs buckled under him, and he swayed on his knees like a chopped tree. Havent hurried to catch him before he clattered face-first to the ground.

The assassin stood now, alone at the center of the sleeping village with a dead guard at his feet. It would have been convenient to hide the body inside the hut, but the disturbance would certainly wake the king and his servant. Havent would only be inside for a few moments anyway. Drawing a steadying breath, he pushed open the door. An inch, then two.

The frail light of the rising sun fell on the king's bed, which was no more than a patchwork of fabrics sewn together and stuffed, Havent guessed, with leaves and feathers. A thick blanket covered the king's bulky form.

All was silent and still.

The assassin stopped the door with his foot and poked his head in. The servant's pallet was empty. She must have taken the night off. Or snuck out to spend time with a guard. Another week of spying would have revealed such habits. Now he was unaware of when she would return.

He moistened his dry lips, opened the door wide enough to admit his body, and crept inside.

***

Avry crouched with Édouard behind a fat trunk on the outskirts of the village. He shifted restlessly in the fog, fighting an urge to swipe moisture off his face and neck. He envied his men, who were too high up in the canopy of leaves to suffer from the damp.

The village was lifeless as a graveyard. The blackened torches around the perimeter had long ceased smoking. Fog crept around the edges, like ghostly warriors testing their opponent's defenses. The twenty conical huts, hunched together in a spiral formation, reminded him of cairns. The doors faced away from him, making the resemblance even more pronounced.

"Where's Havent, sir?" Édouard hissed in his ear.

Avry had asked himself the same question. He squinted through the hazy dawn light. "He's there somewhere, hiding in plain sight." As he spoke, sudden movement made him stiffen.

A female fae, clothed only in a rumpled tunic, darted out from a hut adjacent the king's and stole on tiptoe toward the royal residence. Avry leaned away from the tree, trying to glimpse her between the obstruent huts. He considered signaling to his men to shoot her but decided not to risk it. Doubtlessly, the assassin would take care of her in a more subtle way.

"Sir…"

Avry clapped a hand over Édouard's mouth. "Quiet now. If the king is dead, we'll know soon enough."

"But what if he's not, sir?" Édouard mumbled through Avry's fingers.

"He will be soon."

"And the fem—?"

"Havent will incapacitate her."

***

As Havent stepped into the king's hut, he recognized what his earlier attempts at spying had failed to uncover: the king was not merely fat, but also gravely ill. His lips were the same sickly white as the rest of his face, his breathing shallow and labored. A small pot of what appeared to be expelled phlegm lay on the floor by his head.

The assassin's shoulders sank, and he sighed. He had imagined a healthy, powerful being, not this wheezing slab of rotten meat. His nose crinkled at the foul stench wafting from the wide, gaping mouth.

He would end this quickly.

Fingers steady, he retrieved his box, selected a dart, and reloaded his pipe. But just as he raised it to his mouth, something punched him in the back.

Dropping the box and pipe, he wheeled on his attacker, felling them with a practiced leg lock. The female servant toppled on the floor. Havent's vision misted with anger as he regarded her stunned, half-naked form. How had she approached without his notice? He considered finishing her then turned roughly away and refocused on the king. But as he lifted his pipe, a wave of vertigo struck him, and he found himself on the floor with his head between his arms. He clutched at the pipe and box, his sight darkening. Something wet trickled down the small of his back.

No. He could not have been stabbed. He would not have allowed it.

Sucking in a painful breath, he struggled to rise. Then all of a sudden his pipe was kicked out of his fingers and snapped under a bare heel.

***

A rustle of disturbed leaves alerted Avry that the other teams had arrived.

"Pup…" Avry turned to find the commander squatting on his heels behind Édouard. "Where's the mite?"

"I don't know."

Neville's eyes almost crossed with worry. "You haven't seen him?"

"Haven't," Avry said dryly.

"Has there been any unusual activity?"

Just then, a sound like wood snapping whispered over the treeless space. Was someone breaking twigs for a fire? The thought reminded him that each hut had a hearth, marked by a slight bulge protruding from the back wall.

Neville frowned, started to speak, then stopped. A guard— probably one of the three who took turns guarding the king—had emerged from a hut a few huts away from the king's, fully clothed but lacking half his armor. He walked with a firm step toward the gorge. Halting at the edge of the village, he folded his arms behind his head as if to bask in the rising sun.

The warm light breathed over the stone huts. Shadows sprouted behind them like leaves.

Then the world ripped open and loosed a piercing cry.

***

Havent lay where he had fallen, panting as warm blood seeped down the small of his back to his buttocks, drenching his tunic and hose. He no longer cared whose fault it was that the mission had gone so terribly wrong or that his life was spilling out into the oily dirt. He had failed. A half-naked servant had bludgeoned him with a knife, and he had let her do it. Breath hissed through his clenched teeth. Dimly, he was aware that his limbs were growing cold, his body sinking deeply into shock. The servant had stepped over him and was trying to waken the dead guard outside. Her quiet whimpering made him ache with frustration. If only she had aimed better, he might have died without knowing his failure. But this... If a vindictive god had devised a torture, it could not have been worse.

He blinked as his sight wavered, and it seemed like a thousand tiny flies buzzed in his head. So cold. He hated to die cold.

A rustling of blankets distracted him from his misery. With an effort, he lifted his head and peered around the curved, shadowy space.

The king's eyes slammed into him. Havent flinched, and for an instant he felt a pitiable urge to scurry away. The intensity of that gaze was paralyzing, and he found himself amazed that such a flaccid, sickly creature could contain such fury.

Power does not choose a shape, a voice said from memory. Whose voice? he wondered, then a fond smile touched his lips. His father had spoken those words to him when he was only a lad, a cringing thread of a child who might have been drowned at birth had he been born to less compassionate parents.

What new disaster are you shaping? he asked the king's burning eyes.

Without thought, he thrust a hand into his tunic where he kept his long-range pipe. The movement dizzied him, and he slowed, swaying in the spinning blackness, but somehow his hands kept moving. They knew what to do without eyes to guide them. The king shifted and wheezed as Havent worked then managed to seize some sort of rugged hand bell. But he was too late. The pipe was loaded. Havent fixed it into his mouth, and while cushioning his head on his arm, he used his fingers to aim the shot. He sucked in a breath and blew a deadly kiss at the face wavering before him.

***

"Sir..."
"Shhh."

Avry's knuckles were white as he gripped the tree trunk. Neville had planted a heavy hand on his arm, as if he thought Avry might take off running. And do what? Make sure the king was dead?

If the fae king was not dead, then Havent must be, he told himself, for the little assassin would rather die than fail.

Another cry tore through the still morning air. Édouard gave a hiccup of fear and flattened himself to the ground. Avry peered up at the canopy of leaves. The sky was bare but for a few wispy clouds painted orange by the sun. Then all of a sudden a huge form sailed past, moving silently as a whale under the surface of the sea. Avry lost sight of it for an instant before he glimpsed it flying low over the rock wall.

The White circled the village. The air from her wings batted away fog and snatched leaves off branches. The clearing darkened in her shadow, and the few fae who had ventured outside fell to their knees, as if in obeisance. Avry's hand loosened on the bark, and he swayed, dizzy without knowing why.

In some waking dream, The White tilted her head and met his eyes. Her own were wide, feral, streaked with bright, cold wind and lonely crags. A tiny figure lay curled in a fetal position in one of her pupils. Long, dark hair framed the curve of its back, and its body was draped in damp leaves. He realized with a start that it was Merisande.

Where, he pleaded, wondering if he were only speaking to himself, his own dazed mind. There came no answer. The dream fled, and he gasped as if his chest had been torn open and his heart laid bare.

The White left him that way. With a powerful thumping of wings, she shot back into the sky and disappeared from sight.

The silence she left behind was absolute.

After the length of a few breaths, Neville's hand dropped from Avry's shoulder, and he mouthed a handful of colorful curses.

Avry caught his sleeve. "Listen."

The female they had spotted earlier was stumbling through the village. Her voice drifted tonelessly over the stunned fae who had emerged, half-dressed, from their beds. "The king is dead," she said, again and again.

Neville shot Avry a questioning glance.

"Go ahead," Avry whispered.

At once, the commander leapt to his feet and gestured to the soldiers waiting in the trees.

The army surged forward. Reaching the village, it split off as efficiently as a stream of ants parting to encircle an obstruction. In what seemed like moments, the fae were surrounded, stunned by the forest of arrows aimed at them.

Avry's head dropped forward in weariness. He found the wristband through layers of clothing and gripped it. *Soon*, he promised her.

CHAPTER 28

Gandel dreamed he was underground.

A door had opened in the grass, revealing a shallow crawlspace under the orchard. Curious, he wriggled in, letting the door close over him with a dull thud. The space was quiet and dark, the air cool, smelling strongly of damp earth and moss. His knees sank a little into the loose dirt as he crawled. Tree roots brushed his shoulders and tangled in his hair; he knocked them aside, coughing at the dust he disturbed.

Where was he going? Would the space end, or did it extend past the orchard to the fields beyond Malborne castle? A root scratched his face. Another tore a hole in his tunic, just above the shoulder. He paused, worried that the next would rip open his wounds. Was the ceiling lowering, or were the roots jutting deeper into the crawlspace? He explored the darkness in front of him and was startled to find a wall of solid stone. He trailed a hand over as it curved around. And around. And around. His fingers trembled then fell. He was completely surrounded. How had it happened? Fear surged through him.

He shoved at the ceiling, snapping roots and dislodging chunks of damp soil. Dirt climbed into his nose and mouth. He dragged in a breath and choked. Fire shot down his lungs, making him writhe in pain. A scream built in the fire. It seemed to gather from a distance, as if the pain were not his, but another creature's. He shrank from it even as he cried it out, over and over again.

He woke drenched in sweat, half on the pallet and half off. But it was as if he were still dreaming. The cry shuddered inside him, making his face shake and his hands tremble. He looked around him in panic. Frail light seeped through cracks in the shuttered windows, illuminating rows of pallets occupied by sleeping workers. The peaceful scene should have calmed him. Instead, it was like a gathering thunder, drawing attention to the wrongness inside him.

His lips quivered as he fought to keep from shouting. He clasped his hands together and rocked from side to side.

In a small corner of his mind where he could still think, he grimly assessed his situation. Could there be a mundane explanation for what he felt? He sorted through the possibilities, setting each aside with reluctance until only one remained.

His head shook roughly. It could not be. He had taken steps to ensure it would never happen. He was free now. Hundreds of miles lay between himself and The White. He would not feel the binding.

Or at least, he had promised himself he would not.

But something bore into him. What else could it be, if not *her*?

Like prodding an open wound, he explored the shape the pain took in his mind. As soon as he nudged it, a pathway opened, as if to a memory he had forgotten. The connection felt inexplicably raw and cold, as though violent winds had blown down it, battering it beyond recognition. Open and sensitive, it waited like a frightened child for the slightest touch. Gandel flinched from it in horror, then in a burst of energy he shoved it away, hoping either to destroy it or to thrust it out of him.

Neither happened.

It would have been easier to tear out his eyes than remove the binding strand. He was trapped. The ends of the earth would not be far enough to evade her.

His hands fell, and after a long silence, he wiped tears and snot from his face.

His father was dead.

The fact was oddly meaningless. It brought him neither sorrow nor joy. How could it? How could he feel anything now while being smothered by The White's pain? Desperation was all he had left, a hot poker of despair that would soon drive him over the edge into the realm of madness. What could he do?

Gradually, a solution came to him. His breath shook as it seeped in, settling into his bones like ice.

Moving as if in a daze, he donned his boots and jacket, padded down the gap between rows of sleeping workers, and exited the compound.

A fine misting rain lent the orchard a gray, almost wintry feel. Gandel hunched into his collar as he followed the cart road to the orchard gate. The guard, a tall, rangy man with an excess of facial hair, leaned off a fence pole and greeted him warily.

"Let me through," Gandel said without emotion.

The guard's brows furrowed. "Why? Where are you off to? The morning bell is about to go off."

"I know. But I'm done working here. Let me out."

His mouth fell open. "You're quitting now? But the season's almost through."

"I don't care."

"At least wait until the secretary is in so you can collect your pay."

"I don't need it." He took a step and stared straight ahead until he heard the bolt slide and the door creak open.

The castle gate gave him less trouble. The guards scarcely spared him a glance before letting him through. The doors closed behind him, and he was left standing alone on the hill, staring down at the rising sun. A milky pool of mist enveloped the town and surrounding countryside, giving him the impression that he stood on an island, watching pale waves lap at a distant shore. He raised a hand to wipe rain off his face then decided he did not care.

He stuck to the road until it swerved south then veered off down a grassy slope. Weeds he had no name for flamed with autumn color. Wet vegetation pulled and bit at his legs. He slowed as he spied a depression in the grass where he had buried his belongings. His head sagged then, and he staggered the rest of the way like someone recovering from a grievous illness.

The rock had not been moved. He toppled it with a careless shove and rifled through the contents of the wet sack underneath it. Three coins and a pair of wheel-shaped stones chinked in a small pouch. He wrestled out a rolled-up jacket, soggy with rainwater, and shook it out over the rock. A silver-handled knife flashed in the pale light before it landed by his feet. He grazed its blade with a trembling finger.

Not sharp enough.

He felt around in the sack until his hand closed on the whetstone. Time seemed to slow then. His eyes closed as he recalled long days in the wood, hunting. How many hares, squirrels, and partridges had he cleaned using this knife? And all to feed a doomed man.

Man. He smiled faintly. At least he could say he died human. That choice, at least, had been his to make.

The knife drew blood when he tested it again. It was time.

He lay down flat on his back and rested the blade over the pulsing vein in his neck. The White's silent cry thundered through him still, as much a part of him now as the blood throbbing beneath his skin. With one sure slice, he would sever that connection forever, preventing it from passing to another generation. And he would be free.

He fixed his gaze on the sky. The clouds were burning away, revealing deep patches of blue. He stared at one patch for an endless moment, watching it shake off its swathing and widen into an azure lake. Blood trickled wetly down his neck. If he lay there long enough, he would not have to slice; little by little the blade would work its way through, until...

His fingers tightened convulsively on the handle, then with a wretched cry, he hurled it away from him.

He could not.

And why should he? Why should *he* have to die? Was it his fault that The White had bound herself to his line? If there was any justice, it would be her death, not his, that broke the binding.

He went still at the thought. Could *he* do her in? Did he have the fortitude to go through with such a ghastly task? "Perhaps I don't have a choice," he breathed. It was either him or her. They could not both go on living, not like this.

Though the strength of the cry was supposed to fade over time, he did not know how long he would have to wait before that happened. And would it really diminish enough that he could bear it?

He would not wait to find out.

He flung himself back onto his feet. Warm blood beat back into his face and hands as his resolve strengthened. Three silver coins would get him back to Aure, and he could exchange his knife for a short sword. No, he thought with a grim smile, he did not need such a large weapon. As binder, he could make her take any shape he wanted before doing her in. A rabbit, perhaps. Or a ground squirrel.

He tossed the knife in the sack, wiped blood off his neck, and started down the hill.

***

Avry drifted numbly through the village, his squire trailing behind. All around him, men bustled at their various tasks. The sweet smoke of cooking fires hung in the chill air. A soldier laughed at some jest his comrade had made. Avry grimaced. His own mood bore a close resemblance to that of the villagers, who leaned sullenly against the rock wall, wrists bound in irons.

Neville and half a dozen men had just emerged from the trees lugging bundles of stripped pine branches. These would be bound together with rope to create a sturdy bier for Havent. It was the best they could do for the little man, who had spent his last drop of blood completing his task. Avry might have mourned him were he not so distracted by his own cares.

Avry's archers had confirmed what his own eyes had seen: that The White had not made herself visible until she was almost directly above them. Avry had almost left them then, with his other question left unanswered, but Édouard's perceptive eyes had trapped him like a hook. Avry's tongue fumbled around the words, but he got them out. *Did you feel faint or have visions when the bird flew over?*

To his surprise, several heads had nodded in unison. All admitted to feeling uncomfortably dizzy, and some said they experienced hallucinations, though they did not recall them clearly. The dizziness had been accompanied by an odd smell, which, they said, had wafted from the bird's open wings.

Fighting to compose himself, Avry had thanked them and wandered off. "Haul down the dead fae sentinels," he called back, remembering belatedly the task Neville had given him.

He patted his belt pouch. A small poison box—courtesy of Havent—nudged him like a finger. It was a cold comfort. What good were weapons against a creature that could incapacitate with a smell? He folded his arms to conceal his trembling hands. He still did not know whether he had hallucinated Mer, or if the vision had been some sort of sending. Had the creature taunted him to go after her?

He snorted and shook his head. The White knew nothing about Avry's feelings for Mer or about his plan to confront her. She would have had no reason to single him out. No, he had simply hallucinated.

Focus on the positive, he thought. They had killed The White's binder and routed the fae, and just as Avry had predicted, the bird had refrained from killing anyone. Avry still lacked her location, but that would come in time. One way or another.

The soldiers were emptying the huts, placing the fae's belongings in piles on the ground. Bright swords and armor stood out like the glitter of stolen trinkets in a magpie's nest. The prisoners eyed their belongings with intense, furtive glances. Avry planned to interrogate them after the supper hour, when the soldiers were less alert, less apt to listen in. One of the fae might know The White's location. Their king would certainly have known, simply by virtue of his link through the binding.

As if Avry had summoned him with a thought, the fae king's bloated body made its ponderous way through the village, legs and shoulders supported by several panting men. They hauled him to the rocky edge of the gorge, where a generous pile of wood was growing. Avry frowned. What did Neville mean to do with all that timber? Surely not burn the bodies.

The commander was still supervising the construction of the bier. He grinned as Avry approached. "If that beached whale were full of mead, we'd have enough to do us until the next moon," he said flippantly.

Avry threw a nervous glance at the fae, who were near enough to hear the sordid joke, but if any of them cared, they hid it well. "What," he asked the commander in a low voice, "is the purpose of that wood pile?"

Neville looked at him from the top of his eyes. "We have to burn the bodies, Pup. It wouldn't be right to leave them here like carrion."

His words drew horrified gasps from the prisoners. Avry motioned Neville to the trees, where they could speak out of earshot of the troubled fae.

"Why is this a problem?" the commander demanded when they halted.

"Because the fae don't burn their dead. They lay them on stone shelves and let them decay naturally."

Neville shuddered. "I don't see a place like that here, and we can't drag the bodies back to the city with us."

"No. No, of course not." He pushed a hand through his untidy hair. "I'll talk to them."

The men guarding the prisoners shifted uneasily as Avry approached them. "They want the commander, sir," a guard said.

"Well, they'll have to make do with me." He cast his gaze down the ragged line of fae. Most, he guessed, were soldiers who had guested in Thorsault castle. Their silver-handled swords—heaped now in a glittering pile—spoke of wealth and station. Perhaps they had been related in some way to the king or had done deeds worthy of recognition. All meaningless now. He wondered how they would react if he told them he had helped bring about the downfall of their city. Would they even care?

They seemed beyond caring. Heavy shadows lurked like stains under their eyes. Their skin hung off them, with little meat to prop it up. Even their wings slumped open, as if they had lost the strength to fold them in. He shook his head a little, remembering a line from one of Mer's poems. *Broken blades only cut when shamed.*

He would shame these people no more.

He nearly flinched when one met his eyes. The barefoot female he had glimpsed earlier beckoned him with a finger. She was tall and wiry. Her dark, oily hair fell limply over her face; strands shifted as she blinked. "There is a place for the dead," she informed him.

"Where?"

She pointed her cuffed hands west. "Follow the rock wall for about a mile. You'll come to an opening in the stone. There are three bodies inside and spaces for more." She made a hurried sign over her chest then brought her hands up to her chin. "Please. Just do this one thing. It won't take long."

"An opening," Avry mused, leaning back on his heels. Could this be another door into the mountains? His fingers itched to retrieve the copy of the old miner's map he had tucked into his tunic. Instead, he reported back to Neville, and before long a dozen prisoners were shuffling along the rock wall, burdened down by the carcasses of five fae. Avry's team shadowed them, bows raised.

It was one of the longest miles Avry had ever walked. Despite being freed from their wrist irons, the four carrying the king had so much trouble balancing him that Avry had to order his squire to fetch a sturdy pine bough to slide under the king's back.

They crossed a stream with difficulty and picked their way through an area of spiny weeds and loose stone. The wall curved, and they found themselves in the wood again, wedged between trees and rock. At last, Avry spied a gap in the wall ahead. The fae must have seen it too, for they increased their pace, like runners nearing a finish line.

The gap was shaped like a crooked arrowhead. An ugly crack rose vertically from its uppermost tip, narrowing to a hair until it disappeared from view. Avry's nose wrinkled at a sickly sweet smell wafting out of it.

He gestured for the prisoners to halt. "How long has it been since the last corpse was interred here?"

"Three days ago," one of the fae muttered, refusing to meet his eyes. Another of Havent's kills, Avry thought. He peered around nervously, wondering why the space was so silent and still. A fresh corpse should have drawn the attention of carrion beasts, crows, rats, and vultures. "The others," the fae added, "were interred last month."

"Is the tomb difficult to access?"

The fae jerked his head to the door. "It's right there. Step inside, and you'll see the bodies."

Avry's mouth opened then snapped shut with a click. Being that exposed, the older corpses should have been consumed by now and not carried much scent at all. As for the newer one... Could it smell this bad after three days in chill air? He licked his lips, which had abruptly gone dry.

He might have asked the prisoners to go in first, but the fae had issued what amounted to a dare: *step inside.* If he did not, he would look like a coward.

Édouard nudged him. "Sir, I can—"

Avry silenced him with a cutting motion. "Follow behind me."

Covering his nose with a sleeve, he stepped through the shadowy door.

CHAPTER 29

The tunnel curved before opening into a sizable cavern. "It's so dark," Édouard said.

"We're in the forest's shadow." Avry smiled grimly, pleased his voice did not shudder. He took careful steps, his gaze scouring the walls and floor for booby traps. If he died here, he would have no one to blame but himself and his own wretched pride.

Édouard held his lamp awkwardly while struggling to cover his nose with a sleeve.

"Try to get used to it," Avry suggested. "It won't get any better."

The light trembled as Édouard found the bodies. The wall swept up at one end of the cavern, forming a steep, terraced hill. Four forms, each wrapped in a plain wool blanket, lay on the first uneven terrace. Apart from the hordes of flying insects, none of them showed signs of being tampered with.

Avry's skin tightened. How had they remained untouched? If they were good enough for flies, then they were good enough for beasts. Unless... Had something prevented the beasts from feasting? Something...or someone? He drew his knife. "Move the light around the walls," he breathed.

Édouard's blade whispered out of its scabbard, and they moved forward haltingly. The lamp thrust shadows like dirt away from corners. Avry was so sure he would find some tunnel or hidey-hole that when the light completed its circle he sucked in a sharp breath. It made no sense. Someone had to be watching over these corpses. A fae Havent had failed to count.

Suddenly, Édouard set the lamp down and stepped back. "Sir, the floor."

The circle of light uncovered a river of chewed bones and plucked feathers, some fresh, others dry and dusty with age. Avry snatched up the lamp and swept it over the floor. The edges were littered with tiny bones. Only the center of the cave remained clean. Or nearly clean. A few drops of blood glittered like jewels. Avry examined the terraces again, but their stark lines offered little room for concealment. Only the four corpses—

Four. There were only supposed to be three. As if sensing his realization, one of the bodies moved, its chest rising to take in air. Édouard must have noticed it too, for he charged forward like a loosed bull and leapt onto the swathed figure, pinning it with his knees and elbows while shouting for it to remain still. It would not oblige him. While Édouard fought for control, it cackled and squirmed as if it were being tickled to death. At last, the blanket came free from its head.

A crazed face, mottled with old blood and grime, leered at the boy.

Avry helped his squire remove the blanket. The fae made small sounds of protest as they turned him on his side. His claw-like fingers refused to release the fabric. "Just let him keep it," Avry said. Stooping, he looked the fae in the eyes. "What is your name?"

"Name." He snorted, spraying spittle in Avry's face. "There are no names. None at all."

"Then I'll call you None," Avry offered dryly.

Édouard got to his feet. He paused as he brushed dirt off his tunic. "Sir, look at his shoes."

A pair of worn but immaculately shined boots peeked out from under the blanket. They seemed to be the only clean things on his body.

"He must have been a soldier at one time, sir. Or a guard."

"He..." A word hitched in Avry's throat. Suddenly he grabbed his squire's arm.

"Sir?"

Crazy as a mountain guard.

Could None be one of hers? Avry considered the fae silently. He was utterly hairless. Even his eyelashes and eyebrows were missing, and given the way he kept feeling for hairs on the back of his hand, it seemed safe to conclude he had plucked them. If he was a guard, could he tell Avry where The White nested? Or had madness completely destroyed his mind?

He realized he still gripped his squire's arm and let it go. "Nothing." He cleared his throat. "Let's bring the others in."

The space grew crowded as the last of Avry's men trickled in behind the fae, fanning into the corners. They were disciplined enough not to ask about the bones rustling under their boots or who the demented stranger was, straining in Édouard's arms to get free.

The fae settled their dead onto the ledges and tucked blankets around them.

None stretched his arms out and wailed. The sound, which was like the keening of burning wood, echoed off the rock until it filled the chamber.

Avry's nails bit into his palms. Finally, he could not stand it any longer. "Just let him go, Édouard. He wants to do his job."

As soon as Édouard loosed him, he shot toward the corpses. The other fae fell back as if they had been caught stealing, but respect settled into their faces as they watched None remove the blankets and rewrap the bodies. His hands fluttered tenderly over faces, hands, even genitals, as if he were storing their shapes in his mind. If he recognized the king, he showed no sign of it; all bodies were treated the same. With the dead snug in their blankets, he signed a finger over their chests and muttered what might have been a prayer. The other fae did the same over their own chests. Sadness washed over their faces, and tears glittered in their eyes. Avry, feeling every bit an intruder, loosed a relieved sigh when None finally climbed back down and shuffled into a corner, where he found a fresh bone to chew on.

Avry's voice fell gently into the silence. "All right. Let's head back out."

Once the cave was empty again, or nearly so—None remained hunched in a corner with Édouard standing guard—Avry announced to his men that they would have to wait outside while he interrogated the new prisoner. Then he shooed Édouard out, ordering him to teach the archers a farmer's song so no one could eavesdrop. His squire's brows rose almost to his forehead, but he obeyed without a word.

Avry tore the hem off his tunic and fashioned it into a rough mask. He hoped it would cut some of the smell while still allowing him to speak comfortably with None. He followed the river of bones to the corner, where the guard was still feasting. The fae had exchanged a thighbone for a wing. A few black feathers dangled from it, twitching as he chewed. They reminded Avry of None's sparse, tattered wings. He set the lamp aside so it would not irritate None's eyes, which were accustomed to darkness. He squatted beside him, wincing as bones shattered under his feet. "You are an excellent hunter," Avry remarked.

The crunch of bone continued without a pause. Avry rubbed his chin. Did None know that his people had been taken prisoner? And if so, did it matter to him? If Avry died now, would None drag his corpse onto a ledge and wrap him as tenderly as he had done the others?

Focus.

He flicked a bouncing feather. "Is this a raven's wing? It looks like one. And the first bone you chewed looked like it might have belonged to a rat. Am I right?"

None tossed the wing aside and pawed at the ground. Avry exhaled sharply. He hated to use petty threats, but it seemed he had no other choice. He retrieved the lamp, stalked over to the reposed bodies, and bent as if to examine one. Flies buzzed in his face like a warning: stay away.

Avry stole a glance out of the corner of his eyes. None was watching him intently.

"Don't," the fae hissed.

"Talk to me."

Silence.

Avry drew flint out of his belt pouch and struck it with a knife. A single spark flared in the shadows. While wool did not burn easily, not all the blankets were composed of that material. The king's was a patchwork of fabrics sewn haphazardly together. A single spark could create a hole, or worse, ignite a fire that might envelop the entire body.

None gasped as if he had been hit. "No!" He leapt up, leaving his blanket behind, and wedged himself between Avry and the corpses.

Avry twisted agilely away and struck the flint again, this time dangerously close to the bodies. "Tell me about the animals," he demanded.

The fae's mouth wobbled. "Rats, mice, crows, foxes." He spat each like a curse.

"And how do you see to kill them?"

"I listen."

"Ah." Avry gave a nod of encouragement. "You've been self-sufficient a long time. Were you a mountain guard before you came here?"

None's brows fell, and he tightened his arms around his middle. "Go away."

"Not until you answer my questions." He raised his knife and flint. None made a grab for them, but Avry evaded him, producing sparks as he moved.

"No!" The fae wailed and stamped his feet.

Avry scrambled up onto the third terrace and held the flint and knife aloft. "Were you a guard for The White?"

The fae's bulging eyes glared up at him. "Don't!"

"Answer the question."

His bottom lip trembled open. "The White has no guard."

"Then what were you?"

"Her servant."

Avry's hand clenched exultantly on the stone. Wild excitement surged through him. The cave fled, and he saw himself standing on the edge of the world, blown by the wind of beating wings. Hands trembling, he set the knife and flint aside and drew the map out of his pouch, unfolding it over his knee. "Bring the lamp and come up here." When there was no movement, he snatched up the tools and worked them again. None was beside him in an instant, one hand grasping the lamp, the other reaching pathetically for the knife. Ironic, he thought, that None did not fear the fire glowing in the lamp. Could it be because it was enclosed, just as the bodies were? "I need her location," Avry said.

"Why?"

"Because...I want to be her servant."

None's face went slack, then a giggle popped out of him like a burp. "No. You don't want that."

Avry jammed the tools between his legs and tilted the map into the light. "The village is here." He trailed his finger from the village to the cliffs, then north along what he took to be a narrow ledge inside the gorge. "And here," he added, pausing at a small red 'x', "is an opening into the mountain. Is that where you came from?"

"Will you go away if I tell you?"

"I will. I promise."

None jabbed the map with a chewed finger. "You go in through that door. A narrow canyon takes you to a pretty green valley. Lots of rabbits to eat there, and mushrooms, this time of year. There is a cave beside the valley. If she lets you in, you travel through a tunnel until you get to a bridge." He halted, letting his arm swing back to his side.

"What then? How do I find her?"

"You don't. *She* finds *you*. If she doesn't want you, then you wander in the dreaming place until she does. *She* decides when you come out of the dreaming place."

The fae's voice dwindled to a whisper. Avry coughed to clear his throat. None had traced the same path the miners had taken three centuries before. The cave by the valley was well labeled, showing the area where ore had been found. No mention of a bridge, however.

A tingle of anticipation trailed like cool fingers down his back. He tucked the map into his tunic. "Thank you. That was most helpful."

The fae did not answer. He had curled into a tight ball on the terrace. Avry retrieved his blanket from a corner and tucked it around him, leaving only his mouth and nose uncovered. Pitiful creature. And yet he had not been afraid to speak of his former master. Some soldiers lost their minds after a terrible battle. They would melt at the sound of steel. If The White had turned None's mind, then the slightest mention of her should have shut him down. But it had not.

You will wander in the dreaming place...

Chilled, he took the lamp and rejoined the others outside.

"You left him there, sir?" his squire asked as they began their march back to the village.

"His mind is gone, Édouard. Those bodies are as precious to him now as children. He would waste away and die if we took him away from them." He paused and glanced around. "Do we all agree?"

There was a general murmur of support. The soldiers would be loathe to return to the cave or to lay eyes on the creature again. None, and the knowledge he carried, was safe from Sir Neville.

***

The morning was gone. Avry's team herded the exhausted prisoners back to the rock wall and went in search of food. The village had been tidied while Avry was away. A bonfire had consumed most of the fae's belongings: the poorly tanned hides, old, tattered clothing, scorched cooking utensils. The valuable items had been stuffed into sacks or trussed together with rope. Solders carried the weapons, servants the sacks.

The fae took nothing but their chains. Neville allotted them a generous portion of dried meat and mead before dividing them up among the teams. Avry's team was only given two prisoners, because they had Havent's bier to carry.

Havent was serene. Bathed, combed, and smoothed, he bore an air of dignity that he had not owned in life. Avry was surprised when Édouard offered to be one of his bearers.

"I want to make sure he doesn't disappear," the boy said obliquely. Avry gave him the afternoon shift.

He expected the fae to glance back as they left the village behind, but none did. It had not been home.

Would they ever feel at home again, or would they remain as exiles, just as their ancestors had been long ago? A wry smile breezed across his lips. If Ghislain recovered, he would be sorely tempted to settle the fae on the east side of the arm. It would deter the fisher folk from wanting to roost there.

The thought of the king recovering drove a spike of pain through his middle. Avry's choice to go after Merisande would thrust a wedge between himself and Ghislain once more. He had betrayed his knight's oath the first time he went after her. This latest adventure would reawaken the injury.

But if Avry came back, it would be because he had found Merisande. And he could not apologize for that.

The sun was low on the horizon as they trickled through the gap in the thorn wall to the other side. Neville ordered the teams to break camp. The fae were given meals and blankets. The rest made do with what was in their packs.

Every team set a watch that night. Avry, having got what he needed from None, discarded his plan to question the prisoners. *No need to draw undue attention to myself,* he thought. He would get enough of that tomorrow when the time came for him to break away from the others.

Morning was damp and cold. The overcast sky hung like a sodden sheet. Moisture dripped from the trees onto the company's heads. Boots slid on rotting leaves and slimy mushrooms. The men paused at a stream to refill their bottles then carried on until they broke through the last of the trees and found themselves on the edge of Lord Piercy d'Eleuthère's pasture. A chorus of bleating sheep and cawing crows greeted them. Neville led the teams west until the soil grew uneven and rocky. Rives's cottage was a stone's throw away. The North Road snaked beyond it, vanishing into a green haze of pastureland.

The commander called for everyone to halt and ordered the prisoners to conceal their wings under coats and blankets. Secure them well, he warned, for it would be a long walk to the barracks.

Avry left his team for a few minutes to speak with Sir Neville. His chest tightened as he hiked along the tree line, and he swallowed repeatedly. How many times had he rehearsed this encounter in his mind? And yet it was not the same as doing it.

The commander's broad back turned at Avry's step. "Sir Avry."

Avry shoved his damp palms under his armpits and smiled. At least, it felt like a smile. "A half-score more hours and you'll be back in your bed," he said with as much cheer as he could muster.

"And you."

"I'd like to be, but I can't pass this close to my father's home without paying a visit. I haven't seen my mother since early last month."

Neville chuckled and slapped his arm. "You're a good lad. But must you spend the night?"

"One night, at the very least."

Neville took a step closer and spoke cautiously. "Think on the past few weeks, Pup, the situation with Archard and Patric. The king's uncertain condition. You've been away from the castle for days—"

"Another won't make a great difference."

"It might not. But it might. You'd be wiser to take an hour instead of a day. We can wait for you here."

Avry's jaw tensed. He had known that the commander would make this difficult, but just how far would he push? "I understand your concerns, but I've made a decision, and I'm sticking to it."

Neville considered that with pursed lips and then loosed a quiet snort. "Your mother. I'd wager more than a few coppers you have another lady in mind. Ah, well. So be it. Send the bier over. And your two prisoners; I'll place them in teams that only have three."

"There's no need. My team can convey them to the barracks without me."

The commander's expression sobered. "I can't leave you behind without a guard."

"You *can't?*"

Neville did not seem to notice Avry's sudden stillness, his heated face. "Pup, I shouldn't be the one to tell you this, but you can't go on living like you're still just a knight. A regent shouldn't ride alone. It isn't done, and in these uncertain times, it isn't safe."

Avry's hands had gathered into fists. It took everything he had to keep them under his arms. "I would heed that advice, if the one giving it ever paid the title the respect it is due."

Neville's mouth slackened. He stared at Avry for several moments, then his head sank into his chest. A wisp of shaggy hair fell away from his bald spot and hung over his eyes. "Forgive me. I misspoke, Sir Avry."

There was an uncomfortable pause. Avry's anger collapsed just as fast as it had swelled, revealing the fear and anxiety he knew had propped it up. He tried to swallow, but there was a thickness in his throat. Had he destroyed their friendship with a few poorly chosen words? Unable to speak, he turned away and strode back to his men.

The teams were readying to leave. Backs hunched under blankets, the fae resembled the half-drowned fishermen pulled out of the water after being attacked by the bird.

Avry, having announced he would not accompany his men to the barracks, nominated a new leader for the team. Édouard was speechless. He seemed to choke on words as Avry led him off toward the d'Eleuthères' pasture.

The crows had flown away. Crickets chirped in what was left of the sheep-chewed grass. Avry eyed the ground as he walked to keep from stepping on droppings.

"Are you all right, sir?"

"I'm fine," Avry grumbled.

"Are we spending the night with your family, sir?"

"No. We'll only be there until the teams are gone. I'd like you to lay low for a while. Go quietly to my old chamber and wait for me."

Édouard stared at him for some time before managing a tight nod. "Yes, sir."

The sprawling manor house was peaceful in the early afternoon. Avry slipped through the kitchens, holding a finger to his lips when the cook spotted him. He and Édouard mounted the grand staircase. Reaching the second floor, Édouard slipped into Avry's old room while Avry went on to his mother's quarters.

He knocked lightly on her door. After a few moments, it swung open. The maid, doubtless expecting Lord Piercy d'Eleuthère, gaped when Avry strode in. Once more, he held a finger to his lips. The door closed, and he crossed the space separating him from the figure seated by the hearth.

Lady d'Eleuthère turned at his step. She spoke Avry's name as if it were the only name in the world. Her arms opened, reaching for his.

Avry knelt by her chair, rested his head on her lap, and let her hold him. Her hands were light as butterfly wings. Her slender fingers made paths through his hair, twining, gently tugging. They said little to each other. It had always been that way. Her eyes and fingers spoke better than words could have done.

He did not know how long he knelt there. Time drifted with her fingers, making calm paths for him to tread. Her perfume filled him with memories of quiet afternoons spent reading in sunlight, listening to her hum. He gathered that silence into him, that wordless peace, then he drifted to his feet. Kissing her cheek, he left the room.

CHAPTER 30

Mer reeled as the current caught her again and thrust her into sudden, blazing light—the sun, she thought, baring its naked head over the estuary.

The girl she still inhabited dragged in a breath of sea air and smiled. She was bumping along inside a carriage, her teeth rattling as the wheels shuddered over uneven paving stones.

Mer could count on one hand how many times she had accompanied her father to the city in her uncle's covered carriage. She had been a child of ten the first time, and the last...

A gurgle of pleasure drifted from the adjoining seat.

Jan was there. That narrowed it down to a single trip, taken in the spring of her fourteenth year.

The girl tidily ignored her brother. Her limbs were taut with enthusiasm as she anticipated her visit to the market. She ran her hand over a wrapped bundle on her lap. How much would she get for the dress? A silver would buy her a quality knife, some pens and paper...

Mer smiled inwardly at these thoughts. Simple things. Simple times. If she had known then what terrors awaited her in the future... A wave of depression surged over her. Desperation followed closely on its heels. Usually, these feelings waited until she flailed in The Current, but the memory-dreams did not hold her attention as they used to.

Mer prodded her ghostly presence and sensed growth once more. Not only had her sense of self strengthened, but the girl had lost power. The feeling was elusive, hard to pin down and even harder to explain. When Mer pushed, the girl yielded, not consciously— her younger counterpart was not alive the way Mer was—but as a barred door might yield, little by little, under a firm hand. When Mer concentrated on moving a limb, it gave an eerie tingle. *Almost.* She hoped to gain complete control before finding herself in Thorsault.

If she survived that long.

The driver made a clicking sound, and the horses turned up a busy two-laned street. Scents from the lower market wafted into the carriage. Animal dung was foremost among them. The girl wrinkled her nose. *What a stench.*

Jan cooed again and shifted restlessly beside her.

Watch him, Mer urged the girl, pressing against the confines that held her mind. But even if she could alter the dream, she could not alter history.

A moment later, Jan's delighted sounds changed to panicked screaming. The girl whipped around, her heart thundering against her ribs. Jan was halfway out the carriage window. Outside, a chaos of raised voices mingled with the whinnying and blowing of a horse. The carriage jolted to a stop. The girl tugged on her brother's legs. "Jan, get back in. Get in now!" She peered around his back, trying to see what was going on outside. Another carriage had halted alongside theirs, and the driver was shouting curses at someone.

Just then, Rives stepped down off the front of the carriage, where he had been sitting with the driver and went around to Jan's side. Mer glimpsed his slender back through the window, draped in a freshly oiled leather coat. "Let it go," he said firmly to his son.

Seat springs squealed as the driver of the other carriage stepped off. "If you don't get his filthy hand off my horse, I'll…"

The girl did not let him finish his sentence. Her rage was white-hot, heating her face and making her tremble.

Your fault, Mer the observer thought.

Having exited the carriage, she slammed herself between the driver and Jan. Something in her face must have frightened the driver, because he raised his hands and backed off.

Rives straightened with an audible sigh. "He's snared his fingers in the horse's mane," he told her flatly. "Can you work them loose?"

"I…" Her voice halted as a driver in one of the carriages waiting behind them shouted a curse. "I'll try my best."

Jan moaned. His upper body hung limply over the carriage door. His arm extended out, attaching him like a tether to the docile bay's black tail. The girl ducked underneath him and found his anxious, wet eyes. Strings of snot hung from his lips and nostrils. "Shhh." She wiped his face with her sleeve. "You're safe. Safe, Jan. We're not moving until you're free."

He swallowed and blinked moisture out of his eyes. "Mehhh."

"I'm going to untangle you. Hold still."

His hand was well and truly snared. Clumps of horse hair dampened by sweat and drool were twined around his fingers. The girl worked to loosen them, but it was like trying to peel a mushroom. And his stiff, curled fingers did not help matters. "Jan." She ducked to peer again at his miserable face. "You have to let go. Open your fingers. Let it go."

She repeated the words over and over as she worked, and at last his hand came free.

The world tilted then, and Mer sensed the powerful surge before she was torn away like smoke in the wind.

CHAPTER 31

Avry pilfered half his father's store of smoked meats before returning to his squire. The boy had fallen asleep on the bed. He woke with a start when Avry, stripped of his leather armor and the tightness around his eyes, perched on the mattress.

"I'm sorry, sir."

Avry shook his head. "Sit with me a while." Once Édouard had settled beside him, Avry dove into the grim tale of what had befallen Merisande and Esperance, leaving nothing out. The scent of cured meat unfurled as he spoke, leaving his squire without a doubt of what Avry intended to do.

The retelling ended. Avry tightened his pack strings. As he drew breath to speak, the boy cut in. "Sir, please take me with you. You shouldn't do this alone."

He set the pack gently on the floor. "The last time I made a journey like this, you didn't think I'd return."

"Sir…"

"But I did." He caught the boy's eyes and held them. "What about now?"

Avry was sure Édouard would look away. Hide his doubt behind lowered lids. But instead, his gaze turned inward and his red brows pinched together in a thoughtful frown. He spoke with a measure of surprise. "I think you'll be back, sir. Though I don't know why."

Avry grabbed his shoulders and drew him into a fierce hug. He grinned as he pounded his squire's back with a fist. "I will be back, Édouard."

"Sir, I still think you should—"

"No, Édouard. I need you here." He leaned away, still holding his squire's arms lightly. "I want you to go to Rives's cottage. He'll be expecting you. Stay there for two nights, then return to the castle and tell Sir Neville everything I told you. About Mer. About where I'm going. After that, go to Rives's house and wait for me." He dug a silver coin out of his belt pouch and pressed it into Édouard's hand. "Try not to demolish Rives's pantry."

Édouard gave a tight nod.

"And tell Sir Neville," he added with a dry smile, "that I owe him more than a few coppers."

"Yes, sir."

Avry surged to his feet, infused with sudden energy. "Then farewell, Édouard."

"Sir, at least take your sword!" He unlatched the scabbard from his belt and held it out.

Avry hesitated. He had stashed a couple of sturdy throwing knives—one in his pack, and one secured inside his jacket cuff—and the poison lay like a viper in his belt pouch. Anything more than that would alter his appearance from one of diplomacy to aggression.

But was this worth another argument? He could dispose of the sword later. With a curt nod, he accepted it and strode out the door.

Afternoon sunlight drenched his face as he retraced his steps through the field. The teams were long gone. He had half expected to find archers waiting by his father's front door, but Sir Neville had wisely left him alone. Avry thrust the sour memory of their encounter from his mind. If he allowed himself to dwell on all his failings, he would grow as hunched and maddened as that creature in the cave.

But his mind blew clear. Every step he took now brought him closer to Merisande. He plunged into the trees, following the mash of footprints so that no one could track him. The ghost of Havent's memory flared here and there on the path, taking shape in falls of shadow and light.

Avry did not so much mourn the man as what had been lost by his death. Havent was like a boulder buried in sand. Avry had barely glimpsed his tip, and then he was gone. A piece of the kingdom, lost forever. It made Avry uneasy, as if the assassin's death was part of a curse Avry had carried, just by being king-in-waiting.

Dark thoughts. With an effort, he shook them off and concentrated on the hacked path along the thorn wall. He reached the gorge well before nightfall. Exhausted, he tossed an armful of brush onto the charred remains of a previous night's fire. Once he had a steady blaze, he pulled out a bottle of cider and uncorked it with his knife. He let his mind empty as he peered into the flames, watching them shrink, little by little, against the darkening sky. His eyes heavy, he set the bottle against a tree, wrapped himself in his blanket, and slept.

He woke at dawn. His chilled hands found the cider. He downed it with a few strips of dried pork and an old rind of cheese then slipped the empty bottle into his pack.

North again. He kept to the tracks until they ended at the fae village, then he veered east toward the gorge. If not for the map, he would have assumed there was no way to continue along the edge: the rock wall seemed flush with the wall of the gorge. But as he neared the brink, a narrow ledge came into view. The mountain rose steeply from it. Avry tried not to look down as he plodded forward, trailing a hand over the wall. He could no longer hear the rushing river far below. The cliff on the opposite side gradually ascended until he walked in its shadow.

His hands shook as he stepped over a blackened area of rock where water pooled before it fell. The scent of dirt and moss crept into his nostrils; icy water trickling down the rock wall dribbled over his fingers. He kicked a stone away and watched it tumble down the gorge. For an instant he could not move. Then he placed one foot in front of the other. He imagined the miners walking with him, one in front and one behind. He smelled their sweat, heard the crunch of their footsteps on the stone. They had not known where the ledge would take them. Perhaps they worried it would end abruptly, and they would be forced to retrace their steps. Did one or two beg to turn around? Or did their hope of finding riches drive them on?

A thought startled him to a standstill: if he found Mer and Esperance, they would have to negotiate this ledge, and who knew what sort of condition they would be in? He ran a chill hand over his forehead. He would worry about it when the time came. All he could do now was move forward.

The gorge curved gently east. Eyes fixed on the path, Avry did not see the gap in the wall until it was almost upon him. He halted midstride, his hand creeping to his mouth.

It was as though the mountain had split, like skin that had been pulled too taut. The resulting fissure was thin and jagged. A narrow wash snaked along its bottom, disappearing after a few yards behind a bend in the wall. He swallowed, tasting dry wind and grit. The map indicated that the canyon was several miles long. Miles of that would cost him the day.

At least he had gloves.

"Idiot," he muttered as he fished a lonely pair out of his pack. Even if these lasted him through to the return trip, he still had Mer and Esperance to think about. He should have thought to bring other pairs. "Can't go back now," he told himself. He would just have to figure it out when the time came. Stashing his coat in his pack, he began his long hike through the canyon.

The walls were as fitful as sea waves, swelling out, then pitching in, leaving Avry at times to scramble up the sides like a spider, hands and feet balanced precariously on the uneven stone. Before long, he had ditched his sword in a crack; he did not pause to see where it fell. His footsteps sounded eerily hollow, as if he trod inside a conch shell. Afternoon sunlight oozed down the walls, blinding him with light.

At last, the path widened. Avry, shielding his eyes, did not know he had reached the canyon's end until he found soft green grass under his feet. He stumbled forward a few steps more, then stopped, utterly stunned by what his tired eyes beheld.

A luminous meadow lay in the mountain's craggy palm. Warm sunlight hung over its gently swaying grasses; birds bathed in its winding, glittering stream. Here and there were bright spots of color: autumn flowers, field weeds turned to flame by the cold.

Avry, trembling with exhaustion, waded through the grass to the stream bank. Unshouldering his pack, he squatted on the ground and refilled every bottle he had. His tunic came off next, and then his hose, until he crouched naked in the water, chilled but clean. Belatedly, he realized he had nothing with which to dry himself off. He would not dampen his sleeping blanket. Shrugging, he lay back in the sun-warmed grass, draped his coat over his chest, and slept.

He woke at sunset, cold and hungry. He dressed quickly and hunted for kindling. Some spiny shrubs huddled up against the rock wall. He pulled on his gloves and wrenched a dead shrub out of the ground. Hunched under his blanket, he broke it into pieces and kindled it against the wall.

He regarded the valley thoughtfully as he chewed a strip of dried meat. Sheer stone walls encircled the meadow. The only opening appeared to be the cleft of the canyon, and yet there had to be another. Perhaps it was too narrow to be visible in the fading light.

He winced as he considered what sorts of challenges the next leg of his journey might bring. The word "tunnel" was fairly straightforward, but then so was the word "canyon." "Bridge" would not be any better. And after...? Did The White live above or below the bridge? Was the bridge a door to her "dreaming place?"

He swallowed a hastily chewed bite. Better not to think about it. Keep moving, Neville had always said. Where you stop, you drop.

Neville was wise. Not like Ghislain, but in a rough, practical sort of way. It bothered Avry that he had not noticed it before. What else had he not noticed, not only about Neville, but about everyone he had taken for granted in his life?

He stared with gritty eyes at the burning wood, wishing he had another bottle of cider. But after a time, his dark mood lifted, and his mouth quirked in a self-effacing smile.

He leaned back against the ground with a sigh. The hum of crickets fanned out around him. The violet sunset darkened, and a spray of stars reeled over the curve of the mountain. Avry regarded them thoughtlessly until a footstep wrenched him to alertness.

He withdrew his knife, rolled to his feet, and flattened himself against the rock wall.

The footsteps slowed, started again, then a figure slid like a wisp of smoke in front of the fire.

They eyed each other wordlessly while the purple glow of twilight faded to darkness. The stranger was a young, olive-skinned woman. Her ragged cape, which had been cobbled together from scraps of hide, hung open at the front, revealing the familiar lines of a Thorsault slave's dress.

Avry slipped his knife back up his jacket sleeve and stepped toward her with raised palms. When he was near enough to hear her whispered words, he asked her name.

"Alba," she said, after a silence. "Yours?"

It was a moment before he answered her. Firelight stroked her delicate, symmetrical face. Her eyes had a hunted look. She must have escaped the fae village before Havent got there, he decided, which meant she had lived in the mountains for at least a week, if not longer. "Avry."

Her lips moved, but he did not hear the words.

"Hungry," she said when he asked her to repeat it.

Avry placed several sticks of jerky in her upraised palm. She shoved the meat into her mouth before he had finished dispensing it. He offered her water then forgot his own thirst as he watched her drink. Something about her pulled at him. On the surface, she exuded nothing more than an animal's savage desire to live. But beneath that lurked an alluring darkness. A suspicion crept over him that she could be the skin shifter, but he thrust it firmly aside. Perhaps he deceived himself, but he could not believe that this half-starved slave girl was The White. "Are there others here besides yourself?" he asked.

She shrugged as she chewed. "There's you."

He blinked at the evasiveness of her answer. "I've only been here a few hours."

She took another swig and wiped her mouth with the back of her arm. "Hmm."

"Sit down if you like. It's warm by the fire." He retreated a step and sat carefully, as if she were a skittish colt. Alba followed his example, folding her legs under her voluminous cape. "If you don't mind me asking, how long have you been here?"

"Long."

A week or two probably would seem "long," given her loneliness and apparent lack of food. "Well, you'll be happy to know the village is no more. My people fell on the fae three days ago and took them prisoner. You're free now. You can leave this place."

She offered no response but seemed preoccupied with picking meat out from between her teeth. Avry resisted the urge to draw back the crow's wing of hair that had fallen over her eyes to see what expression stirred there.

"Why are *you* here," she said, setting down the bottle, "if *you* are free?"

The question stole the breath from his lungs. He knew that she asked it in innocence, and yet it held so many shades of meaning that he was left speechless. He jabbed the fire with a scorched twig. "Someone I care about is in trouble. A giant bird carried her off..." He paused, chastising himself for forgetting Esperance. "Have you seen it—the bird, I mean?"

"No."

He tossed the stick into the flames. Somehow he had expected that answer. "When I return, you should come back with us to Aure."

"Why?"

"Because you can't winter here. You won't survive."

"Maybe. Maybe not." Her breath hitched as she uncurled her legs.

Something about the cautious way she moved made him wonder if she were injured. Sure enough, he spied a dark blotch on her skirt, just above her right thigh. He cleared his throat. "It hasn't healed properly, has it?"

Her hand closed over the stain. "No."

"Can I look at it?"

In answer, she hitched up her skirt, baring a pair of well-formed legs. Face hot, Avry bent to consider the injury.

It was deep and old. Pink skin struggled to close over the angry gash, which must have been caused by something sharp. A knife, perhaps, or an arrow. Had she been shot while trying to flee the village? Had she clambered through the narrow canyon with an arrow lodged in her thigh? "How did this happen?"

"I fell on some rocks."

"Rocks." His voice was flat.

"That's what I said."

He shook his head but chose not to argue. Instead, he fetched a flask of gin from his pack, and holding her leg still, dribbled some into the wound. Her muscles stiffened, but she did not jerk away. He tore a strip from his tunic and bound the wound, securing it with a tight knot. "There," he said, drawing down her skirt. "It may heal faster now."

He waited for her thanks, but all he received was a long, impenetrable stare.

"Where do you sleep?" he asked, hoping she would reveal the location of the cave.

"Here and there. This seems like a good place tonight."

He chuckled then offered her his blanket. "Stay, then. This will keep you warm when the fire goes out."

Her lips pursed. "I'll share the blanket. I won't take it from you."

Once more, she left him speechless. He set the blanket slowly over his crossed legs. "That wouldn't be honorable."

"Cold doesn't care about honor."

It was true. He played with a bead of wool, stretching it out and twisting it around his finger. They were alone here. If no one witnessed it, then it did not happen. *You're beginning to sound like*

Ghislain, he thought with a wry smile. He stifled a yawn, feeling self-conscious without knowing why. "Very well. But if you begin to feel uncomfortable, just say so."

She flung him a vague smile then snatched the blanket off his lap and shook it out over the grass. Avry made no movement until she was under it, breathing deeply, then he swallowed a mouthful of gin, tossed it into his pack, and wriggled in beside her.

He did not think he would sleep. The warmth at his back was a torture; in a half-turn of thought, he could have imagined it was Merisande's. What a wonder it would be, he thought, to sleep next to her, to watch her small movements as she slept. That alone would have made him happy. Just that.

The fire settled, and he drifted into a forgettable dream.

He woke with a start, so heavy with sleep that for a time he did not know where he was. Then he felt a warm pressure along the whole length of his body. One leg trapped his waist, the other nudged into his groin. Before he could move, a hot breath grazed his cheek. "Kiss me."

Appalled, Avry ripped himself away, leaving the blanket behind. He crouched against the rock wall, panting.

Stupid stupid stupid. What had he been thinking? A man did not share a woman's bed unless he meant to make love to her. It was as simple as that. He considered apologizing for the misunderstanding then set it aside for the morning. He was not thinking straight. Had not been since the moment their eyes had met. And perhaps the source of his blunder lay there. It had not been a true misunderstanding. A part of him had known what sharing that blanket meant, and he had done it anyway.

The fire was cold. Only a few embers glimmered under a layer of ash. He shifted as close to it as he dared, shut his eyes, and tried to sleep.

Time dragged. The chill air breathed across his face and hands and seeped like brackish water into his jacket. He hunched away from it, but it clawed back, held him suspended on the edge of sleep.

After what must have been hours, he turned onto his back and glared at the sky, which had lightened with the first blush of dawn.

The crickets had quieted and the air was still. The gurgle of the stream flowed painfully over him. It was a cold sound. Cold as his blood. *Get up.*

Three times he struggled to rise. His body shivered uncontrollably; his bones were masts of ice. With a supreme effort, he hauled himself to his feet and leaned against the wall.

Alba was gone.

CHAPTER 32

Avry peeled the blanket off the ground and threw it over his shoulders. Cold. Alba had not lain on it for a while. He stamped his feet until the shivering subsided then crushed some cold strips of jerky between his teeth. With an effort, he thrust last night's misadventure from his mind, but he could not remove the lingering sensations she had left, like stains, on his body. He would have plunged into the stream if he were not so chilled. Scrubbed her off him.

He made a half-hearted attempt to find her trail in the weedy grass then gave up with a sigh. *Just as well.*

Shouldering his pack, he set off to find the cave.

He began near the canyon and edged clockwise. The wall was smooth at first—a sheer rise of gray stone, shot through with slender white veins—then the gray vanished, and grainy, pitted rock the color of sand replaced it. Avry slowed to investigate every shadowy curve and indentation.

He rehearsed what he would say if he stumbled on Alba again. It had occurred to him that she had probably watched him bathe. While Avry could not boast of the bulk Sir Neville possessed, years of training had honed him into the shape necessary to wield a heavy blade. He might not be handsome, but he was young, healthy, and fit—very different from the bony, sallow slave men she would have rubbed shoulders with in Thorsault. Could he blame her for giving in to a moment of weakness, lonely as she was?

His mind cleared, and he found himself grinning, drinking in the cool, sun-touched air.

Dark fissures sprouted in the rock, but none were wide enough to admit more than a finger. He leapt over the shallow stream, which slunk like an animal under the rock wall.

Still no opening.

He passed the remains of his camp and threaded his way back to the canyon. He surveyed the mountain with narrowed eyes. Could the gap be higher up on the wall? He marked a handful of possible spots then set out again with a flutter of nervousness in his stomach. *If she lets you in*, the fae had said. What did that mean? Could The White create an illusion of stone where none existed? Perhaps not an illusion, he thought. She might shape herself to stone, just as some insects mimicked plants.

He trailed his fingers over the wall, not looking, just feeling. His steps whispered over the ground, then stopped.

There it was again: that sensation of being watched. He had not felt it since that night on the cliff edge. His fingers curled around his belt knife. Hardly breathing, he edged around a craggy outcrop.

Nothing.

He rubbed a damp palm over his knife handle then almost jumped at the cawing of a crow.

The feeling of being watched slipped away, but his unease lingered. Not a single place he had marked had yielded an opening. Where had Alba gone?

"Are you lost?"

Avry jerked back as if shot. Drawing his knife, he peered wildly about him. A throaty chuckle drew him around a bend in the rock. He halted midstep, his boot grazing the inky outline of a shadow. Looking up, he found himself inches from a young man who was slouched into a groove in the wall.

The cut of his short tunic marked him as another Thorsault slave. Yet he had retained his voice—he must have just missed going through the ritual—and was anything but frail. His olive-toned skin sat well on his bones; his eyes were bright and focused, glittering with the confidence of a man aware of his worth. Women would have found him attractive.

Avry stepped back and replaced his knife. "I'm looking for a way into the mountain. A door." He managed to keep his voice calm, though irritation threatened to bubble to the surface. Could this man be Alba's lover? Perhaps they had quarreled, and Alba, seeking to hurt him, had endeavored to seduce Avry...

The man folded his arms over his chest. "We all want something."

Avry fingered his bristly chin. "What are you suggesting? That we make an exchange?"

A soft snort. "You have nothing I need."

"But perhaps something you want?" Avry unshouldered his pack and shook it. "I have dried meat and cheese. A few swallows of gin."

Not a flicker of interest. Avry, fighting an urge to slam him against the wall and hold the knife to his throat, rested the pack cautiously against his leg. "I'm not after your hidey-hole. Or," he added, "the woman who shares your bed."

"No? I think you are."

A finger of wind eddied between them. As Avry opened his mouth to reply, the slave made a deliberate movement with his legs, crossing them so that one nudged toward Avry. The material strained over his thigh, revealing a familiar stain and beneath it the bulge of a bandage.

A shudder went through Avry, and he staggered back. The ground tilted under his feet. The slave's head tilted with it, and amusement danced like a glint of flame in his eyes. *Skin shifter.* Avry should have guessed. Should have remembered where The White had been wounded on the day it attacked Aure. Blood thundered through him as he met The White's gaze; he did not flinch from it. "Where are they?" Despite Avry's resolve not to threaten The White, menace crept into his voice.

"They?"

"Mer and Esperance."

"Esperance." His lip curled. "I don't have her. But the *other...* she is indeed with me, under *my* blanket." He let the words drift on a suggestive note. They found Avry like a knife shoved into his stomach and twisted mercilessly. He could not speak. The full meaning of The White's words strangled his voice. Did he hold Mer enslaved somewhere, to be used at his will? The creature seemed to catch the trail of Avry's thoughts. "I would never force myself on anyone," he said flatly.

"Then what are you saying? That she chose to be your lover?"

Another smirk. Avry would have ground it off his face if had the energy to do it, but he felt drained suddenly, sucked dry. His head sagged, and he swallowed back something sharp in his throat.

It was all too possible. If Avry had not been restrained by his thoughts of Mer, Alba would have trampled him like a storm wind. Mer had no such anchor. She had never loved him at all.

Painfully, he sorted through the various ways The White might have seduced her: by pretending to be another of The White's prisoners or appearing while she was captive, and after some days freeing her or by feeding her seductive dreams until, finally waking, she lost control of her mind and...

He passed a trembling hand over his eyes. He was going to be physically sick. "Where is she?" he pleaded.

"With me. In my place. Are you sure she's still worth it?"

Avry's mouth moved, but no sound came out.

"She's safe," the creature promised.

"It doesn't matter. I have to see her." Somehow, he managed to put some strength into those words.

Rock crunched as The White stepped closer. "Why? Why must you interfere?"

The question seemed to reach beyond the moment to all the times Avry had thrust himself in her path. He ran a finger over the purplish smudge on his wristband. The answer formed on his lips before he gave it voice. "Because I love her. That's why."

The White, shaped as a man, held Avry's gaze a moment longer, then his face fell and he stared at his open hands. "I once loved. It brought me nothing but pain."

He walked away.

Stunned, Avry lurched after him. "Wait!"

The slender figure vanished behind an outcrop of stone. Avry turned the corner and halted midstep.

The slave's footsteps trailed off into a gaping hole.

***

Avry fumbled as he lit a lamp. His fingers were stiff and cold. All his movements were jittery, as if he were being shaken by a giant fist. The wick flared at last. He set the lamp on the floor and steadied himself against a boulder.

He was just inside the entrance to a vast cavern. The footsteps were gone. The only sound breaking the silence was the distant drumming of water.

He ground his palms against his eyes. His view of The White had changed: no longer was he—she—the wretched, abused creature who had been compelled to inflict harm on others. Now *she* was the abuser.

His hand dropped, and he stared sightlessly at the shadowy rock. No, that did not sound right. If she enjoyed harming others, she would have remained close to the fae. Instead she had driven a wedge between them. Avry had to be missing something—a crucial piece of information, the key that would explain her actions.

What if everything she had said and done to him in the meadow had been a lie, a test to gauge the genuineness of his love for Mer? If so, then there was another reason she held the lady.

He snorted. It was an ugly sound. *He* felt ugly. Old and miserable, as if he had aged ten years in a day. He had to stop imagining the best and learn to be realistic. The White had long been alone, and recent events would have made that loneliness keener. It would have cost her nothing to snatch up a warm body to take back to her nest.

Perhaps she had even believed she could make Mer happy, that they would grow to love one another.

The White's last words drifted back to him then, like a riddle: *I once loved. It brought me nothing but pain.*

He groaned and beat the back of his head against the boulder. None of it made sense. All he knew for sure was that she had let him into the mountain. He had no choice now but to walk the path she had set him on.

He crossed the cavern, squeezing between jagged boulders while holding the lamp aloft. At the far side, a jagged crack gaped in the wall. He had seen no other signs of an opening, so, securing the lamp to a belt hook, he ventured inside.

His breathing quickened as he stared down the narrow crack. It seemed to go on forever, a wisp of blackness cutting into the deeps of the mountain. His steps sounded loud in his ears as he edged sideways, trying not to bump the lamp against the wall behind him.

An eternity might have passed. At times, the space widened so he could walk freely, and he began to believe that an end was in sight, but then the walls would pitch in again and he would be forced to shimmy between them. His hands slid on the wet stone. Grit caught under his palms. Though he wiped them frequently on his jacket, tiny splinters of rock worked their way in until the skin broke and blood mingled with the icy water. He paused several times to drink, taking small sips in case his bottle was empty before he found a spring.

At long last, the crack ended, and he stepped into another cavern.

He unhooked his lamp and shuddered to the floor. Every part of him ached. He tried stretching his cramped back and winced as pain lanced down it. He needed rest. Only a fool let his blade go dull when he should take time to sharpen it.

Stretching out on the floor, he shoved his pack under his head and closed his eyes. Before sleep claimed him, he reached over and smothered the lamp.

A crunching sound jerked him awake.

He went still in the darkness, hardly breathing.

A tiny crack, like bone snapping, echoed through the cavern. The sound was close, perhaps only a couple of yards away. He drew his knife and waited breathlessly for the intruder either to approach him or pass by.

Neither happened. The snapping and cracking continued but grew no louder. After perhaps a quarter of an hour had passed, he thrust a trembling hand into his belt pouch and retrieved his flint box. He had never felt so exposed. Why had he shut off the lamp? What had he been thinking?

The sounds paused, and a long silence fell. As soon as Avry lit the lamp, he would make himself a target for whatever lurked in the cave. It was probably some sort of animal. Or The White in another guise. Well, he had no other choice. He could not go on without light.

Teeth clenched, he steadied the flint box and went through the motions of making fire, all the while alert to the slightest sound. The wick caught. He raised his knife and stared wildly around him.

He did not have to look far. A red-haired woman sat cross-legged against the opposite wall. As he met her gaze, she lowered a ragged, bloodied bat from her mouth, wiped an arm across her face, and smiled. "Knight Errant. Fancy meeting you here."

"Esperance?"

"How kind of you to remember my name." She rummaged around in the pockets of her stained brown smock, drew out another limp, but apparently unchewed bat, and offered it to him. "Are you hungry?"

He jerked back. "Um, no. Thanks."

"Suit yourself." She shoved the offering into her pocket and resumed gnawing on the first one.

Avry regarded her warily. Could this really be Esperance?

It seemed likely. No one but the wood woman had ever called him "Knight Errant," so unless The White had overheard Esperance say it, she would not know to use the term. Then again, they might have both hit on the same moniker.

She gave a dry chuckle. "You think I'm *her*, don't you?"

So she knew that the white bird was female. Avry stored that intriguing bit of information away. "I don't know what to think," he admitted.

"Wise words. I've heard it said that the only true wisdom is in knowing you know nothing."

"Then I must be unbearably wise." Their gazes met and held. Avry looked away first. "Did the white bird carry you here?"

"I carried myself here."

"Ah." Well, that at least agreed with The White's story. But it did not explain why Esperance had chosen to come to this place on her own. He considered posing the question to her directly but decided against it. Better to feel his way to the answer than risk having her clam up. The little he knew of her had led him to believe she was impulsive and unpredictable. He slid his knife back up his sleeve, dug a stick of jerky out of his pack, and tore off a bite. "We found your ruined cottage."

"Ah." She gave a slow nod. "And now you're here, looking for Mer."

"How did you guess that?"

"Because she was there. And now you're here."

Avry's lips pulled into a tight smile. He could say nothing against such logic. "Did you see what happened?"

"I saw Astrid," she said without meeting his eyes.

He swallowed his meat a touch too sharply. "Astrid. Isn't that the same girl you lost across the gorge all those years ago?"

"There's no other."

"So you got her back." His voice was tinged with wonder. "And then—what happened? Was she carried off by the bird?"

"No." A wing dropped, like a heavy word, into her lap. "Astrid carried Mer off."

Avry's mouth slackened. He stared uncomprehendingly at her bent head. "Are you...are you suggesting that Astrid—"

"I make no suggestions, Knight Errant."

He almost told her she must be mistaken. Astrid was too young to be The White. But then the blood drained from his face, and a cold shudder ran through him.

Astrid did not have to be The White. If Mer had been right all along about Astrid and Esperance changing into deer, if they were both shifters, then they could take shape as birds as well as deer.

The wood woman spat a bone into the corner. "I can almost hear your mind working." She chuckled. "Your friend would have pelted me with questions by now. But you...you make me want to talk. Yes, my daughter can change shape. She inherited that from her mother. And I inherited it from mine." She paused and regarded him expectantly.

Avry jolted as the meaning behind her words hit him. "Your mother is The White."

Esperance grinned. "I knew your head was working."

His hand went to his mouth and then away. Once more, he wondered if his mind was being toyed with, if any of this were true. Esperance's eyes were dark, fathomless as she met his gaze. He swallowed dryly. "Why did your daughter take Merisande?"

"I don't know, but I can guess." She picked something out of her teeth and flicked it into a corner. "Astrid came to the gorge a few weeks ago. She'd been fighting The White's call for some time, though I didn't know it then. She refused to talk to me, you see. Must have known I wouldn't go with her to see my mother. One day I brought Mer to her, hoping she would get her to talk." She sniffed and shook her head. "Poor Astrid; it was as if I'd thrown her a rope. She took it—took Mer so she wouldn't have to face The White alone."

Avry was on the verge of asking why she would not see her mother, why, in fact, The White had called Astrid to her instead of Esperance, but caution stopped him once more. There were more important questions to ask. "Is Astrid still with Mer—and with The White?"

She shrugged. "All I know is that Astrid came here. And I watch for her, as I have always done."

"Do you know why your mother wanted Astrid?"

"No."

Avry's mind raced. These new details added layers of complexity to the problem. "Who was your father?"

She turned the bat over, scraped out a fingernail of flesh, and popped it in her mouth. "That's a story and half, if you want to hear it."

"I'll hear it."

Her hands stilled in her lap, and she dropped her head back against the wall. "He was a miner when he met my mother. One of twenty men who set out hoping to find gold in the mountains. My mother showed up one night like a stray cat, crawled into his camp blanket, and lay against him. She came to him for three nights then disappeared. He never saw her again." She tore some leathery meat off a wing and chewed. Avry shook his head. If she referred to the miners sent out by King Audamar, then Esperance was three centuries old. "After that expedition, he swore off mining and became a farmer. He married a miner's daughter, and they settled into a cottage near the wood. A year later, he began seeing a pale shape in the trees. Of course, he thought it was the woman's ghost come to haunt him. His wife told him to go back to the mountain, find the woman's bones, and bury them, or he'd never have any peace. So after the planting was done, he went off to look for her.

"He found me in the place where my mother had lain with him. There was no mistaking whose child I was, with my red hair and green eyes. His hair. His eyes. But my mother was nowhere to be found, and he couldn't leave me to look for her body, so he took me home with him, and his wife raised me as her own.

"As I grew, my differences became plain. My stepmother grew fiercely protective of me, keeping me in the house even when I screamed to go out. While my father worked, she taught me the control I needed to keep hold of my shape. She was…fearless.

"When I was in my sixteenth year my mother called me to her."

"How did you know it was your mother?"

"I didn't. My father suspected it when I told him what I felt. He and my stepmother were horrified. They thought she had died in the mountains. Now they wondered if she'd died at all. He told me to go, so I went." She paused, her chest quivering as she drew breath. "Do you know The White's story, Knight Errant? You seem familiar with her name."

"I know that one of her binders compelled her to attack slaves."

"But do you know just how many she attacked?"

He shook his head and hunched forward curiously.

"Thousands. And many of them died. That event has festered in her like a putrid wound. For years, she longed to take her own life, but the binding wouldn't let her." Her voice, edged with something raw, menacing, fell like a streak of darkness between them.

Avry shuddered. "She wanted you to kill her," he guessed in a low voice.

"Yes. She thought I'd be strong enough to do it." Her jaw tightened, then her face rippled, and for an instant she let him glimpse the young woman she had been. "Imagine," she whispered, as Avry stared back at her helplessly. "It was a knife in my heart. I couldn't. Though I hated her. Oh, how I hated her." She drew another shuddering breath. "If I hadn't been so loved by my father and stepmother, I don't know what I would have done. Or become."

The lamp hissed and crackled, reacting, perhaps, to the moisture in the air. After a long pause, her voice slid once more into the icy silence. "Pain is the only thing she knows now. Pain has become her binding. She must let it go. If she does not, then one day she'll crack and loose that pain on the world."

Avry's fingers clenched around his water bottle. What could he do against pent-up misery? He had not even been successful at helping Mer through her own painful memories. "Why did she allow herself to be bound in the first place?"

Esperance found a small smile. "Love." She got to her feet then, and tossed the remains of her kill into the shadows.

Avry grasped her arm. "The White still has Mer. Will you help me get her back?"

"I cannot. But you are on the right path." She squeezed his hand. "I'm going to go out, get a breath of fresh air."

"The White's out there."

"We are aware of each other." Her mouth gave a nervous twitch. "Farewell, Knight Errant. Best of luck to you."

***

Avry left the wood woman in the darkness and trudged on.

The cavern shrank to a narrowing tunnel. Dripping echoed down it, soft and persistent.

He thought over all that Esperance had told him. Her mention of a pale shape had called to his mind the ghostly presence he had seen on the edge of the gorge. If that had indeed been The White, she must have spied the sleeping army. Yet she had not warned her binder. The significance of that fact was profound. It meant that she had allowed the attack to happen. Though she had still come to her binder's call, she had been too late to save him. She must have flown far into the mountains that night so she would not reach him in time.

For her, a checkmate.

He shook his head. Esperance spoke of her mother as if she were an animal in pain, not as she really was: intelligent, wily. Made wise by centuries of experience. If she did crack, the fallout would probably be more frightening than her daughter could imagine.

Avry set aside that worrying thought with an effort and focused on Merisande.

What could he give the shifter in exchange for her prisoner? If The White sought permission to die, then he could promise to fetch Gandel. But she would have to release Mer first. Ann was no small place, and the prince could be anywhere.

So much conjecture. He sighed and ran a hand over his eyes. *Stop thinking and just move,* he told himself. She would tell him what she wanted when the time came.

He stooped as the ceiling lowered then straightened as it soared away. The walls opened suddenly, and he staggered to a halt. His light illuminated a vast chandelier of orangey-red stalactites. Heavy drops fell from their sharpened points onto a glassy red pool. Avry tossed a stone and watched it settle on the surface. Not a pool, then, but a congealing mass of whatever seeped from the ceiling.

He considered how best to cross. The liquid occupied most of the floor. The corners appeared dry but so cluttered with piles of loose stone that they were scarcely passable. He slid the toe of his boot over the wet surface. Slippery as ice.

Clenching the lamp handle between his teeth, he lowered himself to a crouch and shimmied forward using his hands to propel him. His fingers slid over the chill fluid, which stank like a physician's medicine chest. When he was halfway across, the surface lost its firmness and yielded like soft jelly under his feet. His boots runneled through the mass until it thickened once more. At last, it ended.

As he shook the stuff off his hands, something wet trickled down his scalp. Grimacing, he ran a coat sleeve over the back of his neck, caught the drip, and chased it up through his hair. Half his sleeve was damp now, sticky. No helping it, he thought. He would not waste water on washing. Stamping his wet feet, he continued on down the tunnel.

He did not know how long he walked. There was no sense of time in the mountain. Even the temperature had steadied to an unchanging damp chilliness, as if day and night had been forgotten. His breath made white puffs in the air. A stickiness between his toes told him one of his boots had leaked. So be it. The wetness would keep him awake.

His eyelids had grown heavy. Must be the bad air, he told himself. Blinking, he pushed on.

Trust me, Avry.

A memory of the king's face leapt at him from nowhere, as though he had slipped into a dream.

Write to me. Mer, peering at him through a gloom of twilight. *I'd like to know how things go between you and the king.*

Of course. Will you write back?

A harsh sound escaped him, and he clutched at the uneven rock. Something was wrong. Was his body reacting to bad air? He took a few deep breaths then drained half a bottle of water. A little better. But not much. His head felt heavy, as if he had spent the night drinking. What would Neville say if he saw him now?

Keep moving. Where you stop, you drop.

"Thanks for obliging," Avry whispered to the memory with a half smile. He was on the floor now, his head hanging over his hands. *Get up.* Panting, he forced himself to stand.

After a few more yards, the tunnel opened into a space the size of Rose Hall. A black chasm split the floor from end to end. The walls, glistening with moisture, ascended toward a shadowy nothingness that seemed to go on forever. Avry stepped out onto a ledge, lamp hoisted over his head.

And there was the bridge.

Two ropes as thick as his thumb spanned the five-yard crack. Scattered planks sat between them, with mesh netting peeking through the gaps. If there had been a hand rope, it was gone now. Avry bent to examine the spikes that secured the bridge to the ledge. They had been driven with great force into the stone. If the rest of the bridge were as sturdy as its pegs, he would have crossed without fear, but it was as worn as a moth-eaten sheet. The wood was swollen, the ropes dark and fuzzy. He would sooner use his own rope and hook.

But not now. First he would eat a light meal and take a nap. The air smelled fresher here. It would clear his head.

He sank shakily onto the ledge and unloaded several strips of meat. The stink of the orangey-red liquid lingered in his nostrils, sullying the taste of his food. Pinching his nose would have only made it worse. Though he had wiped his hands clean, they still reeked of the stuff.

A rustling made him pause and look around. Seeing nothing on the ledge, he studied the rest of the cave, expecting to find a bat or two suspended from the rock. The bridge hung like cobweb, strands glistening in the lamplight. He chewed then swallowed sharply as a protesting creak echoed through the space.

The rope bridge went taut.

Avry shot to his feet, lamp swinging in his hands. "Don't move another step," he warned the wretched creature beginning to cross. Another fae guard, by the looks of him—though looks could be deceiving, but if this was The White, she had outdone herself. The guard's bald head protruded like a turtle's from the neck of his shabby coat. A pair of fleshy lumps were all that remained of his wings. What had become of the feathers?

The fae jabbed a finger at Avry. "You are not allowed here. Begone!" His hands fluttered over his belt, searching for a weapon that was no longer there. There came another creak, then a snap as the plank under his foot split in two. His wings flapped uselessly as he stumbled forward and found his balance on another rung.

Avry's hand closed over his mouth.

A closer look revealed breaks in several places, both in the wood and the rope. The hemp strands pulled away like burning hair, so old they shattered in silence.

The fae kept walking.

Avry jogged to the opposite side and waited breathlessly, eyes locked on the guard. When the fae was halfway across, one of the supporting ropes snapped and the bridge tilted onto its side. The guard caught the netting as he fell and clung to it like a limpet.

"Keep moving," Avry urged him. "Hurry before the whole thing goes."

Mutely, the fae hooked his arm over the supporting rope and inched toward the knight. Avry set his lamp down and crouched between the spikes. Broken planks dropped into the blackness. The fae whimpered, watching them fall. Then, all of a sudden, the far end of the bridge dropped, and the fae fell forward, still clinging to the rope. Avry seized his wrist just as the front end gave way.

It was a mistake.

The guard had somehow become tangled in the netting, so that the entire bridge hung from his body. The weight of it wrenched on Avry's arm like a ship anchor, propelling him over the edge.

The last thing he knew before his thoughts frayed into oblivion was the softness of feathers between his hands.

PART FOUR

THE DREAMING PLACE

CHAPTER 33

The upstairs hallway was hot and stuffy. Blaise's chamber door, swollen with humidity, stank when Avry put his nose to it. He straightened with a yawn and rubbed his eyes. The quiet murmur of his father's voice droned on, rising now and then when Blaise interjected. Avry might have put his ear to the crack and listened, but he could not be bothered. He would get an earful later, and probably a few well-aimed kicks, if his brother was riled enough.

He picked at a chip in the wall plaster. His stomach rumbled, but he dared not wander down to the kitchens. Blaise would expect him to wait around, and Avry would not risk his temper. He rolled up his sleeve and examined the green and purple bruise his brother's knuckle bracelet had left on his forearm. Blaise had not even been angry. *Just wanted to test it out*, he had said.

Avry dropped his sleeve and turned aimlessly. His gaze fell on the door to his father's study.

The hallway seemed to darken. His lips parted and his breathing deepened; his stomach filled with moth wings. How often had he dreamed of exploring that room? If Blaise had more than a finger's worth of curiosity, they might have snuck in together, but no amount of subtle prodding would spark his interest.

Here was a rare chance.

Before he knew what he was doing, he had crossed the space and laid his hand on the heavy brass latch. The door swung open on well-oiled hinges.

Darkness greeted him. Trembling a little, he strode to the windows and opened a shutter then turned. Warm afternoon light spilled over the graceful backs of chairs and the polished lid of a desk. Avry had glimpsed these things before. His eyes shot past them to the cabinet resting like a sleeping animal in one corner.

He paused, listening to the silence. It was now or never.

He padded over, unhooked the delicate glass doors, and drew them open. His father's collection of oddities, purchased over the years from merchants and tradesmen, lay in an orderly array on the shelves. He ran the tip of his finger over a curved tusk, the serrated edge of a spearhead. A tiny wing, lodged in yellow glass, winked at him from behind a jumble of brightly colored crystals. Avry seized the lump of glass and held it to the light.

"You're real," he whispered hollowly to the tangled bees trapped inside. He could almost see them move.

Uneasiness settled in the pit of his stomach. There was something deeply wrong, even wicked, about keeping these creatures imprisoned, forever fixed in one position. He pictured himself inside the glass, unable to move, unable to see anything but what was placed in front of him. Swallowing sharply, he pocketed the lump, closed everything up, and left the room. A drift of voices told him his father and Blaise were still in conversation. Good. It would give him enough time to free the bees.

He flitted like a shadow down the staircase and out the back door. Passing the kitchen, he approached the deserted chopping block. He cast a furtive glance around him. He had to be quick. The servants were not used to seeing him alone. Even without an ax in his hands, he would draw attention. He did not know what worried him more: being found out or being prevented from smashing the glass.

It took longer than he had expected to wrench the ax out of the block, but at last he had it, his small hands gripping the handle exultantly. He set it down long enough to retrieve the lump from his pocket and place it on the block. The yellow looked even brighter against the sun-scorched wood, the two bees even more lifelike as they tangled in their inseparable dance. A few experimental taps with the ax told him the lump was sturdier than he had supposed. He flipped the ax head around, blunt side down, took aim, and chopped.

The lump disappeared.

He dropped the ax and ran his hand over the wood. Had he misfired and knocked it off the block? He turned in a circle, eyes scouring the hard-packed earth. A glint of sunlight tugged him toward the nearby lawn. With an excited cry, he shot down, snatched the shard out of the grass, and held it up to the sky.

A single, lifeless bee looked back at him from its yellow prison. He dug a nail into its body, searching for softness, for a hint that it had ever been alive. But there was nothing. Just cold, hard stone.

A nameless surge of emotion flooded through him then, making his eyes tear. Blaise was right to hurt him. He was an idiot.

All of a sudden, the horizon tilted. The bee blurred as if it had been plunged underwater. With a sickening jolt, Avry was wrenched into a current fiercer than any wind or wave. In the instant he fought to break free, he knew himself, and the memory of what had befallen him at the bridge rushed back like blood into a numb limb.

I'm alive, he thought wonderingly. *She wanted me alive.*

The knowledge drifted with him into his next dream.

***

Astrid flicked a pebble into calm seawater and watched her face ripple and change. Her eyes bulged then thinned; her mouth vanished, only to reappear again like a wedge of overripe fruit.

She was squatting barefoot on a dock north of Aure city. A lone sailboat, wooden hide polished to a vitric sheen, was tied up alongside her. It probably belonged to the nearby lord.

She tossed in another pebble, cherishing her last moments of peace before it ended forever. *You will have no sleep, no peace, and no hope,* The White had promised. Astrid was almost beyond caring. Yet the image of the woman splayed against the crater wall would not go away. *My fault.*

The image had driven her on. In a finch's shape, she had explored the city's less inhabited outskirts, swooping through the amphitheater, weaving between cottages built into the slope of a ridge. When neatly piled stones had given way to green, sloping pasture, she had fluttered down, nestled against a sun-warmed rock, and slept.

Sometime after dark, her sensitive bird's feet were wakened by a rumble of footsteps.

Soldiers.

They turned up a road that led to some military buildings. As moonlight fell on the humped backs of their prisoners, Astrid, soaring in a wide circle overhead, gave a startled flap and wheeled away.

So the fae had been captured at last. And The White had let it happen. Was the fae king still alive? Had he gone into hiding? She wished she better understood the relationship The White had with the fae. Her mother had not elaborated on the nature of that connection. The White had called Prince Gandel "binder's heir." That would make the fae king "binder." What did that mean? And how did this new development affect her hunt for Gandel?

She tossed a frustrated cry at the moon.

Taking a foxes' shape, she trailed the soldiers to a walled fortress built on the water's edge. Her acute hearing picked up the fluttering and creaking of nearby ships sitting at anchor. Lured by a scent of grain, she shaped a brown mouse and slipped through a gap in the base of the wall. A half-dozen buildings came into view. She skittered across a walkway to the one her nose told her contained grain. A cat found her before she could squeeze inside. Changing to a larger cat, Astrid bounded away and was almost trampled under the soldiers' marching feet. The prisoners were being herded into a long, three-story building. *What other fae might be kept there?* she wondered idly. An image of the prince lying half-starved on a bed of soiled straw entered her mind.

Her paws grew slick with sweat. He might be. He just might.

She spent the rest of the night and a good part of the morning scouring every inch of stone and hay. Where she could not walk, climb, or wriggle, she flew. The fae had been divided into three rooms on the top floor of a four-story building. They had no beds, only the shared warmth of their chained bodies and dingy blankets.

A young female whimpered disconsolately at a strand of moonlight. Astrid, drawn to her despair as if it were her own, became a firefly and settled on her finger.

The tears ceased flowing, and wonder filled the female's eyes. Astrid drank it in greedily. It had been too long since she had been admired. Warmth suffused her, and her cold light shone like candle flame. After a time, the female's eyes fluttered closed and her breathing deepened. Astrid was left alone in the darkness.

Another pebble warped her reflection in the water. What shape could free her from The White? The ripples widened to glassy hills before sweeping away into nothing. She wiped her hands together and stood. One more sweep over the city, then she would consider her next move. And it had better be a good one.

***

Avry, flailing once more against the merciless grip of the current, found himself sitting at his father's dinner table, with the scent of spring lamb in his nostrils and the sweetness of brandy on his tongue.

He knew himself now; after being wrenched from one dream to the next, Mer had flitted through. The dream memory had been brief, just a snatch of conversation exchanged at a quarterly dance, but the shock of hearing the full, clear tone of her voice had jolted him back to himself. He had clung to that sound like a rope from dream to dream until he needed it no longer.

He now inhabited his younger body with quiet confidence. Not that he could control it. So far, the dreams had been fixed to specific memories, and he watched like a spectator, sometimes praising himself and sometimes cursing. He had all but given up trying to break free. Questions about the location and condition of his body, and if he were near Mer, only lasted until the next dream, then memory would sweep him up, claiming his attention and interest.

At last, his younger self raised his head and stole a glance across the table.

Merisande.

The older Avry jolted like a caught fish. She was perhaps fifteen, more girl than woman, a flower opening to the first glimmer of dawn. Her skin glowed as if lit by inner light; her lips were soft and pink. She sipped from a goblet of watered wine, her face tilted to the hearth where their fathers stood, engrossed in conversation. A lively gust of his younger self's feelings swept through him: fascination, frustration, a touch of arousal that he tidily ignored. His eyes drifted to her hands. Three scratches marred the underside of one wrist and a smudge of ink stained her thumb. His fingers tightened reflexively on the stem of his goblet. His younger self longed to break her open like a sealed pot, make her tell him where she had foraged, how she had acquired her scratches, what she had written about. But he had no clue how to get her to talk.

He studied his plate, searching for a question she might answer. Lord Piercy was ranting about war again. His opinions were as changeable as the wind, never finding a comfortable place to rest.

Avry cleared his throat. "What do *you* think?" he asked her softly. "Is it moral for a country to want to widen its borders?"

A line formed between her brows, spoiling the expression he had found so alluring. "That isn't an easy question to answer. If we lived in a perfect world, where no one lacked food and shelter, and no country vied for power..."

"But we don't live in that world."

She folded her arms stiffly across her chest. "If you throw meat to a pack of hungry dogs, they'll all fight for a piece of it. If one hangs back and waits for the others to be polite, that dog will starve, and its body will provide food for the others."

There was a silence. Avry breathed slowly through his open mouth. *She sounds*, his younger self thought, *a lot like my father.* "So your argument is that in some circumstances moral values can and must be pushed aside."

"They are now, every day. For instance, most would agree that murder is wrong, yet people are hung for stealing horses. Is the one who delivers that punishment a murderer? Lying, too, is considered morally objectionable, yet people lie all the time. If your father had asked me if I enjoyed the meal, I would have said yes, I did indeed. But that would have been a lie because I hate lamb, and the carrots were overcooked."

At that, he could not stop himself from laughing. He felt a swelling of affection for her, enjoying her bluntness. The older Avry was not so amused. She was plainly trying to turn him off her. That line about dogs eating each other had been particularly telling.

"What?" she demanded. "Do you find me funny?"

"It *was* funny." He fingered the rim of his goblet then looked up to find her brows drawn, her lips a thin line. His head sank. Why did she get so easily offended? This was from both Avrys. "You never answered my question," he muttered.

She replied without looking at him. "It depends on the situation. Few things are black-and-white."

"True."

He swirled his brandy, hoping, waiting. Politeness dictated that she would ask his opinion in turn. But she did not. She did not care at all. All he had done was irritate her. Could he do or say anything that did not rub her the wrong way?

These thoughts came from his younger self. The older self pondered what may have provoked her dislike in the first place. His brother came to mind. Reliving certain memories had given Avry a new and unpleasant perspective.

A loud creak wrenched him from his grim contemplation. Mer had shifted in her chair or perhaps shifted the entire chair so that she faced him. He could not be sure which, since his younger self had not looked up from his cup. Stranger still, no thoughts or emotions trickled through for the older Avry to evaluate. Though his eyes were open, it was as if he slumbered.

Mer cleared her throat. "What do *you* think?"

***

"It depends on the situation. Few things are black-and-white."

"True."

If Mer had teeth to grind, she would have gnashed them down to nothing. Her younger self (a girl no longer) was a willful, condescending brat who would rather soil her reputation than engage the neighbor's son in polite conversation. Avry was a bad smell to her, a punishment inflicted on her by conspiring parents. She did not wish to breathe the same air as him, never mind share a meal.

She flicked a glance at him.

He was frowning into his cup, letting a clump of unruly brown hair tumble over his eyes. Her mouth tightened in annoyance. Was he dissatisfied with her answer?

No, the older Mer thought, he was simply unhappy because she had not been interested enough to ask for his opinion. And it would only get worse as the evening progressed. She had a vague memory of that night, of Avry struggling, like a ship through violent waters, to carry a conversation.

It would be a torment to relive it.

Then don't.

The words whispered through her, raspy and dry. They drifted up from the older Mer, the damaged Mer. Darkness clung to them like cobweb, because nothing inside her remained bright. And yet...

And yet they were powerful.

Could she change it? She longed to finally break out, to take charge. She could not alter the past, but perhaps she could change the memory or at least stop herself from having to relive it.

I can, she thought fiercely, and pushed with all the strength she had, every bit of herself that she had stolen back from her long march of dreams.

It was like shoving a chunk of wood underwater. The younger Mer sank inch by inch, until at last she dipped under the surface, unable to reemerge. The older took a tentative breath and smiled radiantly. Everything felt more vibrant: the firmness of the chair under her bottom, a lingering smell of rosemary. It was beautiful.

She wrenched her chair straight. "What do *you* think?" she asked, wanting to cry at the vibration her voice made in her throat.

The sounds in the hall receded. Even the chatter of their fathers dampened, as if they spoke from a great distance.

Would he answer? Could he?

She willed him to speak.

***

He did not recall this. In all the years they had dined together, she had never once asked for his opinion.

The stillness lingered in his younger self's mind, as though he drowsed. In fact, the entire hall had quieted. Even his father's voice had trailed to silence. Avry, unable to see beyond the empty plate of food, gave his younger self a tentative push.

It was like thrusting at an open door; with a sudden lurch, he tumbled fully into his fifteen-year-old's body, stunned by his newly acquired mobility.

His chest rose as he drank in a breath. It felt so good to be able to move again. He did not know how it had happened, or why, but an improvement in faculty was never a bad thing. It might even help him resist the tide that dragged him from dream to dream. To break free.

"Avry?"

He drained his brandy, set his cup down, and met her eyes.

An exquisite expression had stumbled into her face. Her green eyes sparkled with anticipation; her lips were slightly parted, as if she held her breath. His younger self would have melted like heated butter under that regard.

Avry offered a cautious smile. Was this person his mind's making or a vision of The White's?

Did it matter? For the moment, he was trapped there. He could do worse than be stuck across the table from a dream shape of Merisande.

She waited for him to speak.

"I'll go with your answer," he said, and she gave a faint nod.

Neither moved for a time. Avry rested his palm over his bare wrist where the band would have sat. Soon, he promised her.

***

Mer studied Avry bemusedly.

He was slender and hunched, as if days of reading had fixed him into a curved letter. His jaw line was soft and boyish, his skin sea-foam pale. He did not yet need to shave.

She shook her head. In two years, he would undergo a complete transformation.

"This is a vivid dream," he said, startling her. The same thought had just skittered across her mind. She hoped he would do more than just echo her thoughts.

"It's very real," she agreed. "I've had dreams I thought were real, but this…"

"Which dreams?" he asked idly. "Tell me one."

That was better. She propped her chin on her thumb. "My most vivid ones happened years ago, when I had a fever. There was one…" Her eyes narrowed as she strove to recall the details. "I was in the wood with my father, collecting honey. The bees were all around us, buzzing in our ears and on our clothing. And then they attacked. I woke, still feeling them in my hair and against my cheek. They were everywhere, and then nowhere." She pushed her empty plate aside to make room for her arms. "What about you?"

He sighed and tossed a hand over the back of his chair. "My most vivid dreams were always of you."

"Ah." She ran a finger over the rim of her goblet. "Tell me one. The most vivid dream you recall."

He flashed her an amused smile. Then his eyes lifted to the ceiling and his face darkened, as though he glimpsed death in the shadowy rafters. "Once I dreamed that I found your body in the snow, curled against a tree. The air was bitterly cold, but somehow I knew you weren't dead." His head tilted, remembering.

Mer was spellbound. Even at fifteen, he had an intensity that she recognized she had been consciously pulling away from for years, as if it might shred her like wind dispersing fog or consume her in a blinding surge of light. She was amazed at how well she had reenvisioned him.

"And then?"

He drew a breath. "Then I cut the frozen clothes off you and wrapped my coat around your body. But still, you did not revive. So I ripped your stiff hair off the tree bark and held you against my own body. Gradually you began to warm, and you clung to me, shaking. I opened my coat and wrapped it around both of us so that we were skin to skin. You were still so cold, but you were warm inside as I made love to you."

Mer stared at him, hardly breathing. The image his words conjured crashed into her with unexpected force. She envisioned an older Avry in the dream, the knight with his muscled arms and callused hands.

"I felt terrible the next morning," he went on obliviously, "when I remembered that I had molested you while you were half-frozen."

She swallowed dryly. "Did it feel good?"

"Of course. It felt wonderful."

Now she did not merely see the scene in her mind—she felt it. His warmth, inside her. His heat. And for the first time, she wanted it, and wanting it, she understood it.

She drained her cup with trembling hands. "Did I waken?"

He regarded her for several moments before answering. "Not then. But you will." His fingers clenched around his wrist, as though he held her there.

Was she truly imagining this, or was The White toying with her, using her memories of Avry to create an entertaining puppet? Or...

Her back went arrow-straight. What if The White had captured him, and she and Avry were together somehow, connected in their minds?

She rejected the thought immediately. It was too far-fetched. There had to be a more rational explanation.

Avry regarded her curiously as he scratched his chin.

Mer's heart stilled at the gesture. Avry had not scratched his face that way at fifteen. The habit had developed later, when a day's worth of scruff could catch under his fingernails.

"What are you thinking?" he murmured.

She found her voice with an effort. "I think this conversation is real."

His hand froze. Mer shoved both plate and cup aside and bent toward him. "Where were you when you fell asleep?"

Avry's mouth worked; finally, something came out. "I didn't. I was searching for you in the mountain and The White entrapped me..." He halted, shocked perhaps by the look on her face.

Mer stood abruptly. Her chair made no sound as it hit the floor. The crashing of her heart was all she could hear. "Then this is no dream." Dizziness struck her then, and for the first time, she felt the strands tying her to the dream prison fray. "Avry."

The name came out in a whisper.

CHAPTER 34

Mer stared at Avry across the shadowy table. Then a black wave rolled over her, and she felt a sickening lurch. The candles flared and flickered out. The table fell away into some dark maw in the floor. Something firm was at her back. She tried to whimper, but no sound came out.

The world was black. She could not open her eyes. Her entire body was stiff and confined. She felt so sick, so weak and dizzy. All the power she had gathered was gone. While she felt stone under her feet, she could not be sure if she were upright or flat on the ground. She wriggled her fingers. Something—a crust or shell—coated them. Coated everything. Her arms were pinned to her sides; shifting them even a little taxed her strength. She worked at moving her facial muscles, wincing at the pinching and cracking of whatever encased her. All the while, she continued flexing her wrist, harder and harder, until something snapped—whatever had fixed her hand to her side. She redoubled her efforts, jerking her arm against gummy strands that were buried in the crust. Chunks dropped off her, leaving her stunned skin bare and cold. She struggled on, breath wheezing out of her mouth and nostrils, until with a final snap, her left arm came free.

She touched her cheek and wanted to retch. With excruciating slowness, she picked the broken crust off her face and neck. The chunks were stiff on the outside, and slick, almost slimy, where they had lain against her skin. If a shard fought with her, it was usually because it contained one of the many tough little strands that pinned her to the stone wall at her back. She longed for a rag. Her hand trembled as she mopped slime off her eyelids and nostrils.

At last, face bare and head free, she blinked her sticky eyes open and peered around in the gloom.

The curved wall of the crater swam into view. She was fastened in an upright position into a crevice. Only a handful of feet stood between her and the ledge surrounding the pit. A steady hammer of drips fell from the ceiling, tapping her arms and the back of her head. She could not tell whether it was dawn or dusk.

As she reached across to free her other arm, a wisp of sunlight illuminated a second body, shoved right up against her right side. The shock made her stomach heave, and for several moments she fought another surge of dizziness. As her vision cleared, a familiar figure took shape out of shadow and light.

Avry.

He had not been there long. His crust was thinner and did not reach past his thighs. Silvery strands wrapped around his legs, securing him to the wall like a cocoon. A few of his strands extended to her legs, binding her and Avry together.

Mer dropped her head back against the wall. She had no time to untangle the mass of emotions he wrought in her just by being there. Both of them needed to break free, and soon. It taxed her too much to remain awake. Every drop that fell from the ceiling was like a boulder weighing her down. Her nose was full of the wretched smell. Even her breath reeked of it, as if she had drank it in bucketfuls. She tried to nudge Avry, but her right arm was still confined, and she could barely touch him with the other.

Suddenly, she just had to get free. She tore wildly at herself, snapping threads and ripping crust off in handfuls. She found the edge of her dress and pulled. A terrible sucking noise echoed over the rock as the fabric, engorged with goop, came way from her chest.

Her knees buckled. Without the strands holding her to the wall, she had little strength to stay upright. But if she went down, she would stay down. Her eyes drooped. Snatches of memory flitted through her mind like colored shapes.

"Avry," she breathed, longing for her strong, clear voice. She grasped his arm and pulled, using her weight as leverage. Strands snapped one by one until his arm hung free. Mer gave the underside of his wrist a sharp pinch.

She was rewarded with a hiss of indrawn breath.

"Avry, wake up." His arm stiffened, muscles flexing under her hands. Broken words dribbled from his glistening mouth. She swiped crust off his cheek with a shaking hand. "What did you say?"

"Are you all right?"

Her mouth opened, closed again. His first thought was for her safety, though he was blind, disoriented, and probably dizzy. She leaned her forehead into his shoulder, grateful he could not see her face.

"Mer..."

"I'm fine," she lied. "Try to free your other arm."

In a short time, he had freed his whole body. His eyes, rubbed clean, widened as they fell on Mer.

"Do I look that bad?"

He grimaced. "Probably no worse than I do."

She turned her hand into the frail light and winced. Her skin looked boiled. It was puffy, shriveled, and blotchy, like she had been melting.

A drip from the ceiling spattered on Avry's forehead. He mopped it off with the back of his hand and threw it a disgusted glance. "We have to get out of this crevice and find a way home."

There *was* no way home. No tunnel out of the crater, just steep, encircling walls and the pit at their feet. If Astrid was still around, they could enlist her help, but if not, they were stranded. Their only egress would be in the talons of a giant white bird. "It would be nice," she sighed.

Avry took a cautious step toward the edge of the pit, swayed drunkenly, then took another. Mer watched with her heart in her throat. He halted at the corner of the crevice and peered around. "There's no one else here," he said. His head tilted down. "The ledge is thin, but it widens quickly. If we can brave it, then…ah." He flashed her a hopeful smile. "My pack and jacket, and if I'm not mistaken, your jacket. Do you see them there, on the wider ledge?"

"Not from here," she said tightly, grinding her fingers into grooves in the stone. She was loathe to tell him how weak she was, that she could not walk with him on the ledge. Could they remain in the crevice a little longer? If only she were not so comfortable with the temperature. The air from the pit hung in the space like a warmed breath. It would be colder outside.

"Mer…" He drew her hand gently from the rock. "Squeeze my hand, it'll keep us both awake."

Their fingers intertwined and tightened. Mer breathed shallowly as she observed them, marveling at how well they fit together. Like broken pieces of the same shell.

What a thought to have at such a moment.

"Can you walk?"

"No."

"It's only a little ways." He crouched down and hefted her arm up over his shoulders, taking some of her weight.

"Avry…" Her breath hitched.

"What?"

"Nothing." She wanted to tell him there was no way out of the crater but could not form the terrible words.

He took a tentative step, half-dragging her with him. "Is this all right?"

"Yes. But the ledge is narrow."

"There's enough space. Stay close and we'll be fine."

They turned the corner and crept forward, heaving against the wall. Avry, perhaps sensing the severity of her weakness, slid his arm more securely about her waist and gripped her so hard that only her toes grazed the ledge. Warm steam curled like smoke around her legs; it smelled almost as bad as the orangey-red drops.

Reaching the groove where she and Astrid had huddled, they both collapsed.

Avry's eyes closed, and he shuddered as he fought to catch his breath. Mer hesitated, then slid her fingers through his and squeezed. *For wakefulness.*

***

Gandel, armed with his jeweled knife and a week's supply of rations, turned onto Aure's north road and strode with a brisk step toward his fate.

After leaving the field, he had returned to Malborne and collected what was owed him. He did not want to be left stranded on account of a lack of coin. By midday he had flagged down a wagon carrying casks of brandy and offered the driver an amount he could not refuse. The last of his coin had vanished into the pockets of a gnarled sea captain who had been charged with carrying messages to and from Aure.

All the while, The White's silent cry had thundered through him, full of peaks and swells. He had caught sleep in snatches and ate cautiously to avoid biting down on his tongue.

Even the quiet moments did not belong to him.

Though he told himself he had nothing to do with them, his people's welfare lay like a coiled snake in his mind. Had the king of Aure rounded them up and killed them, or had he taken them prisoner? Or—and this was his worst fear—had his letter failed to reach the king, and his father, rather than die from assassination, succumbed to natural causes, leaving the fae to proliferate in the wood?

Nothing to do with him.

He stroked the knife blade through layers of fabric and imagined the silence it would bring. A bit of blood, then peace. The White's pain would die with her, and he would be freed. His mouth softened, and he cast a weary smile at the rising sun.

He was unprepared for the fierce hand that clamped down on his wrist. He stumbled back, catching his balance by a hair. At the same time, he twisted his arm, hoping to wrench himself free, but the grip only tightened.

When he finally spied his attacker, his face went slack in shock.

A slender blonde girl stood calmly at his side. Memory stirred as he met her watery blue eyes, but he could not connect it to a face.

She sucked in a breath. "You will either come with me willingly or unwillingly. But you will accompany me to The White."

Gandel jerked back as if struck. The name, uttered so carelessly, crackled in the air like dry lightning. "And who are you?" he demanded.

"I am the white doe you spied in the wood outside Thorsault."

Yes, that was where he had glimpsed those eyes. But who was she? Not The White. He still sensed distance in the bond.

The girl's gaze had wandered toward the inland sea. "I've seen your folk. They are imprisoned in some military buildings by the water."

His curiosity about her dissolved in an instant, and the coiled snake raised its head and flicked out a forked tongue. "And how are they being treated?"

She averted her eyes. "How do you think?"

He drifted closer then wheeled away, yanking at her hand.

"Gandel—"

"Whatever you saw," he spat, "imagine worse. Imagine the very worst. That is what my people would do if the tables were turned."

He did not hear her reply. The cry surged again through his tattered bond, punching into him until he could barely stand. He stooped over her arm, his eyes squeezed shut.

An eternity seemed to have passed before it weakened. He lifted his stiff face from her arm and was startled to find tears in her eyes.

"The sooner you reach her, the better you will feel," she said gently, as if from experience.

He was beyond caring. His voice was dull as he spoke. "I'll reach her sooner on my own. Get out of my way." He jerked on his hand then almost tumbled to the ground as she let him go. A thought occurred to him as he strove to find his balance: why was he journeying to the mountains at all when he could just call The White to him, in any shape he liked?

A blast of air struck him then. He had less than a heartbeat to register it before something firm clamped around his middle. The sound of wings filled his ears, scraped like a blade against his heart. He thought he would never miss them, but as the ground gave way under his feet and he lurched into the sky, the place between his shoulders twitched to life, wanting.

The desire lasted only a moment, then anticipation took hold of him. The distance between himself and The White was rapidly closing. The doe-girl, transformed into a bird, arrowed toward the mountains. Gandel's heart flung ahead of her, and the tired strand connecting him to The White buzzed to life. But this time, the call was his.

The end would be his, too.

***

Mer and Avry hunched into their buttoned jackets. Mer's skin itched where her jacket grazed it. Unable to stand it any longer, she undid the top buttons and drew her hand across her sore chest. She sensed his eyes and tossed him a curious glance. "What is it?"

"Nothing. Just that you are here. With me. Alive. I almost wonder…" His mouth snapped shut, and he coughed into his hand.

"What?" She tilted her head and forced him to meet her eyes.

"Never mind."

"You can't say something like that and expect me to leave it."

A fond smile tugged on his mouth before it straightened. "The White takes many forms," he said cautiously. "Even human."

"You think I might be her?"

A pause. "No."

Mer gave a nervous hiss of laughter. "You do. You don't trust that I'm me."

His blotchy face reddened.

She felt a yawn building and quenched it. "Ask me something she wouldn't know."

"I don't need to—"

"Ask me. If nothing else, it will keep us awake."

Avry tugged weakly at the strings of his pack then dropped his hands and lay back against the rock. "What gift did I give you when we last parted?"

"A book you transcribed. One I never got around to reading."

"Ah." His hand, resting on his stomach, sank a long time as he breathed out.

Relief, she thought dryly.

He made another grasp for his pack strings. "We can't linger here. I have rope and a hook. If there's no way out, then I could try scaling the wall…"

"Do you have the strength for that now?"

"No. But I will. Later." His eyes fluttered closed. "It seems hopeless, doesn't it? We don't even have a lamp."

Mer gave him a pained stare. There was Aure's future king, lying sprawled in a crater. Probably because of her. "How did you get here?" she asked.

He told her then about his ill-fated journey through the mountain. "I thought I was dead when I felt myself fall. But she caught me and brought me to you." A note of mystery crept into his voice. After a silence, he asked, "How long were you fixed to the wall?"

"I don't know. Since Astrid tore out of her mother's cabin and brought me here."

She kept them both awake by recounting the story. Avry nodded along, looking thoughtful rather than surprised. But whatever his thoughts were, he kept them to himself.

At last, he worked his pack strings open and drew out two bottles of water and a pouch of dried meat. The scent, rather than stir her hunger, made her draw back with nausea. Avry drained what was left in one bottle and passed her the second, which was nearly full.

He caught it as it slipped through her hands.

"I can't. It's too heavy."

"Can you drink a little?" He pressed it to her mouth, and she took a few cautious sips. A sudden cramp made her push the bottle away.

Avry touched her shoulder. "How do you feel?"

"Not well. I can only drink a little at a time, and the thought of eating makes me sick."

He gave a slow nod. "I think the crust was keeping you alive, nourishing you somehow. A little while longer, and it would have done the same to me." He fingered a week's worth of scruff.

Mer sighed and leaned back. "Do you think The White produces it—the orangey stuff, I mean?"

"I don't know. I've seen it in other places in the mountains, dripping from tunnel ceilings, oozing from the rock. It might be what turned her guard's minds."

"Perhaps she doesn't produce it, then. But surely the strands are hers. I wonder if she turned into a giant spider to make them."

"That's certainly possible."

After a pause, she admitted, "I almost want the crust back. I feel...wrong without it. Bare, and weakening."

He grew restless at that, his gaze flitting around the crater. "We have to find a way out of here."

"You keep saying that." Her spine stiffened. "Are the fae still on the edge of the mountains?"

"No. We killed their king and took the rest prisoner. Gandel's father no longer controls The White."

Mer sagged back in relief. Then her father and brother were safe. The thought drifted away, and she knew no more until Avry grunted like someone awakened from sleep. Mer's head jerked up.

"We can't stay here," he said for a third time.

The day was brightening. A shine of light burnished the eastern edge of the crater. There was something raw, primal about the ancient wall of curved stone. Enormous power had shaped it, and perhaps it still lingered, like a sleeping dragon curled around its treasure. "Watch the sun with me," she said.

So they did, until fire blossomed like the first dawn. She turned away and found his eyes on her, soft and repentant. "I'm sorry about what I said in the dream. I thought you weren't real, so I just... spilled out."

Her lips trembled with a suppressed smile. "You said many things."

"You know what I mean."

"About spilling out. Yes."

He stared at her incredulously then flushed from neck to forehead. Still, she would not let him off. It was too much fun. "I should've let the conversation continue. Imagine the dreams I could've pried out of you." She grinned at his discomfort then sighed as she recalled her uncle's words. She ought to remember that Avry was not hers. He could not marry the voiceless daughter of a disinherited lord. The king would not let him. To avoid unrest, Avry would have to marry into the house of Audamar.

She looked away, not wanting him to glimpse the unhappiness in her face. "It didn't offend me," she said.

A shadow fell over the crater.

Avry loosed a startled shout as a form descended like a blanket from the sky, deposited a body on the ledge a few feet away, then dwindled away to nothing. No, not quite to nothing. A white shrew skittered into a cleft in the wall.

"Astrid," Mer breathed. She was about to call the shrew back when the body on the ledge unfolded, and with the caution of someone weakened by dizziness, got slowly to his feet. A premonition fluttered in Mer's belly as he turned and looked at them.

Mer hissed out a name, one she had not uttered aloud for many months.

"Merisande." The wingless fae gaped at her. "Why are *you* here?"

She could not find an answer. Relief swelled in her throat; tears welled up behind her eyelids.

"Binder," Avry said.

The word prompted a violent twitch. Mer noticed the strain in the prince's face then. Sweat glistened on his brow, and deep circles rimmed his eyes. The binding had found him after all, even from as far off as Ann. What did he intend to do?

Gandel's head tilted, as though he scented something in the air. No, not a scent, she thought. A sound. A scratching and scraping whispered up from deep in the pit. Mer covered her ears, but it sank through her palms until her whole body itched. It ended at last with a whoosh of displaced air and a dull thud. She let her hands fall, opened her eyes, and stared.

CHAPTER 35

A fair-haired woman stood on the edge of the pit wearing a simple brown frock and black leather shoes. Something about her looks tugged at Mer's memory. Esperance. That was who she resembled. But the similarity did not extend beyond her face. Esperance was a knobby tree next to this creature, who exuded grace with every breath. She was the white doe, wild and ethereal. And she was the bird, powerful, deadly, shaped by a ragged knife of pain. Deep wrinkles fanned around her eyes and mouth, marring her otherwise youthful appearance. Something inside Mer stirred at the sight of her raw, weary eyes. *Those old bones.* Mer saw herself in them. Her own seed of pain, cracked open and laid bare.

The woman took a step toward Gandel then fell to her knees.

The action seemed to free him from thrall. His hand dove into his tunic, and out came a large, jeweled knife. The woman sucked in a breath. Emotion blazed in her face, then her eyes squeezed shut and she flung her head back, baring the smooth column of her throat. "Please."

Gandel readied his knife.

Mer froze. A terrible pressure built in her chest. If she could scream, she would have. Despite what The White had done to her, her whole being protested what Gandel was about to do. She felt like *she* were the one kneeling there, neck ready to accept the bite of the blade.

"Do it," The White said.

The knife shook; sunlight sparked on its jewels, flicking color onto the ledge. Gandel hesitated. The White must have sensed it, for her face blurred, like water contorted by waves, and something hideous took shape: her lips crumpled; her skin bulged and sagged, gathering in her neck like a cock's wattle. She raised bulbous, beseeching eyes to him, and begged for the death owed a suffering creature.

The knife steadied. Gandel's lips firmed, and his arm stiffened to strike. Mer, unable to watch, threw her hands into her face and loosed a voiceless moan. She could not explain why this felt so horribly wrong. The woman had agreed to it. Did she not have the right to end her pain? More than once, Mer had desired the very same thing.

There was a clatter of metal.

The knife, Mer thought, falling, bloodied, to the floor. But a peek through her splayed fingers revealed it was not so. Gandel had not slaughtered The White. Instead, he had tossed aside his blade and dropped to his knees beside her. He reached a hand behind her head and brought her chin forward. There was a helpless fury in his eyes. "I can't."

She gave no response. Her lids remained tightly closed, as if she still believed he would do it.

No one would willingly caress such a face, and yet that was exactly what he did. Cupping her head with one hand, he ran the other down her cheek, across her forehead, along the bridge of her nose to her mouth and chin. He smoothed away the ugliness until no trace of it remained.

The woman's eyes opened at last, and they regarded each other hopelessly.

***

Gandel's father had never warned him of this. Nothing, either in writing, or in conversation with his forebears, had hinted that this disaster could happen.

The moment The White came to stand at his side, it felt like a lid had slammed down over him. The vast ocean of The White's pain swallowed him, became him, so that he could not disentangle himself from it. She was him, and he was her. They were one.

That was bad enough. That alone would finally have stopped his hand, for he was unable to kill himself.

But then, those eyes...

They reached into him like an old lullaby, something the bones remembered, even when the mind did not. He had not met those eyes before, and yet something in him jerked awake at the sight of them. An imprint, perhaps, from generations of bindings. He could have fallen forever into those eyes. His hands ached to touch her and to keep touching, no matter what shape she took.

He wrenched away from the feeling, wrenched away from her gaze so that a hair's breadth of distance stood between them. He stared at his trembling hands, not knowing what to do, wanting death because she wanted it. Unable to walk away, because she wanted him there.

A soft breeze touched him, and he glanced up at the crater rim. Somewhere, across thousands of miles of ocean, lay the land of his ancestors. The White's presence made it seem closer, for she had been birthed there.

"Home," he heard himself say.

"Hethare?"

"Yes," he whispered. "That home."

A touch of longing moved through him. *Mine or hers?* he thought. Then, *Does it matter?* He gripped her arm. "Let's go back, take what's left of my people, and just go."

"Do you think they'd fare better in Hethare?"

"I don't know. They're imprisoned now. There, at least my own people can judge them."

"And what of our binding? How will they judge that?"

He forced himself to meet her eyes squarely. Once more, the warm feelings coursed through him, confusing his thoughts. He swallowed tightly. "We'll have to destroy it."

He did not believe they could. But if the prospect made her hope, then at least he would not have to endure the blast of her torment any longer.

"Destroy it." She regarded him with parted lips. "We can't."

He ran a finger along her chin. "Don't say can't. Not when we haven't tried."

She did not pull away from his eyes. In the building silence, the hope he waited for trickled in, until it overwhelmed all other feelings.

It terrified him. For in an instant, he knew that if they failed to do what he had promised, she would crack.

Her voice gained strength as she spoke again. "Then we should try it. We should try it now."

***

"Now..." Gandel breathed.

Avry had stiffened, and Mer wondered if he would interrupt the conversation to protest the prince's demand, but he remained fixed where he was. What could either of them do against such a creature anyway, weakened as they were?

"Now," The White said. "If we succeed, then I'll do as you ask, but out of my own free will."

Gandel's chin rose, and Mer shuddered at the fear and hope in his eyes.

He reached behind his neck and untied a string that had been concealed under his tunic. A pair of wheel-shaped stones emerged, their faces joined as tightly as clasped hands. One of them had graced Mer's throat for nearly a decade. He upended them onto his palm. "My father gave me these, years ago. They belonged to Genningas. I kept them to remember the place my people came from. They are yours now." When she did not move to take them, he pressed them into her palm.

Light flashed as the woman pulled them apart and placed one into his hand. Her fingers closed on the other. "Nir imen, Gandel."

Murmuring a reply, Gandel rose and stepped back several feet, as though his proximity to her made breaking the binding more difficult. Their eyes locked then, their fists tightened, and they both began to tremble.

Time slowed. Beads of sweat gathered on the prince's brow. His breathing turned harsh, ragged. His lips drew back, revealing tightly clenched teeth. Mer hardly noticed when Avry dug her hand out of her sleeve and gripped it with sudden fierceness, as if they were both about to tumble off a precipice.

Gandel's disembodied voice, welling like steam from the pit, made them both flinch. "Let it go," he pleaded. "Please. Please let it go..."

A grimace of pain contorted The White's features. Her hair shook as she trembled. She sucked in a breath. As she loosed it, light flashed between gaps in her closed fingers and then died. They both cried out. Their voices, blending, echoed over the curved stone walls. Gandel's eyes lost focus, and he swayed to the ground.

The White did not move to help him. She had turned into a statue of herself. Only her face moved, like ice splintering on a still pond. A sound quivered behind her closed lips, gradually built until her mouth opened, and burst out. The shout, which seemed a blend of pain and joy, was scarcely human, yet it sang through Mer's bones like a familiar chord. As it trailed to silence, the woman's face cleared, and she rose on steady legs to her feet. A memory of power glittered in her eyes. The sky arched above her, a pale cyan darkening to navy. It was another kind of sea, Mer thought, one navigated by wings instead of fins. Wind stirred the woman's hair. Her fingers eased open, and she regarded the broken and bloodied stone on her palm.

She smiled. Such a smile. Mer's eyes closed on tears, and a sensation of wind, of vast open spaces where sunlight danced and the air ran clear, moved through her, leaving her feeling scoured but as bright as flame. She refused to wipe her face, to make any movement at all that might distract the woman. Through a blur of tears, Mer watched her close her hand and step off the edge into the pit. There came a whooshing sound, and hot, stinking air blew into Mer's face, making her cough. Her wincing eyes opened, fixed on the prince, who was struggling to rise amid the chaos of wind and steam. The white bird shot out of the pit, plucked him up as she climbed, and vanished over the lip of the crater.

Gone. Just like that.

Mer swallowed. Her wet lips trembled with a smile that nothing could erase. Not even Avry's quizzical look. She had felt *herself* fly out of the pit, like something dead come back to life. Perhaps she *had* been dead.

Avry stirred.

"I'm fine," she snuffled, answering his question before he could ask it.

"Well, that makes one of us." He smiled wryly. "The barracks are about to receive an unwanted visit, and I've done nothing to prevent it."

A scraping sound made them both start. Just as Mer remembered Astrid, the slender youth wriggled out of a crevice, strode to the pit's edge, and looked up at the sky.

A single tear fell from her chin into the empty space.

CHAPTER 36

Ronal, guard to Barrack Block Donatien, tipped his helmet down to shade his eyes from the relentless sun.

The yard was quiet. Most of the men were in the refectory, breaking their fast. No one stirred in the block Ronal guarded. He was not surprised. The guard he had just relieved said that the prisoners had had no peace until the early hours of morning, and while Ronal had not been given details, talk was that at least one female kept the lot awake, night after night, with her whimpering. Provisions sent up to them by Commander Neville had not made a difference. The fae sobbed on mattresses now, with soft blankets to dry their faces. They should have been grateful just to be alive. Ronal judged himself an even-handed man. But even he balked at the generosity that had been shown the prisoners. Everyone knew the stories. The pubs had buzzed for months with Sir Avry's account, until it seemed to have blackened the walls. But no amount of retelling could ease the chill Ronal felt whenever he recalled the ritual that had destroyed the slaves' voices, or the hive of tiny, dank rooms the men and women had endured, separated from their loved ones, buried in stone. It was the stuff of nightmares. And yet here they were: the slave masters. Could anyone be blamed for feeling uneasy in their presence? Or less than merciful?

He hunched into his coat. A chill wind broke the morning's stillness, plucking at his warrior's tail. Sudden gales were not uncommon in Aure, and this time of year they came down from the mountains, carrying a whiff of snow instead of brine.

This smelled like neither. His nostrils flared as he sniffed. Some sort of musk, he decided. But where...?

The thought frayed. Dizziness struck him like a mallet. His vision blackened, and he felt himself fall. A wretched numbness spread over him, until he could scarcely feel his body. With a great deal of effort, he forced his eyes open.

Nothing. The yard was undisturbed. It must be him. Had he been poisoned?

The thought had barely formed when the slender legs of a man came into view. He crouched at Ronal's side, giving the guard a view of worn brown shoes. Ronal wheezed as he tried to shout. He could not feel what was being done to him. For all he knew, the man could have knifed him in the belly.

Keys jangled. Was he going to free the fae? Who was left inside to guard the prisoners? Two men, he decided. The others were breakfasting in the refectory.

He heard the familiar thud of the block's door closing, then nothing. His eyes drooped, and he drifted in and out of consciousness.

Time dissolved into a sticky sludge of shapes and color. The brown shoes reappeared as the stranger walked by, a sparrow hopping along behind him. Darkness again, then a forest of shadows marching soundlessly over the ground. Did he dream?

He must have slept, for he woke to the jab of a boot in his shoulder. Horns were sounding; booted feet clambered on the pavement. He groaned and rolled over then flinched as he met the barracks captain's deep-set eyes. Ronal made a weak attempt to salute, his hand flapping like a fish before dropping back to his side. It was over. He was ruined. Three years of training washed away like a winter's snow. He would have to find work at the docks, or worse, hire himself out to tenant farmers. With his reputation in tatters, he would never again be employed as a guard.

He waited for the captain to lean in and sniff for brandy. But the man seemed distracted, his attention torn between Ronal and the gate. "Are you able to speak?" he asked finally.

Ronal's lips wobbled. "Cap-capchan, I wash poishon—"

The captain waved his hand impatiently. "Yes. You and a score of others. Larin!" he shouted, his head swinging back to the gate. "What news?"

The runner's shadow leapt over Ronal's face. "They're nearly at the mouth, Cap'n," he said breathlessly, "with the *Marietta* and *Modeste* lagging far behind."

The captain's voice rose in consternation. "How did the bastards get there that fast? Did they figure out how to hoist the sails, work the oars?"

"The bird, Cap'n—

"Should be dead by now. Between the crossbows and ballistas..."

"Easier said than done, Cap'n. She's dragged that ship as close to the east bank as she can get without running it aground. That far off, anything that hits her won't be on mark."

Ronal fought not to smile as he lay there, slack with relief. A bird attack. Surely he would not be blamed for succumbing to the creature's poison. And he was far from alone. A score of other men...

"They'll have better aim at the mouth," the captain said.

"Talk is, Cap'n, that those at the mouth haven't been trained on ballistas. No one thought the bird would..." His words trailed as another series of horn blasts floated in the air.

"The devil's hairs," the captain breathed.

There was a lengthy silence. The booted feet on the cobbles had stilled. Only the wind spoke, tugging at flags and shutters, scattering leaves over the ground.

"Ann's patrol ships might still catch them..." the runner said weakly.

"No, Larin. The ships are too far off. She would have to run into them." The captain paused then lowered his voice to a whisper. "Perhaps we should say good riddance."

"Good riddansh," Ronal agreed, and promptly fell back asleep.

***

Mer was resigned to the fact that she would pass out. She had done so the first time Astrid had carried her over the mountains, and she had not been weakened as she was now.

So it surprised her that she held out for as long as she did. The crater rim vanished under her, and with it the last wisp of warmth. She gritted her teeth as icy wind snapped against her tender flesh. She writhed to keep herself warm, to hold back the numbness, but it crept over her all the same.

How would Avry fare? Astrid had promised to go back for him after dropping Mer at Esperance's cottage. The young woman refused to take them anywhere else, and there was no sense arguing with her.

As if Mer had conjured him with a thought, another pair of talons lowered into her line of sight. And there was Avry. A giant red wing beat down, obscuring him for an instant.

Red bird, white bird, Mer thought and found a thread of a smile on her chill face. Esperance had come.

The recognition instantly prompted another: Esperance was The White's daughter.

"Of course," she breathed. "Of course she is." Then her vision blackened, and she knew no more.

***

Mer woke, shivering at the touch of cold water on her skin. A fire crackled nearby, heating one side of her body. A cloth swiped down her arm, and she stiffened.

"Be calm, girl." Esperance's gruff voice was almost soothing. "I'm just giving you a needed bath. I'd strip the clothes off you too, if it weren't for that one."

Mer slid her arm off her face and squinted through the jumping flames to see who she meant. Avry, in the midst of rinsing his shirt, paused and regarded her shrewdly.

They were huddled around Esperance's fire pit. The cottage had been cleared of debris. Sunlight poured in through the open roof, casting a fuzzy halo on Avry's short, wavy hair. Astrid squatted over their jackets, setting them over piled wood so that they faced the warmth of the fire. She glanced up as if she felt Mer's gaze and met her eyes.

"Thank you," Mer mouthed.

Astrid's response was to snatch up a chipped mug and scurry around the fire to Mer's side. Mer managed with Esperance's help to sit up and drink. Avry passed her some dried meat, and she chewed it slowly, rinsing it down with what was left in the mug.

No one spoke for a time. Esperance's cloth worked its way over Mer's neck, down her back, and through her knotted hair.

"You don't have to do this," Mer said at last. "You have my gratitude, but..."

"Hush, girl."

Mer, noting an odd hitch in her voice, swiveled to look at her. Her mouth fell open. Tears streaked Esperance's cheeks and gathered in the corners of her mouth.

Esperance's eyes narrowed at Mer's stunned expression. "What are you gawking at, girl?"

Mer did not know what to say. Did the wood woman grieve over the fact that her mother was gone? Or were these tears of joy? Was she happy that The White had pushed past her pain and broken free? She swallowed tightly. She felt she ought to say something. Her mouth opened then snapped shut again as Astrid crossed to her mother, knelt down, and gathered her into her arms. Esperance did not resist the hold. She did not even struggle as her daughter rocked her back and forth, smoothing her hair and cooing in her ear.

The fire rustled and snapped. Mer caught Avry's gaze and smiled helplessly. Avry, too, looked like he had forgotten how to breathe.

At last they pulled apart, and Esperance kissed her daughter's face. "Will you stay?"

She buried her forehead in her mother's shoulder. "Do we have to stay *here*?"

Esperance sighed and looked around at the ruins of her cottage. Wiping tears from her face, she murmured, "Time for a change."

CHAPTER 37

At noon, Mer and Avry gathered their things and hobbled out the cottage door. Astrid took the shape of a large white doe and waited patiently for Mer to find a comfortable place on her back. Avry flatly refused to be carried by Esperance, but she walked with him all the same, while Astrid drifted ahead, threading her path unerringly through the trees.

Mer pressed her face against the deer's warm neck and watched the flaming leaves swirl by. Her life looked back at her, clear as an image in a mirror. Every memory sparkled anew. She eyed it all from a distance, detached and flowing free. There was no pain left, no darkness. Just the world gliding by, as it would probably do for the rest of her days.

Hoofbeats thudded behind her. The red deer caught up with the white and paced her. Avry, splayed on Esperance's back, threw Mer a sheepish grin.

"I didn't want you to get there first," he said.

Mer simply looked back at him, wondering how much time they had left together.

The deer left them at the field behind Rives's cottage and slipped back into the trees.

Eager to see her father, Mer tugged on Avry's arm, and together they lurched and swayed across the stony yard.

"How are you feeling?" he asked as they mounted the front step.

"Better. I think I might even be able to walk on my own."

"Do you want to try?"

Someone must have heard Avry's voice, for the door burst open, and a red-haired youth materialized in the hazy light. As soon as he saw Avry, he dropped to his knees at his feet.

Mer was speechless. Who was this stranger, and where was her father? She peered past the boy into the smoky gloom. No Rives, no Jan.

Avry threw her an awkward glance. "This is Édouard, my squire. I arranged for him to stay here until I returned."

"Does he know where my father went?"

"Probably. I'll ask him."

She thought he would order the boy to rise, so it surprised her when he stooped down and laid a gentle hand on his shoulder. "Édouard."

"Sir, you came back."

"I said I would."

"You did, sir. You said that."

"Where are Rives and Jan?"

"Out, sir. Trapping." He lifted his head then, and regarded Avry with a face stiff from suppressed emotion. Avry's answering smile could only be called fatherly. It stunned Mer, who had not know that side of Avry existed. He had written once or twice of his squire's achievements, but ink could not contain the regard he clearly held for the boy. Her lips pursed, and she shoved down a mortifying twinge of jealousy.

"Are we leaving, sir?"

He did not seem to notice how Avry clung to the door frame to steady himself. "No, Édouard. Not today."

"It's been busy around here since you left, sir, with soldiers and trackers and the like. Would you like me to report?"

"No, not at the moment." Avry's brow furrowed. "Has there been any...activity... today?"

"Yes, sir. A runner was here at noon." A shadow stirred in Édouard's face. Anticipation? Worry?

"Out with it, Édouard."

"There's been another bird attack, sir. The prisoners escaped and stole a ship. Then The White tugged them out of the harbor like an ox hauling a plow."

Avry's mouth crooked wryly. "Is that all he said, or is there more?"

"That's all, sir. The man was in a hurry to move on." Édouard paused then slipped a scroll out of his tunic and handed it to Avry. "This came for you today. I was to hold it until you got back."

Avry took one glance at the wax seal and dropped the scroll with a hiss of inhaled air.

"What is it?" Mer asked, tilting her head as she tried to make out the image stamped into the wax.

Avry caressed it with a trembling finger then broke the seal and unrolled the letter over the door frame. Mer averted her eyes to allow him privacy. "The king is alive and lucid," he said at last.

"Did you think he was dead?"

"I—no. Not dead exactly, but not alive either."

"I see." While she searched for a suitable response, he rose with a grunt and offered her his hand.

"Did you leave us anything to eat, Édouard?"

He grimaced. "There's not much, sir. A bit of rabbit on the spit and a jug of water on the table."

"More meat," he sighed, dismissing the pitiful state of Rives's table with an easy grace. "That's all we've had lately."

"If you like, sir, I can run over to Lord Piercy's estate…"

Avry nodded. "If you can sneak into the kitchen without being seen then bring us some carrots and berry preserves, and whatever else you can lay your hands on. But mark a good place to hide before you go in. And if you're caught, make up some likely excuse. I don't want anyone to know that we're back yet."

"Yes, sir."

Mer stared at him after his squire had gone. "That was kind."

"What was?"

"The way you drew attention away from my father's table and placed it on your own preferences."

"To be honest, I was kinder to Édouard than to your father's table. The boy isn't without coin. At the very least, he could have given Rives enough to buy a few chickens. I know he wanted to be here in case I returned, but that's no excuse for not earning his keep."

She loosed a snort. "Rives would never have allowed it. I'm going to my room to change. Take some of my father's clothes if you like. They won't fit well, but at least they'll be clean." Saying that, she moved past him into the shadowy innards of the cottage, snatched up the water jug, and hauled it to her room before he could offer to carry it for her. Her improvement surprised her. Hours ago she could not have taken three steps, never mind carry a jug. She set it on the floor and shut the door soundly. Then she slipped off her jacket and soiled frock, yanked a cloth—still damp from whoever had been using it during her absence—off the lip of her wash basin, dunked it into the pitcher, and began swabbing what Esperance had missed.

The water was the color of fall leaves before she was satisfied. With an effort, she wrenched open her clothes chest and took whatever lay on top.

Clean and draped in a worn green frock, she unhooked the shutters and examined herself in the full light of day. Her skin was no longer swollen and patchy, but an even, sun-baked orange. The stain would recede, she thought. Just as the numbness had. She rubbed her hands together, enjoying the renewed sensation in her fingers.

"I saved you a leg," Avry offered as she dropped into one of the two chairs at the hearth. He must have visited the well. His hose clung wetly to his skin, and he sipped from a refilled bottle of water.

He stared at the letter as she chewed.

"Is there a problem?" she asked, tossing a bone in the fire.

"He wants me to return at once. I will, but tomorrow."

Her mouth pinched. She should, she told herself, urge him to go. The last time he disobeyed a summons, he was confined to his chamber for two months. "What will you do?" she asked hollowly.

"What do you mean?"

"He'll be angry at you."

He chuckled. "I don't doubt it."

"Then…"

"What did Rives do when you came home after running off to Thorsault?"

He had held her, weeping. "Rives is my father," she pointed out.

"And Ghislain is mine. In every way that counts."

Mer frowned. He had never mentioned that before. Was it new? Perhaps being nominated the king's successor had drawn Avry and Ghislain closer.

"What bothers me more," he went on, "is the pain I've likely caused him, the damaged trust. I left after…" His voice trailed off.

"What? After what?"

He handed her the bottle. "A lot happened while you were gone."

He told her about it while she sipped, his narration rambling off in different directions before returning, unerringly, to the root. It reminded her of his letters.

She might have followed that thought down into a bleak place if the tale had not been so riveting. Mer gripped the bottle with both hands and stared at the fire, seeing Patric's men in the flames, the gate opening to admit them, Avry chained in a cell, waiting for death. It had come too close to disaster.

"Mer…?"

Her eyes closed briefly. "Yes?"

"What are you thinking?" His tone was hesitant, as though he worried that she judged him.

"Just about how close you came to death and may do so again."

"You sound like Édouard." He scooped up the poker and nudged the charred bones into the fire. "You never told me how you felt about my appointment."

"I congratulated you."

He threw her a look that made her smile.

"You don't want my honesty," she warned. "You've never liked it."

"I want it."

"Very well." She took a long pull of water. "I was shocked and horrified."

He spat out a laugh. "That was exactly how I felt when I learned about it." He fell silent then, frowning. "So you think I would be that terrible a king."

"No, not at all." She shook her head firmly. "In fact, I can't think of anyone who would be better suited to that role, though that's not saying much."

"Then..."

"I felt as though you were being exiled to some far-off land, and I would never see you again." Friends missed each other, did they not? "Silly, I know. After all, here we are, sitting at my father's hearth."

The hand holding the poker had gone still. Had she said something wrong?

He set the tool down slowly, perched on the edge of his chair, and caught her eyes. "What is it that you feel for me, Merisande?"

His words reached in and snared her. Pressed under the full weight of his searching gaze, a part of her mind fled to a corner and keened.

She could not admit the truth.

If she confided her feelings, Avry would have to carry the knowledge of her love for the rest of his days. It would ruin him. Her throat swelled as she contemplated that. Contemplated Avry married to another woman. It was impossible. Those amber eyes belonged to Mer, as surely as if they were her own. And yet she had no right to them. To any part of him. He belonged to the kingdom. "I..."

"Just say it," he said, pain creeping into his voice. "I need to know."

His doubt was a jagged blade, twisting in her middle. If she had a voice, she would have groaned. She clapped a hand over her mouth.

"Mer—" His tone had gentled.

A tear trickled over her finger. She would sooner find her own blade and do herself in than lie to him. "I love you," she blurted, and found that she could breathe again.

Avry's mouth fell open. He stared at her speechlessly.

"You don't believe me?" she said as the silence lengthened. Frustration seeped into her. It had cost her so much to admit the truth. He could at least acknowledge her feelings.

The door creaked open then, and her father entered with Jan in tow. Catching sight of her, Rives dropped a partridge and brace of rabbits onto the table, crossed the room, and dragged her into his arms. He smelled of the wood and fresh autumn air. Mer hugged him back weakly while Jan patted her arms, making excited sounds in his throat.

"Are you all right?" Rives murmured into her hair. "You don't seem hurt…"

She had not framed a reply when the door opened again, and Édouard's plaintive voice gusted toward the hearth.

"I'm sorry, sir, but I couldn't filch a single thing. I waited a long time, but the kitchen's crawling with folk smoking and bottling, and…" His voice faltered on an odd note.

Mer twisted to look at Avry's face, wanting to see what Édouard saw, but the knight suddenly lurched out of his chair, stumbled to the table, and snatched up the rabbits. "I'll skin these," he offered hastily, his face averted.

Rives's reply was muffled by the sound of the door closing.

A silence fell. Édouard's mouth hung open gracelessly. He took a step toward the door and halted. "What happened? What's wrong with him?"

Mer turned to Rives. "Did you see his face?"

"I only saw that he was here. Then I saw you and nothing else mattered." *You are still all that matters,* his eyes said.

Édouard collapsed into a chair by the table, still staring at the door, as though his master might come charging through at any moment. Mer, feeling an urge to busy herself with a task, left the warmth of the fire and her father's arms, grasped the partridge by its twiggy legs, and hauled it to the pantry to be plucked. As always, Jan knelt beside her and tried to help. He played with the feathers he plucked, brushing them against his cheeks and lips, enjoying the soft texture of the down. Mer had buried herself in his world so completely that she jumped when Rives touched her arm.

"Mer—"

"Let me be," she begged. "Please."

There were a hundred questions in his eyes, but he forced them all down—as he always did, Mer thought—and wandered off.

The bird had been plucked, cleaned, and put in a pot before Avry graced them again with his presence. Mer, kneeling at the hearth, stirring pickled turnips into the pot, did not turn to look at him. She listened to the murmur of voices, to her brother's soft sounds behind her, and all the while she watched the fire, begging it to burn away her thoughts. She stiffened as the floor creaked behind her, but whoever it was said nothing.

She could not avoid him at dinner.

Rives had asked Avry to stay the night. He and Édouard could sleep by the hearth, he said. Just move the chairs, throw some blankets down, and they would be snug and warm. He chattered as he ate, filling Avry in on the latest gossip, which he had picked up from visitors who dropped by to speak with Édouard. Avry nodded vacantly to Rives while his eyes strayed to Mer's as if they had been calibrated that way. The look he gave her left her breathless and unsteady. She had often felt his intent gaze throughout the years, but this was different. This time he held nothing back.

Rives reiterated what Édouard had said about the bird attack, hoping perhaps that Avry would confide what had happened in the mountains. Avry dropped a few words here and there, but his retelling was punctuated by long, distracted silences, and after a while Rives simply let him be.

Mer should have kept her feelings suppressed. Once loosed, she could not call them back. Tomorrow Avry would return to the city and continue his life. Would he beg the king to let him court her? She imagined the pain he would feel when Ghislain refused his request. The subject of marriage might arise naturally then, and

Avry would be faced with the prospect of being bound to someone he did not love.

The thought of him marrying another sent her reeling into a darkness she could not come up from. She slid out of her chair, turning away before anyone had time to respond, and took her plate to the fire to scrape her leavings into the pot.

Avry's voice behind her, soft as a coal rustling in the grate, made her flinch. "We need to talk."

"Yes. I know."

"When?"

She pushed a hand across her eyes. "I don't know. I don't even know if I want to." He said nothing after that, but she still felt him there: a warm breath, a steadiness at her side. Suddenly she became aware of the crashing of her own heartbeat. Her dry lips parted, and she caught his gaze. "I'll come to you later," she said. "When everyone is asleep."

***

Rives, aware, perhaps, of how weary Mer was, tucked Jan in earlier than usual. Jan whooped when he discovered that his father would sleep in the same room with him again. Édouard had occupied Rives's bed while Avry was away, and Rives had slept in Mer's.

His familiar scent had permeated her covers; it was the smell of home, of companionable silences by the hearth on winter days, of riddles flung across stacks of cut logs. She lay on her back in the darkness, breathing in his smell, and gradually her tight muscles relaxed and her pounding heart stilled.

She would not allow herself to think. Instead, she drew on her brother's ability to focus entirely on the moment. The future did not exist for him; the here and now was all there was.

Her lips curled ruefully. Actions had consequences, as Jan had once so aptly demonstrated when he loosed the bull that charged across Lord Piercy's field, causing a score of sheep to leap to their deaths over the gorge. And so...

She did not have the answer.

The house was quiet. It was time. She dragged in a steadying breath then flung off the blankets, padded to the door, and opened it just enough to let her slide through. Stepping over the cranky floorboard, she tiptoed to the hearth where Édouard and Avry lay side by side. The squire snored softly, his body curled toward the grate, in which a low fire still burned. Avry shifted at her step then drew off his blanket and sat up. She knelt in front of him. Neither spoke. Was there anything to say? The air was warm, and she felt herself drift toward him. Then, as if it were the easiest, simplest thing in the world, their lips met and clung. Her hand slid behind his neck; his flowed across her shoulder blades and up through her unbound hair. Heat flooded her then, and she could not get close enough. Her weakened muscles strained as she surged against him. His breath was warm against hers; his lips teased her with an infuriating gentleness, brushing, tasting, gently prodding. She scarcely knew herself when he drew away.

"Could we go outside?" he begged in a breathless whisper.

They tugged on their boots and tiptoed out the door. Avry guided her around to the back. The moon was bright and round, showering his face with soft light. Mer did not feel the cold, and neither, she guessed, did Avry. His warm hand trembled against her cheek as he found her lips again.

They reeled against the wall, tangling, untangling, devouring each other with mouths and hands until, with a suddenness that left her gasping, he stopped and pulled away.

"How are you?" he asked.

Words. She did not need words. "Fine." She quested for his mouth again, but he evaded her.

"You still smell like the crust."

She choked out a laugh. "Is that why you stopped?"

"No, of course not." His breath tickled her ear. "Marry me."

She jerked back with a sharp intake of breath. "What? Can we?"

"We can. We will. Tomorrow."

"Tomorrow!"

"Yes. That would be best."

"You wish to elope?"

"Not exactly." He captured her face in one of his callused hands. "You'll have to trust me."

He fell silent, looking at her—still waiting for an answer, she realized. She strove to gather her thoughts. "My father would be left alone with Jan. In this house."

"That would have to change. He couldn't keep living this way, even if he wanted to. Once he becomes my relation, abandoning him to poverty would appear an intentional act."

"Yes. I can see that." She fingered the wispy hair at the nape of his neck. "I thought the king would force you to marry someone else. A woman from Ann or Audamar..."

"Knowing that you loved me? I'd sooner flay myself alive." He paused, frowning. Was he remembering the fact that Ghislain had married his own daughter off to the Prince of Ann, despite her protests?

"I didn't think you'd have a choice," Mer said.

"It's not a matter of choice. I couldn't pledge vows to a woman while loving another. The words wouldn't come out of my mouth. Even if the king demanded them."

"That may be. But the king could prevent you from marrying me."

A trace of a smile breezed across his lips, as if he welcomed the challenge. Mer's head tilted. For an instant, she thought she grasped the essence of his relationship with Ghislain, but then it floated off like a errant sunbeam, and she felt herself caught up instead in Avry's heady enthusiasm. Anything seemed possible just then. He made it so. "I trust you."

Was that an answer?

Avry's mouth straightened. "Your life won't be easy, Mer. Everything will change. Things you took for granted will be gone: your freedom, your privacy, your liberty to be yourself. You will feel closed in and in danger. Always. And these things will never go away. They will become your life, and you will have to find your stroke or drown."

Warmth deserted her as he spoke. She found herself enclosed by cold stone. High walls. Whispering voices. There were no trees; the wind tugged on banners instead of branches. "That will be your life, too."

"Yes. It *is* my life."

"Then it'll have to be mine. I can't stay here and let you live like that alone. It would cut me to the quick."

"Mer…" He shook his head and cupped her face in his hands. "I had no idea you felt this way. You stopped writing me…"

She sighed. "I did. And for all the wrong reasons." She winced inwardly as she thought back to her conversation with Thierry at the quarterly, all the spiteful rumors spread by Audamar…

"What reasons?" he asked cautiously.

"Never mind. I don't want to talk about it now." She tugged away his hands and held them. "Avry, are you sure we'll be able to marry? You once told me that Ghislain views everyone as chess pieces, each with an assigned value. I don't think he'd consider this a good move."

"I'm not going to give him a choice." He caressed her hand with his thumb. "This is my game now, Mer. My move. *Trust me.*"

It was the second time he had said it. She leaned her head into his shoulder and drew a long breath in. "All right."

"Tomorrow then." He kissed the top of her head then swooped down and took her lips. He broke away an instant later, leaving her aching to respond. "Dress in the best you have. Leave the rest to me."

CHAPTER 38

Mer did not think she would sleep that night. Too many dragons weighed on her mind—the possibility that something would go wrong, or that nothing would go wrong but that she would come to hate her life and blame Avry for her own ill-conceived choices. She worried about Jan too, and that thought roused her fear that her first child would be a halfwit.

On and on it went. And if these distractions were not enough, her face still tingled where Avry had placed his lips. The awakening of her body amazed her. She buzzed. She burned. She did not think she could live another day without touching him, and that frightened her because their marriage was not assured.

Despite all this, she drifted off and awoke staring with wonder at the glimmer of light trickling in around her shutters.

Shivering in the chill air, she washed herself thoroughly from the basin Rives had brought in the night before. From her clothes chest she selected the cream-and-burgundy gown she had worn to the last quarterly. Avry, she recalled, had not seen it. She scooped her silver pendant out of a drawer and latched it contentedly around her neck. It draped her skin like spider silk. Hair brushed and plaited, she pocketed her bell, snatched up a pair of shoes, and left the room she had inhabited for two decades without a glance behind her.

She walked into the sitting room, blinking at the brilliant sunlight. Rives had flung open all the shutters. He stood at a window with his back to her, a dark figure surrounded by light. Something about his posture told her he had already spoken to Avry.

She glanced at the hearth. As she had expected, the place was deserted, the blankets folded and stacked. Avry and his squire were out arranging things.

Mer threw a blanket over her shoulders and joined Rives at the window.

"I hope the fair weather holds," he murmured.

Neither moved as they regarded the sky. A dark line of clouds had settled like a mountain range across the southern horizon. A cold breeze touched her cheek. Rives turned suddenly and drew her into a tight embrace.

"Everything changes," he said wistfully into her hair.

She waited for him to ask her if she was sure about her decision, perhaps to remind her of how different her life would be, but he said none of those things. It was as though he had already removed himself from her path to let her walk freely down the road she had chosen. The thought made her throat burn.

"I'll miss you," she said.

"I'll miss you too." He broke away, dashing tears from his face.

"Did Avry talk about your living?"

He hissed out something between a laugh and a cry. "Yes. He gave me two options. Either allow a new house to be built on this site or move into a place in the city. In either case I will receive servants and a monthly allowance."

Mer turned in a slow circle, attaching memories to every crack in the wall, every stain on the floor. "Well, I suppose you'll need a bigger place, with servants living here."

"Mer, I chose the city."

She wheeled, her eyes bulging. "But this is your home. I thought you liked it here."

"I've never liked it here. How could I, Mer? I was brought up in a wealthy home. I had everything I wanted." He must have noticed the pain in her face, for his eyes gentled. "I don't regret marrying your mother. My life with her, and you, has made this all worthwhile. But it's useless to me now. A few pine boards sitting atop some stones."

"I understand," she said, but her words felt forced.

He touched her cheek. "Remember my life, Mer, when you're up on that windy hill missing your wood. Remember: home is where you are loved."

She swallowed painfully, her own eyes threatening to tear up.

The sound of carriage wheels made them both straighten.

"That would be Barret and Lisette," Rives said. "Could you greet them? I have to dress Jan."

Mer caught his arm. "How many did he invite?"

"Only a few. His family, mine. You should eat something. It will be a long ride..."

Mer barely had time to greet Barret and Lisette before the Eleuthères arrived, their sleek team of bays turning off the road and up the bumpy path to Rives's cottage. Avry rode behind on a chestnut gelding, his oiled leather armor glinting in the sunlight. Where was his squire? Mer thought. And why had he traveled to Rives's cottage on horseback instead of in his family's comfortable carriage? Surely he did not plan to ride into town.

The d'Eleuthère carriage halted, and a servant stepped off and approached her. "Lady Merisande, Lady Belle wishes to meet you."

Few things shocked Mer nowadays, after all she had been through, but at these words she took an involuntary step back. Avry's mother, inflicted by some debilitating illness, had been confined to her home for more than a decade. Mer had never laid eyes on her. "Lady Belle d'Eleuthère is in that carriage?"

"Please, Lady," he said, ushering her forward with a sweeping gesture.

Mer did not recall walking to the carriage, but suddenly she was there, the door was open, and a delicate face bent toward her. The lady searched Mer's eyes, hoping for a glimpse, perhaps, of something words could not convey. Sincerity, or courage. Mer gathered both into her heart, drew the lady's hands off her lap, and squeezed them. She did not know what her expression conveyed, but it wrung a smile from Belle.

The lady retrieved her hands and lifted a creamy garment off her lap. "He said that your jacket was damaged. Take this one. Take it," she repeated, noticing Mer's hesitation.

Mer unfolded the garment and stared. It was of the finest white wool, silk-lined, and finished with mother-of-pearl buttons and ermine trim.

"It should fit," the lady said. "We are of a height."

She was right. It fit as though it had been made for her. Mer thanked her fervently, offering thanks to her husband too, who had been watching from the shadows. The carriage door closed. Mer turned and just about walked into Avry.

His eyes were red, his lips soft, vulnerable. She judged that he had observed the entire exchange. He finally found his voice.

"Have you eaten?"

"No. I suppose I forgot to."

He pulled a sack out of a saddlebag. "There's some bread and cheese. A flask of brandy." He cleared his throat. "How are you?"

He was either nervous, she thought, or trying to hide some overpowering emotion. She accepted the sack. "Impatient. Every step that stands between here and the altar seems like an impossible odd." She tore off a chunk of bread and chewed.

He watched her bemusedly. "Try not to think about it," he suggested, then added in a quieter tone, "You look enchanting in that."

Rives jogged over and crammed an armful of something into a saddle pack. "Spare clothes," he muttered before returning to Jan in the second Ivry carriage.

Mer, looking from the gelding to her father, grasped in a painful flash what Avry's plan was. She caught his arm. "Are we to ride together on that horse all the way to…to…?"

"Yes."

A crawling sensation swept down her back. He wanted to draw people's eyes to them. The protective shield of a crowd.

"You'll be fine," he promised. "Think of all you've been through lately. What you've been able to accomplish."

Her brows drew together. "What *have* I been able to accomplish?"

"You freed us both from the Dreaming Place."

So I did, she thought. "I'd wager that won't be the story Ghislain will tell."

"It'll be the story *I* will tell."

She ran her hand over the horse's silky flank. Could her weakened body bear such a lengthy ride on horseback?

She was mortified to learn that she could not even mount without assistance. Avry helped her gain the saddle, then she leaned back so he could mount in front of her. The horse was at least eighteen hands high—easily the largest she had ever ridden. Geldings of that sort were bred to haul the weight of heavily armed men, so it did not surprise her when the beast lurched forward and fell into an easy trot. The carriages fell in line behind him, wheels creaking as they turned off the path and onto the cart road.

Mer steeled herself not to look back.

The smudge on the horizon was inching west. Sunlight shimmered on it, accentuating the deepness of the shadow. The contrast reminded her of all the old homes in Aure. Light, resting on darkness. Locking her arms around Avry's waist, she sank into the rhythm of the horse.

"Are you worried about how your life will be?" he asked after a lengthy silence.

"No."

"I said some things last night that I probably shouldn't have. I was thinking about my own life when I said them. My challenges this past month. But it won't always be so bleak."

She nodded against his shoulder.

"I love you," he said.

She smiled, thinking on her father's words. "I love you too."

They paused at a stream to water the horses. Mer stretched her stiff legs and peered down the road behind her. At least a dozen carriages now trailed them, with solitary riders following alongside.

She snagged Avry's arm. "Did you invite all these people?"

"No. But your aunt asked if she could send servants to invite her family and friends. I told her to do as she wished. My father," he added wryly, "didn't ask."

They mounted again, Mer biting her lip as pain lanced down her thighs. But she did not complain. What was the use?

They encountered few on the road: wagons hauling grain; a farmer herding pigs; a highway patrolman who, after a short exchange with Avry, chose not to return to the city and report to his superior what he saw; Jacques, the messenger. Most pulled off the road at Avry's approach and stared.

They were about a mile from the city road when Édouard overtook them. "I got it, sir," he said, a foolish grin sprouting on his freckled face. "Barracks captain handed it right over as soon as I gave him your message."

"And he agreed to keep my presence secret for a few hours?"

"He did, sir."

Avry pulled up as Édouard dismounted. The squire flipped open his saddle pack and drew out something wrapped in cloth. The fabric slid as he carried it to Avry, and a crack of silver glinted in the sunlight.

Mer stiffened. Avry must have felt it, because he turned and threw her a guilty look. "I should have said something earlier but—"

"You want to wear fae armor to our wedding." Her whisper was flat, her mouth a thin line.

"Only until we get to the church."

Édouard peeled open the fabric. A pair of foot-long vambraces lay on the cloth. Avry did not move to take them. Mer, gaze drawn to them as to the hypnotic eyes of a snake, whispered, "I know why: they identify you."

"I won't wear them if it makes you uncomfortable."

She drummed her head against his shoulder. If they helped him, then she would endure it. "Wear them."

He paused a moment longer then held out his arms. Vambraces shielded the wrists and forearms, leaving the fingers bare. These were in perfect condition, neither dented nor warped. Their owner, Mer guessed, still lived and was at that very moment skimming across the open sea.

Straps fastened, Édouard bowed and mounted his horse, then they were off again, the train rattling along behind.

They climbed a low hill. At the top, the vista of the city opened like a flag unfurling. The castle looked more inviting than it had in her mind the night before. Its smooth white stone shone; its towers stretched gaily into the sky. "The damaged tower roof has been rebuilt," she pointed out.

"Yes. It was nearly finished when I last saw it." His voice was light and untroubled; his fingers trailed over hers as though playing an instrument.

Mer, lingering on the glittering arm of the sea, on the fishing boats looking as tiny as toys, felt something deeper than contentment seep into her. This could be home.

She glanced back as they turned off the old north road and headed into the city. The train had doubled. Not only were there twice as many carriages and riders, but commoners also ran alongside, some carrying small children on their shoulders. This day, she realized, was bigger than her and Avry. Their future titles, though still misted by the uncertainties of time, lay in people's hearts as if fully formed. The same urge that had drawn them to the king-in-waiting ceremony had brought them here. Avry had not merely understood this—he had relied on it.

They had not traveled far down the city road before soldiers appeared: a pair of mounted guards, observing Mer and Avry's approach from the mouth of the castle road. Despite herself, Mer's shoulders tightened and her hands chilled.

"They won't stay," Avry said. And he was right. An instant later, they had spurred their mounts and cantered up the hill.

"They'll inform the king."

"They'll inform someone," he agreed.

Passing the road, they pressed on into the thickest part of the city.

Mer thought she knew what it felt like to be stared at, but this was an entirely different animal. Shutters were flung open, people spilled out of open doors, wagons, and carriages to collect along the sides of the road. The air shook with a commotion of raised voices, whoops, and tossed congratulations. But the worst was yet to come. As the markets neared, it was as if a gear shifted in an enormous machine. From her height, Mer watched the road ahead of her clear and the sides thicken with bodies. An excited flow of people streamed between buildings, out of carriageways, and down one-wagon streets toward the train, like rivers draining into a sea. Avry's vambraces flashed in the sun, drawing people's attention.

But Avry was not the only one being gawked at. Mer was forced repeatedly to stretch her lips into a smile as folk tried to snare her attention: girls propped on their father's shoulders, grubby fishwives, even richly dressed women standing near their carriages.

A farmer raced into the road after his runaway goats, eliciting a rustle of laughter. Mer smiled truly then. But it faded as five men on horseback appeared in the throng of bodies. Four were obviously soldiers, and the fifth was dressed in knight's regalia. Folk regarded them warily, reluctant to make way.

"Let them through," Avry shouted, and miraculously, a path opened.

The knight rode up alongside Avry, his eyes flicking nervously at the crowd.

"Sir Fennick," Avry greeted him cheerfully. "Does the king know I'm alive yet?"

Fennick licked his lips nervously. "He may, sir. I came when you were sighted. The standing order is to escort you back as soon as you are sighted."

"And it just happened to be you."

His mouth twitched. "Sir."

"Fennick, I'm here. I'm back. I have but one stop to make, and I'll be at the castle door."

Fennick did not immediately reply. The muscles around his eyes tightened. "Sir," he repeated stiffly, and bowing, he turned his horse.

"Fenn, tell the king to come to the church if he can. Tell him it would be important to me!"

The words had reached the throng. People shouted at Fennick as he passed them, "The king! Tell the king to come!"

Fennick glanced sharply back at Avry, and the crowd swallowed him.

***

King Ghislain's chamber was shadowy, despite the brightness outside. All the shutters were closed except one. The latch had come loose in the storm, and no amount of tightening could fix it. Fennick stared at the shutter so he would not have to see the king's face, which had turned the color of stewed tomatoes.

He told himself that he had done nothing wrong. He could not have arrested Avry with four guards. Not even with twelve. A crowd as massive as the one he had just waded through could turn in an instant. Avry, reckless as always, had wrapped himself up in it as though it were a cloak.

He glanced at the king and felt a twinge of sympathy for the frail old man. He had only been lucid four days, and half of that time had been spent arranging a complicated expedition into the mountains. Six teams would have left that evening to search for the king-in-waiting's body.

Enter Sir Fennick, with news that Avry was alive. Ghislain had heard the rumor, but it had not been confirmed until that moment.

The king had lost his mind. He had lurched out of bed, reaching blindly for his cane, only to drop back down into the covers. He had repeated the action three times before his servant had come to pat his hands and tuck the blankets around him. Cursing, Ghislain had shoved him away with more energy than Fennick thought he possessed.

The king had regained his senses after that and pelted Fennick with questions. Most had concerned Avry's state of health, which Fennick had failed to ask after. After a full report, the king had gone silent. His jaw had clenched, and his cane had thudded on the floor, harder and harder, as if in time with an accelerating heartbeat. His face had darkened until it had turned the shade it was now.

Fennick cleared his throat. "My Lord, you could have a company escort him to the castle. With enough men, the crowd may be brought to heel."

The cane ceased thudding. "Be silent."

Fennick bowed and waited.

A breeze rose, carrying with it the clamor of the throng. Ghislain bent his head toward it, his wrinkled mouth twitching.

***

"Mer!"

Avry's head swung toward the boyish shout. Mer's cousin, Thierry, was jostling through the crowd with a dozen students in tow, all of them attired in their school uniforms. Mer waved to him weakly.

"Come to the church," Avry called, knowing it would be Mer's wish. Then he added, "Your friends, too." These were the heirs to the houses. They would remember this day.

The long journey was nearing its end. The church, which had been built near the shoreline, cast a pointed shadow over the water. A scent of brine touched the air; sea birds wheeled. Avry cast his gaze over the bustling city. The crowd was astonishing. In a daring effort to glimpse the wedding couple, some men had crawled onto the roofs of fishing huts and warehouses. Others watched from the masts of their docked ships. Avry shook his head. He had worried that the recent bird attack would have scared people away. But the opposite seemed to have happened: folk had grasped onto hope, like a drowning man sucking in a breath of air.

The thought of someone drowning wrenched his thoughts back to Mer. Her arms had slackened. She no longer clenched him but rather sagged against his back as though she slept. He untangled her chill fingers and rubbed them between his own, which were scarcely warmer. Guilt stabbed him. Had he demanded too much of her? Would she even be able to stand to give her vows?

They turned a gentle corner. And there was the church. Its doors had been flung open. The deacon, standing to one side and gripping the door frame, watched Avry's approach as if the knight were the grim reaper come to harvest his soul. Avry pulled up his tired horse and found the energy to dismount. He caught Mer as she drooped forward and hauled her into his arms. Édouard was beside them in an instant, offering water and bread. Avry tried not to be aware of the crowd as he set Mer on her feet and let her lean on him. "Can you still do this?" he asked quietly.

He bent close to catch her answer. "Of course. Why would you ask me that?"

He bit back a nervous chuckle. "All right. Try to stay on your feet. I'm going to walk toward the door."

Somehow, she found the strength to walk with him. Avry's heart swelled with pride as he observed her straight back, her set mouth. Was there a stronger woman in Aure? He doubted it.

The deacon bowed as they neared the door. "A fine day to marry, sir."

He probably wondered why Avry had chosen this ancient church instead of the fancy one on the hill. "Indeed. Do you have a stable?"

"Certainly, sir. I'll have a man tend to—er—these two horses."

Avry tossed a glance behind him. With nowhere to go, the carriages had planted themselves where they had stopped, and folk were disembarking. He walked Mer inside the church and left her on a bench then went back outside to see to his mother, who was limping along under a servant's arm. Having settled his parents, he turned wearily to the others pouring in through the doors.

Édouard touched his shoulder. "Sir, I know the order of houses. And relatives," he added with a grin. "I'll settle them for you."

Avry's eyes closed. "Thank you, Édouard."

As the boy wandered off, Avry peered out one of the small round windows at the front of the building. The throng was growing, the road disappearing under a carpet of bodies. His fingers trembled as he unfastened the vambraces and shoved them under his arm. He longed for Ghislain to be there. The desire had come over him swiftly, unasked for, and he could not tear it from him now. He felt like a child who had played a prank, only to learn that someone had got hurt because of it.

"Sir..."

The world crashed back, like cold, gushing water. He looked around him.

The pews were full to brimming. The crowd had closed in around the entrance, darkening the once-bright space. "Keep the doors clear," Avry warned, and people reluctantly obeyed.

The priest waited at the front with folded hands. Mer struggled to rise as Avry approached her.

He rested a hand on her shoulder. "Not yet. Just wait a little while longer."

"Why?" She searched his face.

"The king is weak. He'll need time to get here."

"Avry, the king won't come. You blindsided him. Did you think he would celebrate that?"

"I—I suppose not." Pain bloomed in his chest.

"Avry—"

Her whisper died as a trumpet blast sounded, clear as sunlight through the air. The crowd quieted, and from somewhere far away came the clopping of hooves. Closer, closer. Mer's hand tightened on his.

Suddenly, the clopping ceased and booted footsteps sounded on the cobblestones. A shadow fell over the space.

Heart thundering, Avry shot to his feet. "Stand for the king!" he shouted, just as a gilded sedan chair swept through the doors, with two lines of knights marching on either side. The guests obeyed, wide-eyed.

The chair was lowered, and Ghislain, leaning heavily on a cane, stepped out and seated himself in the space Mer and Avry had just vacated.

A silence fell. The crowd outside had grown so still that Avry could hear the gentle creak of fishing boats nudging against their moorings. A bird landed in one of the arched windows and sang a few notes into the hazy light that lingered in the curve of the vaulted ceiling. The king's face tilted to the sound. His gaze found Avry's. There was no anger in his eyes, no tightness or mockery. Only a gentle glint of amusement.

Throat burning, Avry turned to Merisande.

It was enough.

It was more than enough.

ABOUT THE AUTHOR

Canadian novelist W.K. Greyling lives in the maritime province of Nova Scotia. When she's not writing, she spends her time curating the music library for Ancient FM, an online medieval radio station.

Printed in Great Britain
by Amazon

27871749R00202